PRAISE FOR COLIN

'A fantastic read'
Wilbur Smith
'Spectacular historical fiction, blazing with intrigue, romance and dramatic action'
Booklist
'Makes dry history into a real rip-roaring read'
Forum
'Living history at its best'
Good Reading
'Falconer's grasp of period and places is almost flawless'
The Australian
'Poignant characterization, dazzling dialogue and impeccable research'
Bibliotica
'Truly made this historical era come alive'
Historical Novel Review
'Nothing short of brilliant!'
History and Women
'Sure to find its way onto the bookshelves of lovers of a thrilling tale'
Liverpool Daily Post
'Moves along at a cracking pace, the narrative fraught with action and tension at every turn'
Bookmuse
'Beautifully written in typical Falconer style with plenty of snap and sharpness, and wonderfully researched'
Great Historicals
'A great read'
Martina Cole
'A magisterial tale'
Daily Mail UK

ALSO BY COLIN FALCONER

Epic Adventure
Silk Road
Stigmata
Lord of the Atlas
Harem
When We Were Gods
Colossus
Feathered Serpent
Venom
Fury book 1
Fury book 2
Fever Coast
East India
Ends of the Earth
Converso
An Ambush of Tigers (sequel to Fever Coast)

Other historical fiction
The Unkillable Kitty O'Kane
Loving Liberty Levine
A Vain and Indecent Woman
Isabella: Braveheart of France

DI Charlie George crime series
Lucifer Falls
Innocence Dies
Angels Weep
Cry Justice

AN AMBUSH OF TIGERS

COLIN FALCONER

EPIC ADVENTURE SERIES BOOK 15

Cover design by Ben Prior

This book is for Lise, who made all my dreams come true.

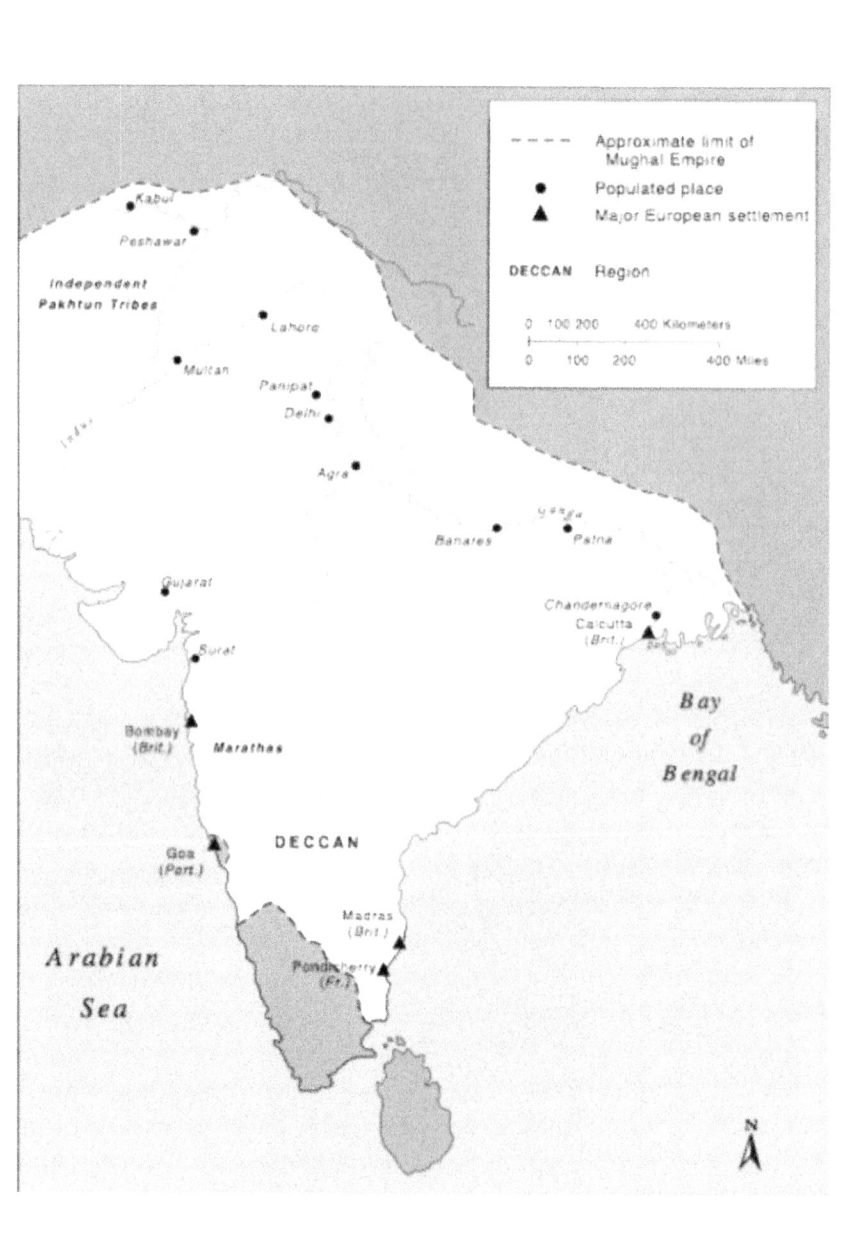

Prologue

1752: The Mughal Empire is in rapid decline, riven by internal disputes. Regional powers such as the Marathas are in open rebellion. Meanwhile, in Bengal and the Carnatic, the British and the French vie for supremacy through their various client princes.

Lachlan McKenzie has returned to Madras a hero, having commanded a successful defence from Chanda Sahib and the French at Karimkot. Through his efforts, the British have kept a precarious foothold in the south of the continent. A tentative truce follows. But with the Empire falling apart, there is far too much at stake for peace to last for long...

Part 1

THE TIGER OF KARIMKOT

CHAPTER 1

Madras, 1752

On the day of the murders, Lachlan woke long before the crows.

When the birds finally took up position on the veranda rail right outside the bedroom window, he guessed it must be nearly dawn. He threw back the mosquito net, went to the nightstand in the corner of the room and splashed water on his face from an enamel bowl. He felt like he was suffocating. His skin was damp with sweat and the sun wasn't even up yet.

He went out onto the veranda and the crows launched themselves into the air, cawing in protest. He stared over the walls of the fort towards the ocean. There was a faint leeching of light on the horizon. A flock of parrots took off from a stand of banana palms and flew screeching towards the Black Town, dark shadows against an indigo sky.

He sat on one of the wicker chairs, propping his leg on a stool. The wound still ached. The Company surgeon had told him that it would be a few weeks yet before the muscles knitted properly and he got full use of it again.

He wondered how he would tell Catia that he was reconsidering Channing's offer. He couldn't put it off any longer. She wouldn't like it, and a part of him agreed with her. In his heart he wanted to leave this blighted coast as much as she did.

But he couldn't rely on his wife's inherited fortune to get by in life. She always said the plantation in Africa was as much his as hers, but they were just words. A man had to make his own way in the world, that's what his father had told him.

Catia reached out a hand to Lachlan's pillow. When she realised he wasn't there, she sat up and swung her legs out of bed. She walked into the living room and saw his silhouette outside. He was holding a glass of *arrack*.

'It's a little early for that, isn't it?' she said.

'I didn't sleep well.'

She sat down on his lap, taking care to put her weight on his good leg, and kissed his cheek. 'Did the ghosts come again last night?'

He nodded and downed the rest of the *arrack*.

'They will leave you alone as soon as we are away from this place.' She brushed the hair away from her eyes. 'I can't wait to go home.'

He took a deep breath. 'I was thinking. Do we have to be in such a hurry about it?'

She stared at him, trying to make out his expression in the half-light. 'You're serious?'

'Channing spoke to me again. He's pushing me to reconsider staying on. No wait, hear me out. Everyone thinks I'm mad. They say this job offer is too good to pass up. It's like having your own mint, they tell me. And don't I deserve something for what I did for the Company at Karimkot and all I've been through? After what we've *both* been through.'

She jumped to her feet. 'No. You promised me.'

'You do understand what he is offering me, offering us? This is not just a raise in pay. I'll get a commission on all the supplies coming into the fort. Everything. Even *arrack*. Do you know how much the average soldier drinks? Imagine it. Five to ten per cent in our pockets. In a few years, we can go back to Africa with an absolute fortune.'

'We don't belong here, *meu amor*. Look at this place. We have to look over a wall to see the ocean.'

'That's just it. Channing has promised us our own bungalow, away from the fort, with our own servants. It will be almost as good as the *prazo*. What difference will it make whether it's in Africa or India? We may never get a chance like this again.'

'You told me that after you killed Napoleon Gagnon we would go home to Novo Santiago. Well, you found him, and you did what you had to do. So now we go home.'

'My father said that Hindustan is the future, not Africa.'

'You cannot live your life for your father anymore. It's not your fault you're alive and he's dead.'

Lachlan shrugged his shoulders. 'I feel like it is, a little. I wonder if I owe him this.'

'He wasn't even...' She trailed off.

He knew what she was going to say. *He wasn't even your real father.* But he was. He had raised him and treated him like his own and done his best by him, even though Lachlan had another man's blood in his veins. And that was all that mattered.

'We need to leave here,' Catia said. 'I have a bad feeling about this place. If we don't go soon, I think I will die here.' She went back into the bedroom, closing the door softly behind her.

She still had not come out by the time he had dressed. He called to her, but when she didn't answer, he left the apartment and went looking for Charlie Mathieson.

The mess hall was empty. Everyone was at church. A two-month-old copy of the *London Gazetteer* lay on a table. Lachlan picked it up and scanned the front page. There was nothing that interested him much, something about the coronation of the new King of Sweden and the founding of a new colony in the Americas. They had called it Georgetown.

He tossed it aside and took a billiards cue from the rack. He placed the white ball on the table and attempted a two-ball cannon but missed both the red and the yellow. His own ball clattered into the pocket. He swore under his breath.

'That's not like you,' a voice said from the doorway. 'Something bothering you?'

He looked over his shoulder. 'Morning, Charlie.'

Charlie Mathieson was one of those fresh-faced Englishmen who looked as if they were straight out of grammar school. In fact, he had been working his way up through the Company ranks in India for five years. He was practically a veteran now, and Channing had made him his *aide de camp*.

'Didn't expect to find the Tiger of Karimkot on the prowl this early.'

'Please don't call me that. I'm no hero, Charlie.'

'Tell that to the ladies.' Charlie laughed. 'Couldn't sleep?'

'I had a difference of opinion with my wife.'

'Very unwise.' Charlie chalked the end of his cue and bent over the table. He potted the red ball with the yellow, a losing hazard. 'What was the cause of this disruption to your domestic harmony?'

'I broke a promise.'

Charlie winced. 'Dear God. Don't ever do that.'

Lachlan took his ball from the corner pocket and slid it across the table. 'I told her we'd go home after I had done what I came here to do.'

'And you have, haven't you?'

'I want to renege. But I have good reason.'

'You mean Channing's offer to make you Clerk of the Market? I agree, it's a golden opportunity for any man. But you're not any man. Your circumstances are complicated. Catia has her heart set on going back to Africa, and after all, a promise is a promise.'

'I can make thirty, forty thousand pounds in a single year. Five years and we could go back to Novo Santiago and live like kings.'

'Meanwhile, what will Catia do here in Madras?'

Lachlan frowned and shrugged his shoulders.

'You told me her father left her an entire plantation.'

Lachlan nodded.

'She gave up a lot for you, and she doesn't seem to me the kind of woman who will just tag along forever. I doubt if you would have married her if she was.' He put the yellow ball back on the table, lined up a shot and sent the ball down the far pocket with a sound like a pistol shot.

'I'll never find another like her,' Lachlan said.

'Hard to disagree.'

A sergeant major was drilling his sepoys outside on the parade ground. It was already getting warm, and the sun was barely over the walls. Lachlan tugged at his collar. 'So, what should I do?'

'Supposing you stay here, and she goes back to Africa, what will you do with your fortune? It will buy you no end of bad women, of course. Will it buy you a good one?'

'It's only for a few years.'

'Have you walked around the cemetery recently? How do you know you have a few years? Some count themselves lucky to last three monsoons.'

Lachlan put his cue back on the rack on the wall. 'You're right. I'd better go and talk to Channing and tell him I can't do it.'

'It's what I'd do.' Charlie grinned. 'A man should never break a promise to his wife.'

CHAPTER 2

To Adelaïde, the British fort didn't look very different to the battlements of Pondicherry, with its pepper pot bastions and crowds of natives milling around the sea gate. There was the usual *foule* - hawkers with bananas and rice cakes, peddlers, *paan* sellers, beggar women far too old for the babies they carried on their hips.

Narain Singh shoved them all roughly aside to clear a passage for her.

A *masula* boat was battling its way through the surf. For a moment she thought it must surely tip into the boiling froth of water, but somehow the native crew managed to ride the breakers to the shore where a gaggle of servants waited with umbrellas and concerned looks.

An Englishman in a top hat was helped out of the boat, followed by his hysterical wife. She was pale and shaking. Her husband marched up the strand ahead of her, imperious and seemingly unaffected.

Adelaïde remembered what her father had said about the English: *Cut them open and what comes out is nothing like blood. It is a thick, white paste, tinged with resentment and spite.* She had thought he was joking until she was old enough to see for herself.

Narain stopped when he saw the sepoys at the gate. 'They are checking everyone who goes through,' he said. 'The native servants all have paper *chitties*.'

They were mercenaries by the look of them, Portuguese perhaps, or Armenians. They looked slovenly and their uniforms were ill-kept. Adelaïde knew their type well. Most of them were lazy and useless in a fight. They could also be unpredictable and vicious.

'We don't need a *chitty*,' she said.

'Be careful, *mem'sahib*. You put yourself in great danger.'

'If they try to stop us, say we have been visiting one of the bazaars in the Black Town and you are my bodyguard.'

They approached the gate. One of the sentries saw them and was about to throw out an arm. Adelaïde gave him a look and he thought better of it. The crowd parted for her, and they went in.

Suddenly they were in another world. It was deathly quiet, the boom of the surf from the beach muted by the high stone walls.

'Are you ready?' Narain said.

'I'm ready,' she said. She was holding a rag doll. She hugged it to her cheek and felt inside it to satisfy herself that the pistol was there, well-hidden and ready for use.

Catia sat on the rocker next to the four-poster bed, staring at the whitewashed wall. Soon, in Africa, it would be *Nyenyanyana*, the month of the baby birds. The women would be singing on their way to the well. On clear mornings you could hear the crack of a sail from a dhow out on the ocean.

That is where I belong, she thought. Not this place.

So much had happened since the day she had found Lachlan half-dead on that deserted beach. What had been done to him was unthinkable, and she had understood his need to find the man who had murdered his family.

But that was over now. The man he had sought out was dead. She had kept her promise to support him. Now she expected him to keep his.

It was not just that he wanted to stay here in Hindustan. What frightened her was the reason. Greed would corrupt him like it had corrupted everyone in Madras. All they ever thought about here was money.

Did Lachlan expect her to do whatever he said? She loved him with all her heart, but she wouldn't give up her soul to please him. She couldn't be an English wife. So, what was she going to do about it? She had to talk to someone, but she hadn't a single friend in Madras, even after all this time.

She saw her mother's silver cross lying on the bedroom table. They would be coming out of the church soon and she would have it to herself. She supposed the English protestant god wouldn't care that she was raised with a rosary. Perhaps an hour there might help to quiet her mind.

She heard their servant, Aadhimi, moving about the main room setting up the *tatties*, the woven grass mats everyone used on their windows to keep their houses and barracks bearable in the heat of the day. They would be dampened with water later to cool the hot breeze from the eastern ghats.

She put on a loose-fitting muslin gown and tied her hair on top of her head, then went downstairs and up the street to the church.

If the outside of the fort reminded Adelaïde of Pondicherry, inside it was quite different. There were broad avenues of tamarinds and palm trees, and the white stone mansions had shaded porches. The streets were swept clean. Even the flower beds looked ordered, like soldiers on a parade ground. The place was dull and bloodless.

She heard the chatter of a mynah bird from the branches of a flamboyant. The blood red flowers seemed to be the only colour in the whole of the White Town.

The needle of the church spire towered over the walls of the star shaped bastions. Large cranes strutted about the maidan in front of the Residence, looking much like the English themselves, superior, thin-legged and dismissive.

'Hold my hand,' she said to Narain.

'*Mem'sahib?*'

'It must look as if you're my protector.'

Narain looked uncertain but did as he was told. He would not have dreamed of touching her until now. She would have had him horse whipped.

'Where do we go?' she said.

Narain had paid ten rupees to a subaltern's cook to draw him a plan of the fortress, with the Tiger of Karimkot's apartment marked in red ink. He had committed the plan to memory. The cook had assured him that most people would be at church, except for McKenzie and his wife. They rarely went. This was the perfect time to catch him unawares.

'It won't be easy,' he said, as he led the way towards one of the broad avenues beside the church. 'This man. He is a warrior.'

'And I am just a sweet, lost little girl,' Adelaïde said. 'That is where I have the advantage of him.'

She thought about her father. He would be proud if he could see her now. But he couldn't because this man had murdered him in cold blood. She didn't even know where they had buried the body. An accounting was long overdue.

They passed a barracks for the East India officials and unmarried officers. Some young men came tumbling down the stairs and spilled into the street in front of them. She felt Narain tighten his grip on her hand, alarmed. But the English passed either side of them, not even sparing them a glance. They were barely into their twenties, and by the state of their clothes and the deathly pallor of their faces, she guessed they had all been out until the early hours drinking and whoring in the Black Town.

As they turned a corner, another couple came towards them. The man was bewigged, and the woman's face was so thickly powdered it looked like a death mask. She was wearing a ridiculous low-necked silk gown.

'It is up here,' Narain said and pointed to some stairs.

They went up slowly. The door to the apartment was open. Adelaïde pulled her hand free of Narain's and went in.

She looked around at the bare whitewashed walls and the hardwood floors covered with dusty carpets. There seemed to be a layer of sand over everything. The grass screens on the window threw the room into semi darkness.

She went into the bedroom. There was a four-poster bed and a rocking chair. Where was he?

She heard someone in the kitchen. She pushed the door open. An old woman was throwing dirty sheets into a wicker basket.

A servant, Adelaïde supposed, or the laundry woman.

The crone looked around and grinned, showing tombstone teeth stained with betel. 'Hello, *mishti*,' she said. 'Who are you?'

'Hello Mother,' Adelaïde said.

Well, this was unfortunate. She glanced at Narain. He nodded. The command was implicit in her look. Nothing needed to be said. It was a pity, but she was raised to be practical. She supposed the old woman was not long for the world anyway.

Narain moved quickly, stepping behind the woman and clamping a hand across her mouth. He took his kris knife from his belt and drew it expertly across her throat, severing the neck veins. He stepped aside to avoid being sprayed with blood.

It was a quick death. The old woman's heels drummed on the floor. Narain closed her eyes with his fingertips. He stepped over the body, went to the night table and washed his hands in the enamel bowl.

He searched the rest of the apartment while Adelaïde waited.

'I have looked everywhere,' he said when he had done. 'He is not here.'

CHAPTER 3

Catia hurried across the square but stopped halfway, feeling faint. A *tonga* swept past her, almost knocking her off her feet. She glimpsed a councillor sitting in the back with his wife. The woman gave her a look of distaste from under her parasol. The man was someone Lachlan knew well, but there was not even a backward glance to see if she was all right. Her husband might be the Tiger of Karimkot, but they couldn't forgive her for being Portuguese.

She waited in the shade, steadying herself against the wall with her hand. The world seemed to be spinning.

'Are you alright?'

She looked up. Charlie took off his tricorn hat and bowed.

'Charlie. I'm glad it's you. I feel unwell.'

'Perhaps you have a fever,' he said. 'Where are you going?'

'To the church.'

'You look pale. I think the good Lord might prefer it if you went home to rest.'

Catia hated feeling helpless, but the thought of collapsing here in the street and giving the other wives reason to gloat overcame her pride. She held out an arm. 'If I may lean on you for a moment.'

'Certainly.'

As they made their way back along St Thomas Street, he said, 'I saw Lachlan not a few minutes ago. He was quite out of sorts.'

'So he should be.'

He laughed. 'You're very direct.'

'Did he tell you why he was upset?'

'We had a long talk about it. Afterwards, he said he was going to see Channing.'

'To see if he could have me shot?'

'I don't think that's allowed under Company rules.' He smiled. 'I think rather he was going to tell him that he couldn't accept the post as Clerk of the Market and that he was going back to Africa with you. By the way, you didn't hear that from me.'

'Is that really what he said?'

Charlie nodded. 'I told him a man should never take his wife for granted. Especially a wife like you.'

They had reached the apartments. It was cooler in the shade, and she felt a wave of relief at what Charlie had just told her. The blood stopped pounding in her ears and her breathing came easier.

She let go of his arm. 'Thank you.'

He tipped his hat in acknowledgment. She started up the stairs.

'Let me help you rest of the way.'

'No, I'll be all right,' she said. 'Aadhimi will be there to help if I feel faint again. It's just the heat and the worry. Thank you again. Everything is fine now.'

As Catia walked into the apartment, a girl came out of the kitchen. She was dressed in white muslin and holding a rag doll. Catia was shocked to stillness. The girl stared back at her, unblinking, a pale, pink-eyed wisp of a thing. She looked like an angel.

'Who are you?' Catia said, finally.

The girl didn't answer. She proffered a beatific smile. Catia smiled back, unsure of what was happening, then looked over the girl's shoulder and saw an outstretched hand on the floor of the kitchen.

'I shouldn't go in there if I were you,' the girl said.

'What have you done?' Catia said and pushed past her. There was blood everywhere. It had sprayed up the whitewashed wall and lay in congealing puddles on the cold tiles. Aadhimi lay stretched out on the floor, flies already settling around the gaping wound on her neck. Her mouth was open in her final, silent scream.

Catia ran out of the kitchen. She heard a man's voice say, 'We must finish this now.' A tall Sikh in a red Company uniform was blocking the doorway. There was no way out.

'I'm sorry,' the girl said. 'This wasn't meant for you.'

Catia wanted to scream, but her voice closed over in terror, and she found she couldn't make a sound. She tried to back away across the room, but her heel caught on the edge of the carpet and she slipped.

The girl stepped towards her. 'I'm Adelaïde,' she said. She reached inside the doll and drew out a flintlock pistol. She cocked it and aimed it at Catia's chest. 'And this is for my father.'

Catia watched the world recede. It happened slowly and in silence. She felt herself leaving along a long, dark tunnel. The borders began to turn black even though she knew her eyes were wide open.

Lachlan was there, calling to her from the end of the tunnel. His face was so twisted he barely looked like him. He was shouting something. She supposed he was calling for help, or perhaps he was telling her not to go. She felt him shake her.

But it was too hard. She couldn't keep her eyes open.

There were other people in the room now, some Company clerks she recognised from the dining hall. She saw the horror on their faces and felt sorry for them. They were just out from England, boys.

Poor Lachlan. It wasn't fair that this was how it ended. She wanted to say to him: don't cry, it's all right, it doesn't hurt anymore. But most of all she wanted to say: I'm sorry about this morning. I told you once that I'd love you till the day I died and look, I really did.

But she couldn't stay awake. She was so tired. She was going to sleep now. Just for a while.

CHAPTER 4

The president's secretary ushered Lachlan through a set of carved rosewood doors. Liveried native servants stood on either side in powdered wigs and heavy woollen jackets.

Channing leaped to his feet when he saw him and came round the desk to shake his hand. 'How are you?'

Lachlan wondered what he was supposed to say to that, so he just shook his head. The truth was he didn't know how he was. It was as if he was looking at the world through the wrong end of a spyglass. Where was the rage, the grief?

'Sit, sit,' Channing said. He looked embarrassed and flustered.

Lachlan felt dazed. He looked around the room as if he had never been there before, at the wood panelled walls, the pen and ink set on Channing's expansive desk, and the bronze bell he used for summoning his aides. A *punkha-wallah* laboured fitfully in the corner. Through the window he saw a squadron of sepoys in red uniform jackets tramping over the parade ground, raising a dun cloud of dust.

'Terrible business,' Channing said. 'Terrible.'

Lachlan had never seen the president looking so discomfited. He supposed this was a duty he wanted over as quickly as possible, yet propriety demanded he take his time and show an adequate amount of sympathy.

He felt sorry for him. What could you say to a man whose wife had just been shot dead in broad daylight? They were all accustomed to arbitrary death in Madras, but not something as awful as this.

There was a long silence. A grandfather clock chimed the quarter hour on the far wall.

'How are you holding up?' Channing said finally.

'I'm not really. I think I'm coming apart.'

Channing looked away and cleared his throat.

Lachlan realised that wasn't what he was supposed to say. But when he had lost his family in the attack at Delgoa Bay, Catia had been there to see him through the grief and loss and make him hope again. This time he was on his own.

Channing put his thumbs in the pockets of his waistcoat then took them out again. 'This is a shocking crime, shocking. Who would do such a thing?'

'Gagnon.'

'What?'

'Napoleon Gagnon. He would do it.'

'The French mercenary? But he's dead.'

'Someone close to him. This is a reprisal. The bullet was meant for me. Do we know how they got in?'

'Simpson has been looking into that,' Channing said. He looked at his secretary who was standing by the window, staring out at the sea, his hands clasped behind his back.

When he heard Channing say his name he turned around. He wanted to get this over with every bit as much as the president did. 'One of the sepoys remembers seeing a Sikh officer with a young European girl,' he said. 'He thought the man was her bodyguard. He said the girl gave him such a look that he was afraid to challenge her. I'll have him and the other sentry flogged for this.'

'Please don't. It will serve no purpose now. Tell me about the girl. How old was she?'

'He couldn't say. Young enough to go to school, not old enough to marry.'

Lachlan couldn't make sense of it. He supposed the officer was one of Gagnon's former mercenaries and he had used the girl as a way of getting inside the fort unchallenged.

'How did they escape?'

'We don't know. By the time the alarm was raised, it seems they were well away from the fort.'

'The girl at least should have been easy to spot in a crowd.'

'There was no sign of her,' Channing said. 'It looks like the whole thing was very well planned.' He was about to say something else but trailed off. He looked like an actor who had forgotten his lines. He turned to Simpson, hoping for a prompt.

Simpson could come up with nothing.

'Take as much time off as you need,' Channing said.

'Right. Thank you, sir.' Lachlan got up to leave.

'Time heals all wounds.'

'Yes, sir,' Lachlan said. He thought, but didn't say, that whoever believed that had never been wounded.

They buried her the next day, late in the afternoon, in a corner of the British cemetery alongside the clerks, Company soldiers and other adventurers who had died young a long way from home. She was given a plot a little apart from respectable Anglicans. Channing impressed on Lachlan how many strings he had had to pull to arrange for her – a foreigner and a Catholic - to be buried there.

Afterwards, he assured him that it had been a good turnout. He meant in the circumstances. She might have been a half-caste Portuguese, but she was also the wife of the Tiger of Karimkot, so everyone came. The men wore their frock coats or their uniforms and some even brought their wives. Six shots were fired over her grave by a squadron of redcoats.

Her name had been burned into a wooden cross and they put a heavy stone over the turned earth to stop the jackals getting to her. Lachlan put a finger to his lips and touched it to the cross. Even as he did it, he thought what an empty gesture it was. Love was not romantic words or kisses. It was what you did that counted, and what she had wanted him to do – what he had promised her he would do from the very beginning – was take her home again.

He made his way back to the fort alone.

Night fell quickly in the tropics and by the time he got to the apartment it was already dark. Her night gown was folded over the back of a chair on the veranda, where she had left it. He held it to his face and breathed in her scent while he still could.

The surf beat rhythmically on the sand on the other side of the walls. It made him think about another beach, far away at Novo Santiago. The waves were gentler there, just a froth of white rippling the shore like lace. He remembered Catia pulling him down onto the sand beside her and making love to him for the first time.

The day they sailed for Hindustan, he had honestly believed that one day they would go back and be happy there forever. But it seemed life punished you when you took too much for granted.

'Want some company?'

He turned around. Charlie stood in the doorway. He could barely make him out in the dark.

Charlie held up a bottle of *arrack*. 'I thought you might need some of this.' He set the bottle down on the table in front of Lachlan. 'You'll get bitten to death out here.' He went back inside to fetch a candle and made his way around the apartment lighting the incense burners.

He was right. The little buggers were swarming. Lachlan had hardly noticed.

Charlie came back with two glasses and opened the bottle. 'To Catia,' he said, and raised his glass in a toast.

'To Catia,' Lachlan said.

'No one can believe it. Who'd do something like this? It's barbaric.'

'This has something to do with Napoleon Gagnon.'

'But you didn't kill him. I did.'

'I meant to kill him. I crossed an ocean to do it. Everyone knows it. The fact that you were the one who finally pulled the trigger, well, that's just detail. No one knew that except you and me.'

'I understand someone coming after you. But what kind of man murders a woman in her own home?'

Lachlan thought about Delgoa Bay. The bones of his mother and sister were still there somewhere, bleaching in the sand. 'I think I know the kind of man. There's just more of his kind than I realised.'

The candle guttered in the evening breeze.

'I saw Catia,' Charlie said, 'in the square outside the church a few minutes before it happened. She was feeling ill, so I walked her back. I should have come up with her.'

'It's not your fault, Charlie.'

'I keep going over and over it in my head though. If only. Do you what I mean?'

'Those kinds of thoughts can drive you mad.'

Charlie poured them both another *arrack*. 'What are you going to do?'

'I don't know.'

'If it was me, I don't think I'd rest until I found whoever did it.' He toyed with his glass, tapping it against his knee. 'Look, there is something. I probably shouldn't be telling you this.' He paused. 'We have a man in Pondicherry.'

'You mean a spy?'

'An intelligencer, we call him. If this has something to do with Gagnon, then he will know who did it and where to find him.' He leaned in, eyes bright. 'All you'd have to do is get inside the city. You speak Tamil like a native. You could disguise yourself as a pedlar or something...' He trailed off.

'And then what?'

Charlie stared at him, puzzled. 'Surely, you're not going to let this stand.'

Lachlan thought about his father. He hadn't deserved to die the way he did, but he hadn't been entirely innocent either. He had stolen another man's wife. What goes around, comes around. Wasn't that how it worked? 'It's just that I wonder where it will all stop. I'm so tired of it.'

'They have to pay,' Charlie said.

'That's what Sasavona said.'

'Who's Sasavona?'

'He saved my life the day Gagnon and his men arrived in Delgoa Bay. Afterwards, he made me swear to take revenge, for my sake, for his, for everyone who died that day. And I did. I should be... what? Happy? At peace?' He shook his head. 'I feel like a rat on a wheel, Charlie. I'm back where I started. I moved heaven and earth to find Napoleon Gagnon and now he's gone but it didn't change anything. It didn't bring any of my family back. In fact, it made it worse. Now I've lost Catia as well.'

'So, you're just going to walk away? You can't go through the rest of your life knowing you let her killer walk free. It would be like, well, like she didn't matter. Like she'd never been.'

Lachlan tipped back the glass of *arrack* and poured another. He stared blankly at the wall.

'What would Catia say?' Charlie said.

'She'd probably say: Go home, *meu amor*. Enough is enough.'

'Well, if that's what you think, you're a better man than me. Or someone much worse. Right now, I can't decide which.'

'The Hindustanis believe in this thing called karma. Do you know it? If you do wrong, it comes back to haunt you.'

'An eye for an eye like the Bible.'

'No, that's vengeance. This is different. The way they talk about it, it's more like the scales the traders use in the markets. It weighs the good and bad of everything you do and balances it all out. There's no anger to it, no blame. No right and wrong. It just is. Hurt someone and you'll get hurt. Take a life and a life will get taken from you.'

'You don't believe that mumbo-jumbo?'

Lachlan shrugged.

Charlie stared at the bloodstains that had dried into the floorboards. 'They slaughtered Catia, and she was innocent. They killed her in cold blood. How can you stand it?'

'That's the problem, I can't. She was my second chance. I think my chances are all used up now.'

'Don't talk like that.'

'All right, I'll just think it.' He splashed more *arrack* into his glass. His hand was shaking and some of it spilled onto the floor. 'I think I'd like you to go now. I'm not very good company.'

'Do you think that's a good idea?'

'It's the only idea I have. Please, Charlie. I'm tired of talking. You've been a great friend to me, but right now I need to be alone.'

Charlie stood up. 'Are you going to be alright?'

'I don't know, and I don't really care.'

Charlie patted him on the shoulder. He wanted to say something else but couldn't find the words. He hesitated at the door. 'Just think about what I said. At least speak to our man in Pondicherry. You have to find out who did this, Lachlan.'

CHAPTER 5

Pondicherry

The French Quarter was a neat grid of cobbled streets between the ocean and the canal that divided the European sector from the *Ville Noir*. There were sun dappled avenues shaded with poinciana and sandalwood trees. Ornate villas, their high walls painted in pastel shades, clustered on either side. It was as if some giant hand had scooped up an acre of provincial France and placed it gently down among the tropical palms.

A platoon of infantry in blue coats with white facings marched towards the fort. It was not much different from the Residence in Madras. It had its own star fortress with pepper pot bastions and high battlements, though Lachlan doubted that it could long withstand a prolonged siege from a seasoned Company army.

He made his way along the Rue St Martin, past an arched gateway and a whitewashed wall with cascading purple bougainvillea. He was no longer recognisable as a gentleman and an officer of the British East India Company. He wore a dirty white *kurta* and a long skirt-like *veshti*, with a grubby *angvastra* thrown over his shoulder, trying to cover up as much as he could. A turban hid his blonde curls. Any bare skin he had rubbed every night with a mixture of earth and boot black before he set out from Madras. He had dispensed with his silver-topped cane, and instead, fashioned his own walking stick from a long shaft of bamboo. He carried a dirty bundle in his left hand. He had even grown a moustache as part of his disguise, since no Tamil man would go out bare faced like an Englishman.

He kept his head lowered and his shoulders hunched. So far no one had looked twice at him. Just another pedlar, down on his luck.

AN AMBUSH OF TIGERS

He turned onto the Rue Labourdonnais and stopped in the shade of a banyan tree. Squirrels chattered and scampered in the branches above. It was a Sunday morning and the White Town was quiet. The air was heavy with the scent of spice from the warehouses.

The house he was looking for was like all the others in the street, with wooden shutters and wrought iron balconies. Colonnades beyond the gates led to the entrance. He sat on his haunches and settled down to wait. He mixed some *paan* on a betel leaf and popped the wad into his mouth to chew.

After about an hour, a horse and chaise swung through the gates and pulled up outside the entrance. A man in a frock coat and white wig stepped down and went inside the house.

That must be him, Lachlan thought. Jean-Jacques Monsabert, diamond merchant and spy.

He waited a few minutes then crossed the road and rang the bell at the servant's gate.

A Sikh watchman scowled at him through the bars. 'What do you want?' he said in Tamil. 'We've no alms for the likes of you.'

Lachlan reached into his robe and took out a letter. He handed it to him and said in French, 'Give that to your master. Now. And if you ever speak to me like that again, I'll pull your beard out by its roots.'

The man's eyes went wide. He took the letter and disappeared into the house. A few minutes later he reappeared and unlocked the gate. 'This way,' he said.

Monsabert studied Lachlan with the look of a man who had just opened a basket and found a live viper inside it. He still had the letter in his hand. 'What are you doing here?' he said. 'You have put us both in great danger.'

'I need information.'

'Everything I know I pass along to President Channing in the usual way.'

'This is a different kind of information.'

Lachlan looked around the room. Monsabert lived in some style. There were high raftered ceilings, Bengal rugs on the black and white checkered tiles, and endless rows of leather-bound books on the bookshelf. The desk was carved in teak and inlaid with mother of pearl.

He wondered if greed was the reason this man had been attracted to espionage. Perhaps even the diamond business didn't realise sufficient profit for his expensive tastes.

Monsabert got up from his chair and shut the door. He also closed the blinds. An unnecessary precaution, in Lachlan's opinion. It seemed to him that the Frenchman's nerves were shot. The man had no business being a spy with such a temperament.

Or perhaps I'm the odd one here, he thought. He had stopped caring what happened to him, and this sudden indifference to life had given him a heady sense of freedom.

Monsabert was a curious man. He had the small, pinched features of someone who had spent too much of his life squinting at diamonds and account books, and the quick, nervous movements of a man expecting the police to knock on his door at any moment.

He went to the liquor cabinet in the corner and took out a bottle of brandy. He held it up in silent enquiry. Lachlan nodded. The cut crystal glasses rattled as Monsabert poured a generous amount into each. 'So, speak. Tell me why you're here.'

'My wife was murdered in Fort Saint George three weeks ago.'

Monsabert's demeanour changed. 'That was you?'

Lachlan nodded.

Monsabert handed him the glass of brandy. '*Desolé, monsieur.*'

'I don't want your sympathy, just a name.'

Monsabert swallowed half of the brandy in one gulp.

'It seems you already know about this,' Lachlan said.

'All Pondicherry knows about it. But what can you expect of such a girl?'

For a moment, Lachlan wondered if he had heard correctly. He remembered what Simpson had told him about the girl who had been with the Sikh. 'What girl are we talking about?'

'She is the daughter of a man called Napoleon Gagnon. This man was a mercenary, and a highly successful one by all accounts. He died at the Battle of Karimkot.'

'Wait. A woman murdered my wife?'

'Hardly a woman. Fourteen years old, I think. No more'

'No, there was a Sikh with her. He killed her.'

'I am never wrong about such things. Besides, she has openly boasted about this. The whole town is talking about it. It is a scandal.'

'What about the Sikh?'

'Narain Singh? He goes everywhere with her. I am sure he is capable of such a thing, but not in this instance.'

'And who is he?'

'He was employed as a *subadar* in Gagnon's private army. His older brother, Ram Singh, was Gagnon's right-hand man. Before Gagnon left for Karimkot he appointed both brothers as guardians to his daughter if he didn't come back. He must have had a premonition.'

'So, what happened to Ram Singh?'

'He died along with Gagnon at Karimkot. The job of guardian fell to Narain. Gagnon must have thought a lot of him because he didn't trust many people.'

'And you're sure it wasn't him who killed Catia?'

'Why would she boast about it if she didn't do it?'

Lachlan drained his glass. The brandy set fire to his throat. He went to the window and stared through the trees at the walls of the *Gouvernement*. He felt numb.

A girl did this.

'Write down her address,' he said, finally.

Monsabert picked up a pen from his desk and dipped it in the inkpot. He scribbled a note on a piece of paper and blotted it. 'Here. But I warn you. Go anywhere near her, and her *subadar* will kill you.'

Lachlan closed his fist around the note. 'Or I will kill both of them.'

CHAPTER 6

Lachlan found the villa easily enough, on a corner along the Rue Suffren. It was one of the largest villas in the French quarter.

He squatted against a wall on the far side of the street and watched and waited. It was getting on towards sunset and though he had attracted little enough attention in his native clothes during the day, he supposed that would change after dark. Many of the local people who worked here, the servants and the cooks, would be heading back to the *Ville Noir* by now. He would have to find a way to get inside before the curfew.

The villa was surrounded by a high wall, impossible to climb. A pair of wrought iron gates led to the portico at the front entrance. There were also two wooden gates at the rear for the kitchens and trade. The gates were locked when they weren't being used and there were uniformed guards with muskets patrolling the gardens.

This wasn't going to be easy.

He saw a bullock cart loaded with firewood rumbling down the street. Two servants appeared at the villa's gates and unlocked them so the cart could get in.

He got to his feet and walked quickly across the street. He jumped on the back of the cart and sat down, his legs swinging over the edge of the tray as if he were the driver's labourer. As the cart bumped through the gates, the two house servants didn't spare him a second glance.

Once he was inside, he dropped from the tray and followed the cart until it was in the shadows of the house, then slipped away into the gardens. He hid behind a tree and watched the drayman stop outside the kitchens, jump down from the running board and start unloading.

No one had seen a thing.

He smiled grimly. He took off his peasant clothes and hid them in the bushes. In his bundle he had a black *kurta* and black *pajama* trousers. In moments it would be night, and he would be invisible.

A servant lit the oil lamps that hung from the branches of a mango tree. Moths swarmed around them, throwing themselves against the glass. Bats flickered and swooped through the garden. A peacock screeched in the bushes.

Lachlan kept to the shadows, watching the house for movement. A silhouette appeared for a moment at the curtains of one of the soft-lit upstairs rooms, then was gone. He peered through a ground floor window and saw more servants moving about inside, lighting sticks of sandalwood incense to keep the mosquitoes away. He heard the cooks in the kitchen shouting to each other in Tamil over the clash of pots and dishes as they cleaned up after the evening meal.

Where was she?

He made his way slowly around the side of the house. He could hear voices from inside, through an open window. One of them was a girl's. 'Narain, we must leave now.'

'I am coming, *mem'sahib.*'

The wrought iron gates creaked open. Four porters shuffled through with a palanquin on their shoulders and set it down under the *porte-cochere.*

Lachlan moved silently through the bushes and positioned himself in the shadows a few paces away. He took the pistol from the waistband of his breeches and felt in his pocket for one of the charges he had brought with him. He bit off the paper twist, spat it out, then poured a few grains into the frizzen pan and the rest of the charge down the barrel. He locked it down again.

He looked up to see if the porters had heard him, but not one of them had looked around. They were more concerned with massaging their raw and blistered shoulders. He could fire a cannon, and they wouldn't care.

He made sure the ball was slotted firmly down the barrel with the ramrod, pulled the cock back to its firing position and held the pistol, barrel upwards, next to his cheek.

He could hear his heart hammering against his ribs. It seemed so loud to him he wondered that the whole house couldn't hear it.

He knew that he would only get one shot and that there would be no time to reload. When it was done, her guards would come at him, and the only other weapon he had was the dagger concealed inside his shirt. His chances of escape were negligible, but then getting out of Pondicherry alive had never been an essential part of the plan.

Someone stepped out onto the portico.

Lachlan could see him clearly in the light of the coach lamp hanging above the door. He was a tall Sikh with a thick black beard. The uniform he was wearing – a light blue jacket and grey breeches - sent a chill through him. He remembered it only too well from the day Gagnon's men had swarmed Delgoa Bay. There was a curved sword with a pearl handle at his belt, and he was wearing more gold braid than an admiral of the fleet. A ruby glinted in one of his ears.

A girl stepped out of the villa behind him. She looked as fragile as a china doll. She was wearing a bonnet, and her white hair hung straight down her back from beneath it. She went towards the palanquin. 'These men are slovenly,' she said, 'We should employ our own.'

'Yes, *mem'sahib*,' the Sikh said. 'Next time.'

She was no more than ten paces away.

Lachlan raised the pistol. Flintlocks were notoriously unreliable at a distance, but this one had a rifled barrel and at this range he could not miss. He aimed at her head.

The porters picked up the palanquin and the Sikh stood to the side to help her into it.

Now, Lachlan thought.

The girl took the Sikh's hand and stepped up into the sedan. She pulled the curtain closed and the porters set off through the gates, the Sikh body-guard marching alongside.

Lachlan lowered the pistol.

He couldn't do it.

Madras

'McKenzie,' Channing said, 'so, you have decided to grace us with your presence once more. We all wondered what had happened to you.' He tapped on the edge of the rosewood desk with his pen.

Charlie had told him that Channing didn't know what to do with him. How could he throw the Tiger of Karimkot in prison for deserting his post, especially when his wife had just been murdered inside the fort?

'I left Madras,' Lachlan said.

'Without permission.'

'You said I could take as much time as I wanted.'

'I did not say you could leave the post.'

Lachlan nodded and offered nothing else. He watched the play of confusion on Channing's face.

'Where did you go?'

Lachlan didn't reply.

'You went to Pondicherry,' Channing said.

Why are we playing these games, Lachlan thought. Monsabert would have already told you all this. 'Yes, sir.'

'That was damned stupid.'

Yes, it had been stupid, especially as he had spectacularly failed to do what he had gone there to do.

'If the French had discovered you, you would have been shot as a spy. To deliberately put yourself in such danger borders on madness. What were you thinking?' When Lachlan still didn't reply he said, 'Our intelligencer says that you were looking for the person responsible for your wife's murder. Well?'

'That business is done.'

'I'm glad to hear it.' Channing shook his head and tutted. 'You performed sterling service at Karimkot, but this will blot your record I'm afraid.'

'I understand, sir. And with that in mind, I have respectfully decided to forego the position you offered me. I can't remain on post after all that has happened. I hear that Captain Clive is to take an army against the French. I should like to go with him.'

Channing realised that his reprimand had gone unheeded. He shrugged his shoulders, at a loss. 'I thought you'd had enough of military life.'

'A change of heart.'

'Are you sure about this?'

'If I stay here in Madras, I shall go mad.'

If only it had been the Sikh, he thought. I would have pulled the trigger, and it would be done with. But does a man of conscience kill a young girl in cold blood? Charlie had understood. *How can you stand it.* That was the problem. Right now, he couldn't.

But the latest developments in the Carnatic had given him a way out. Despite the victory at Karimkot, Madras was still under threat. The French and their ally, Raju Sahib, had captured Conjeeveram and had tried to retake Karimkot while Lachlan was in the hospital recovering from his leg wound. Reinforcements had arrived from Bengal, and a Company captain named Robert Clive had marched out of Fort David to confront the enemy. He had roundly defeated Raju Sahib at a battle at Arni and was in pursuit of the remains of his army in the south.

Channing chewed his lip, thinking it over. He really had no choice. 'Clive is already halfway to Conjeeveram.'

'Then I should like to leave as soon as possible. With a good horse I could catch up with him in a couple of days.'

'If that's what you want.' Channing looked perplexed. 'I understand you've suffered a great loss, but you're still young. You will get over this in time.'

Lachlan nodded, eager to escape. 'Thank you, sir. I'll remember that.'

CHAPTER 7

Vendalur

Robert Clive sat in a camp chair in a sun-faded red jacket chewing a dry chapati. He looked up as an aide lifted the tent flap and ushered Lachlan inside. 'Ah, the Tiger of Karimkot,' he said.

Lachlan saluted.

He had heard a lot about Robert Clive. Rumour had it that he had been thrown out of school for violent conduct and that he had even run a protection racket in the village where he had grown up.

His first impressions of the man didn't disappoint. There was a restless energy about him. He looked to be the sort of man always ready for a brawl or a thirty-mile march.

'I heard you were on your way,' Clive said. 'I'd offer you a chair but there isn't one. I see you're limping.'

'Souvenir of Karimkot.'

'As long as it doesn't slow you down. I need as many good men as I can get, so your timing is perfect. One of my officers has just expired from fever. His bad luck is your opportunity.'

'I know these men well. They fought with me at Karimkot.'

'You mean the Fusiliers? Not them, I'm afraid, I need you with my sepoy regiment.'

'Are they reliable?'

Clive grimaced. 'We'll soon find out. Most of them are new recruits. I'm afraid you'll have your work cut out.'

Lachlan closed his eyes. Dear God.

'You'll be fine. I've put one my best sergeants in charge of them for the time being. He'll give you every assistance.' He turned to his aide de camp. 'Bring Baker in here, will you?'

Sergeant Baker was ushered in. He saluted and stood to attention, ramrod straight.

'Baker, this is Lieutenant McKenzie.' Clive nodded towards Lachlan. 'He is to take command of your regiment. Find him a tent and introduce him to the men.' He turned back to Lachlan and clapped his hands enthusiastically as if they were about to go into town drinking and whoring. 'Great days! Get some rest, McKenzie. Channing says you're eager to get into action again and I'm sure we shall not disappoint.'

The sun was sinking behind the clouds, turning them rose pink. Flocks of parrots wheeled overhead, landing skittish and quarrelling in the palm fronds. Spider monkeys howled in the forest.

As Lachlan walked through the camp, he recognised the familiar, acrid taint of woodsmoke and horses. A few of the men had started cook fires, while others lit their pipes and tried to massage the stiffness from their calves and their feet.

Baker introduced him to the *jemadars* in his new command.

Lachlan spoke to them in the bastard Portuguese that was the common language of the Coromandel. He was pleased to find that the sepoys had been well kitted out with Brown Bess muskets and socket bayonets. Quite a few of them also had their own swords, sturdy weapons with distinctive curved blades that they called *talwars*.

When his impromptu inspection was done, he bent down and lit his cheroot from one of the campfires. He followed his new sergeant to a tent not far from Clive's.

'This is yours for tonight, sir,' Baker said.

'Thanks, Sergeant. Do you have a first name?'

Baker raised an eyebrow, surprised that an officer would be interested. 'Thomas. Friends call me Tommy.'

'Where are you from?'

'East End, sir. Born and raised.'

'The east end of what?'

'London,' Tommy said, as if that should have been obvious.

'Never been there. What's it like?'

'Shit hole, sir, pardon my French.'

Lachlan slapped at a mosquito. 'Worse than here?'

'Different shit. Different hole.'

'So how long have you been with the Madras Regiment?'

'The natives, sir? Only since Captain Williams went to feed the worms. I was brought across from the Fusiliers.'

'The Fusiliers? You weren't with me at Karimkot.'

'No sir. I was shipped down from Calcutta after that was all over. You were the toast of Madras when I arrived.'

Lachlan noticed that his new sergeant was still standing as if he was on the parade ground. 'At ease, Tommy. Do you want a cheroot?'

'Thank you, no sir. I prefer my pipe.'

'Well, alright. I'll let you go off and relax. I'm going to turn in. It was a hard ride from Madras.'

'Yes, sir. By the way. Commiserations, sir. I heard what happened to Mrs McKenzie. Bad business, that. You must be eager to settle the score.'

Lachlan hesitated. 'Whatever that means,' he said. He ducked under the tent flaps and fell onto the bed.

A few hours later, he woke to shouting. Clive's scouts had returned with the news that they had located Raju Sahib's army at Conjeeveram.

Bugles echoed around the darkened plain as Clive roused his seven-hundred-man army.

The Fusiliers marched in file along the road in their heavy, red serge jackets and white cross belts, their muskets over their shoulders and bayonets fixed. Their uniforms were dark with sweat and coated with ochre dust. The heat was enervating. Several of them had dropped out of the line and were on their knees by the side of the road calling for water.

Lachlan's own sepoys, in their sandals and baggy native trousers, might not look as smart, but in his opinion what they wore was a hundred times more practical than the stockings, gaiters and heavy shoes of the European regiment.

But it was not their turnout that concerned him. The Fusiliers had months, if not years, of hard training behind them. His levies were raw recruits. He wondered how many of them would be able to load and reload quickly and efficiently in a real firefight.

The sweat was pouring out of him. It ran down his face and into his eyes. He hoped that Clive might call a halt, but it was soon clear their captain had no intention of it. He kept them going right through the afternoon. At sunset they got a short rest, then he urged them on again.

Lachlan let the other officers ride ahead without him and walked alongside his new detachment, leading his horse by the reins.

'Horse giving you bother?' Tommy said. 'Don't trust them myself.'

'The horse is fine. Just thought I'd march with the men for a while. For the sake of morale.'

'The men's or the horse's, sir?'

Lachlan laughed. It had been a while. He thought he might get to like his new sergeant. 'I don't know how you manage it. Marching all day and night in those uniforms.'

'You get used to things, sir. Hot, cold, it's all the same to me. In Limehouse none of us kids ever had shoes, even when it snowed. You manage. No point complaining. No one listens.'

'I've never seen snow. What's it like?'

'It's very fucking cold, sir, pardon my French.'

'Is there anything you've never got used to?'

'Mosquitoes. Can't abide the little bastards. And officers. Begging your pardon, sir, I'm sure you're not like the others.'

Lachlan laughed again. 'I'll try not to be.'

They reached Conjeeveram just before dawn. Lachlan was anticipating a fight, but thankfully the bulk of Raju Sahib's army had already moved on towards Arcot. As soon as the native garrison that Raju had left behind saw them coming, they ran up a white flag.

Just as well, Lachlan thought. The men were all too exhausted to fight. Most of them were too tired even to build campfires. They just lay down by the side of the road and slept. They had marched almost fifty miles in two days.

Late in the afternoon, the bugle sounded. The pack ponies and mules were brought up, along with the bullock carts and the coolies with folding tables and camp stools balanced on their heads.

Clive was ready to march again.

CHAPTER 8

I t was just on sunset, and the air was heavy with the tang of fruit. Lachlan dozed in the saddle. The mosquitoes and sand flies began to swarm, and he slapped irritably at his neck.

Suddenly, flames flickered along the line of mango trees away to their right, followed a heartbeat later by the boom of heavy cannons. The ground erupted in front of him, and he saw men, or pieces of men, flying through the air. For a moment he was too stunned to react.

Clive had led them into an ambush.

'Get the ranks into cover!' Clive shouted.

The men hardly needed encouragement. Most of them had already thrown themselves into the ditch on the other side of the road. Lachlan jumped off his horse and led it down the embankment.

He started counting in his head. Like every man who'd been in battle before, he knew how long it would take the gunners to reload. He would only have to count to thirty if they were French, perhaps to a hundred if they were natives.

So, for all our sakes, he thought, let's pray they're not French.

He peered over the top of the ditch. Clive was ordering one of the lieutenants to get the supply train to the rear, while two redcoats were dragging a body off the road. The man's legs were gone and there were just meaty stumps protruding from his breeches. He was still conscious and screaming.

Lachlan turned away.

Clive came to stand at the top of the ditch, one hand on his hip. He was tapping his foot as if he was impatient with the enemy gunners for taking so long to reload.

Dear God, Lachlan thought, the man has ice in his veins. He stood up and went to join him.

Twenty-eight, twenty-nine...

He saw another blossoming of flame and smoke as the guns in the tope roared again. A rush of heat sent him and Clive toppling sideways into the ditch.

When he sat up, he saw an ensign lying on his back, his head hanging over the lip of the trench. He pulled him down out of harm's way. He was surprisingly light, and then he saw why. There was nothing left of him below the chest.

Someone shouted a warning. Lachlan looked up. There were French infantry heading towards them along the channel. He saw the flash of musket fire as shot after shot zipped past his head in the dark.

Tommy appeared beside him and pulled him back to a bend in the watercourse, where the rest of the men had taken refuge. 'Fix bayonets?' he said.

'Not yet,' Lachlan said. 'Let's see how much fire those Frenchies have in their bellies. Load and fire at will.'

He watched the sepoys go about their business, firing down the trench then ducking back for cover. The French fired back from their own positions but stopped their advance.

They had each other effectively pinned down.

A three-quarter moon appeared from behind the clouds, making it light enough to see the silhouettes of Raju Sahib's cavalry on the other side of the ditch. They were galloping from one flank to the other, but never quite forming up. Their presence meant that Lachlan and his sepoys could not advance or retreat without leaving themselves vulnerable to a cavalry charge.

Two of his new recruits were cowering in the ditch, unnerved by the noise of their first battle. He remembered his own baptism of fire at the fort in Delgoa Bay. That day, he had learned to block out the screams and the crack of musket fire, so he could get his limbs moving and think his way through the battle.

He ran over to the two men and shook them roughly by the shoulders. 'Load and fire,' he shouted . He stood over them and showed them how to do it, reminding them of their drill. He pulled a paper cartridge from the pouch at his side, bit off the end, then poured some of the powder into the pan of his musket. He rammed the ball and the rest of the wad down the barrel, aimed and fired.

'Now do it,' he said in Portuguese, and they roused themselves from their panic and copied his movements.

Once he was satisfied that they knew what to do, he clapped them on the back and moved off. He had gone barely ten paces when there was an explosion of dirt and smoke behind him, and when the smoke cleared, one of the men lay in pieces. The other was screaming with half his leg gone.

Lachlan stumbled backwards onto his haunches, and looked down, expecting to see blood. But he seemed to be unharmed.

The man was still screaming as the bearers carried him away. His foot and lower leg lay in the mud, meat and bone.

'Sir. Sir!' Tommy was shaking him.

Lachlan nodded and got back to his feet. 'I'm alright,' he said, though he scarcely believed it himself. 'I'm alright.'

It was the gunners who were taking most of the casualties. It was clear that the French battery in the mango tope was overwhelming them. Lachlan guessed they were twelve or sixteen-pounders. They were simply being outgunned.

He peered over the lip of the ditch. Grapeshot raked the corpses that littered the road, turning them into butcher's meat. The gunners leaped over ramrods and sponge pails to manhandle their field guns onto their limbers and move them up and down the road after each salvo to prevent the Frenchies getting a mark on them. The sulphur stink of powder clung to the night mist.

He felt a hand on his shoulder. It was one of Clive's runners, motioning for Lachlan to follow. He went after the man in a crouching run.

Clive and the other officers were huddled in conference behind a huge banyan. 'Even if I was of a mind to,' Clive was saying, 'it is impossible to retreat. The guns would butcher us, and their cavalry would come over the top of us. What we must do is attack.'

'How do we do that?' someone said.

'We get behind the French guns. My scouts say they are undefended on their left flank.' He turned to Lachlan. 'Lieutenant McKenzie, I want you to take fifty men back along this ditch and circle around their guns.' He grabbed Lachlan's tunic and hauled him up to show him. He pointed to the dark silhouette of the mango tope on the other side of the rice paddy. 'Stay low and stay quiet until you are close enough for a charge. Do you think you can do it?'

'We can do it,' Lachlan said. He would have said yes even if Clive had asked him to charge the guns alone, armed only with a pistol.

So, this is how it ends, he thought. He made his way back along the ditch, eager to be at it.

'So much for our scouts,' Tommy said.

Lachlan lay on his belly in the dirt and peered into the dark. Clive's scouts had reported that the French battery was undefended on its flank, but Lachlan could make out what looked to be an entire company of infantry in the grove between them and the guns. He wasn't surprised by this turn of events. He had never really believed that any French officer would be so foolish as to leave the flanks of his artillery exposed.

'Tell the men to follow me.'

'Sir?'

'Our orders are to charge the guns. So that is what we are going to do. Only instead of coming from the flank, we'll take them from the rear.'

'But if we keep going and we're spotted, we'll not be able to retreat. It's suicide, sir.'

'Just follow me, Tommy. And if it all goes to hell, look on the bright side. The mosquitoes won't ever bother you again.'

Lachlan set off, crawling on his belly, without waiting to see if his sergeant had obeyed. Tommy was right, of course. If they were seen, they would find themselves in a hand-to-hand fight, heavily outnumbered and cut off from the main body of their army. Yet he felt curiously detached from the outcome.

A few minutes later, he was a hundred paces past the French infantry outposts. He peered back across the paddy. The moon had disappeared behind the clouds again, and it was difficult to make out the French positions. The mango tope was now to his left. He doubled back towards it.

The moon reappeared, and for a moment, the battlefield was bathed in a silvery luminescence. He made out the French gunners standing at their positions around the cannons. They think they're untouchable, he thought.

He looked over his shoulder. He half expected to find himself alone, but to his surprise he could make out the silhouettes of his fifty men on their bellies in the dust behind him. Good lads, these. He hoped he hadn't led them to their doom. He raised himself on one elbow and shouted 'Charge!' Then he stood up and started to run.

Because of the din of the cannons, he was only a few yards from the battery by the time the French gunners saw him. Their faces registered a mixture of shock and disbelief.

He drew his hanger and charged at the first gun in the line. Their captain produced a pistol from his belt and aimed it at Lachlan's head. Lachlan could have thrown himself aside, but he didn't. Sparks flew from the frizzen, but there was no shot.

A misfire.

Lachlan kept his hanger straight out from his arm as he ran. It took the French captain in the middle of the chest and piled him back against one of the trees.

Something hit him hard from the side. Another French officer was standing ten paces away with a drawn pistol. Lachlan realised he had been shot. He went down onto one knee.

A French gunner ran towards him holding a handspike. He raised it over his head. Lachlan closed his eyes and wondered if there would be much pain. But nothing happened.

When he opened his eyes again, he saw Tommy pulling his bayonet from the Frenchman's body.

Suddenly, there were red jackets everywhere. His men had followed him right into the teeth of the guns.

Tommy knelt down beside him. 'You're bloody mad,' he said.

CHAPTER 9

The Company Hospital, Madras

A minister with a Bible was passing along the beds. He was attracting good custom. Nothing like a shave with death to make a man think about the hereafter, Lachlan thought. When the minister came up to his bed, he waved him on.

He vaguely remembered waking up in the field hospital and the surgeon saying he was lucky. How did getting shot constitute good fortune?

Then there was the long trip back to Madras on the back of a wagon, men moaning and vomiting and bleeding everywhere. It was mostly a blur. Finally, arriving here, being thrown into a bed and told to rest.

There was no rest to be had in this madhouse. Every hour or so, a man would start screaming and raving and have to be held down. The captain in the bed opposite him snored day and night. His head was entirely covered in bandages, and an orderly told him it was grapeshot and there wasn't much of his face left. Lachlan realised the poor bastard wasn't actually snoring, he was just trying to breathe.

There was the constant wearying attack of the flies. They crawled all over his face and into his ears and nose, without pity. They even flew into his mouth when he was asleep. Countless times he woke up choking.

Munro, the surgeon in charge of the hospital, was rarely there. Sometimes Lachlan heard him and the orderlies laughing, drinking and playing cards down the corridor in Munro's office. At night they went into the Black Town for further entertainment. When they got back in the early hours of the morning, some of them were so drunk they would haul one of the other ranks out of their bed so they could sleep it off in comfort.

Charlie Mathieson came to see him. He said the lead ball had passed straight through the flesh on his shoulder and that he was luckier than most. There was that word again. Luck. If this was being lucky, what would it be like the day it finally ran out?

On the third day he caught a fever. He thrashed and tossed on the bed in delirium, shivering with cold and burning up by turns. He lost track of time. He didn't know when he was awake and when he was dreaming. It all bled into one.

One day he woke briefly and saw Tommy bending down next to his bed. 'Tommy, what are you doing here?'

'Got the ague again so they sent me back here. Fever broke last night so I'm getting out of this place. I came to see how you were doing. Not too good by the looks of it.'

'I don't remember much.'

'Do you remember charging the guns on your own, sir? You could have given me fair warning. Was a hell of a business getting the men to follow.'

'What happened?'

'The Frenchies bolted when they saw us coming. We rounded up a few of them, but the ones that got away put the frighteners up the rest of them. Ran like Irishmen from a bath, they did. All thanks to you. The Tiger of Karimkot.' He lifted the bandages and sniffed at the wound. 'Oh, good lord. Like a side of beef that's been left out in the sun. What's that quack been doing to you?'

'He bled me, I think. Yesterday.'

'You'll do no good here. We have to get you out. Hold steady.' Tommy hauled him upright and manhandled him over his shoulder. 'This will hurt a bit,' he said and walked out of the ward.

No one challenged them. There were no guards, and Munro and his orderlies were whoring in Black Town. Lachlan wanted to ask where he was taking him, but he didn't have the strength anymore. He slipped in and out of wakefulness. Every step sent a vivid spasm of pain through his shoulder.

Finally, he blacked out.

When he woke, he found himself lying in a bare room with mud walls. Chevrons of light filtered in through a tattered bamboo blind. He lay on a simple charpoy, lathered in sweat.

He listened. It sounded like he was in the native quarter. He could hear a smithy beating copper with a hammer, a hawker shouting for customers. A bullock cart rumbled past the window.

After a while, an old man came in wearing a *dhoti* and a white robe. He was carrying a wooden jug with some steaming liquid in it. Lachlan shook his head. He was boiling up. The last thing he wanted was *chai*.

'Bullocky *sahib* says you can speak Tamil,' the old man said.

Lachlan frowned. 'Who?'

'Your *jemadar*.'

Lachlan realised he meant Tommy.

The old man sat down on the edge of the charpoy. 'The wound in your shoulder is suppurating. There is every which kind of dirt and muck in it. If we don't clean it, you are going to die. Do you understand?'

Lachlan nodded. 'What is that?'

'It is *ghee*, clarified butter. It is still hot. I am sorry, *sahib*. This is going to hurt very much. But it will save your life.' He pulled back the filthy dressing on his shoulder. 'Are you ready?'

'No. Wait. What are you going to do?'

'It cannot wait, *sahib*,' the old man said and poured the steaming butter into the open wound.

Lachlan lost an entire day as he lay on the charpoy shaking with cold or boiling up with fever, yelling at the phantoms that came to torment him. But the next morning when he woke, he felt as if he had walked out of thick fog into the sunlight. His mind felt clear as he watched the sun inching across the mud floor. He found he could remember things again, the battle at Kaveripauk and the field hospital where they had taken him after he and his men had attacked the French field battery.

He remembered the old Tamil and the boiling butter. Who the hell was he?

There was no pain until he tried to sit up. When he did, he gasped and lay back again. His skin erupted in a cold, oily sweat, and after that there was no position he could lie in that would relieve the agony. He had never experienced anything like it. He heard old the man moving about outside and he called out.

The door opened. The man came in, holding a brass cup of steaming liquid.

Lachlan put up a hand, ready to get off the cot and fight him. 'No,' he said, 'you're not going to do that to me again.'

The old man grinned. 'No *sahib*, this is *chai*. You like *chai*?'

'Better than I like *ghee*. Can you give me something for the pain?'

The old man nodded and left the room. When he came back, he was holding an opium pipe and an ivory box. He sat cross-legged on the grass mat next to Lachlan's charpoy and laid the pipe and the contents of the box in front of him.

There was a small, brass lamp which he lit with a flint. He took a needle and a ball of black, sticky opium from the box and held it over the flame in the lamp, turning it round and round. The opium started to soften and evaporate. He placed it into the saddle of the pipe and handed it to Lachlan.

He hesitated. He had heard about the opium dens in the Black Town and seen the skeletal addicts collapsed outside. Opium frightened him. Charlie had once told him about a Company man who had got addicted to it. Before they could send him back to England, he had disappeared from his rooms, and no one had heard from him again. Rumour had it that he was living in rags somewhere in the native quarter.

But he needed something. One pipe wouldn't hurt. After all, this was just medicine. He took his first draw and even as he watched the grey blue tendrils of smoke drift towards the thatched roof, he felt the pain magically dissolve. He let out a long sigh and drifted off to sleep.

Lachlan sat up. His shoulder was so stiff that he could barely move it. But he could smell no putrefaction from underneath the bandages, and the fever was gone.

The old man stood at the bottom of the charpoy and gave a curious head wobble that Lachlan knew could mean just about anything. 'I'm going to live?' he said.

Another bob of the head.

'What's your name?'

'My name is Balu, *sahib*. I am a healer. Bullocky *sahib* brought you here.'

Lachlan remembered now how Tommy had put him over his shoulder and carried him out of the hospital. 'Why do you call him that?'

'That is what everyone in Black Town calls him.'

Lachlan smiled. He supposed his sergeant's wide shoulders and the way he walked, with his head down and get-out-of-my attitude had spawned the nickname. 'You know him well?'

'Oh yes. He brings me many patients. He says bad things about Munro *sahib*. He calls him Doctor of Death.' Balu looked at the fresh pink wound on Lachlan's leg. 'You have many wounds for a young man. On your back, also.'

Lachlan pointed to his thigh. 'Battle.' He jerked a thumb at his back. 'Vulture.'

Balu's eyebrows shot up. 'Then you are very fortunate.'

Lachlan shook his head. 'That's me. The luckiest man alive.'

'You do not think you are blessed?'

'Not really, all things considered.'

'Ah, I see,' Balu said. 'You are feeling sorry for yourself. Something bad has happened to you?'

'I've had more than my fair share of bad happenings.'

'Who says what is a fair share?'

'I don't know. God perhaps?'

'You are a religious man?'

Lachlan shrugged. 'Not particularly.'

'When you leave here, look around you, *sahib*. You will see lepers with no faces, beggars with no feet. Yet you have a friend who will carry you all the way across Madras on his back to save your life. What kind of man has such friends? A very fortunate one. Also, you are young, and you are handsome. You have come from a big battle where men have lost their lives and their legs. But not you.

'You are just a spoiled *feringhee* who expects too much from life and from the gods. In a week, you will walk out of here and no one will know you were ever hurt. Whatever these bad things are that have happened to you, you have not had more than your fair share. More than some perhaps, less than others. So bless your good karma, *sahib*. You have a second chance at life. Be thankful for it.'

CHAPTER 10

A s soon as Lachlan walked into the teak-panelled mess hall, he found himself surrounded by wide-eyed young writers wanting to shake his hand. It seemed the Tiger of Karimkot had added to his legend with his exploits at Kaveripauk.

The older men looked up from their games of seven card loo, frowning and muttering among themselves at the unseemly commotion. Charlie came over and rescued Lachlan from the crush. He steered him towards the billiards table.

A turbaned butler brought a glass engraved with the Company coat of arms. 'Your lime juice and water, *sahib*,' he said to Charlie. He looked at Lachlan.

'*Arrack*,' Lachlan said. 'Bring the bottle.'

The butler nodded and silently withdrew.

Charlie chalked his cue. 'You've made a spectacular recovery. The last time I saw you in the hospital you were raving like a madman from fever. Munro said you were not long for this world. Then I heard you'd disappeared. Where on earth did you go?'

'I went looking for a second opinion.'

Charlie nodded. 'A wise decision. But you can't keep disappearing. It's hard to keep up.'

'Does Channing still want me to be the next Clerk of the Market?'

Charlie laughed. 'Not likely. Tiger of Karimkot be damned. These days he thinks you're reckless, unreliable and a possible troublemaker.'

'Like Clive?'

'Channing will only indulge one renegade at a time and Clive has seniority.'

Lachlan looked up at the walls. Portraits of former presidents and Leadenhall Street dignitaries glowered down at him, all of them as disapproving as Channing.

The windows were open and as Charlie leaned over the baize, he paused his shot to slap at a mosquito.

'I'm not killing any more Frenchmen,' Lachlan said. 'I've had enough of butchery.'

'Of course. He can't send you back to the battlefield anyway, not in the state you're in. It looks like the warring is nearly over anyway. Have you heard the news?'

'Has Clive relieved Trichinopoly?'

'Not yet, but it's only a matter of time. When he does, the French and their bevy of Indian princes will have to come to the treaty table, and it will all be over. How's your Parsi?'

'What?'

'Your facility for languages has not gone unremarked. I told the Board that you speak Tamil and Portuguese like a native.'

'Why would you do that?'

'There's an opening for a new Resident in Murshidabad. The last poor chap caught a fever and is now representing our interests in the Hereafter.'

'Channing thinks I'm suitable for a diplomatic posting?'

'I wouldn't go that far. He has severe reservations about your mental state, but I managed to persuade him that your bout of madness was temporary.'

'Why would you do that?'

'Because you need to get away from Madras, and the Company needs someone of your resources. Do you think you're up for a new challenge?'

Lachlan drained his *arrack*. 'What do I have to do?'

'Your job will be to ensure that the nawab there remains sympathetic to our ambitions in Bengal. A thankless job, but it won't involve killing any Frenchmen. Or killing anyone, we hope. Sir Roger Drake, the president in Calcutta, has requested we send someone urgently.'

'I know nothing about diplomacy.'

'Think of it as kissing someone's feet and twisting their arm at the same time. You're a smart fellow, I'm sure you'll get the hang of it. First, you'd better find yourself some books on grammar, and a good teacher. They only speak Persian in the Mughal court.'

'Can I take my own staff?'

'Well, you'll need an adjutant, at least. Who do you have in mind?'

Lachlan's arrival in the regiment mess hall caused some consternation. He pushed the *tatties* aside, and the three men playing cards at a table immediately leaped to attention. 'I'm looking for Sergeant Baker,' he said.

'Go and get Tommy,' one of the men said and the youngest of them took off down the corridor to the dormitories.

Tommy appeared moments later in his shirtsleeves, smoking a pipe. 'Lieutenant McKenzie,' he said, his face registering his surprise.

'Yes, alive and kicking, thanks to you. Could you step outside for a moment?'

'I'll get my jacket.'

'It's like a furnace out there, Sergeant. Come as you are.'

When they got outside, Lachlan heard laughter and saw some young men climbing over the wall of the fort. Munro was with them.

'Heading into the Black Town again,' Tommy said. 'Gallanting the ladies they call it. Others call it whoring. I wouldn't mind what that piss prophet does on his own time if he spared a thought on occasion for some of my lads that are in his hospital.'

'You saved my life, Tommy.'

'No, Balu did that.'

'How did you come to know him?'

'One of my fellow sergeants told me about him. He cured him of a very nasty dose of clap. I've taken several of the lads to see him since. And not just for clap. For all sorts.'

'I'd like to repay you.'

'No need, sir. Only cost me a few *annas*. Couple of bottles of *arrack* should do it.'

'I think I can do better than that. I've been ordered north, to take up a diplomatic posting in Bengal. I'll need an adjutant. It means a significant raise in pay and prestige.'

'Me, sir?' Tommy sucked vigorously on his pipe. 'I've never been anyone's adjutant before, sir. What am I expected to do? Hope there's no buggery involved, begging your pardon.'

'Buggery is on your own time, Tommy. When you're in uniform you'll be expected to run my household and generally keep me out of trouble. You've been doing that well enough already. Only now you'll be paid for it.'

Tommy took his pipe out of his mouth and saluted. 'Right you are, sir. Adjutant it is.'

CHAPTER 11

Lachlan reined in his horse and looked over his shoulder at the two hackeries rumbling behind them. The bullocks hauling the carts slumped along barely above walking pace.

Dear God, it would be quicker to crawl to Bengal on our hands and knees, he thought. But what was under the oilskin covers was unfortunately indispensable. The carts contained presents for the Nawab of Bengal. No diplomatic mission in India was complete without bribes, though Lachlan was privately unimpressed with the Company's idea of bounty.

There was a rather ordinary sword, a portrait of King George II looking as if he had just sat on a pin, and an account of the English, Scottish and Irish ecclesiastical councils from 446 to 1717 in four volumes, bound in red calfskin. And a walnut longcase clock. Aside from the hackeries, they had several cartloads of supplies and half a dozen porters.

Their escort took up the rearguard - a dozen mounted sepoys on nags that should have gone to the knackery long ago. A *subadar* carried the red and white striped Company flag.

Lachlan surveyed the dull, torpid river below them. Flights of stone steps led into the water, and there was a crowd of local people bathing there, the men in simple white dhotis, the women wearing their bright coloured saris.

The character of the countryside was changing. He had seen several small and slightly garish Hindu temples through the trees, but now they were side by side with sedate, red brick Mohammedan churches, their minarets bone white against the vivid green of the jungle.

Tommy rode up beside him, jerking at his horse's reins as if he were trying to pull a crate of bricks up a steep slope. 'This fucking horse, pardon my French, sir.'

He and Tommy had been given two big Marwari horses from Jodhpur. They were both fifteen hands and fine-looking beasts, though Lachlan's had the better temper and didn't constantly champ at the bit like his sergeant's. An hour into each day's ride, Tommy was already red in the face from battling with the reins.

'Use your knees to guide her, Tommy.'

'I'd rather use my musket.'

'Then you'd have to walk.'

'Walking might be easier.' The mare twisted her head and tried to bite him over her shoulder. 'She hates me.'

'I can send you back to Madras if you like. It's the horse or back with Clive, tramping all over the Coromandel at his whim.'

Tommy laughed. 'A lot of similarities between Captain Clive and this horse, not least the temperament.' The mare finally settled, and he leaned over the withers to catch his breath.

'Come on, no time for lazing about.' Lachlan spurred his horse down the slope.

Further along the valley, they passed several mounds of raised earth marked with a stone. They were well-tended, and the grass had not been allowed to encroach. Lachlan knew they were *sati* stones. He had seen them before. They marked the spot where a wife had thrown herself on her husband's funeral pyre. Some of them even bore the woman's sculpted handprint. The families of such women were proud of her sacrifice as it reflected well on them, so they kept the stones and the area around the memorials in good order.

He thought about Catia's sacrifice. He felt ashamed of himself.

'Penny for your thoughts,' Tommy said.

'I was calculating distance,' Lachlan said. He consulted his map and showed him the river and the nearby village. 'We should be in Murshidabad the day after tomorrow. A fresh start for us both, Tommy. When we get there, remind me to get you riding lessons.'

The long, dusty road seemed endless. By nine o'clock Lachlan could barely sit straight on his horse, his throat was parched and his lips cracked. He poured water over a towel and draped it around his neck, but in minutes it was dry again. Even the sepoys were swaying in their saddles. It was impossible to continue.

He saw a grove of tamarind trees ahead of them and signalled that they would make a stop. They would continue again later in the afternoon after the scorching wind had died down.

The servants set up his tent. When it was done, he collapsed into his camp chair and tore off his jacket. He pulled the cloth from around his neck and dropped it into a bucket of water. He rinsed his face with it then squeezed the water over his head until it ran down his neck and off his chin. Then he put the towel back around his neck.

He reached for his cheroots. He offered one to Tommy, who shook his head. He lit it and watched the sepoys settle down under the broad shade of an ancient peepal tree. Its twisted roots had been exposed by the monsoon rains, and they squatted between them, laughing as they prepared *chai*.

'Did you know they're Brahmins?' he said.

'They're what, sir?'

'Those sepoys. They're all Brahmins. In the Hindu caste system, they are at the top of the hierarchy. See those brass pots they're drinking from? If you or I took a drink from them, they'd have to throw the pot away because we would have defiled it. Do you know why?'

'Because we're foreigners?'

'Because we're beneath them. In their eyes, we are untouchables, no different to beggars and street cleaners. And yet they take orders from us and fight for us and die for us. Don't you think that's strange?'

Tommy stared at the sepoys and frowned. 'I knew the officers thought I was untouchable. I didn't know the men thought that as well.'

'I wonder why they do it,' Lachlan said. 'Why fight for us and not their own kind?'

'Perhaps the money's better.'

'I suppose so. Seems everyone's got a price. Well, not quite everyone.'

'Sir?'

'When you carried me out of the hospital, you weren't motivated by money. If someone had seen you, you would have been in a lot of trouble. There was nothing in it for you and you did it anyway.'

'No chance of getting caught, sir. I know my way around that fort blindfold.'

'So, you'd do that for anyone then?'

Tommy shrugged. 'Perhaps I thought you were worth saving.'

'I'm amazed that you think that.'

'I know you've had some bad luck in your life, but I can see the day a man such as yourself will recover from his losses and be rewarded for his doggedness. I wouldn't want anything to get in the way of that.'

Lachlan smiled. 'You should have been a philosopher.'

'All I know is, no matter what kind of trouble a man finds himself in, he must hold on and hope for the best. There's always tomorrow.'

'What if tomorrow is worse?'

'Then you be patient and wait for the day after that.'

'That's been your experience, has it?' Lachlan studied him. 'How has life treated you?'

'Not too bad, all things considered. I could have ended up doing the hangman's jig like my brother, but instead the Company gave me a musket and a pair of boots and here I am. I've not much to complain about if you don't count the heat and the dysentery.'

'So, you'd never go back?'

'To Limehouse? I'd rather stick my cock in a fire ants' nest. The army's my family now. Besides, you can't go back, can you? You know the saying, you can't swim in the same river twice.'

Lachlan nodded. 'Good advice, Tommy. I'll take it on board.'

CHAPTER 12

Murshidabad, Bengal

Lachlan drew breath as Murshidabad came into view on the far shore of the Cossimbazar River. This misty, watercolour world of white cupolas and palm trees was so different from the Coromandel. The city was much bigger than he had expected, even though Charlie had warned him that Murshidabad had as many people as London. He had thought he was exaggerating.

Bengal was like coming to India a second time. There were sights and sounds he had not seen before. As they rode down the valley, he heard the Muslim call to prayer echo from the minarets, a sound he supposed he would grow as accustomed to as the church bells of Saint Mary's in Madras.

A snaking file of Hindu women with clay jugs of water balanced on their heads made their way down the road from the ghats. This was an everyday sight around Madras. What was new to him was the bright-painted elephant, with a turbaned Moslem noble in the swaying howdah on its back, passing the other way.

They reached a large rainbow-shaped lake. A harem barge, curtains drawn, drifted across the mirrored surface. Fishing boats, propelled at the bow by a single oar, weaved around it. Bee-eater birds flitted, vivid green, through the clumps of bamboo that grew along the banks.

They rode through the outskirts of the city, past the tumbledown hovels filled with the usual goats, children and chickens. The smells were much as he had become accustomed to in Madras - dust and rotten fruit, piss from the alleys and incense smoke from the temples. But the white Mohammedan churches and the men in their turbans and women in *purdah* told him he had come to another world, one where he had to learn new ways if he was to do the job that they had sent him here to do.

There were ghats and sentry posts all along the banks of the river, and the domes of two Mohammedan churches, one gold and one silver, rose above the walls of the fort.

A massive pair of iron studded gates loomed ahead. An officer in a green turban advanced to meet them. He had an escort of soldiers behind him, their long-barrelled rifles over their shoulders and swords tucked into the sashes at their waists. The officer seemed disappointed to find their papers in order. He waved them through.

The gate was tall enough for an elephant. As they rode under it, Lachlan heard trumpets and kettle drums and cymbals playing above his head from a concealed musicians' gallery. The clash of sounds was jarring, and Tommy made a show of putting his hands over his ears. 'Begging your pardon, sir,' he said. 'But I think my ears are bleeding.'

'You'll grow accustomed,' Lachlan said.

'I'll go deaf first. See if I don't.'

They came out on a large, sandy parade ground. To the north was a vast wooden palace surrounded by several red brick buildings, with canals, flowerbeds and fruit trees.

A regiment of the nawab's troops had been drawn up in formation. There was a ceremony taking place. Lachlan could tell by the tension in the air and the looks on the faces of the soldiers, that it was a punishment and not any kind of celebration.

'You think it's a flogging?' Tommy said.

'I think it's worse than that.'

They walked their horses to the edge of the maidan and watched on over the heads of the assembled troops. There were ten cannons lined up facing the ranks of infantry. Their gun crews stood at attention beside them.

The flutes and drums stopped, and an eerie silence fell over the parade ground. Lachlan felt his mouth go dry, as it did before a battle.

There was movement from the barracks room on the far side of the maidan and a group of ten prisoners were led out. Their guards handed them over to the gun crews one by one. The artillerymen took hold of them and roped them to the barrel of their guns with the small of their backs over the muzzle.

'I don't know how good those gunners are,' Tommy said, 'but I don't think they can miss from there.'

Some of the condemned men stood silent, indifferent to their fate. Other struggled and fought, shouting and spitting curses at their executioners.

The guns were loaded with powder but no shot. Behind the cannons, the gunners stood with lit fuses, waiting for their orders. Two of the captives had the nerve to look over their shoulders and try to confront their executioners, but the men avoided their eyes.

A regiment of infantry was drawn up facing the guns. Two more companies made up the remaining sides of the square. Their uniforms were identical to the ones the prisoners were wearing. So, this was not just a punishment then, Lachlan thought. It was also a warning to the men watching.

He studied the officer in charge of the proceedings. He was dressed like a prince, in a gold breastplate and white robes braided with gold so that he glittered in the sun. There was an egret feather in his powder white turban. He sat on his horse, smiling through his thin moustaches, clearly enjoying himself.

It was his age that shocked Lachlan. He could scarcely have been out of his teens.

He drew a jewelled sword from his sash and raised it above his head. He held it in the air for an inordinate amount of time. The condemned men's eyes were inevitably drawn to it.

The seconds dragged past. Everyone waited.

Finally, he lowered the sword.

The cannons roared and the maidan filled with smoke. Lachlan saw a head fly tens of feet into the air. Something landed in the sand near his feet. It was a leg, blackened with powder burns.

Tommy covered his nose. The stench of gunpowder and burning flesh was appalling.

As the smoke cleared, Lachlan saw that the front ranks of infantry facing the cannons were covered in gore. Flesh and intestines dripped from their uniforms into the sand. The gunners themselves had fared little better as they had neglected to put up backboards. They had been sprayed with hot blood and burned flesh as well. Now several of them were on their knees, retching.

The officer walked his horse past the cannons and over a blasted corpse. Just a boy, but he had a look of depravity about him. Lachlan noticed that his eyelids were lined with *kohl* like a *nautch* girl.

When he saw Lachlan, he dipped his head and gave him a mock salute. Then he threw back his head and laughed.

CHAPTER 13

The *durbar* glittered with jewels and silks. Polished marble reflected the vaulted ceiling, and thick Persian carpets lay underfoot. Frankincense burned in silver saucers all around the room. The fragrance was overpowering.

The nawab, Alivardi Khan, lay on a canopied divan stroking a white Persian cat while near-naked hench boys fanned him with peacock feathers.

He was wearing a turban of turmeric yellow with a huge ruby clasp, topped with feathers. There was a jewelled ceremonial dagger in the sash of his long-skirted silk tunic. He had a short, grey beard and his mouth was turned down at the edges, as if permanently disappointed with life. His face was as lined as an old tobacco pouch and he looked frail among the gaggle of courtiers, bodyguards and clerks.

But his eyes were still shrewd and watchful.

Lachlan was also watchful. He noticed that Tommy's attention had been drawn to the corner where some *nautch* girls were sharing a water pipe. Their breasts were bare and their nipples had been dusted with gold leaf. Gold chains looped from the piercings in their noses. He quickly nudged him and brought his attention back to the proceedings at hand.

Alivardi Khan regarded them from the *divan* with a look of profound distaste.

The vizier stepped forward and introduced Lachlan, who took off his hat and bowed. 'Allow me to present myself. I am Lieutenant Lachlan McKenzie, envoy of the British East India Company to the court of His Honourable Majesty, Alivardi Khan.'

'Another Englishman,' Alivardi Khan said. 'God's bounty knows no limits.'

'My king sends you his warm regards. He has sent gifts.'

The vizier leaned forward and whispered something in the nawab's ear. Lachlan supposed he was telling him about the clock and the calfskin books Lachlan had brought with him.

Alivardi Khan looked at the vizier, then back at Lachlan. 'Where is the Englishman who usually pays homage to us at our *durbar*?'

'I'm afraid he's dead, sir. He was sent back to Calcutta with a fever. It appears he succumbed to it.'

'And your king sent you here in his place?'

Lachlan nodded. 'He wants to ensure that the good relations between your majesty and his beloved Company are maintained to everyone's mutual benefit.'

'The last one wanted me to sign a treaty giving you sole trading rights in Bengal.'

'In return for our protection.'

'You should care more for protecting yourselves against the French,' someone said.

Lachlan looked around. It was the boy who had officiated over the execution on the parade ground. '

'The British are like bees,' the young man went on, turning to the nawab. 'They smother you with honey, but if you don't do what they want, they sting you to death.'

Alivardi Khan held up a hand to warn the boy to silence, then returned to Lachlan. 'This is my grandson, Siraj. He has less patience for you *feringhees* than I do.'

'I hope he will learn to love us, in time,' Lachlan said. 'We have only your best interests at heart.'

My first day at the court, he thought, and I have lied three times.

'I will consider your treaty,' Alivardi Khan said.

'I was told that you were already considering it. Since last year.'

'No, it was two years before that. Some things require much consideration.' He waved a hand airily and the vizier turned to someone else. Lachlan realised he had been dismissed.

He hated his new job already.

Cossimbazar, near Murshidabad

Lachlan sat at his desk in the Company factory and accustomed himself to the view from his window. Out on the river, royal *budgerows* with figureheads of horses and elephants, glided between the freighters waiting for the next load of silks or ivory.

The factory was on a bend in the river, just south of Murshidabad. It was a two-storey, grey stone building with Greek columns and a grand, white portico. Lachlan thought it might be mistaken for a palace, except for the bastions at each corner of the walls, all of them mounted with cannon. A red and white striped Company flag whipped from the flagstaff.

The French and Dutch factories were nearby but were not nearly as grand and were not fortified. They were just large houses with low walls to keep out grazing cows.

I can see why Alivardi Khan does not trust us, he thought.

Tommy stood at attention on the other side of the desk. A steward brought *chai*.

'Sit down, Tommy. Make yourself comfortable.'

'Doesn't feel right, sir.'

'Oh, for God's sake. You saved my life. The least I can do is offer you a cup of tea.'

Tommy sat down, ramrod straight, his tricorn balanced on his lap.

'So,' Lachlan said, 'what did you make of today? I noticed you were much taken with the *nautch* girls.'

'I thought these Muslims hid their women away and put sacks over their heads. Those girls hardly had a stitch on.'

'They're court dancers. The rules are different for them.'

'First time I've seen a proper nawab, too. He doesn't seem well disposed.'

'No. He's clever. His aim is to keep us and the French in conflict with each other. That way he keeps a fine balance. What the Company fears is what will happen when he dies.'

'Which doesn't look to be far off.'

Lachlan tapped a fingernail on his glass cup. 'No.'

'I don't like this fellow Siraj.'

'Neither do I. Unfortunately, he's the crown prince. The nawab has recently announced him as his successor, so one day we may have to deal with him directly.'

'Doesn't the nawab have any sons of his own? I thought his lot had wives like a dog has fleas.'

Lachlan shook his head. 'He's an unusual man. He has just one wife. They have three daughters together, but he's outlived all his sons-in-law, so he's settled on that strange bastard as his successor. In the Company's view, he's the worst possible choice. It's my remit to try to change the nawab's mind and persuade him to revisit his decision. Find someone more amenable to England.'

'Well, I'm sure you know what you're doing.'

'But here's the thing, Tommy, I don't. I've never been an ambassador before, I've never been to England, and I don't give a damn about the Company.'

'Then what are you doing here, sir?'

'Good question. In truth, I feel like I've been washed up here by the tide. Just lying around waiting for someone to pick me up, brush off the sand and weeds and find a place for me.' He saw the look on Tommy's face. 'Tell me something, what do people say about me?'

'They think you're a hero, sir.'

'No, they don't. Not everyone. It's all right. I'm giving you permission to be honest with me.'

Tommy cleared his throat. 'Well, most think you're a bit odd. There are all sorts of stories about you. About Africa. And everyone still talks about what happened to your wife. Sorry to bring it up.'

Lachlan got up and went to the window. The warehouses were bursting with raw silk and opium, cotton and saltpetre, betel nut and indigo. The writers would be hunched over their desks, scratching away with pen and ink in the ledgers while the sweat ran down their faces. Strange to think it was barely two years ago he was doing the same thing.

'Life's a funny thing,' he said. 'Do you ever wonder about your purpose on earth, your destiny?'

'Not really, sir. We don't have destiny where I'm from. People would think you were getting above your station.'

'My father never seemed to think about anything else.'

Hamish had said a man could make his fortune in Hindustan, and he had been right. As Company Resident in Murshidabad, there would be ample opportunity for him to do some trading on the side and line his own purse, just as Channing had offered in Madras.

Yet it all seemed so futile now.

Lachlan sat on a mat on the floor of his bedroom, his head in his hands. He was exhausted, but he was terrified of falling asleep. The dead still came to him in his dreams - Sasavona, Katherine, his mother, Catia. He thought about what Channing had said. It was easier to talk about moving on than to actually do it. A man might let go of the past, but what if the past wouldn't let go of him?

The house they had given him was silent and empty, and by now the servants were all asleep. From somewhere he heard the curious, coughing yip of a jackal in the forest.

He stared at the lamp, the needle and the little ball of black resin. His hands shook as he reached for his opium pipe. Only his poppy dreams were sweet. A small voice in his head told him to put the pipe back in its velvet lined box. Pack everything away and fight the demons himself.

But he couldn't. He didn't have the strength. This was the only medicine he had. He needed this.

As he watched the opium sizzle over the flame, he felt a prickling on his skin from his hands and up his arms to the base of his skull. He lay on his side and brought the pipe to his lips. Just one pipe, just tonight.

He exhaled the blue-grey smoke through his nose, and the pain deep in his gut seemed to dissolve like mist in the sun. He felt suddenly relaxed and content, and the world was once again a safe and wonderful place.

Pondicherry

'We should have gone back and killed him,' Narain said. 'The woman was of no account.'

Adelaïde turned from the window. 'It would have been too dangerous. The British doubled the guards on all the gates after her death. We would never have gained entrance a second time.'

'He cannot remain behind the walls of the fort forever. We must come up with another plan.'

She shook her head. 'The British have already sent him away.'

'How do you-'

'Does it matter?'

He stared at her, puzzled. 'But I thought that-'

'I want to show you something.' She picked up a candle from the table and lit it. 'Come with me.'

He followed her into the garden.

She had found a scorpion in a nest of leaves under a frangipani tree. She used a long stick to move the leaves aside.

'Watch,' she said.

She built a wall around the creature with the detritus of leaves. Its sting curled venomously over its head as it sought out its tormentor.

Deftly, she used the candle to light one leaf, then another, until the scorpion was surrounded by a circle of fire. It turned and turned again, trying desperately to escape the flames, but the heat drove it back. Soon, the leaves were burning brightly, and the scorpion was trapped.

Mad with pain, it froze, trembling, then drove its sting into its own back. It gave a shudder, then it stiffened and rolled over, dead.

'You see,' she said. 'We do not need to destroy him. We have caused him indescribable pain by taking his wife. Now we let him destroy himself.'

Part 2

THE HUNT

CHAPTER 14

P ondicherry, three years later

Adelaïde listened to the cook girls working in the kitchen, grinding spices and making *naan*. She remembered how she used to sit out here in the courtyard like this with her father when she was a little girl. His breakfast had never varied: strong black coffee and a slice of pineapple with a peeled, quartered orange.

A peacock screeched and thrashed in the branches of the tree above her. Her father had hated that thing and was always threatening to shoot it, but he never did. She resolved to do it herself. She resented it for being alive when he was now long buried. If those English pigs had bothered to bury him at all.

Narain brought her breakfast. Coffee, pineapple and an orange, quartered. He bowed to her with a hand on his heart. 'Will you be needing me today?'

She shook her head. 'I am staying home.'

'You are not going to church?'

'I am a little tired of God.'

'Well, you only have one. It must become monotonous.'

As he turned to go, she said, 'Don't forget, I have the governor's party tonight at Fort Louis.'

'You are still going?'

'Why would I not? De Leyrit has invited me. It would be churlish to refuse.'

'His secretary invited you. And that man has his own reasons for wanting you there.'

'I can look after myself.'

'If it were a duel at fifty paces, I don't doubt it. But this is different.' Narain shook his head. 'They will never accept you. As they never accepted your father.'

She waved him away. 'I am not my father, and I have my own way of doing things. Have a *tonga* ready. I am to arrive at six o'clock. That will be all.'

Fort Louis

The *Gouvernement* was a blaze of light. Her *tonga* went through the gate past two saluting *topasses* and stopped behind the gilt and curtained palanquin that had arrived just in front of them. One of the town's chief *dubashes* emerged from it, gowned and turbaned, clutching a ceremonial sword in the sash at his waist.

Narain helped her step down from the *tonga,* and she took a moment to arrange herself. She was wearing a green silk gown that set off her pale complexion. Pearls were threaded into her hair with a spray of jasmine.

She went up the steps into the great hall. The walls were gilt and there were curtains of fine emerald lace over the windows. Ionic columns soared to the ceiling like a forest of marble.

She joined the line of guests at the foot of a winding staircase where liveried servants were taking the men's tricorn hats and their canes. Each of the guests had their own servant and she felt Narain's reassuring presence beside her. He wore a white turban to denote his high caste. Not that these people would care much about that, she thought.

De Leyrit and his wife were waiting at the top of the stairs to greet everyone. A steward stood beside them, taking the visiting cards. 'Miss Adelaïde Gagnon,' he announced when she reached them.

She saw heads turn and for just a moment there was a hush in the ballroom.

'Your reputation precedes you,' Narain said.

'My father's reputation.'

She accepted the governor's somewhat cool greeting and went in. A buffet table had been set out, piled with local dishes, mostly *pilaus*, curries and tropical fruits. It was decorated with frangipani flowers.

There was a monstrous *punkha* more than thirty feet long, creaking high above everyone's head. Its wooden frame was painted with gilt. *Wallahs*, hidden from sight behind bamboo screens so their presence did not offend the sensibilities of the guests, worked frantically trying to drive cooler air into the room from the open windows. The ropes and pulleys they used to control the motion of the massive fan were covered in red silk.

The room was lit by giant candelabras, and there were sashed curtains on the windows. Mildewed, she noticed. What did they expect? These people seemed to think they were still living in France.

Musicians had set up in the corner near the dance floor and had begun tuning their flutes and violins.

She fanned herself. Despite the *punkha*, the heat in the room was unbearable. She had never grown accustomed to wearing these shifts and petticoats and ruffled sleeves the other women wore. She was told that it was the very fashion in France. Madness. In France right now it wasn't ninety-five degrees.

The clammy society matrons looked as if they had been poured into their silks and satins, and only their stays held them together. Some of them even had plumed headdresses as if they had escaped from the chorus of an opera. They were all wearing thick layers of face powder.

'I'm the only one here,' she said to Narain, 'who does not look like a corpse.'

Even the men were red in the face. The army officers were buttoned up in their dress uniforms, while the government people wore heavy brocade coats, waistcoats and powdered wigs. They turned their backs on her as she passed.

By now, de Leyrit had dispensed with his duties at the door and was wandering around the room, looking at the busts and portraits as if he had never seen them before. So far, he had not deigned to speak to anyone. He had a goblet in one hand and a handkerchief in the other, which he bit down on nervously from time to time like a man with a sore tooth.

There was a large silver punch bowl, and waiters were circulating with trays of champagne. Adelaïde tried to catch the eye of one of them without success.

'You see,' Narain said.

She watched the dancers forming up. Not a single worthy had approached her so far.

'They've all been warned off you,' Narain said. 'It's like me and that punchbowl. I should very much like a glass of it, but my religion will not allow it. It's the same for them. Taboo is more powerful than desire. We should go.'

Perhaps Narain was right. But just as she turned to go, she saw the governor's secretary, Fontaine, making his way across the room towards her holding two champagne flutes.

He bowed and kissed her hand. 'You're not leaving us so soon, *Mam'selle* Gagnon?'

'The heat is unbearable,' she said.

He offered her one of the flutes. 'Some chilled champagne to help you cool off. There, I hope you will grace us with your presence a little longer. I thought you should enjoy this evening's entertainments. It wasn't easy to get you an invitation.'

'Why?' she said.

'Well,' he began, and his cheeks flushed with embarrassment.

'Am I not welcome?'

'For myself, I find your company most pleasing. In fact, I was hoping you'd have space for me on your dance card.'

The orchestra began a sarabande. The governor was pried away from a portrait of a French king by his wife and manoeuvred onto the dance floor. Several other couples joined them.

Fontaine held out his arm.

Adelaïde shook her head and took out her fan. 'I need some air.' She turned to Narain. 'Wait here.' She went to the doors leading onto the terrace, Fontaine following eagerly behind her.

Outside, it was scarcely cooler with only the faintest breeze. The night smelled earthy - ripe with fruit, curries and waste. The shadows of bats flickered through the trees.

Fontaine stood as close to her as he dared. 'I had hoped to see you here,' he said, keeping his voice low. 'I am an ardent admirer of yours.' There was sweat on his upper lip.

'I have been eager to see you also,' she said. 'There is something I wish to talk to you about.'

'And what is that?' He tried to touch her hand.

She stepped back. 'Government policy.'

'What?' he said and looked suddenly lost.

'I need to know. Is there going to be another war with the British, do you think?'

'A war? Is that what you're worried about? You're quite safe in Pondicherry.'

'When Governor de Leyrit arrived here, he brought two thousand French soldiers with him. What does he plan to do with them?'

'Why are you interested in such things?'

'Why wouldn't I be?' She held his gaze.

Finally, he shrugged and gave in. 'Well, the Crown, you see, has directed the governor to bring the struggle with the British to a close. The king wishes to free our trade from the encumbrances of war.'

She stared into the dark. That was disappointing.

'It's not like it was in your father's day,' he said. 'No one wants another war with the British.'

She stared at him curiously, as if he were some exotic animal she had never seen before. 'Well, they should,' she said.

She handed him the empty champagne flute and went back into the ballroom.

CHAPTER 15

H e was surrounded by a group of young *fonctionnaires.* They were all shouting at the top of their voices except him, even though he seemed to be the cause of their ire.

He stood out from the rest of them. His clothes were well cut and clearly expensive. He had on a suit of blue silk over an embroidered waistcoat, and his breeches were overstitched with voided velvet. The gold ring on his little finger was set with a cabochon cut ruby that must have cost a tidy fortune. His long dark hair was loose and clubbed, tied with a black ribbon at the nape of his neck. There was a vivid scar over his right eyebrow which somehow only added to his good looks.

Adelaïde stopped and listened to what the fuss was about.

'If you think the British will confine themselves to Madras,' he was saying, 'then you are very much mistaken.'

'We can throw them out any time we want to,' one of the clerks shouted back, leading the chorus of disapproval.

'You think so?'

'We have an alliance with the Nizam of Hyderabad. We control most of the Northern Circars and everything around Pondicherry. What do the British have? A mudflat in Madras.'

'Do you also control the sea routes around India?' the dark-haired man said. 'You don't. And if there is another war, that will be critical, because then all your scheming and alliances will mean nothing.'

Adelaïde looked around at Fontaine, who had followed her inside. 'Who is he?' she said.

'His name's Gerard Kilcannon.'

'He is Irish?'

'His grandfather was. He has a French mother, minor nobility. Because of her, he considers himself some sort of aristocrat. He's nothing but a rogue and a dilettante. Stay away from him.'

Kilcannon looked up for a moment and caught her eye. He smiled.

Fontaine raised his voice. 'There will be no war. We have a treaty with the British, signed just last year. Our new governor is not like the last one. He wants no trouble.'

Kilcannon turned to Fontaine. 'The last governor. Marquis Dupleix. He was recalled, I believe?'

'Because he was corrupt.'

Kilcannon shook his head. 'Because he changed the rules. For years, we all followed a policy of appeasing the local princes. But Dupleix changed all that. He tried to use the army to usurp them, and the British beat him at his own game. Dupleix didn't lose his post because he was greedy but because he was incompetent. He lost the war. Now it is too late. The British have learned from us that they can get what they want with cannons instead of presents and treaties.'

One of the *fonctionnaires* shouted, 'Even if there is another war, our soldiers are more than a match for the British.'

Kilcannon looked at the young man. 'Are they, my boy? You see, the other problem you have, gentlemen, is that there is not a single honest man in this room.' He raised his hands and laughed as they all yelled at him in outrage. 'I do not mean to insult you. I include myself in this accusation. The difference is, I know that I am dishonest. It is the one thing I am honest about. But how many of you will confess also? How many of you have secretly bled off money that was meant to pay the troops?'

The uproar subsided and was replaced by a shuffling silence.

'Everyone takes a little something, yes? Nothing wrong in that, you tell yourselves. Everyone does it. Only because of this, the soldiers go hungry. Hungry soldiers quickly lose discipline and lose their taste for a fight.'

Fontaine had had enough. 'The king has given the governor strict orders to confine himself to trade. There will be no more fighting.'

'You really think the British care what the King of France wants or does not want?' Kilcannon said. 'The British have a parliament, *m'sieur*, and many of its members have invested in British East India Company stock.

They are making massive profits for themselves, and they will do anything to protect their investments. They will give the Company everything it needs to break the French hold on the Coromandel coast and on Bengal. They will even send navy warships and regular British troops. You may want to sit on your hands, but I assure you, they will not.

'No gentlemen,' he finished, looking around the room, 'there is going to be a war. And that is when you will need someone like me.'

Adelaïde walked out onto the balcony. Kilcannon was standing in the shadows. The sound of music and laughter from inside was muted by the terrace doors.

'Those people,' she said. 'They are all so pointless.'

He turned and smiled at her. 'We will never be the same as them,' he said. 'People like you and me, we see things from above like gods, while they are bound to the earth like the muddled little people they are.'

'Why do you bother with them?'

'They are my prey,' he said casually, as if it was obvious. The air was steamy hot and the trees cacophonous with the sound of insects. 'Can you smell that?' he said. 'Everything around us is sprouting or decaying, mating or dying. Everywhere you go in Hindustan, you breathe it in, don't you think?'

'I have never noticed.' She stared at him, and he did not flinch and look away as most people did. 'I'm Adelaïde Gagnon.'

'I know who you are,' he said. 'You are notorious in Pondicherry. Just like your father.'

'What about my father?' she said.

'He was a half breed who sold guns and soldiers to the highest bidder and was detested by most of the people here. Am I right?' There was that mocking smile again. 'You were tolerated after his death because you were very young, but then a little while ago, you committed an act of extreme violence and even boasted about it afterwards. Now people are afraid of you.'

She stared at him, unblinking. 'Did you call my father a half breed?'

'I meant no disrespect by it. I am a half breed also, as *M'sieur* Fontaine has no doubt told you.'

'He also said you were a rogue. Are you?'

'Most assuredly.' He bowed from the waist. 'Count Gerard Kilcannon, *mam'selle*. I served the Jacobite prince at the battle of Falkland Muir against the English and fought with the French army under the great Marshall de Saxe at the Siege of Maastricht.'

'Yet you have no uniform.'

'You are looking at a man who has exchanged his ideals for profit. Does that disturb you?'

'You must know that it does not. Judging by your clothes, you have done well from your private affairs.'

'I specialise in selling armaments. No one ever lost money doing that. It's like prostitution or making wine. There will always be a need.'

'You said in there that the government is going to need men like you. Why?'

'I can see the future.'

'You can read the cards?'

He smiled. 'A man doesn't need magical powers to read the future, just common sense. Anyone can do it if he is prepared to put his prejudices to one side and think practically without his ideals getting in the way.' He took the crystal glass from her hand. 'Empty. We should get you another.' He lowered his voice. 'We have much in common, you and me.'

'We do?'

'We are both exiles among our own people and we both value personal enrichment more than the approval of others.'

'Is that what you think?' she said.

'It's what I know.' He held out an arm. 'May I have the next dance?'

She hesitated, then looped hers in his.

Nothing was said on the way home. Narain was silent, though his disapproval clung to him like stale sweat. A servant boy holding a flaming torch ran in front of their *tonga* through the darkened streets. Adelaïde swayed with the movement of the *chaise* as the wooden wheels rumbled over the cobblestones.

But once they were inside the house, Narain could no longer contain himself. 'You should stay away from him,' he said, trying to keep his voice flat.

'You are my guardian,' she said, 'not my father.'

'And as your guardian, it is my duty to warn you about that man.'

'I am tired. I am going to bed.'

'I took the liberty of making enquiries about him when I saw how much attention he was paying you.'

'And who assisted you in your enquiries? Fontaine?'

'I don't like the governor's secretary any more than you, but he knows everything that happens here in the colony.'

'And he puts his own interpretation on it.'

'Kilcannon has a reputation with women. He is a seasoned seducer, and you are still an innocent.'

Adelaïde blinked slowly but said nothing. It was curious how Narain still thought of her as a child.

'Fontaine says he has ruined several girls' reputations in Paris.'

'Of course he would say that.'

'He also said that he had to leave France in a hurry to avoid the debtor's prison. He is a renegade, unprincipled and untrustworthy.'

'They said the same about my father.'

'Your father made me vow to protect you.'

'Go to bed,' she said. 'I know what I'm doing.'

Narain clearly wanted to say something else but bit it back. He bowed and left, albeit reluctantly.

A single candle burned on a stand in the hall, throwing grotesque shadows around the whitewashed walls, but the high ceiling was lost to the dark. Somewhere in the house she heard the Comtois grandfather clock chime the hour. She stood at the foot of the stairs, turning over the evening's events in her mind, making sure she had retrieved all the useful information.

She closed her eyes and saw a regiment of highly trained recruits in smart blue and grey uniforms, armed with the latest flintlock muskets. They were formed up next to three eight-pounder field guns, each with its own seasoned artillery officer and crew.

What had been once could be again.

Yes, Gerard Kilcannon would perfectly fit into her plans. Her papa would be pleased.

CHAPTER 16

H er palanquin made its way slowly through the afternoon streets, her porters bumping shoulders with beggars and buffalos. The copper sun was still fierce even as it dropped towards the ocean.

They were passing the Capuchin cemetery when she ordered the porters to stop. She got out and told them to wait for her, then went the rest of the way to the church on foot.

She hurried across the forecourt, past the statue of Mary with a sari wrapped around her waist. A jackal lurked in the shadows among the brick-and-mortar tombs. There was a fresh grave without a stone on it. If the monks didn't rectify that, the jackals would be clawing at the earth as soon as it was dusk, digging up the corpse for their dinner.

The church was a long way from being completed. The walls were finished, but there was still no roof. The interior was mostly empty. A plain wooden crucifix had been fixed high up on the wall where the altar would one day be.

It would be another four or five years before they held the first Mass, but a priest came once a week to take confession behind a curtained alcove in one of the transepts.

Adelaïde dropped to her knees in front of the cross and closed her eyes. She tried to compose the words to a prayer in her head, but she couldn't do it. She didn't know where to start or what she wanted to pray for. It had been a long time since she had been to Mass, but some words came to her, unbidden. 'Only say the word, and I shall be healed.'

She heard a noise behind her and jumped to her feet. A priest must have been taking confession. The door banged as the penitent hurried out of the church.

'Father,' she said.

'I know you,' the priest said, gently. 'You're Napoleon Gagnon's daughter. I'm surprised to find you here.'

'I wanted to see how the building of our new church is progressing.'

He looked around. 'Slowly.' He spread his hands. 'I only came here today to hear confessions. Now we are here, may I ask how long since...?'

'A long time, Father.'

He pointed towards the alcove. 'Then we should make a start.'

'I would be wasting your time.'

'Saving souls is never wasted time.'

She moved past him towards the door.

'Your father had that same look on his face the last time I saw him. He came to me once. Do you know that?'

She stopped and turned around. No, she didn't know that, and it shocked her. 'When?'

'Before he went to fight the British at Karimkot. I tried to persuade him to cleanse his soul, but he was determined to hold onto his sins, just as you are.'

She hesitated. 'Would a donation towards the building works serve as recompense?'

'Anything you can do to help the Lord's work will be welcome. But you can't buy your way into heaven, Adelaïde.'

'That's purely supposition on your part, Father. Has anyone ever proved it either way?'

The door closed quietly behind her.

Kilcannon's villa was on the corner of Roman Rolland and Dumas. He was there to greet her at the gate, dressed in a silk *choga* of gold and dark blue, his servants lined up behind him.

He stepped forward and kissed her hand. 'I didn't think you would come.'

'Did you not receive my acceptance to your invitation?'

'I thought you would make some excuse at the last moment.'

'Why would I do that?'

He nodded curtly to Narain standing behind her. 'Because there are some who think me unsuitable company for a young lady. Come, let me show you my house. I am very proud of it.'

It was quite unlike any of the other villas in the White Town. He told her it had once belonged to a wealthy *dubash* and had been built in the native style. The vast expanse of the ground floor was surrounded by a gallery made entirely of black teak wood and supported by elegantly carved pillars. The polished timber floors were covered with silk carpets.

The furniture was mostly rosewood, and statues of various Hindu gods nestled in niches in the pale blue plaster walls. The heady scent of jasmine flowers filled the room from the garden. It was rich and indulgent and princely, and she wasn't at all surprised.

He led her upstairs. Here the furnishings were less oriental. In fact, they were unashamedly masculine. A collection of hunting rifles hung on the walls. She stopped to admire them.

There was a heavy-bored Jager with a walnut stock, and a Matheus Gram with an octagonal barrel and gold inlays, as well as a beautiful piece from Zellner of Vienna. She recognised an Esterhazy from the coat of arms on the brass shield on the stock.

'You like hunting, *mam'selle*?'

'I have accompanied my father on many *shikars* ever since I was a little girl. It is in my blood.'

He seemed impressed. He showed her the rest of the gallery, which was lined with sombre portraits of his ancestors, many wearing military uniforms. Most seem to be missing an arm, a leg, or an eye. For a renegade he seemed excessively proud of his heritage of Gaelic chieftains. He claimed he could trace his family line back to the High King of Ireland in the second century.

'And who is this?' she said.

'That is my grandfather, Sir Thomas Kilcannon, the last official Count of Kilcannon. After the Jacobite war in Ireland, he was one of the 'wild geese' who fled to France. That's where he met and married my grandmother. Like me, he joined the Irish Brigade and fought for the French.

I was with the Brigade when we captured the colours of the Coldstream Guards at Fontenoy. Some say it was our proudest moment.'

'Do you?'

'No, I say it was just a bloody slaughter for no reason, and I resigned my commission as soon as I could. That was twelve years ago.'

She looked around at the bevy of servants, the silver plate on the walls, the gilt on the ceilings. 'It seems to have done you no harm.'

He nodded. 'Indeed, it hasn't. And unlike my ancestors, I have all my moving parts. Shall we go into dinner?'

It was a torrid night for so early in the year. The dining room shutters had been thrown open to the faint sea breeze, and frankincense burned in copper bowls around the room to keep away the mosquitoes.

Adelaïde was aware of a heady aroma of spices from the warehouses on the other side of the street, where the *Compagnie* stored sacks of cardamom pods and cumin and cloves ready for shipping to France.

A small table had been laid, set with silver plate and crystalware. Kilcannon clapped his hands, and a stream of servants filed into the room carrying dishes of local Tamil delicacies - okra in buttermilk, *brinjal*, seafood spiced with ginger, turmeric, cloves and red pepper.

He took a key from his pocket and gave it to his steward who unlocked a rosewood liquor cabinet and took out a bottle of wine. He handed it to Kilcannon for inspection. He glanced at the label and nodded.

The steward filled their glasses.

'Madeira,' Kilcannon said, smiling. 'A *sercial*, single varietal. I find it lighter and more pleasant than the Burgundies our countrymen serve. It is not easy to find a bottle that has not despoiled on its way from France.'

'How did you get the scar?' Adelaïde said, taking a spoonful of the okra.

'A duel. A certain gentleman of my acquaintance was cheating at cards and took offence when I accused him of it. He had drunk too much and challenged me to a duel. When he sobered up, I believe he thought better of it, but it was too late. The next morning, we met at the proscribed place and paced out the ten steps as required by convention. But he was shaking with nerves and fired too soon. Poor fool. As you can see the lead ball grazed my forehead and no more.'

'What did you do?'

'What do you think? He had to stand there and let me have my turn. I took my time and shot him through the heart.' He helped himself to the *brinjal*. 'After that, I had to leave France for a while. It's how I found myself in India.'

'Not Pondicherry?'

'No, Surat. I married an Armenian woman there. Her father had made a lot of money buying and selling jewels among the Mughals. It was she who taught me to speak Persian.'

'What happened to her?'

'She died. A fever.'

'She left you her money?'

'I have my own means.' He leaned forward. 'Her name was Mariam, and I cherished her. I think about her every day. She taught me that marrying for love is too painful.'

He drained his Madeira and his eyes glittered. 'I shall be far more practical when I choose my next wife.'

CHAPTER 17

Through the windows Adelaïde heard the devilish screeching of the jackals in the Capuchin cemetery. She imagined that she could hear them grinding fresh bones between their teeth.

'Can I borrow one of your guns?' she said. 'If you furnish me with some powder and shot, I will quiet that din for you.'

Kilcannon seemed unsure whether or not to laugh. 'It's night. They're on the other side of the street, half obscured by a wall. You wouldn't hit an elephant.'

'We'll see.'

They went out into the hall. She chose a flintlock musket with a pewter-grey patina and a rifled octagonal barrel. It had both a rear and fore-sight, and beautiful brass mounts carved with hunting scenes in bas-relief. The inlay was signed *Joseph Hauer in Bamberg*.

He reached up and handed it to her, then snapped out an order to one of the servants, who returned moments later with a powder horn and a canvas bag of ammunition.

Still half amused, he told the man to give it to the *mam'selle*.

He watched as she poured a measure of powder down the barrel, then took a ball and wad from the bag and loaded it, tamping it down tight with the ramrod. She snapped the ramrod back into place then pulled the hammer back to half cock and opened the frizzen cap. She poured a little more powder into the pan and closed the lid. She pulled the hammer back to full cock. When he heard the click, the servant who had brought the powder jumped back a full two steps.

'That was quick,' Kilcannon said. 'You have done this before.'

'Of course.'

She returned to the dining room and leaned out of the window, letting her eyes adjust to the dark. She brought the rifle up to her shoulder, but she didn't aim, not yet. She could hear them out there. She imagined it was her father's bones they were splintering between their stinking jaws.

She could make them out now, dark shapes outlined against the cemetery wall. She took a breath, held it, and emptied her mind of everything as her father had taught her to do.

There were four of them down there. Two of them were moving, the others were crouched, feeding. She chose the one that offered the best shot.

She waited until she felt a stillness overtake her, then blinked slowly, letting the muscles in her arms and shoulders relax. Her finger squeezed the trigger mechanism very gently.

The stock kicked back into her shoulder, and for a moment she was blinded by the shower of sparks from the frizzen. The smoke from the charge hung in the room, and she saw two of the servants hold their noses and turn away. In the close confines, it smelled like woodsmoke and rotten eggs.

Narain rushed into the room, his sword drawn and his eyes wild.

'It's alright,' she said. 'I offered to kill a jackal.'

'Tell him to put his sword away before he takes someone's eye out with it,' Kilcannon said. He looked at his steward. 'Go over the road and see how *mam'selle* has fared.'

The man hurried away. Narain followed.

'Did your father teach you to shoot?'

'He taught me many things.'

'I can teach you many things as well.'

She felt his hand on her back. 'Have you ever done anything you regret,' she said.

'Such as what?'

'When you killed that man in the duel, did you feel any remorse at all?'

He seemed confused by the question. 'No. I rather enjoyed it, in fact. Is that terrible to you?'

'No. Papa was like that. He always said it's just business, but I saw the look on his face sometimes, when he was about to kill. He enjoyed it, too.'

'And you,' he said. 'Do you have regrets?'

'What would be the point of that?'

She turned back to the window. Kilcannon's steward had ruined his uniform climbing the wall to the cemetery, but his efforts were not in vain. He was holding something in his right hand. He held it up by the tail. It was a jackal.

Kilcannon shook his head. 'You are to be commended. You are a very remarkable young woman.' He touched her arm with a finger. 'I knew it from the moment I saw you.'

I have you, she thought. Now it is just a matter of being patient.

'Why did you leave Surat?' she said.

They were on the balcony. The moon seemed to shiver in the night sky and fireflies glittered in the trees like sparks.

People are overly taken with fireflies, she thought. Close up they are ugly little worms that even predators find too distasteful to eat.

He raised his glass. 'I left looking for opportunity. There are fortunes to be made here. For the right man.'

'And are you the right man?'

'I speak Persian so I can talk to the Mughals. I am French so I can talk to your *M'sieur* Fontaine, even though he despises me. And I have access to what everyone wants, French or Mughal.'

'What is that?'

'Guns. The French need them to rid themselves of the British. The Mughals need them to rid themselves of each other. There will be war here for the next fifty years, and war is the greatest commercial enterprise there is. If you make bread, you pray for a famine. When you sell guns, you pray for war. And here in Hindustan, a man never has to pray very hard.'

'You sound like my papa.'

'Your father did more than supply weapons to the Mughals and the *Compagnie*. He had his own private army, did he not?'

'Not an army. A regiment. But they were very well trained.'

'What happened to them?'

'Why, do you want to borrow them?'

'If they are available, I'm sure I could find clients willing to pay the fees for their services.'

'Then I must disappoint you. The regiment was dissolved.'

'And the leases on the three ships?'

She did not answer. He was remarkably well informed.

'I'm told he took you with him on all his adventures. But now here you are, this last few years, living all alone in your villa on Dumas Street, reading poetry in the garden and listening to the birds. It must be very lonely and very tiresome.'

'I don't read poetry.'

He smiled. 'Forgive me, I did not mean to make fun of you. Quite the reverse. But it seems to me that you are in a curious position. You shoot a rifle better than any man in Pondicherry, and yet you spend most days shut up in your villa, shunned by your inferiors. You deserve more.' He turned and saw Narain through the double doors, patrolling the landing outside. 'He follows you around like a tiger on a leash.'

'That's what he is paid to do.'

'And who pays him?'

'My father trusted him to run the estate until I am eighteen.'

'And when is that?'

'Next year.'

'That's a lot of trust. How do you know, when you open the books for yourself, that there will be anything left of your father's fortune?'

'Is that where your interest lies?'

Kilcannon spread his hands and looked shocked, like a man accused of stealing silver at a dinner party. 'There are so many things for a man of means to admire about you. Money would not be one of them.'

'Good. You seem to know so much about me, now tell me more about your own business.'

He shrugged as if it was of no consequence. 'I help men make war on each other, much like you father did. He showed what was possible with a little daring and imagination.'

'And you have both?'

'Better than that, I have contacts. My brother is highly placed inside the Académie de Marine at Brest. He sources everything I need through his friends and colleagues and assists me with its transport. I do the rest.'

'Your king allows this?'

'Our king does not know. Military men like to keep their secrets to themselves, along with the profits.'

'This is why *M'sieur* Fontaine does not like you.'

'No one in the government here likes me, but they need me. The king says he will not finance a war. The *Compagnie des Indes* must find a way to keep the British at bay somehow.'

'So, you are not a patriot?'

He smiled and shook his head as if the very idea was absurd. 'I never met a patriot without meeting a fool at the same time.'

'You should be careful, *m'sieur*. In Pondicherry people love the king, and they love France.'

He shrugged. 'It's true that some people think their country is better than others because they were born in it. But there is only one cause that I would ever die for, and you are looking at him.'

Adelaïde sat at the bureau in her father's study. Everything was just as it was when he left for Karimkot - the bell he used to summon the servants, his writing set, his personal stationery in the top left-hand drawer. Even his brandy, on a silver tray at one side, was untouched. She picked up his velvet-lined cigar box and breathed in, but the smell of tobacco was fading now.

'You understand, don't you?' she said.

You are only seventeen, he said. This man is twice your age. I have provided for you. You do not have to take such a risk.

'But what is life without risk?' she said. 'You always took me everywhere with you. You raised me to be like you. And now you think I should sit around this empty villa watching the world from the window?'

As a woman, she could not negotiate with moghuls and princes and governors. The world would not countenance it. So, she needed a man who was ruthless, ambitious and without conscience who could help her do the things she could not do.

'Someone just like you,' she said to the shadows.

CHAPTER 18

A delaïde left Narain behind, over his protests, and made her way outside the city alone.

There were villas and parks for miles all around. The spot chosen for the governor's garden party was shaded by a bower of apple and sandal trees. Carpets had been laid out on the grass, and a three-piece orchestra was playing a gavotte. White jacketed servants were busy taking around trays of champagne in silver cups.

The governor himself had just arrived in his gold painted coach, escorted by a company of sepoys in royal blue jackets. The chief *dubash*, Ananda Pillai, was being helped down from the *howdah* of an elaborately painted elephant.

But their arrival was not greeted with as much interest as hers. As she climbed down from her *chaise*, she heard several of the women draw breath. Even the musicians seemed to lose their way for a moment.

Fontaine pounced on her as soon as he saw her. 'It's so good to see you again,' he said. 'We thought we had lost your society. I hear you have been spending an inordinate amount of time with that rogue, Kilcannon.'

'Have you set your spies on me?'

'I don't need to, *mam'selle*. All Pondicherry is talking about you. They can't decide if he's after your money or you're after his. You are young, and you have no one to protect you. You should take care of such men.'

'I have Narain to take care of me. And please do not underestimate me, *m'sieur*. My father gave me a good education in the realities of life from a young age. He once had me castrate a kitten. He said it would be good practice for when I grew up.'

Fontaine blanched and gave her a nervous smile. 'Where is *M'sieur* Kilcannon?' he said.

'He has left for Bengal. He has business there.'

'He can smell money.'

'Gerard said there will be a war in Europe soon. Britain and Austria are rattling their sabres, and he believes they will drag us into the war with them.'

'To fight in a war is glorious,' Fontaine said. 'To profit from it is despicable.'

'So, the *Compagnie* does not expect to profit from its wars here against the nawabs and the British Company?'

He dabbed at his forehead with a handkerchief and looked around for inspiration. 'Time weighs heavy in this part of the world,' he said at last. 'We lack for entertainments. Do you like to hunt?'

'On occasion.'

'I am told you have a marksman's eye.'

'Where did you hear that?'

'All Pondicherry knows that you shot a jackal in the dark at fifty paces.'

'Seventy-five.'

He bowed in acknowledgment. 'Tomorrow, I have organised a hunting party. Perhaps you would care to join me and put your skills to the test on more worthy game?'

A group of French officers were standing in the broad shade of a banyan. Before she could answer, one of them detached himself and came over.

'This is Captain Le Roux,' Fontaine said, with a look that said he'd rather the captain was somewhere else. He was a head taller than Fontaine and without the soft belly. He stood ramrod straight and kissed Adelaïde's hand with a knowing smile.

Despite the heat, he was wearing full dress uniform, blue woollen tunic with white facings and brass buttons. His white trousers were tucked into his knee-length boots. She could see her face in the polished leather.

'Captain Le Roux is a celebrated officer in the army of the *Compagnie*,' Fontaine went on. 'He fought at Srirangam. The engagement was lost unfortunately. They were bested by the British.'

Le Roux shot Fontaine a look. 'Have you ever served in the army, *m'sieur*?'

'I haven't had the honour.'

'Then you wouldn't understand that winning battles is not as easy as some seem to imagine.'

'Your commander is a fool.' Fontaine said. 'He retreated from an almost impregnable position to an island where he was completely cut off from his allies and from which it was impossible to escape.'

Le Roux's cheeks coloured. 'He did not acquit himself well, it is true. Nevertheless, a civilian should not opine on military matters.'

Fontaine took the rebuke in his stride. 'I understand logistics well enough,' he said.

'Then you will know how important it is to have the right equipment at the right time. The muskets my men were supplied with were ancient matchlocks, full of rust. That *petit salaud*, Kilcannon! If he were here now, I should like to knock him down.' He bowed in apology to Adelaïde. 'Excuse my language, *mam'selle*.' He walked off.

Fontaine looked pleased.

CHAPTER 19

Gudachatram, near Pondicherry

The sun rose, a menacing white ball above the flat of the horizon. The village women were already at work grinding corn. Others glided through the tendrils of mist like wraiths, with earthenware pots on their heads. Parrots clustered raucously in the trees.

The village headman came out to meet them wearing a simple white *dhoti*, stark against the leathery folds of his skin. He had no teeth and his smile was ghastly, his gums and lips stained with betel. He put his hands together. '*Varuka.*'

'*Varuka*,' Fontaine replied in Tamil.

The headman said his name was Aravinth. He led them towards a peepul tree in the centre of the village where they were urged to sit down on a cloth that had been spread on the ground in the shade. They were offered water served in halved coconut shells.

Adelaïde looked around. Piles of cowpats had been laid out in front of the huts to dry in the sun. The villagers would use them later as fuel for their cookfires.

Aravinth appeared sombre when Fontaine told him that they wanted to hire some young men to act as beaters for their *shikar*.

'He said we should be careful,' Fontaine said to Adelaïde. 'There's a tiger in the forest. He says they can hear him at nights.'

Adelaïde frowned. 'I know what he said.'

Fontaine turned back Aravinth. 'We're just after deer.'

Aravinth spat a quid of betel juice onto the ground. 'The tiger doesn't care what you want,' he said. 'A tiger does as he pleases.'

He found three young men to act as their beaters and a price was agreed on. While Fontaine hobbled the horses, Narain began priming and loading the muskets. The village children looked on, curious.

'Don't use shot,' Adelaïde said. 'Load them with ball in case we come across this tiger. I should be pleased to have its skin for my wall.'

They had been walking through the jungle for less than an hour when they saw a *chital*, a spotted deer, eating leaves from a peepul tree. They had come upon him downwind. He was a male stag with huge antlers, his golden back covered in distinctive markings. His belly, rump and legs were completely white.

Fontaine stopped and put up his hand. He imagined taking him back as a prize to Pondicherry, having that proud head forever on display in his dining room. He was magnificent.

It should have been his shot, but he could feel Adelaïde glaring at him. Such a tiny thing, pale and pink, yet she frightened him. Had she really killed that woman in Madras? Some people said it must have been Narain. An empty boast from a silly girl.

Or was it?

He decided to let her take the shot anyway. He nodded to her.

Adelaïde put out her hand and Narain handed her a musket, primed and ready to fire. As he stepped back, he trod on a fallen branch. It sounded like a cannon shot in the oppressive silence of the jungle. The stag's ears twitched. It knew something was wrong. It froze.

Adelaïde brought the rifle quickly up to her shoulder and sighted along the barrel. Her father had taught her that a head shot would bring down a deer instantly, but if her intended target made even the smallest movement as she pulled the trigger, she might only wound the animal and lose it.

She aimed instead for a point high on the shoulder. Her rifle was loaded with a heavy calibre lead ball, so a good shot would snap the spinal cord and rip through the lungs.

She slowed her breathing. She was aware of the sounds of the forest - the buzzing of cicadas, a flock of parakeets fussing over some wild plums. A troop of monkeys crashed through the treetops above her.

Suddenly the birds and monkeys fell silent. She glanced up. A crow peered down from its high branch, its head twisting one way then the other. It had seen something.

She looked back at the stag. Just as her finger began to squeeze the trigger, it darted away through the forest.

In moments, it was gone.

'What happened?' Fontaine said.

She shook her head. 'I don't know. Let's go after him.'

'Is this wise, *mem'sahib*,' Narain said, but she had already gone after her prize. She knew he would have no choice but to follow with the porters.

The stag had fled into a ravine. The ground dropped sharply away, and it was hard going. Adelaïde eased her way down, musket at the ready, taking care not to step on any deadfall as Narain had done.

The foot of the ravine was gloomy, completely in the shadow of the tall trees, and there was not a breath of air. Sweat ran into her eyes. She blinked several times, trying to clear her vision. A deathly hush had fallen over the jungle.

Narain pointed. There were some marks at the base of a teak tree, where a tiger had sharpened its claws and left deep gouges in the iron-hard wood. One of the boys found some fresh pug marks. The tiger must be close.

Adelaïde smiled. If the fat French matrons in the *Gouvernement* thought her liaison with Kilcannon was a scandal, they would burst veins in their eyes if she came back to Pondicherry with a tiger skin.

Fontaine appeared beside her. 'Something is not right,' he whispered.

'You're frightened.' she said.

'No,' he said, but he was.

'Good. Let's go on then.'

The undergrowth was dense, with wait-a-bit thorn bushes and lantana matted together. Adelaïde inched her way through. She followed the tracks to a dry *nullah*. Suddenly she lost the spoor.

'We should turn back,' Fontaine said.

There was a raucous cry. A bird flitted down from the branch of a tamarind tree, then up again.

Something was there.

She took a few tentative steps, pulled down a branch and peered into the gloom. A fresh kill lay ahead of them in a clearing - the half-eaten remains of a goat or a small deer. There were drag marks on the ground around it. The animal had been killed elsewhere and carried here by its predator. She felt the hairs prickle at the back of her neck.

One of the bearers pointed. There was more tiger spoor on the ground. It was fresh.

'He could have doubled back on us,' Fontaine whispered, looking over his shoulder. His hands were shaking.

Adelaïde waited, totally still. The sun was higher and hotter now. A bead of sweat made its way from the nape of her neck to the small of her back.

And then she heard it, a low primordial rumbling that seemed to vibrate up through her feet and into her bones. It echoed down the length of the glade like thunder.

'Holy God,' Fontaine said. He brought the musket to his shoulder and turned a full circle. The bearers crouched down and started to talk animatedly to each other in Tamil. One of them tried to run back to the village and had to be restrained by the other two fellows.

'We should go back now,' Narain said.

Adelaïde felt a prickle on the hairs along her arms and the back of her head. She felt as if she was being watched. Even the cicadas had fallen silent. Suddenly, there was a flurry away to her right. She spun around in time to see a sambar run across the trail and dart down into the *nullah*.

'Leave him,' she said.

'We came here to shoot deer,' Fontaine said.

'I want a tiger.'

Then, out of the corner of her eye, she saw the barest whisper of movement, the shivering of a feathery tuft of grass fifty paces away. Yet there was not even a hint of breeze.

She brought her musket to her shoulder and concentrated on the long grass. She waited. Breathe gently, slowly, she heard her father say. Let him come to you.

The minutes dragged by.

Sunlight burst into the clearing. The jungle seemed to let out a sigh. The crows and the cicadas started up their din once again.

The tiger had gone.

'Let's go home,' Fontaine said. He sounded relieved.

Narain nodded and led the native boys back the way they had come. Adelaïde followed. She stopped once to look over her shoulder.

'I'll be back for you,' she said.

CHAPTER 20

The day was limp, exhausted. A few pale stars appeared in the sky above the flat horizon of sea. There was a flash of bright blue as a kingfisher dipped over the languid waves along the beach.

Adelaïde sat with Kilcannon in the back of a *tonga*. They rode south along the shore past the endless small villages that hugged the coast. Some fishermen were squatting on the beach mending nets. They stopped for a moment to watch them.

The fishing boats were moored along the muddy foreshore, half out of the water, resting on their keels. The day's catch had been laid out on drying racks and the air was ripe with fish, salt and smoke.

'How was Bengal?' she said.

'Not as exciting as here, apparently. I heard that you almost bagged a tiger.'

'I think someone has made more of the adventure than it was. We heard the animal close by in the forest, that was all. But we didn't actually see him.'

'You seem sure there was only one.'

She studied him intently as if he had said something profound. 'What do you call a gathering of lions?'

'A pride.'

'And jackals?'

'Well, a pack. What is your point?'

'What about a gathering of tigers?'

He shrugged. 'I have no idea.'

'No. No one does. Because a tiger almost always hunts alone.'

They rode on for another few minutes and then Kilcannon had their driver stop on the far side of the village in the shade of a spreading banyan. The evening cook fires had been lit outside the palm-thatched huts but there was no wind. They watched the sun set through the layered drifts of woodsmoke.

A three-masted barque was heading towards the jetty at Pondicherry. The red, white and blue France ensign hung at the stern.

'Do you see that ship?' he said. 'At this very moment there will be dozens like her riding at anchor at Port Lorient in Brittany. On the dockside will be countless barrels of wine and water and supplies. The longshoremen will be rolling them up and down the gangplanks, day and night, while squadrons of marines embark from the quayside. There will be cannons and mortars and crate after crate of ammunition all going down into the holds. And do you know why? Because the King of France knows that war is inevitable, not only in Europe, but in the American colonies and all over the world.

'A little apart from the other ships at Port Lorient, on the seaward edge of the harbour, there are three more Indiamen. And in their holds, nestled in crates packed with straw, there are fifty cannon, two thousand flintlock muskets, and ammunition enough to start not only a small war, but a very large one. They are not meant for the French navy or even the *Compagnie*. Well, they were once, but not anymore. Now they belong to me. And soon, I will have them here in Hindustan, waiting for the right buyer.'

'Is that why you went back to Bengal?'

'Of course. It's where the money is.'

Behind them, the land was already dark. Adelaïde could smell the river somewhere close by, dank and fetid. Parakeets flew noisily to their roosts.

'Who are the guns for?' she said.

'A man called Aziz Khan, one of the nawab's most trusted generals. He is acting secretly for the nawab's grandson, Siraj ud-Daulah. When Siraj takes the throne, there will be a war. He hates the British and is spoiling for a fight. What he lacks is the means. I will provide it.'

'I applaud your foresight.'

He took her hand. 'This little war is going to be very profitable. And soon there will be other wars. If the nawabs and the British spill enough blood, within five years I shall be the richest man in Asia.'

'You are to be congratulated.'

'Not yet. There is something missing.'

'And what is that?'

'A wife.'

'Once you are the richest man in Asia, the governor will have to send in troops to organise the queue of women suitors into orderly lines.'

'I don't want something decorous clinging to my arm. I should be bored inside a month. I want someone who sees the world the way I do. Someone extraordinary.'

'And do you know such a woman?'

Kilcannon threw up his hands. It was a theatrical gesture, and she was surprised he felt the need to resort to it.

'You are making this hard for me. I am talking about you.'

'You want to marry me?'

'I won't insult you by talking of love and other sweet things. I know you are of practical mind, as I am. I desire you, of course I do. But I have more to offer you than caresses and sweet words. Neither you nor I are of the ordinary round. Together we can do things other men and women can only dream of.'

He tried to kiss her. She supposed he felt obliged to. She put a hand on his chest and gently pushed him aside. 'As you say, we are both of a practical mind, and a kiss is impractical by its very nature.'

He kissed her hand instead. 'I shall not sleep until I have your answer.'

Adelaïde made him wait a week.

Finally, she invited him to her villa on Suffren Street, where she formally accepted his proposal of marriage.

The wedding took place a month later at St Andrew's church. Narain was there to give her away. No one came except their servants.

And Fontaine.

CHAPTER 21

Murshidabad

Lachlan felt groggy and dispirited as he always did when the effects of the opium wore off. He struggled into his *banyan* – a white linen coat that the natives wore - and loose *pajama* trousers, and shuffled out onto the veranda.

He squinted against the glare. It was a fine day with no breeze, the mist clinging to the surface of the lake. He heard boatmen calling to each other across the water. Cattle with broad, bony hips grazed on the lawn outside, regarding him with dreamy, faraway eyes. It was cool at this time of the year, and the *punkhas* were not yet required. The place was almost liveable.

It was almost three years since he had arrived in Murshidabad. Time seemed to have stood still. He didn't flatter himself that he had achieved a great deal. Whenever he attended Alivardi Khan's *durbar* he found himself making excuses for the Company and for President Drake in Calcutta, who seemed inclined to provoke the old man at every opportunity. It was thankless work, and he suspected that Channing had only sent him up here to get him out of the way.

He tried not to smoke too much opium. It wasn't easy. It was the only way he could dull the pain he still felt over Catia. He felt ashamed that he had not straightened himself out. He must have flouted the accepted time limit on shame and grief by now.

It wasn't a bad life he had fallen into. The bungalow they had given him was luxurious compared to what he had been accustomed to in Madras. His sitting room was the size of a small church, and all the doors and windows had mesh screens, like the ones on meat safes, to keep out the insects. There were thick Persian carpets on the floors.

He had an abundance of servants. Some of them were already busy in the central courtyard, sweeping and washing and chattering with no thought for those who wished to sleep till noon.

His biggest problem was that apart from Tommy, he lacked for good company. He had started talking to the frog that had taken up residence in his bathing room. He had christened it Callum, after his brother.

He was also host to a massive spider, large enough to have its own personality according to Tommy. It had walked into his bedroom on the night he had arrived, looked him over and walked out again. Since then, they had agreed on an uneasy truce, the spider keeping to itself high in a corner of the main sitting room.

He wondered what to do with his day. Perhaps a good gallop on one of his Arabs before lunch, then the usual cursory visit to the factory at Cossimbazar. Then a few hours sprawled on the day bed or in one of the white wicker chairs.

He saw a horse in the distance and frowned. As the rider got closer, he saw that he was wearing a red uniform jacket. It had to be Tommy. He frowned. What could he want so early in the day?

He went back inside. A rosewood box lay open on the table and his pipe, oil lamp and needles lay spread out beside it. He quickly packed them away and hid the box in a drawer in a wooden cabinet in the corner. He locked it and put the key in his pocket.

He heard Tommy stamp up the front steps to the veranda in his heavy boots. He went out to meet him and saw the look of disapproval on his face. He wondered if it was because he could smell the opium on him or because he was wearing native clothes. Well, he wasn't going back to wearing breeches and serge jacket to keep his sergeant happy. The Muslims, it seemed to him, dressed for the climate and no sensible man should do differently.

'What bring you here so early? It can't be good news.'

Tommy shook his head. 'A messenger came this morning from Aziz Khan. He wants to see you.'

Lachlan sighed. It was almost certainly something to do with that fool Drake in Calcutta. He rubbed his face. 'Tell the servants to get my horse ready. Wait here while I get dressed. And take that look off your head, Tommy. You're not my mother!'

General Aziz Khan was an impressive looking man. He was powerfully built with a deep growl of a voice. He had a black beard with not a hint of grey, and a ruby glinted from the gold ring on his index finger. He was wearing a green silk *jama* with an orange sash and a pure white turban.

Lachlan would rather have been in his own *jama*, but this was Company business and so his dress uniform was obligatory - red serge jacket with gold facings and cuffs.

The general did not seem to mind Lachlan's discomfort. He left him standing before his *divan*, his tricorn under his arm and sweat running down his face.

Lachlan waited while he conferred in whispers with his secretary, the two men occasionally throwing long and baleful looks in his direction. The tension was palpable.

But if one must melt from heat and hostility, he thought, then this is a beautiful room in which to do it. The stonemasons who had sculpted the walls and ceiling had somehow made the marble appear as delicate as sea foam. It had been fretted into geometric patterns that allowed even a zephyr of breeze to pass through. There was a faïence of blue and yellow tiles around the room, polished mirror bright.

Finally, the general turned and addressed him without preamble. 'The nawab is furious,' he said.

Lachlan shifted his weight to his other foot. 'I am saddened to hear it,' he said, while his mind raced ahead, trying to fathom what might have caused Alivardi Khan's ire.

'Our nawab has shown great forbearing in the face of many provocations from your President Drake.'

So, as he suspected, Drake was the cause of the problem.

'He continues to fortify your fort at Calcutta despite the nawab's orders that he desist.'

Lachlan tried to figure a way to defuse the situation. It was a delicate matter. There was a long-standing agreement between Bengal and the Company that Calcutta would be used as a trading post only. Over the years, of course, walls and bastions had been built, and Alivardi Khan and his predecessors had chosen to overlook the strengthening of the fortifications for diplomacy's sake. But clearly the nawab felt that things had gone too far.

Aziz Khan signalled to his secretary. The man stood up and approached Lachlan with a letter which he produced from his robes. As he did it, a *purdah* curtain behind the general was gently moved aside and Lachlan saw, for just a moment, a pair of beautiful black eyes watching him. They held his gaze for what seemed like an eternity and yet could only have been a moment. Then the curtain was replaced.

The secretary was impatiently waving the letter under his nose.

'It is from your President Drake at Calcutta,' Aziz Khan said.

Lachlan read it quickly through:

> We cannot think of submitting to a demand of so unprecedented a nature. For this century past, we have traded in the nawab's dominions, and have always paid obedience to their orders, that it gave us concern to observe that some enemies had advised his Excellency, without regard to truth, that we were erecting new fortifications.

Technically, Drake was right. He wasn't building new fortifications, he was repairing walls that were already there. But by the terms of their agreement, he should have first sought permission from Alivardi Khan. It was what Lachlan would have done. Then he would have carried on with the repairs anyway, without waiting for an answer.

All the nawab wanted was to be shown a little respect.

Aziz Khan nodded at the letter in Lachlan's hands. 'Your President Drake goes on to suggest that he is preparing for a war against the French. Is this true? Because the nawab is not amenable to foreign nations fighting each other on lands that belong to him. We have all seen for ourselves what damage these wars have done in Madras and in Trichinopoly. Let me be clear. We do not want your wars here.'

'I'm sure there has been a misunderstanding,' Lachlan said.

Aziz Khan shook his head. 'The only one who misunderstands is President Drake. The nawab believes he is not only fortifying Calcutta against the French, but against us. And that cannot be allowed.'

'I will notify him immediately of your concerns.'

The general waved a hand in dismissal. 'Do that and remember that things may not always go so well for you British. May God forever delay the hour, but one day there may be a new prince sitting on the throne of Bengal. And we both know that unlike his grandfather, Siraj ud-Daulah is not renowned for his patience or his restraint.'

Lachlan bowed formally.

Aziz Khan inclined his head. 'May God protect you.'

As Lachlan turned to leave, he saw another slight movement of the *purdah* curtain. And then it was still.

The rooms in the *zenana* – Aziz Khan's harem - fronted onto an enclosed garden. There was a fountain with fat goldfish swimming in it, and flocks of tame pigeons that fluttered around the court all day, pecking at the sunflower seeds the girls scattered for them.

Nafisa and her niece, Yasmin, reclined on a bed of gold silk cushions. Two servant girls knelt beside them, keeping away the flies with large peacock fans.

Aziz Khan stormed in. 'What were you doing, letting Yasmin watch my private discussions?' he said.

Nafisa was accustomed to her brother-in-law's temper. She waved a hand at him as if brushing away a fly. 'She was curious. She has heard a lot about the Englishman.'

'What? What has she heard?'

'That he is not like the others who have come here. In private, he wears proper clothes like us, and he can speak our language faultlessly.'

'He is also an opium addict,' Aziz Khan said. 'So, he can speak a little Parsi. That means nothing. He is just another Britisher. Soon we will be rid of all of them.'

'He is very handsome,' Yasmin said.

He stared at his daughter in astonishment. She had not been asked to express an opinion. Nafisa waited for the inevitable explosion but this time her brother-in-law restrained himself.

He satisfied himself by giving Yasmin's cheek a gentle slap. 'Don't be stupid,' he said.

Lachlan stood on the terrace roof of the fort, smoking a cheroot and listening to the call to prayer echo over the city. It happened five times every day, giving cadence to life in Murshidabad. He would miss this when the time came for him to leave. He suspected that day might not be far off.

It was dusk and the parade ground below was deserted. As the sun dipped below the roofs of the city, it turned the clouds magenta and pink. The final notes of the *maghrib* prayer faded away, and the crickets and frogs started up in the forest on the other side of the river, all but drowning out the sound of a bugle as two redcoats lowered the Company flag.

He watched a *mor-pankhi,* a pleasure boat, making its way back to the city. It was painted gilt and blue, and its bow was long and curved in the shape of a peacock. Its passengers would be someone's women, forever hidden from the outside world.

He thought about the eyes behind the *purdah* curtain

Behind him, Tommy coughed to remind him that he was there.

'Sorry Tommy. Miles away. That's all for the day.'

'Yes, sir. Thinking about General Aziz, I suspect.'

Lachlan nodded. 'What did you make of President Drake's letter?'

'Didn't understand a word.'

'In short, Drake was saying that the nawab's claim that he was building new fortifications was a lie and that even if it wasn't, the nawab couldn't tell him what to do.'

'Was that wise?'

'Not very. But President Drake is not widely renowned for his intellectual capacity. He's played right into Aziz Khan's hands. The man hates us so much it makes his teeth ache, and that letter gives him more ammunition to sully our reputation with the nawab.'

Tommy shrugged. 'So, what are you going to do?'

'I don't know. Our esteemed bloody president in Calcutta has led us all into a real mess. In every dispatch I've sent him since I've been here, I have tried to warn him that we are walking a fine line. He seems not to have paid a damned bit of attention.' He stubbed out the cheroot. 'Siraj is lapping it up, just biding his time.'

'There's going to be trouble when the old boy gets put to bed with a shovel.'

'Tommy, you have your ear to the ground. What do they say about Siraj in the bazaars?'

'The talk is that whether you're a prince or a princess, you have to keep your back to the wall, or he'll be up there. Apparently, he has not a care for position, gender or species. But it's his sabre rattling they like. I suppose you can't go far wrong promising people a war and telling them they can't lose.'

'He wants us out of Bengal, there's no two ways about it.'

'What's the answer?'

'We'd better send a message to the vizier. Tell him I need an urgent private audience with the nawab himself. Tomorrow.'

'Double the sentries tonight?'

Lachlan shook his head. 'Nothing will happen until the nawab dies.'

'In that case,' Tommy said, 'we don't have long.'

CHAPTER 22

Pondicherry

Narain sat astride a grey Arab mare. He had hired a string of half a dozen mules to carry their supplies. Six of the servants were to follow on foot as porters.

Adelaïde appeared from inside the villa, wearing a long white muslin dress and a broad-brimmed hat. A palanquin with four bearers waited for her in the forecourt.

'Did you bring my Toradar?' she said.

'Yes, *mem'sahib*,' he said.

'I want to go by the Kamatchi Amman temple.'

Narain frowned. 'I thought we were hunting for deer.'

'Later. First, we go to the temple.' She climbed into the palanquin, drew the curtains and lay down on the cushions.

Narain walked alongside her, deep in thought, leading his horse by the reins. Suddenly he stopped and pulled the curtains aside. 'You must forgive me,' he said, 'but I have great concerns for your wellbeing.'

'I have a husband. My wellbeing is his concern now.'

'With respect, I fear he married you for your money.'

'Your job is to look after my money.'

'I don't trust him.'

'Neither do I. Is that all? The sun is getting in my eyes.'

'There is one more thing.' He hesitated. He did not want to overstep his position. 'You have asked him to spy on the Englishman, McKenzie.'

'How do you know that?'

'Is it not true?'

'He brings me news. It is hardly spycraft.'

'I worry that while Mckenzie is alive, you make yourself a target. One day the hunted may become the hunter.'

'Be assured, the only reason I allow him to live is so that he can suffer. If he should ever stop suffering, I will kill him. I have noted your objections.'

Narain knew the conversation was over. He drew the curtains, mounted his horse and rode ahead.

They crossed the canal into the *Ville Noir* and stopped outside the Kamatchi Amman. The massive pink entrance tower, the *gopuram*, threw a long shadow over the entire street.

Narain climbed down from his horse and drew aside the palanquin's curtains once more. 'What now, *mem'sahib*?'

Adelaïde pointed to an old leper woman who was squatting on her haunches at the temple entrance. 'Do you see that woman?' she said. 'Give her this.' She gave him a handful of coins.

He blinked. It was a lot of money for a beggar. 'You know her?' he said.

'Yes,' she said. 'It's my grandmother.'

Gudachatram

The villagers were huddled around something they had found in an irrigation ditch on the edge of a paddy field. As Adelaïde came closer, she saw that it was one of the village cattle. There was not much left of it. It had been disembowelled and the meat off its hindquarters had been eaten. The air was murmurous with the buzzing of fat green flies.

Aravinth saw her and came over, hobbling on his bamboo cane. He spat a quid of betel onto the ground. 'It is the tiger,' he said. 'It came out of the forest yesterday just as the sun was setting and attacked our cattle. The guards were asleep over there.' He pointed to the tamarind trees away to their right. 'One of them woke and threw a spear at it to try to scare it away. It fell short and the tiger turned and chased him. Then it came back to eat the bull. It was already wounded and could not get away.'

'You have more cattle,' Narain said.

'It was my bull,' Aravinth said. 'It used to take my cart to Pondicherry on market days. Now what will I do?'

'It must be a very large and very cunning tiger,' Adelaïde said.

Aravinth nodded. 'The guards said it knocked the bull down with one swipe of its paw and then broke its neck with its jaws. It dragged it here as easily as a jackal taking a chicken.'

She looked to where the old man was pointing. The beast must have hauled the massive bull across a deep *nullah*. The strength it would have taken to do that was terrifying.

'I have a bad feeling about this,' Narain said.

'You sound like a girl,' Adelaïde said. 'If my papa were here, you would never dare say that.'

'I am thinking of you.'

'Let me think about me. And I think I want to shoot a tiger.'

They brought three young men from the village as guides and made their way into the forest. That first hour, they made slow progress through thick brush and impenetrable stands of bamboo. Once, Narain yelped as a fire ant dropped down the front of his shirt, startling every animal within a hundred yards of them.

Adelaïde gave him an icy stare.

'There are some temple ruins near here,' one of the guides said. 'We think perhaps he goes there to sleep during the heat of the day.'

Adelaïde nodded. 'Show us.'

The temple was surrounded by a thicket of teak trees. To one side of it was a giant tamarind which was being slowly throttled by strangler figs. There was a carpet of decaying leaves all around it.

The temple itself had been all but reclaimed by the jungle and only a few ancient, grey stones were visible. The rest of the structure was almost completely hidden by the grasses and young trees that had taken root in the cracks. The lolling tongue of a female deity and the stone-worked face of a devil protruded from a tangle of vines.

Two of the villagers they had hired approached the dark mouth of the sanctuary, holding long branches they had cut from saplings. They started beating the ground around the entrance. If the tiger was hiding inside, the noise and movement would draw it out.

Narain handed Adelaïde the Toradar, and she crouched down with her back to the trunk of a wild mango tree. Once the tiger appeared, she would have a clear shot.

But as she looked around, she felt that something was wrong. If this really was the animal's lair, then there should be a litter of animal bones scattered about, evidence of its recent meals. But there was nothing.

The beaters were making a lot of noise. If there was anything hiding inside the temple, it would have come out by now.

It had been cool when they started the hunt. Now it was close to midday and the heat was suffocating. There were flies crawling in her nose and her mouth. Sweat ran into her eyes, making it hard to see.

Something made her look to the side. Two white tufts protruded from the undergrowth about fifty paces away. They were unlike any grasses she had ever seen before. Slowly, the tufts rose and flicked briefly at the air. She realised they were ears.

In another moment, she was staring into the unfathomable golden eyes of a tiger.

Perfectly camouflaged in the dappled shadows of the jungle, it emerged from the brush. It was a female, imperious and beautiful. She opened her jaws and snarled, baring her yellow tusks. Adelaïde could see the sinews in her back and shoulders rippling beneath the glossy orange and black coat.

When the guides saw her, they turned and fled.

Adelaïde raised her musket, sighting along the tiger's shoulder. It was the ideal shot. She imagined the lead ball tearing straight through to her heart.

As she was about to pull the trigger, she was distracted by another movement behind the beast. A cub appeared from between her legs, then a second, now a third, clownish and boisterous. Two of them tussled with each other while the other fell over its own feet. It rolled onto its back then looked around, startled, as if looking for an aggressor.

Suddenly, the other two cubs stopped their tumbling and stared straight at her. One of them hissed, showing its tiny teeth as if they were the deadly tusks of its mother.

The she-tiger stopped, her belly almost touching the ground, eyes glowing like coals. A deep rumble came from her chest. Adelaïde could feel the vibration through her feet. She willed herself to pull the trigger, but she couldn't do it.

She lowered the gun, keeping her eyes fixed on the tigress. She felt confused and bewildered. She had never hesitated to kill before. She backed out of the thicket.

When the tigress was out of sight, she turned and struggled through the tangle of vines and bamboo. Finally, she reached the fringe of lantana bushes and date palms that bordered the bund beyond the native village.

Narain was waiting for her. 'Are you alright?' he said.

'Where were you?'

He held up the spare musket. 'I was covering you the whole way.'

Liar, she thought. You ran with the rest of them. I always thought I could trust you with my life.

I was wrong.

CHAPTER 23

Murshidabad

Lachlan was shocked by the change in Alivardi Khan's appearance. The old man was almost swallowed by the cushions and pillows around him on the *masnad,* the throne platform. His silk robes hung loose on him. He looked frail.

There were fresh-cut jasmine flowers about the room, but they could not disguise the smell of death that clung to him. A slave with a silver-handled whisk made from a yak's tail fanned away the flies that seemed to be swarming in anticipation.

But the old man's mind was still as sharp as ever. He recognised Lachlan immediately and motioned him to kneel on a pillow beside him.

Lachlan had prepared a long preamble, as was customary. But it seemed the nawab knew that time was short. He dispensed with the usual pleasantries. 'I know why you are here,' he said, his voice no more than a croak. 'My grandson.'

Lachlan nodded.

'Speak.'

'Siraj has caused great concern in many quarters. All know that he is neither clever nor kind. You take a great risk naming him your successor.'

'It is true that he does not like you British,' Alivardi Khan said. 'So why would you like him?'

'My commission here is to ensure good relations between Bengal and my employers. Siraj will make my job impossible.'

'The next nawab of Bengal must rule as he sees fit, without interference from foreign powers.'

'Majesty, you have spent almost your entire reign at war with the Maratha tribes in the north. It ravaged your country and your treasury. You know very well that wars serve no one. That is why you have worked so hard to keep the peace between Bengal and the Company. It has required a singular touch. But your grandson, may God bless and keep him, is neither a great tactician on the battlefield, as you were, nor is he a diplomat who can treat skilfully with the foreign powers on your doorstep when you're gone.'

'It is no concern of yours. You British are a little people, only good for haggling and keeping ledgers.'

Lachlan shook his head. 'Believe me, Majesty, you do not want a war with the Company. For the future of Bengal, I beg you. Think again about the man who will replace you.'

'There is no one else.'

'You have another grandson. Shaukat Jung.'

'He drinks.'

'Yes, but all know it is your daughter, Ghaseti Begum, who will rule him from behind the curtain. And she is wise of politics and people. She will ensure the legacy you have built endures. When you have left this earth and are living in repose in Paradise, as is your just reward, you will be revered in Bengal for all that you have done. Your treasury revenues have increased by almost half since you took the throne. You have finally defeated the Marathas and brought peace. There is just one man who may yet destroy everything you have built. His name is Siraj.'

There was shouting from outside the *durbar*. As if waiting for his cue, Siraj appeared, dishevelled and red in the face. He pushed past the guards and pointed at Lachlan. 'What is he doing here?'

Alivardi Khan looked saddened rather than shocked by his grandson's sudden appearance. 'You should not be here,' he said.

'Why did you give him audience?' Siraj shouted. 'He is trying to poison your mind against me.'

'I decide who I can and cannot see.'

'We do not need these British. They are building a fort at Calcutta to make war on us.'

'The fort was built to protect us from the French,' Lachlan said. 'And you do need us. It is through us that you sell your silk and cotton and indigo all around the world. You need our ships, and you need the money we bring to your treasury. Your grandfather understands this.'

'Let me finish with him now,' Siraj said and drew his sword

'Put down your weapon!' Alivardi Khan shouted. The strength in his voice shocked everyone. Two of the guards immediately positioned themselves between Lachlan and the crown prince. Siraj reluctantly sheathed his sword.

'Leave us,' Alivardi Khan said.

There was an uneasy silence after he had gone. Lachlan let out his breath.

Finally, Alivardi Khan said, 'He is a good boy. A little headstrong, perhaps. But he has always loved me.'

'Majesty,' Lachlan said, 'he is impulsive, ill-informed and out of his depth. I do not doubt that he loves you, but that is not reason enough to commit Bengal's future into his hands.'

'Plain speaking. I could have you flogged.'

'But you won't. And that's the difference between you and him.'

Alivardi Khan raised his hand.

Lachlan knew he was dismissed. He's not long for this world, he thought. I pray to God he heard me. If not, there's going to be trouble.'

The oil lamp beside the bed sent shadows dancing around the walls. After a while, they formed themselves into uniformed men holding muskets, running up the strand towards a wooden fort. Another shadow became his sister. She fell to the sand, a red stain blossoming on her blouse.

Lachlan sat up, fighting for breath.

Napoleon Gagnon was staring down at him, a pistol in his hand. There were stains on the carpets. Catia's blood had leaked everywhere.

He heard her father's voice: *The girl was standing right there. Why didn't you pull the trigger?'*

He lay down again, the heat sapping every bead of moisture from his body. He felt as if he was peering at the world through a thick fog. His eyes wouldn't stop watering, and his nose ran as if he had a heavy cold, but there was nothing wrong with him, not in that way at least. He squeezed his temples with the flat of his hands, trying to stem the waves of pain in his head.

There was only one way he could stop this. He got up and went to the rosewood case in the corner, fumbled the key into the brass lock.

He reached for the pipe, laid it on the table beside the bed and lifted the silver locket from around his neck. Inside was Catia's portrait in miniature and a ball of black opium resin. He took a needle from the box and skewered the opium with it, then held the resin over the candle next to the bed. It would be better to use the lamp in his kit, but the wick needed trimming, and his hands were shaking so badly he knew he wouldn't be able to manage it.

He turned the needle until the opium softened and began to melt. Then he lay on his side, one hand reaching for the pipe. With the other he brought the bubbling ball of opium towards the bowl and inhaled.

As he breathed out the smoke, he felt his muscles relax. The trembling in his hands stopped.

His last thought before the opium worked its magic was, I should have pulled the trigger.

CHAPTER 24

Pondicherry

Kilcannon climbed down from the *tonga*, throwing his cane and tricorn to one of the servants. He took the ribbon from his queue and shook his hair free, then tossed his jacket to another of the servants who were crowding around him.

He saw Adelaïde and gave her a disarming smile.

'A long journey,' she said.

'But worth it when you are waiting at the end of it.' He swept her up in his arms and kissed her.

This would not do in front of the help. 'We should walk in the garden,' she said.

'We ran into a storm two days out at sea,' Kilcannon said. 'I thought I should never see land again.'

'Well, you are here now. Your journey was a successful one?'

'In Murshidabad they feted me like a prince. They all want to throw the British out of India and know I am the man who can help them do it. I will make a fortune and become an Indian saint at the same time.' He took her around the waist. 'But I don't want to talk about that now. Every day without you has been a torment. You were all I could think of.' He reached up, took a flower from a frangipani tree and placed the buttery yellow bloom in her hair.

'The servants have prepared your dinner,' Adelaïde said.

'I'm only hungry for you. Famished.' He kissed her neck and squeezed her breast through her dress.

'Stop.' She put up her hand. 'The servants will see us.'

'I don't give a damn,' he said. He scooped her up in his arms and carried her inside.

Adelaïde lay naked on their four-poster bed. A *punkha* with a deep double frill swung lazily overhead. Its silken rope passed through a hole in the wall into the next room, where two *wallahs* had taken turns to keep it moving through the night.

A bead of sweat trickled between her breasts. 'Tell me about Murshidabad,' she said.

Kilcannon turned from the window in his silk dressing gown. Behind him the light seeped into the sky over the pantile roofs of the *Ville Blanche*. 'It's a tinderbox waiting to explode. Everyone thinks the war for Hindustan will be fought here in the Carnatic. They're wrong. It will be decided in Bengal.'

'What about the British Company. Are they ready for war?'

He laughed. 'That's the beauty of it. Their president in Calcutta, Drake, is a half-wit. He's only concerned with lining his pockets. The Company bigwigs in London have warned him to prepare for trouble, but he pays them no attention. It's astonishing.' He sat down and stretched his arms above his head. 'You haven't asked me about McKenzie.'

'I knew you would tell me in your own time.'

'On the days he shows up at the *durbar* in Murshidabad, he seems sharp enough, but I'm told that privately he's still smoking far too much opium and slowly wrecking his health. Satisfied?'

'For now.' She played with her hair a moment. He recognised it for the calculated gesture it was, but it stirred him just the same. 'I want you to do something else for me,' she said.

'I won't kill him for you. That's not my business.'

'If I wanted him dead, I would arrange it myself.'

'You should want him dead. He'll come after you one day.'

'That's what Narain thinks. But it won't happen while he's choking on his own poppy fumes in Murshidabad.'

'So, what is it you want now?'

'Your brother in France...'

'Yes,' he said, warily.

'I want you to order a consignment of arms for me. Can you do that?'

'For what purpose?'

'I intend to bring my father's regiment of mercenaries back into service. Narain will help me find recruits and train them. But finding modern equipment may prove difficult.'

He shook his head. 'What?'

'I also want three six-pound field cannons.'

'Why would you need to revive your father's business? I can look after you.'

'I want quality, Charlevilles, not the museum pieces you sold to Le Roux at Srirangam. Narain will give you my requisition later today. I have made a detailed list.'

'You could not possibly afford such a purchase.'

'I would not order items I could not afford. On delivery of the shipment, I shall furnish the funds in full.'

'Where will this money come from?'

'That is none of your business.'

'Of course it's my business. I'm your husband.'

'Those two things do not follow. Get me the guns and the cannons and I will pay you.'

'Are you hiding money from me?'

'You are tense,' she said, and laid back on the bolster. 'Come back to bed.'

It was not in his nature to reject any woman's advances, but for once he had quite lost his appetites. His first instinct had been to laugh off her ridiculous request, but he knew her well enough to know that she never made frivolous demands.

'I'm hungry,' he said. 'We should go down to breakfast.'

'Don't forget my guns,' she said as he closed the door.

They took breakfast on the patio. A flock of crows sat in the mango trees above their heads making their usual din.

'So, there's going to be war in Bengal,' she said.

Kilcannon nodded. 'Everyone's just waiting for the nawab to die. When Siraj takes the throne, the first thing he will do is throw the British out of their factory at Murshidabad, then he'll set his sights on Calcutta. He'll need muskets and cannons, which I shall be happy to provide.'

'If you can get guns for the Nawab of Bengal, then you can surely get them for your wife.'

'You make it sound so easy. It's not like buying rice in the market.'

'I wouldn't know. I've never bought rice in the market.'

He sipped his coffee. 'Narain tells me you went hunting for tigers again while I was away.'

'Without success.'

'You should be careful. It's a dangerous pastime.'

'I know what I'm doing.'

'Perhaps I should I get you a proper musket for such a venture?'

Adelaïde called to one of the servants and told him to fetch her hunting rifle. When he returned, she indicated that he should give it to Kilcannon.

He allowed himself to look impressed. 'That is quite a gun,' he said.

'It's a Toradar. It was a gift to my father from the Raja of Jaipur.'

Kilcannon weighed it in its hands. It was five feet long, and heavy, reinforced with iron side plates. It was more than a firearm, it was a work of art. It had a delicately painted stock with birds and animals detailed in gold against a white background. It had been signed by its smithy, Haji Sha'ban.

What was truly remarkable was the gold damascened barrel which was square and not rounded.

'You can fire this?' he said, thinking she was too fragile to wield such a heavy weapon.

She stood up and took it from him, swinging it easily to her hip. 'The stock is too small to place against the shoulder. It must be held under the arm, like this.' She pointed it at him.

Alarmed, he scraped his chair backwards out of the way.

'It's alright,' she said, 'it isn't loaded.'

'*M'sieur.*' Narain said.

Kilcannon was relieved at the interruption. He had not heard her *je-madar* step out onto the patio.

Narain held out an envelope. 'This came for you, *m'sieur*. It arrived this morning on a packet boat from Surat. The courier who brought it said it was urgent.'

Kilcannon took it from him and tore it open. It was a single page, and he read it through quickly. Then he refolded it and put it back in the envelope.

'Is everything all right?' she said.

He gave her a tight smile. 'Just a small complication with one of my cargos. Everything is fine. You must excuse me.' He pushed his breakfast away, jumped up and went inside, calling for the servants to fetch him a *tonga*.

CHAPTER 25

T he heavy teak doors were flanked on either side by saluting sentries. Kilcannon went in.

De Leyrit studied him from behind a rosewood bureau. He wore a powdered wig and heavy frock coat, the same one he wore every day. Dear God, he stinks, Kilcannon thought. He had never seen the man smile. A bureaucrat through and through.

His predecessors, the former governors of Pondicherry, were ranged behind him on the panelled walls, from La Prévostière to Dumas. There was an empty space on the wall where Dupleix should have been. The *Compagnie* did not reward failure. They had blamed Dupleix for losing Trichinopoly to the British, and the previous year, he had been recalled in disgrace.

De Leyrit consulted the piece of paper that lay on the polished surface in front of him. He studied it as if it contained some mysterious cypher that might lead him to discover the meaning of life.

Finally, he said, 'Can you perform miracles, *M'sieur* Kilcannon?'

This was not the opening gambit Kilcannon had anticipated. He blinked. 'I am afraid not.'

'Neither can I. Yet that is what they expect from us in France. Miracles. I am to keep the peace with the British, though it is quite clear they are not planning to keep the peace with us. I cannot attack them, but I am convinced that soon they will attack me. And what do we have to defend our interests?'

De Leyrit looked down at the piece of paper and ran a finger down the handwritten list. 'Here in Pondicherry, we have ten infantry companies and a further three in Mahé. That is a little over a thousand men. We have several thousand native troops also. But men are not the issue. The issue is what do we have to put in their hands? Our men need muskets, and they need ammunition. We need cannons, also. But in France they say we are to keep the peace, so they will not spend their precious *livres* on something they say we do not need.'

'They are all idiots in Paris,' Kilcannon said.

De Leyrit inclined his head slightly. 'That may be so. I am not at liberty to offer an opinion. But it has left me with a problem. How may I equip my army? You came to me several months ago and said you could provide me with a solution. You asked for a generous downpayment, and I agreed to provide one. So where are my guns, *M'sieur* Kilcannon?'

'They are on their way.'

'Are they?'

The two men stared at each other.

'I heard a whisper that you had received a letter from your agent in Surat. You seem surprised that I know of this. Don't be. I may not have guns for my army, but I do have abundant spies, at least here in Pondicherry.'

'What did your spies tell you?'

'They told me that your ships, with my muskets and cannons on board, had foundered off the Malabar coast in a storm.'

'Your information is incorrect.'

'I hope so. Because if you cannot deliver on time, I shall need my downpayment returned immediately.'

Kilcannon held the other man's gaze and tried to keep his voice even. 'And you will have it, should it prove necessary.'

De Leyrit nodded. 'Good. The dungeons downstairs are full of men who made promises they could not keep. *Bon journée, M'sieur* Kilcannon. Do not attempt to leave Pondicherry until I have what you promised me. Do you understand?'

Kilcannon stared at the cards in his hand. It was hot in the room, too hot. He rubbed his eyes and tried to concentrate. He wondered if someone had put something in his drink.

He looked down the table. It must have been a grand piece once, but now it was marked by a hundred wet glasses and its polish removed by a thousand elbows.

The young officers were playing high, one hundred-and-fifty-rupee points. Which was fine when he was winning. Losing five thousand rupees on a rubber of whist was not what he needed right now.

'Come on, Gerard,' one of them said, 'let's play.'

Only a few minutes before, the four men had been laughing and joking with each other, but as the stakes grew, an uneasy silence had fallen over them. They were guarding their cards, their eyes on the fat pot of money in the middle.

Kilcannon blinked and looked around the table. 'Something's not right,' he said.

'What do you mean?' someone said.

'Who shuffled these cards?'

The man on his right grew impatient. 'Just play the game.'

Kilcannon's eyes went to the money in the pot. Game? This was no game. 'I thought I was playing with gentlemen,' he said.

'What are you talking about?'

'You get me drunk and then you try to cheat me.'

'No one's cheating you.'

Kilcannon studied his cards, then laid them down. He licked his lips as if he could taste something foul, put his hands underneath the rim of the table and pushed it over, spilling cards, brandy and silver rupees everywhere.

The others shouted in outrage and leaped to their feet. But Kilcannon had already staggered away from them into the hall and was shouting for the madam. He almost fell. One of the young women who worked there reached out an arm to steady him. He swore at her and pushed her away.

'I'm fine, damn you,' he said. 'Where's Lily?'

Madame Peloise came down the stairs. She wanted no trouble and the *m'sieur* was a regular customer. If he wanted Lily, then he could have her.

Of course, her name wasn't really Lily, it was Vishnupriya, and her father sold *paan* in the Black Town. She could speak not a word of French. Her popularity derived from the skills she had learned in the bedrooms upstairs. The girl would know how to calm him down, in fact she was expert at it.

She went into a back room to fetch her.

Lily emerged in a diaphanous silk wrap. Her arms and legs were tattooed with henna and her breasts were bare. There was gold jewellery on her wrists and ankles.

She smiled at Kilcannon, took him by the hand and led him toward the stairs. Meanwhile Madame Peloise went into the gaming room to console the guests that Kilcannon had upset with his antics. Some free champagne should settle their tempers.

Half an hour later, she heard screams coming from upstairs. She called for her *securité,* Jean-Pierre, and ran up to the first floor.

When she threw open the door to Lily's bedroom, she found Kilcannon kneeling half-naked on the bed. Lily was underneath him. He was holding her hands above her head with his left hand, and with the other he was punching her repeatedly in the face so hard that the blood ran.

Jean-Pierre appeared on the landing a few moments later. He had been a sergeant in the *Compagnie* until grapeshot had taken his left eye and most of his arm. The wound had ruined his looks but not his usefulness. He was the size of a small horse and had the strength to match it. He ran into the room, grabbed Kilcannon with one giant hand and threw him against the wall.

Lily ran screaming from the room.

Kilcannon lay crumpled in the corner, breathing hard from his exertions. The ribbon had been torn from his queue in the struggle and his long hair fell loose around his face. He was sweating and his face was swollen and red with rage and with drink. He looked like a madman.

'Get out,' Madame Peloise said. 'Get out and don't ever come back.'

Kilcannon sighed as if he had been done a great injustice, got slowly to his feet and reached for his breeches. When he had dressed, he turned to Madame Peloise. 'I shall not be returning if this is how I am to be treated,' he said. Adjusting his frock coat, he set his shoulders and walked out.

As he passed Jean-Pierre in the doorway, he nodded to him as if he were an old acquaintance. 'If you ever want a job,' he said, 'come and see me.'

CHAPTER 26

It was a hot morning, and the servants were already busy throwing water on the *tatties* to cool the rooms. Chevrons of light angled in through the louvred blinds.

Narain received a summons to Kilcannon's study. The Irishman was sitting behind his desk when he walked in. He wore just a loose linen shirt over his breeches and his hair fell around his shoulders. He had piled several accounts ledgers on his desk alongside his quills and a pot of ink. He was poring through one of the account books, running his fingers down the columns and carefully totalling the figures.

He looked up and smiled. It worried Narain, that smile.

'Where is the *madame*?' Kilcannon said.

'She's still in bed,' Narain said.

'I've been going through the accounts.'

Narain nodded and said nothing. Down in the street he could hear a hawker selling *paan*.

Kilcannon leaned back in his chair and stared at him. Narain heard the clock in the hall sound the hour. The silence went on and on.

'So,' Kilcannon said finally, 'where is all her money?'

'I don't understand.'

'You understand perfectly. There are obviously two sets of books.' He sorted through the papers on his desk. 'And the house on the Rue Suffren. It seems she doesn't even own it. It was leased from Ananda Pillai. So where is all her father's estate?'

'It has to be protected.'

'From whom? From me?'

'From everyone.'

'I'm her husband. Her worldly goods belong to me now.'

'She said you would think that.'

Kilcannon gripped the edge of the desk as if he must hold on to something solid to stop himself from grabbing Narain, anyone, by the throat. 'Let me tell you what I think. I think she's using us both.'

'She's just a girl.'

'Is she? I believe she married me because I have certain business connections that she wants to avail herself of. And as for you, she'll reach her majority soon. How long will you be needed after that?'

'She will always need me.'

'Are you sure of that? Even if you're right, explain to me how her appreciation for your services is going to enrich you.'

'Not everything is about his money.'

Kilcannon laughed out loud. 'Of course it is, you sorry fool. Listen to me. You pay yourself a salary out of the estate, correct? Well one day, when you have outlived your usefulness, I hope you have put enough of it away that you can maintain your present lavish lifestyle.'

'I gave an oath to her father. He was a great man, and he was very good to me and my brother.'

'A great man who is long dead and in his grave. Or eaten by jackals if you believe the rumours.' Kilcannon leaned back in his chair and regarded Narain through half closed eyes. 'Does she know how much you've stolen from the estate this last five years?'

Narain fought the urge to blurt out some denial or excuse. He had to give himself time to think. He shifted from one foot to the other. 'That is just the daily accounts. The ingoings and outgoings. I take a small commission.' He paused. 'I earn it,' he said, deciding to brazen it out.

'Perhaps. But it's not what her father proscribed in his will, is it? You were to get a salary, quite a handsome one in fact. Nowhere does he say you could take a cut from every trader and supplier who comes to the house.'

'It is nothing compared to what she has elsewhere.'

There was a deathly silence. Narain realised what he had said.

'I can imagine,' Kilcannon said. He jabbed a finger at the pile of ledgers. 'When the *madame* finds out about this, what will she do, do you think?'

'She will be angry.'

'Angry?' Kilcannon shook his head. 'She will come after you with her elephant gun. We will have to scrub you off the wall with putty knives.' He leaned forward and put his elbows on the desk.

Here it comes, Narain thought.

'The *madame* has many talents,' Kilcannon said, 'but numbers are not among them. She will only discover your perfidy if someone tells her.' He slammed the ledger closed. It sounded like a musket shot in the tiny room and Narain jumped, despite himself. 'You expected more, didn't you? The last five years of your life you dedicated yourself to protecting her, and yet she still takes you for granted. She married me against your advice. Correct? She doesn't listen to you anymore.'

'I promised her father I would look after her.'

'You broke that promise when you started stealing her money. Now it's too late. You cannot undo what has been done.'

'What do you want?'

'I want your services, and I am prepared to pay for them. I can make you a rich man, Narain. Do you want to be wealthy, truly wealthy, like these fat *dubashes* you see riding up and down the streets on painted elephants, or do you want to be a servant all your life?'

Narain closed his eyes and told himself to be strong.

'She's a vindictive little bitch. She might even report you to the governor and you'll end up with your neck in a noose. I wouldn't put it past her.'

Narain wanted desperately to sit down, but he knew his life depended on staying calm. 'How will working for you be different from working for her?'

'First, I need to know where her money is. Once I have it, twenty per cent goes to you, straight away. After that, you will work for me and do whatever I tell you to do. Everything we make, you get the same terms. One fifth. How does that sound?'

Narain did the sums. When he had confirmed his share in his head, the total made him light-headed. He slumped into a chair. The silence stretched.

Kilcannon lit a cigar. He watched the smoke drift lazily toward the ceiling. 'When is she going hunting again?'

Narain stared at him. 'Tomorrow.'

Kilcannon got up and came around from behind the desk. He leaned close and put an arm around Narain's shoulder. 'Hunting is a dangerous sport. People get killed all the time.'

'No.'

'Yes. But it's up to you. Untold riches working for me or hanging from a gibbet in Fort Louis. Men are always free to choose their own fate. That's the wonderful thing about life.'

CHAPTER 27

Gudachatram

'What is going to happen to me,' Narain said, as they rode towards the village for that day's *shikar*. 'Now that you are married, everything has changed.'

'I do not mean for Gerard ever to replace you,' Adelaïde said.

'But he will. As you can replace me when you reach your majority.'

'There will always be a place for you in my household. When I reform my father's regiment, I shall make you *subadar*. You will never be without employ.'

'So, more fighting then.'

'Yes. That is what God made you for.'

Narain glanced angrily at her, but she didn't notice. She had seen something up ahead.

The tiger had killed again. The entire village had congregated in the paddy field. Something lay on the ground, covered in a bloody shroud. Aravinth separated himself from the crowd and came over. His face was contorted with grief.

'What has happened?' Adelaïde said.

'The tiger,' he said.

'Who is it?'

'It is the husband of my youngest daughter. He went into the fields to bring in his cows. That is all that is left of him.'

She got down from her horse. The crowd parted for her. She knelt and pulled back the sheet. Much of the young man's lower body was gone. At the sight of him, the howling from the villagers started up anew.

The old man replaced the sheet. 'What are we going to do? We have no guns to defend ourselves. Please, help us.'

Then she heard it, as if on cue, a low rumbling like distant thunder that built to a roar and shook the ground under her feet. Everyone looked up and fell silent. A cow, panicked, broke into a run and headed off down the dusty road.

An hour later, Adelaïde and Narain set off into the jungle with their bearers and five of the young men. The men were wearing masks made from tree bark, but instead of putting them on their faces, they had them on the backs of their heads. Aravinth said that a tiger would never attack someone who was looking directly at it, so this way it could not stalk them from behind.

They led them towards the ancient temple again, skirting a dense clump of bamboo, its feathery flowers overhanging a sombre glade, thick with a carpet of rotting leaves.

Adelaïde could hear them ahead of her, blowing horns and banging drums, their shouts echoing through the forest. She carried the Toradar loosely at her hip. This time, I won't hesitate, she promised herself. It will be my first tiger.

After a few minutes, one of them raised his hand. He had seen something. He put his finger to his lips. Adelaïde waited, and then she heard it again, that low, rumbling growl.

Narain was behind her, breathing hard. 'He has lost all his money,' he said.

'What?'

'*M'sieur* Kilcannon. Everything. The three ships his brother sent from France were lost in a storm off Malabar. He is ruined.'

Adelaïde stared at the jungle of lantana and thorns in front of her. Was there something moving there? She wiped her face with the back of her arm and tried to make sense of what Narain had just said. Why was he telling her this now?

'He tried to win some of the money back at cards but has only got further into debt. He had to do something.'

'What are you talking about?'

'I tried to warn you when you first met him. He is not a good man.'

'If he was a good man, I would not have married him.'

'What I mean is, you have made a mistake.'

'I never make mistakes,' she said.

She turned away from him and tried to focus again on the jungle, looking for movement. Her father had told her time after time: *when you are hunting, whether it's a man or a dangerous animal, never allow yourself to think about anything else. Set your mind only on the kill. Nothing must cloud your mind.*

'This time you have made a big mistake. And there is nothing you can do, not now.'

She heard the unmistakeable sound of a trigger being cocked behind her. She looked over her shoulder. Narain was pointing his musket at her head.

'What are you doing?' she said, more puzzled than alarmed.

His hands shook as his finger tightened around the trigger, and in that moment, she realised what had happened. She didn't know how Gerard had got to him, only that he had.

'I'm sorry, *mem'sahib,*' Narain said.

Just as he said it, he looked from her to something that he could see over her shoulder. He took a quick breath and his eyes went wide.

She threw out a hand to grab the barrel of the gun and turn it away, but he dropped it and ran.

She heard a roar behind her.

The tiger exploded from the undergrowth, its teeth and talons exposed. She saw a blur of gold and black before it hit her very hard on the shoulder and knocked her down. She felt hot, fetid breath in her face and a moment of unimaginable pain.

Then blackness.

Part 3

THE TRAP

CHAPTER 28

Murshidabad

Water murmured from a fountain in the courtyard and sparrows fussed in the mango trees around it. A peacock strutted across the garden, its fan of tail feathers rustling as it spread them on display. The breeze carried with it the fragrance of roses, jasmine and sandalwood from the surrounding pickets and bowers.

'We have a problem,' Aziz Khan said.

Kilcannon chose a fig from the silver platter between them. Things were going well. His wife's tragic demise had given him the funds he needed to pay off de Leyrit and return to Bengal. It had not been easy to put this transaction together for Aziz Khan, cultivating relationships with corrupt French officers, buying muskets, cannons and ammunition meant for the *Compagnie* and diverting them to his own warehouses ready for delivery to Siraj.

Meanwhile his protégé, Narain, had more than justified the faith he had put in him. He had sent him to Calcutta with bribes for any malcontents inside the houses of the rich merchants living there. Once the city fell, there would be loot to be had, and he wanted to get more than his fair share of it.

Narain had reported back that he had found such a man, in the household of Ashin Das, one of the wealthiest merchants in Calcutta. He was reputed to have more gold and jewels in the vault under his palace than the president of the British Company himself.

If all went well, and Siraj made good on his threats to attack the British, Kilcannon would make a handsome profit on the shipment of arms, and with Narain's help, he would make a second fortune when Ashin Das was forced to flee Calcutta.

He was close to the sort of riches that could make a man's head spin. But so much could still go wrong. And looking at Aziz Khan's face, he suspected the blow was just about to fall.

'What sort of problem?'

'The English Resident. It seems he has Alivardi Khan's ear and has proved persuasive.'

'McKenzie? He is a hopeless opium addict.'

'Whatever you have heard, he is not hopeless. He keeps his wits about him during the day. Enough to persuade the nawab to change his choice for crown prince.'

'You're not serious?'

'The nawab has told me he is contemplating a decree in the coming weeks, naming Shaukat Jung as his successor. It is McKenzie's doing.'

Kilcannon tried to hide his panic. This couldn't be allowed to happen. Everything depended on Siraj assuming the throne after Alivardi Khan. If Siraj lost his place at court and cancelled their contract, he would be bankrupted.

'We must keep McKenzie away from Alivardi Khan,' he said.

'He trusts him. He likes him.' Aziz Khan leaned forward and tapped the carpet between them to make his point. 'If Siraj does not take the throne, you and I will fall out of favour in the *durbar*. Shaukat Jung will give preference to McKenzie - the man who won him the throne - and the Company that sent him here.'

Kilcannon said softly, 'Then we should kill Alivardi Khan now, before he makes the decree.'

'Many have tried over the years, and many have failed. Killing kings is a dangerous business. Perhaps there is a better way.'

Kilcannon braced himself. Here it comes.

'It will be expensive,' Aziz Khan said.

'For you or for me?'

Aziz Khan spread his hands. 'If our arrangement with Siraj does not go ahead, it will be inconvenient for me. But we both know it will ruin you.'

He said it with the smile of a man moving his piece to checkmate in a chess game.

Kilcannon thought it through. 'What do you want?'

'What can you offer me?'

Kilcannon wanted to pull the other man's liver out through his nose. 'I am already paying you a handsome commission on the guns.'

An almost indiscernible shrug.

Kilcannon didn't want to tell him about Narain's dealings in Calcutta, but he had no choice. 'You know of a merchant called Ashin Das?'

'Of course.'

'I have a contact inside his household. On the day Siraj takes Calcutta, I plan to liberate what is hidden in his vaults before the general soldiery can get their hands on any of it. Get rid of McKenzie, and I will be happy to share some of the profits with you.'

'You mean share them equally.'

It wasn't a question. It was a statement.

Kilcannon clenched his fists. Aziz Khan had him over a barrel. He thought he was going to choke. 'Agreed,' he said.

There were eight double pillars along the length of the *zenana*, which was spread with silken carpets. Brass lamps were scattered around the floor, each holding scores of candles. Aziz Khan sat at ease, his elbow resting on a padded bolster, surrounded by cushions of plush velvet.

Nafisa entered first, barefoot, Yasmin following. His sister-in-law still wore the nose ring his brother had given her on their marriage day.

Today, his attention was solely given over to his daughter. As she knelt in front of him, he appraised her in a way he never had before. She was wearing a white *chador*, wrapped so closely around her that only her eyes were visible. But what eyes! Black and unfathomable.

'Remove your veil,' he said.

She did as he ordered, and he nodded in satisfaction. He had forgotten how lovely she was. She would suit his plans perfectly.

He turned to Nafisa. 'I have been thinking.' He waited for one of her biting rejoinders, but she simply smiled and said nothing. Perhaps she was finally learning her place. 'I wonder if it would not be a bad thing to make an alliance with the British hat-men.' He used the disparaging name the Mughal court used for all Europeans.

'I thought you had sided with the French,' Nafisa said.

'Politics is a matter of checks and balances.' He looked at Yasmin. 'She is curious about the English Resident. How curious?'

For once Nafisa seemed lost for words. 'The Englishman?'

'He is an option that we should perhaps explore. Is the idea displeasing to her?'

'But Yasmin is already betrothed to Mir Najaf.'

'On reflection, Mir Najaf may not be as useful as the Englishman. Should the marriage not take place, he and his family will be compensated.'

'You think to marry your daughter to an Englishman?' Nafisa reached out and took Yasmin's hand. Yasmin kept her eyes on her lap.

'It might be a judicious alliance if I could make it come about.'

Nafisa stared at him. 'You would use her in such a way?'

'I have to use her some way, and at this moment this is the way I consider best.' He got to his feet. 'I have business to attend to. Talk to the girl. Make sure she understands what is required of her.'

He was pleased with how easily he had been able to manipulate Kilcannon. Yasmin, of course, would do whatever he said. That only left the Englishman to misdirect. He would be here shortly, but it would be good to keep him waiting.

As soon as he had gone, Yasmin looked up at her aunt. 'Do you think he means it?'

Nafisa shrugged. 'I never know what he means.'

'But do you think this is even possible?'

'You have noble blood. You should marry a prince like Mir Najaf.'

'I do not like Mir Najaf. He has a temper. He kicked one of his mother's dogs. I saw him through the curtain when he thought no one was watching.'

Nafisa had no answer. Mir Najaf came from a wealthy and influential family, but that was all the good she could say about him if pressed.

'Tell me,' Yasmin said. 'What was it like for you with uncle?'

'I was sixteen. I didn't even see him before our wedding day. He treated me reasonably well, until he found out I could not give him a son, then he turned against me. I must tell you I did not weep many tears when he died. Your father took over his affairs and his property, and since then, I have been in this rather pretty prison. There, that is the bare truth of it.'

'I don't want a life like yours, Auntie. I don't want a brutish husband. I don't want to spend my whole life in a *zenana*. Tell me you have never wished things had been different.'

Nafisa did not know what to say. It was true. She lived every minute of every day with the sour realization that her time on earth had been wasted. Yet she was afraid for her niece. 'Yasmin, you have everything to lose. Should your father be serious about this new proposal, it puts you in great danger. You see a handsome and exotic young man in a uniform. I see exile and abandonment away from the protection of your family.'

'I don't want to be shut away, playing on swings and feeding peacocks.'

'Then what do you want?'

'There is another world outside of this one. I want to see it. I want to be a part of it.'

'You are just a woman. Leaving your father's protection will put you at great risk.'

Yasmin shook her head. 'I know the risks.'

'You know nothing of risk,' Nafisa said, but she thought, I wish I had had her spirit when I was her age. Despite everything I have said, perhaps it is not too late for her.

CHAPTER 29

L achlan climbed down from the saddle of his horse outside Aziz Khan's palace and saw a well-dressed European waiting for a servant to fetch his mount from the stables. He knew him only by reputation. This had to be Gerard Kilkannon. He had been in Murshidabad several times over the last year, trying to peddle guns.

He forced a diplomatic smile. It would be good to know why Kilkannon was meeting with Aziz Khan.

'*Señor* Kilkannon,' he said in Portuguese, 'I didn't know you were back in Murshidabad. Business or pleasure?'

'*Señor* McKenzie. We have not been formally introduced. I have heard a lot about you.'

'From the general?' Lachlan said, nodding towards Aziz Khan's palace.

'From my wife, Adelaïde. Her father was Napoleon Gagnon. I believe you knew him.'

Lachlan felt as if he had been kicked in the stomach by a horse. He tried to keep the shock from showing on his face.

But Kilkannon knew he had caught him off guard and smiled wolfishly. 'Did you not know?

'Gagnon's daughter is your wife?'

'She was, God rest her soul.'

'She's dead?'

'Sadly, yes. In tragic circumstances.'

'I hope she died screaming.'

Kilkannon's smile did not slip. 'If it pleases you, I imagine she did. Are you satisfied? Justice is done, and you can sleep easily again knowing you are safe from her.'

A servant brought his grey. He put one foot in the stirrup and hoisted himself into the saddle. 'Why did you never come after her? I warned her, you know. I said, as long as that man's alive, you will always have to watch your back. You should finish him first. Do you know what she said?'

Lachlan wanted to drag the smug bastard down from his horse and throttle the life out of him. 'Enlighten me.'

'She wanted you to suffer. She thought death would be an easy escape for you. His grey wanted its head, but he hadn't done yet. He jerked on the reins and brought the horse under control. 'We held a memorial for her at the church before I left Pondicherry. Not many people came. Nothing left of her you see, and people do like to see a coffin, don't they?'

'Nothing left? What do you mean?'

'She was taken by a tiger.'

Lachlan felt the blood drain from his face. He should have done it himself. He stared at Kilcannon. He was enjoying this.

'Now she is gone, I imagine I will be spending much more of my time in Bengal. Murshidabad is a pleasant city, don't you find? In fact, I may relocate here permanently as soon as the last Englishman is gone. Once Siraj takes the throne, I shouldn't have to wait long.' He looked over his shoulder at the palace. 'Are you here to bow and scrape to Aziz Khan as you do to the nawab? Surely the Tiger of Karimkot has grown tired of having to put on a smile just for show?'

Lachlan couldn't think straight. He said, almost mechanically. 'There are many ways a man might serve his country.'

Kilcannon leaned down from the saddle. 'Come now, you don't have a country. You're a renegade like me. It is only an accident of birth that put us on different sides.'

'Believe me, the difference between us goes a lot deeper than that. Honour. Morals. These things mean a great deal to me. They mean nothing to you.'

'You're right, they don't. I take that as a compliment. But you must excuse me. I am taking up too much of your time.' He lowered his voice as if he was about to divulge a secret. 'A word of advice about the general. Don't believe a word that bastard says.'

'General Aziz is renowned for his honest dealings.'

Kilcannon laughed out loud. 'Very amusing. I like a man with a sense of humour. He's had me on a string for months. Now he's sent me away empty-handed. I hope you have more luck than I did.'

Lachlan watched him ride off.

Tommy appeared at his shoulder. 'Are you alright, sir? You look like you've been filleted with a carving knife, don't mind me saying. What did he say to you?'

Lachlan tried to get control of himself again. His breathing was ragged. 'He told me that a mutual acquaintance had passed away.'

'Sorry to hear that. My condolences.'

'None are needed. Tommy, have you ever heard the story of the Hydra?'

Tommy shook his head.

'It's a monster from an old Greek myth. It had a hundred heads, but if you cut one off, it grew two more. You just saw one of the heads.'

'Not sure I get your meaning.'

'It doesn't matter.' Lachlan took his tin of cheroots from his jacket pocket and lit one from Tommy's pipe. His hands were shaking. He needed a minute. He couldn't go in to see Aziz Khan feeling like this.

He tried to make sense of it all, but he felt the same as he had when Gagnon himself died, a profound sense of relief mixed with disappointment. He had thought he would feel like all his burdens had been lifted, but he didn't, not at all.

One of Aziz Khan's ushers came to fetch him. He stubbed out his cheroot and followed him through the gates.

The man led him to a summerhouse built of white marble. There were cusped arches and fretted screens worked into the stone. It was situated in the middle of an ornamental pond, with a marble walkway connecting it to an avenue of tall and majestic cypress trees. Carp and goldfish nibbled at the dark green pads of lotus flowers floating on the surface of the water. A silver swing hung under one of the mango trees. It was an oasis of tranquillity.

The garden was surrounded by a high stone wall. Lachlan knew that by Mughal tradition the walls of a harem garden had to be high enough that a man standing on the back of an elephant couldn't look over the top. He realised with shock that he must be in the *zenana* garden, forbidden to everyone but the general himself.

He felt the stirring of alarm. Just by inviting him here, Aziz Khan had put him in a highly compromising position. What was the sly bastard up to?

The general lounged comfortably in his *jama* on a bed of green and tangerine silk cushions, languid as a *nautch* girl.

Lachlan was dressed formally in a heavy maroon coat with breeches and silk stockings. He felt light-headed in the crushing heat. He tugged at his collar and flicked at a bead of perspiration above his eye.

Aziz Khan waved a hand, inviting him to take a seat on one of the cushions beside him.

They exchanged the usual pleasantries while servants hurried across the lawns with platters of mango and plantains, carefully arranged on palm leaf platters. There were frosted jugs of lime and rosewater. A servant with a large peacock fan kept them cool.

'Alivardi Khan is dying,' the general said finally, getting down to business.

'There have been rumours about him dying ever since I first came here,' Lachlan said. 'He may yet outlive us all.'

'Come Englishman, let's stop playing games. These are not rumours. We both know the end is near. A sad day for him. It will be worse for those left behind.'

'Is this about the repairs to the fort in Calcutta? I expect an answer imminently.'

'It is too late for that. Whatever your President Drake says, when Siraj takes the throne, everything will change. The French will take advantage of his enmity towards you British and ally with him. There will be a war.'

'A war like that serves no one. A diplomatic solution would be better for everyone.'

'For once, I must agree with you.' Aziz Khan leaned forward and whispered, for effect, as there was not another soul within a hundred paces. 'You have more sympathizers than you believe.'

The sudden turn in the conversation took Lachlan off guard.

Aziz Khan pushed his advantage. 'I know you have been busy cultivating many friendships inside the *durbar*. You have championed the cause of Shaukat Jung, and you are friendly with Mir Jafar. But sadly, you and I have never shared the same affinity. It has been remiss of me.'

'To my eternal regret also.'

'Ah! Spoken like a true diplomat. You don't like me. That is all right, I don't like you. But we have a common interest.'

'Which is?'

'For a long time, I supported the crown prince, Siraj. But lately his behaviour has become erratic. I have had a change of heart. I am afraid now of what will happen to Bengal if he should take the throne.'

'You want a foot in both camps.'

'Excellently put.' He clapped his hands.

On cue, Lachlan saw two figures make their way towards them across the lawn.

'I should like you to meet my sister-in-law, Nafisa Begum. The young woman with her is my daughter, Yasmin. I must tell you she is a pearl beyond compare and the very light of my life.'

The two women stepped gracefully into the pavilion and knelt on cushions a respectable distance away. They were both wearing *chadors*. All Lachlan could see of Yasmin were her eyes. He realised they were the same bewitching eyes that had watched him from behind the *purdah* curtain. He felt a thrill of both excitement and alarm. He looked away, trying to gather his thoughts.

'They tell me that your wife died and left you without sons,' Aziz Khan said.

'Yes. Three years ago.'

Aziz Khan took a sip of lime juice and reached for a mango before leaning back on the cushions. 'Every man of good position must have a wife. I understand that in your religion you may take only one, but as yours has passed, have you not considered remarrying?'

Lachlan dared another glance at Yasmin. She held her veil across her face. For just a moment she let it slip, perhaps accidentally though probably not, and he was afforded the briefest glimpse of her face.

I am being played here, he thought. Like a fish on a line. 'I am not presently looking for a wife,' he said.

Aziz Khan shook his head. 'But this is not just a wife, Englishman. Excuse my immodesty, but my daughter is considered the most beautiful woman in all of Bengal. I am offering her to you. With her comes my tacit support for your efforts to persuade the nawab to choose someone else as crown prince, and my support for your Company if Siraj becomes the nawab. Because then you British will need a friend, and in Bengal I am one of the most powerful friends you can have.'

Lachlan blinked. This proposal was unexpected, to say the very least. 'I shall have to consult with my superiors in Calcutta,' he said, wondering what Drake would make of such an arrangement. He knew he could not let the prospect of taking such an exotic and beautiful bride blind him to the diplomatic consequences.

But it was an astounding offer.

It had been three years since he had lost Catia, surely long enough to mourn. No one could ever replace her, but he was only flesh and blood, and men had been asked to do much worse in the service of their country.

Yet something told him to tread carefully. As Kilcannon had said, the general could be as slippery as an eel.

Tommy was waiting for him with the horses in the shadow of the gate. He sat with his back against the trunk of a banyan tree, smoking his pipe. He jumped to his feet and saluted when he saw Lachlan.

'You don't have to salute every time, Tommy. I've told you. Only at the fort.'

'Right you are, sir. Are you all right? You look a bit glassy eyed.'

'Actually, I need a little time to think. Let's get back to Cossimbazar before the heat kills the horses.'

'What happened in there?'

'General Aziz just offered me everything I've been asking for these last three years. Even an alliance against Siraj. On top of that, he tried to sweeten the deal with his daughter. I said I would have to seek permission from Calcutta.'

'You need to ask Calcutta for permission to marry?'

'As Resident, I can't marry high born princesses just like that. It would have major political ramifications.' He looked back at the palace. 'Also, I don't trust him an inch.'

CHAPTER 30

L achlan woke to someone shaking him by the shoulder and calling his name.

'Lieutenant McKenzie sir, you must wake up. Come on, sit up now, sir. You have work to do.'

He opened his eyes. The sun was high in the sky. He had slept too long. Slowly, he remembered who he was and where he was. Reality flooded back, bringing with it a familiar feeling of disappointment. 'What is it, what's happening?'

'Aziz Khan is on his way to see you,' Tommy said. 'I rode as hard as I could. Come on, you must get up.' He kicked the door shut and pulled off Lachlan's nightclothes. He threw him a thin cotton towel.

Lachlan wiped at the sheen of sweat on his skin, but it did no good. His head was fogged by opium dreams. He went to the bowl of lukewarm water in the corner and upended it over himself.

Tommy's eyes went to the opium paraphernalia besides the bed. 'Does you no good that stuff, sir.'

'I know what is and what isn't good for me, Tommy,' Lachlan said. He heard voices. Someone was coming. He quickly pulled on his uniform and ran outside onto the veranda.

A richly carved teakwood palanquin had arrived at the end of the drive, carried on the shoulders of half a dozen porters. There were red wheals on their shoulders from the chafing of the bamboo poles. He supposed they must have come all the way from the city.

The palanquin was accompanied by a bevy of servants liveried in orange. Aziz Khan climbed out, magnificent egret feathers swaying from the turban on his head.

Lachlan finished buttoning his uniform and stepped out to greet him. 'This is a great honour, General,' he said. 'If you had given me warning, I could have prepared refreshments.'

Another palanquin appeared, just as magnificent as the first. This one was screened and its curtains tightly drawn.

'I have brought Yasmin and two of her servant girls,' Aziz Khan said. 'She has shown an interest in seeing your gardens.'

'They are not worthy of remark,' Lachlan said. He looked at the second palanquin in consternation.

'We will let her be the judge. You would do her great service if you would show her around.' Aziz Khan strode inside and threw himself onto one of the daybeds.

Lachlan sent the servants hurrying to the kitchen to bring *sharbats* and sweetmeats, fighting down a wave of panic. How do I get out of this, he thought. I cannot offend him by sending his daughter away.

He signalled to Tommy. 'Go inside with the general. Attend to his needs.'

Yasmin was helped out of the palanquin by her servant girls to the jangling of gold jewellery. Her arms were covered with armlets and bracelets, and there were rings on all her fingers as well as her toes. She also had a large number of small bells strung on a cord around her ankles.

She was wearing a gauze *kurti* over a tight-fitting silk bodice, with crimson brocade *pajama* trousers, tight at the waist, flaring into extravagantly wide cuffs. Over it all was a *dupatta*, a diaphanous full-length veil that enhanced rather than disguised her figure. Once again, all that was visible were her eyes, which she had darkened and accentuated with *kohl*.

Lachlan took a deep breath to steady himself.

'McKenzie *sahib*,' she said. 'Thank you for inviting me here.'

He looked back at the bungalow. Was that what Aziz Khan had told her? 'It is a great honour. As you can see, the Residency is humble in comparison your father's palace. I hope you will not be too disappointed in the gardens, such as they are.'

Yasmin lowered her voice so that her two escorts could not hear her. 'Oh, we both know I have no interest whatever in flowers and trees.' She made her way across the lawn. Her chaperones ran after her, one of them holding a *chatra*, a golden fringed parasol, to shield her from the sun. She waved them away.

Lachlan followed.

'You are surprised to see me here,' she said. 'I know my father has proposed a union, but he said that you wanted to meet me first. I think that is very wise. After all, you know nothing about me.'

'And you know nothing about me.'

'I know a little. I asked my auntie, Nafisa. She knows everything about everyone.'

'What did she tell you?'

'That you are English, but you were not born there. Not here in Hindustan either, but in some other place across the Persian Sea. She did not know the name of it. She said your wife was murdered by a French assassin and that you are considered a great warrior by your people.' She seemed breathless as if nerves had the better of her. 'You have been wounded twice in battles, and you can speak Tamil, Portuguese, English and Parsi, though I have noticed that when you are speaking to my father, you still make many grammatical errors. You are also very handsome in your uniform. That I found out for myself.'

'It seems you know more about me than my adjutant does, and he has been by my side for three years. Yet I know nothing about you.'

'There is very much less to tell. My mother died when I was young, and I was raised by my aunt. They say I can trace my bloodline back to the Prophet, which my father makes much of. My aunt said I should tell you I am headstrong so that you are forewarned.'

Her eyes and her voice were more alluring to him than any *nautch* girl with painted nipples. But he didn't trust her. She was Aziz Khan's creature, and he could not imagine that she had had no hand in his manoeuvring.

He looked over his shoulder. Her chaperones were keeping their distance. They had taken shelter from the sun under the spreading branches of a mango tree a hundred yards away.

'There's something you should understand,' he said. 'Your father did me great honour by proposing this marriage, but it has put me in a rather delicate position.'

'In what way?'

'What has he told you about our conversation?'

'He said that you were well disposed to the idea but that you wanted to ascertain my qualities for yourself. That is why I am here, is it not?'

'He dissembles. I need first to seek the advice of my employers.'

'On whom to marry?'

'In this case, yes. What your father is doing is first and foremost a political manoeuvre. I suppose he did not tell you this.'

'He didn't have to. I'm not some silly girl. You should be careful of my father. He doesn't like you.'

Lachlan nodded in acknowledgement. 'Yet, it was he who suggested a betrothal.'

'He is always scheming. He has visitors night and day in his *durbar*, generals and viziers smoking *huqqas* and drinking coffee and whispering. I overheard him telling a French *sahib* about you. He said you are a grasping Englishman who wants to ruin us all.'

'And what do you think?'

'Nafisa says you are a man, and all men except the Prophet are lechers and bullies. But she thinks you are of the more harmless sort.'

'That was kind of her. Thank her for me.'

Yasmin's laugh was genuine, and her honesty took him off guard. She was not what he had been expecting at all.

'It's good to talk to someone who is not a eunuch or a servant,' she said.

'It must inflate my modest virtues out of all proportion.' He smiled, couldn't help himself. 'Apart from my grasping nature, what was your father's main complaint about me?'

'He said that your wife was murdered by the French, but you did nothing about it. He found that unfathomable. He also said that the legends of your exploits in battle were idle boasting.'

'He's right. When I heard the first shot fired at Karimkot, I ran and hid under a hedge.'

She gave him frank appraisal. 'You do not look the kind of man who would run from anything.'

'None of us should trust appearances. But I am saddened that he has such a poor opinion of me.'

'He also complains regularly that the nawab likes you too much.'

'I'm not sure about that. Who was this French *sahib* he was speaking with?'

'Ah, you wish to recruit me as your spy already. Should you not at least wait until we are married?' She made a motion with her fingers and the henna butterflies on the back of her hand took wing. 'You're right, I would be a good spy. I know more than people give me credit for. I listen to all my father's conversations. I do it because I am curious about the world outside.'

Lachlan looked over his shoulder to check that her servants were still in place and watching. He could sense a trap but could see no way out of it. He wanted to ask her again, who was this Frenchman, was it Kilcannon, but something told him to bide his time. Besides, he supposed he already knew the answer.

'They say you English only have one wife,' she said.

'That is our custom.'

'And you keep her in your bed even when she is old. That seems a good custom. Of course, I would not expect you to do the same. But you may find over time that you might learn to like me a little.'

He saw her eyes soften. Was that a tear? He couldn't be sure.

'I have to get away from this place,' she said, looking at the lake and the palaces as if they were the ditches and hovels of Black Town.

Lachlan followed her gaze. One of the gilded harem barges was gliding across the mirrored surface. There was a flag at the stern. He recognized it. It belonged to Siraj.

He realised it was on a collision course with a rickety ferry that the local people used to cross the lake.

'Good Lord,' he said. 'What are they doing?'

The royal barge did not deviate. It crunched straight through the ferry, slicing it in half. He thought the pilot must surely turn around and come back for the passengers, who were flailing on the surface of the water, but he continued northwards on the lake towards Murshidabad.

Even from where they stood, Lachlan could hear the screams of the women and children who made up the bulk of the ferry passengers. 'They can't swim,' he said.

'That's why Siraj does it,' Yasmin said.

'He told his pilot to deliberately ram the ferry?'

She bowed her head as if she was somehow responsible for it. 'Such things give him pleasure.'

Lachlan turned around, thinking he should run back to the bungalow and sound the alarm. They should send a boat out to pick up survivors. It was only then he realised that Yasmin's escorts had disappeared.

They were quite alone in the garden.

Tommy hurried up the lawn from the house, red-faced. 'It's the general, sir,' he gasped when he got there. 'He's gone. Him and the servant girls. They took off. Nothing I could do to stop him.'

Lachlan took just a moment to admire the beauty of the trap Aziz Khan had laid for him. He shook his head. Was there anything he could have done about this? Probably not. He turned to Yasmin.

'I am so sorry,' she said.

'Did you know about this?'

'Of course not! I would never have been party to such a miserable thing. Never.'

Somehow, he believed her. He looked at Tommy. 'Ride to the fort. Find a palanquin for the lady. We need to take her back to her father's palace in Murshidabad. Perhaps we can get her away from here without anyone seeing.'

'No,' Yasmin said.

They both stared at her.

'I am sorry,' she said. 'I know my father and I see what he has done. Look outside the gates. Tell me there is not an old woman selling bananas by the road, or a farmer taking papaya to the market. Only they are not really selling bananas or papaya. They will be Alivardi Khan's spies. As soon as I leave here unescorted, they will run back to the palace and tell him what they have seen, just as my father planned.'

'Then it's too late,' Lachlan said. He felt the trap close.

CHAPTER 31

Aziz Khan sipped his coffee, black and sweetened with honey. His *huqqa* was at his side, and occasionally he took the tube in his mouth and puffed gently on it. He savoured his moment's peace.

This was his favourite place in the harem. It overlooked a courtyard with several small fountains of murmuring water. To one side was a corridor of archways hung with filmy *purdahs* that bent softly to the cool breeze coming off the river. The room appeared almost dream-like through the haze of *huqqa* smoke and filtered sunlight. A soft breeze rustled the leaves of the date palms and cypress trees in the garden.

The tranquillity was disturbed by the sounds of an argument. Two of his wives were fighting over the basket of mangoes he had given one of them. There was always something. It was supposed to be an oasis of pleasure and peace. It gave him neither. A man might as well try to enjoy his leisure moments in a cage full of tigers.

It was said the Prophet had nine wives, but the Qur'an permitted just four. Even the holy scribes had learned from experience.

He saw Nafisa hurrying across the courtyard. There was only one thing this could be about. He sighed. 'Please sister, sit. I will have the servants bring *sharbat* and some refreshment.'

She flicked a hand to send the servant away. 'I want nothing.'

'What could be troubling you on this warm afternoon?'

'What have you done?'

'You know what I have done. If I may say so, it was a masterstroke. Alivardi Khan has finally stopped his dithering about the crown prince and has named Siraj. It was the perfect solution. The Englishman's meddling had to be stopped somehow.'

'You have disgraced your own daughter.'

He made a face. 'Yes, she is disgraced. But it is not me who will take the blame.'

'All this to trap the Englishman?'

'The nawab's spies saw her leaving the British Residence unescorted, and they say she had been in there almost an hour. The nawab is enraged. He has sent a blistering letter of complaint to their Company President in Calcutta saying that their Resident has raped a descendant of the Prophet. He also claims that he has dishonoured our religion and besmirched the reputation of a beloved princess. He is demanding that he be hanged. He says he would do it himself, but he does not want a war with the British, though that will come soon enough.'

'You used her.'

'What is the point of a daughter if she cannot make herself useful?'

'But she is dishonoured forever!'

He shrugged his shoulders. 'Siraj knows that I have saved him, and he will be more than grateful when he becomes nawab. When he makes me the second most powerful man in Murshidabad, no one will remember this little indiscretion. Men will be beating at our doors wanting her as their wife or rather wanting me as their father-in-law.'

'You care nothing for her.'

'She is hardly thrown out on the street.'

'This is untenable.'

'And you are ungrateful. Now leave me. I wish to drink my coffee in peace.'

Tommy knocked, threw open the door and stamped to attention.

'Please stop doing that,' Lachlan said. 'You and I have known each other long enough to dispense with formalities.'

'You did say to salute you while we were at the fort, sir.'

'Only when there are other Company people around. What is it?'

'There is news.'

'News or rumour?'

'They say the nawab wants you shot from a cannon.'

'No, that's just rumour. The actual truth is he wants me hanged. He says I raped Aziz Khan's daughter.'

'But you didn't sir. I was there. I would have seen something.'

Lachlan smiled. 'Yes Tommy, with your acute powers of observation I am sure you would have done. But as Yasmin pointed out to us at the time, what happens is not as important as what is believed. Aziz Khan will claim ignorance of the whole affair. Indeed, he is shouting to the rooftops that I abducted his daughter to satisfy my carnal lusts, and most people here think that is exactly what a *feringhee* like myself would do.'

'How would you have done that?'

'Satisfy my lusts?'

'Abduct her. He keeps his women under lock and key, day and night.'

'No one seems too bothered with the details.'

'So, what's going to happen?'

'Alivardi Khan has written to Drake in Calcutta. I dare say I'll be removed from my post.'

'What can they do to you?'

'I'll be sent back to face the music. Charges of gross misconduct probably. A court martial perhaps.'

'They can't do that. You're not proper army.'

'I am a Company employee, and the Company does whatever it wants.'

'That is an injustice. I can be your witness, sir.'

'I appreciate your concern Tommy, but nothing you say is going to make the slightest difference. This is about politics, not justice.'

'I suppose there is no point going to the nawab and telling him your side of the story.'

'None whatsoever.'

There was a knock. A clerk came in and handed Lachlan a letter. He tore open the envelope and read it. 'It's from Aziz Khan. He wants to see me.'

'Shall I come with you?'

'That won't be necessary. It seems he doesn't want to see me at his palace this time. We are to have a private conversation on his barge.'

'Perhaps he's going to offer you a way out.'

'I doubt it very much. More likely, he wants to show me how to get myself in even deeper.'

Lachlan went to meet Aziz Khan in full fig and made his way alone down the lawns to the lakeside. It was shallower at this southern end and choked with lotus pads, many with long pink flowers reaching for the sunlight. In the distance, through the morning haze, he could make out the palaces and *chhatris* and sculpted gardens of the great nobles of the Murshidabad court.

He watched the general's barge cut its way through the limpid water. The bow was carved in the shape of a peacock, freshly painted in blue and gilt. The barge's occupants were customarily concealed behind a curtained pavilion in the centre of the barge.

There was just one servant at the oar to steer, and a single armed guard, in the burned orange livery of Aziz Khan's house. Lachlan guessed he had been chosen as much for his imposing physique and impressive black beard as his martial abilities. He had a jewelled sword in the yellow sash at his waist.

As the barge nudged the jetty poles, Lachlan jumped easily aboard. The guard lifted the curtain aside and he stepped in. The man whipped it shut again behind him.

Lachlan had been expecting to see Aziz Khan himself, so he was shocked to find a woman reclining among the cushions. He did not try to hide his surprise or alarm. He felt the barge pull away from the jetty. Another trap.

It was already too late to escape.

CHAPTER 32

The woman was completely covered. At first, Lachlan thought it might be Yasmin. But as he grew accustomed to the half-dark of the pavilion, he realised it was not her. They were not her eyes.

'Who are you?' he said.

'My name is Nafisa. I am Yasmin's aunt. We have met only once, yet I feel I know you very well. Please, McKenzie *sahib*, sit, relax. There are no assassins waiting behind the curtains.'

'Assassins might be preferable.'

'You are frightened of a woman?'

'For the British Resident in Murshidabad, being alone with a woman from a noble family is terrifying. As you well know.'

'I am not my brother-in-law. He has left for Chandernaggar. He has gone there to receive a supply of thirty cannons from a French arms smuggler. Gerard Kilcannon. You know him?'

'I have had that doubtful pleasure.' So, Aziz Khan hadn't sent Kilcannon away empty-handed after all. 'It was you who sent the message, not the general?'

'I am sorry for the subterfuge. But it was necessary. We need to talk.'

Lachlan kicked off his boots and sat warily on the cushions facing her. The sunlight, filtered through the curtains, cast the pavilion into a roseate dusk.

Nafisa lay on her side, occasionally placing a *huqqa's* mouthpiece between her lips and breathing the smoke out slowly through her nose.

Since he had been in Murshidabad, he had learned that the Muslims were fond of perfumes of all kinds. Here on the barge, the scent of attar of roses mingled with the plumes of fragrant Persian tobacco was overpowering. He began to feel lightheaded. He tried to focus.

'I am sorry for what happened to you,' Nafisa said. 'It was my brother-in-law's doing. Yasmin and I had no hand in it. You must think badly of us.'

'I should have been more careful.'

'You are an outsider. How could you have known? There was nothing you could have done.'

'Nevertheless.'

'He is cruel, my brother-in-law. Why should I be surprised? He and my husband emerged from the same womb.'

Lachlan felt a bead of sweat trickle down the side of his face. 'Why am I here?'

'I want to suggest to you that there is a way out of your predicament, though it perhaps benefits Yasmin more than you.'

'What do you mean?'

'My niece is very unhappy. She has hopes and dreams far above what her father intends for her. But her fate is totally in his hands and until now I have been powerless to help her.'

'Sometimes life knows what's best for us.'

'I disagree.'

'So, how does this concern me?'

'You will have to leave Murshidabad very soon. Yasmin wants to come with you.'

Lachlan stared at her. He shook his head. These bloody people. Did they never stop intriguing? 'That's impossible.'

'No, it is difficult, but not impossible. There is a difference. Difficulties can be overcome if one has the will.'

'I am already in serious trouble with the Company. Why would I want to make more for myself?'

'This is no game for her. She thought the match was genuine and wanted to go through with it. She still does.'

He shook his head. 'I can't do that.'

'She is a lively companion and as smart as a whip. She also happens to be the most beautiful woman in all Bengal.'

A part of him wanted to leap at the chance. But there was another wiser, saner voice telling him to get as far away as he could from Bengal and never look back. 'Beauty is only part of being a wife,' he said.

'With most men, beauty is the whole thing. But very well, if it is important to you, she can also read and write in Persian, English and French and she has a good head for figures. She can keep your household accounts for you while she soothes your spirits.'

'Aziz Khan is a very powerful man in Bengal. Who Yasmin marries will have profound political implications.'

Nafisa leaned in. There was a faint look of amusement in her eyes. 'I don't think you give a damn about politics. When I look at you, I see a renegade who has been marking time here in Murshidabad while giving his wounds time to heal. I think it would give you a great deal of satisfaction to thumb your nose at my brother-in-law and your President Drake.'

Lachlan inspected a piece of lint on his cuff.

Nafisa pressed her point. 'She is not asking to be your wife in the English manner. Many of you European gentlemen have taken wives among us - Hindu and Muslim. *Bibis*, as you call them. Some of you have several, after our custom. Yasmin expects you will no doubt do the same.'

He shrugged. 'They're not real wives.'

'What is a wife? You put a roof over her head, she gives you children, and if you get tired of her, you get another one and let them argue with each other. And so on. But at least with you, she won't be locked away, and if you are a good man, as we both suspect that you are, you will take her with you wherever you go and treat her kindly. It is a gamble but one we are willing to take.'

'We?'

'That is the only condition. I must come with you. When my brother-in-law finds out what I have done, he will want to kill me.'

The water pipe bubbled.

'You said it was a way out of my predicament.'

'When you get to Calcutta, we can speak for you. We will tell your *sahibs* that you did not dishonour her. Her presence with you will put the lie to all the vile accusations against you.'

Lachlan stared at her. 'I need time to think about this.'

'Listen to me. Every night at sunset for the next seven nights, I will sit with her at the blue gate at the end of the gardens. From there we can see the lake. Should you decide to take us with you, we will be waiting.'

'And Aziz Khan?'

'He will not be back for another month, and he has left the *zenana* in my charge. He will not know about this until it is too late. By then we will be far from his reach.'

The barge nudged against the jetty. They were back at the Residency gardens.

'It is up to you,' Nafisa said. 'Fate has shown you two roads. You must decide which one you will walk down.'

Lachlan strode out in his dress uniform. His horse was waiting. He rode with an escort of four Company troopers along the lake and past the ghats, entering the city by the Chowk gate.

When he got to the nawab's palace, he dismounted and approached the sentries. The guards crossed their lances. He waited.

The captain came out from the shadow of the main arch. 'McKenzie *sahib*,' he said. He put a hand over his heart and gave a stiff bow.

Lachlan took off his tricorn and put it under his arm. 'I'm here to see Alivardi Khan.'

The officer looked discomfited. He shook his head. 'I have orders not to admit you. A thousand apologies.'

There was a commotion behind him. Siraj galloped out through the gates on a white Arab, his robes whipping behind him. He took out his *talwar* and rode straight at Lachlan, only reining in his horse a few yards away, showering him with sand and grit.

'Englishman, what are you doing here?' he shouted.

'Your Majesty,' Lachlan said.

'You violated a daughter of the Prophet.'

'I did no such thing. It is why I am here. I need to speak to the nawab and explain to him what really happened.'

'My grandfather does not wish to see you. He curses you. He curses your children!' Siraj waved the blade of his sword in Lachlan's face. 'Draw your sword.'

'No.'

'I thought so. You have no courage.'

'I have more sense.'

Siraj laughed. 'I shall see you in Calcutta, hatman!' He rode back inside the palace. The gates slammed shut.

Well, that was that. The die was cast.

CHAPTER 33

Cossimbazar

Lachlan went out onto the balcony of his office at the fort and fed crumbs from his breakfast chapati to the sparrows waiting for him on the rail as he did every morning. He looked down into the yard and watched the servants taking horses to the stables and unpacking the wagons that his visitor had brought with him.

He had been notified in advance of the man's arrival. He had met him once, in Madras. His name was Chalmers, and he was one of Drake's proteges. A man who looked as if he had spent his whole life sucking lemons.

There was a knock on the door and a clerk showed him in.

Lachlan came in from the terrace but didn't rush to shake Chalmers' hand. He sat down and regarded him across the desk.

Chalmers threw a letter down in front of him. 'It is from President Drake in Calcutta,' he said, unnecessarily.

Lachlan didn't trouble himself to open it.

'You are to be replaced.'

'By whom?'

'By me.'

'As of when.'

'Let me put it in another way,' Chalmers said. 'As of this moment you're sitting in my chair.'

'Would you like to be briefed on the situation here?'

'Not by you. President Drake wants you to return to Calcutta immediately to explain your conduct. I understand you are to face charges. I am to take over here in the interim until a suitable replacement can be found.'

Lachlan got to his feet. 'Don't forget to feed the sparrows,' he said on his way out.

The Company had sent a small sailboat, a *pinnace* from one of its warships, upriver to retrieve Lachlan. She had a shallow keel, ideal for river work, two masts and a copper-bottomed hull. There was a crew of twenty men including a skipper and a cook.

Lachlan's quarters below deck were surprisingly spacious and well appointed. Tommy and the rest of the crew were to sleep on deck.

'I asked the captain when we're leaving,' Tommy said. 'He said we were to stay here overnight.'

Lachlan nodded.

'May I ask why?'

'Are you my adjutant or my mother?'

'Just curious, sir.'

Lachlan stared across the water to the northern shore. 'Some guests will be accompanying us on our journey.'

Tommy smoothed down his moustache. 'Guests of the female sort?'

Lachlan nodded.

'Is that good idea, sir?'

'Probably not. But the decision has been made.'

'I would have thought you were in enough trouble.'

'Exactly. So, what's a little more?'

'For the record, I consider this a reckless action on your behalf.'

'Duly noted.'

The sun fell behind the trees. There would be a brief, mauve dusk and then the mosquitoes would swarm. He had better cover up despite the heat. He decided he would sleep on the deck tonight with Tommy and the crew. It was where he would be spending the next four nights, so he might as well get used to it.

He was awake long before dawn, pacing the deck, smoking one cheroot after another. He tamped down a thrill of excitement and fear, as he would before a battle. He knew that should something go wrong, and he was caught, they would kill him on the spot and be damned the consequences.

But it was not only the danger of what he was about to do that bothered him. He would never demean himself by smoking opium openly, so this would mean four days without it, and he was not sure he could manage it. By the time they reached Calcutta, he might not be able to function. He could not imagine meeting Drake when he was in one of the funks that overtook him when he was short of supply.

The skipper indicated that they were ready, and two of his crew dropped the painter over the side. Lachlan clambered in after them. They started to row towards the shore.

He searched the darkness. Tommy was right, of course. This was madness. He decided that if he couldn't find them easily, he would abandon the idea.

The lake was silent. Not a light anywhere.

No, wait. There.

He saw the glimmer of an oil lamp off the port side. He pointed it out and the two crewmen rowed towards it. When they reached the shallows, he jumped into the water and made his way up the bank, the liquid mud oozing between his toes. Something shot out of the reeds at his approach, startling him.

A wild duck.

'Nafisa Begum?' he whispered.

'Here, *sahib*.'

They were hiding in the tall grasses by the water gate as she had promised. Two more shadows appeared out of the dark. Of course, he thought. A lady of her position wouldn't go anywhere without servants.

'You will have to carry us,' Nafisa said.

'Is that allowed?'

'It is a little late to worry about modesty, McKenzie *sahib*. In the eyes of the world, you have already shamed my niece. You might as well shame me. I would rather risk dishonour than get mud on my good clothes.'

He carried her to the painter and returned for Yasmin.

'Thank you for coming, McKenzie *sahib*,' she said.

Lachlan smiled to himself. This might be madness, but there was great satisfaction in it. Aziz Khan had played him for a fool, ruined his career and perhaps put his life in danger, so helping Yasmin escape couldn't help but give him a certain satisfaction. It also didn't hurt that she was beautiful.

He was aroused by the heady scent of her perfume. Attar of jasmine. Unlike her aunt, she nestled into him, her arms tight around his neck. He let her gently into the boat. She clung on to him till the last.

The servants splashed behind him through the mud.

A few minutes later, they were all aboard the *pinnace*. The captain ensured the four women were safely closeted away in Lachlan's quarters below deck and got ready to leave. He hoisted a foresail, and the yacht glided silently across the lake towards the river.

By the time the sun rose, Murshidabad had disappeared into the morning mist.

Lachlan woke the next morning on the stern decking, curled awkwardly between a capstan and some thick coils of rope. Tommy was standing at the rail, smoking his pipe. Lachlan stood up, stretched, and went to join him. For a long time neither of them spoke.

'I have noticed during my time in uniform,' Tommy said at last, 'that some men are drawn to trouble.'

'I can recruit another adjutant, if that's what you want.'

'Begging pardon sir, but I don't think there's many in the service who will be rushing to fill my role once we get to Calcutta. In fact, I suppose that I shall be ordered back to my regiment in Madras as soon as we arrive there.'

'I think you may be right. I shall miss you.'

'Will they really hang you?'

'I don't know what they'll do. Yasmin's presence in Calcutta might save me or it might make my situation a lot worse.'

'You do have a plan?'

'My plan is to offer to resign and get out of India with her and her aunt as soon as possible. Go back to Africa and my wife's plantation there. It was what I had intended to do before I let President Channing sway me.'

'That sounds like a very happy life to me. I hope you manage it.'

Lachlan lit a cheroot. 'Unfortunately, every time I am faced with the possibility of a happy life, the Devil sends one of his creatures to get in the way of it. And on this occasion, I think that creature might be called Drake.'

CHAPTER 34

Whenever they passed a village, naked children appeared from nowhere, running alongside and waving. Some dived into the water and swam out to the *pinnace*, hands outstretched, shouting for *baksheesh*.

At some of the larger villages, stone ghats jutted out into the river and local women in bright saris squatted there beating their laundry on the rocks. Others trailed in and out of the forest with stone jars poised effortlessly on their heads.

Occasionally, they saw the ancient, ochre dome of a Hindu temple, almost hidden in the shade of a sacred peepal tree.

Below, on the sandbanks, crocodiles basked in the sun, still as logs. Massive buffalo wallowed up to their necks in the water. Tiny birds, balanced between their horns, helped themselves to the clouds of flies that circled their hides.

The two women and their servants made no appearance, keeping out of sight below decks until the second night, when their skipper decided they would make camp on the shore.

He chose a spot high enough up the banks that they were safe from the crocodiles and the tigers that came to drink at the river. He sent half a dozen men into the forest to fetch firewood, and they set up their tents.

The night fell quickly. The crew built a fire to ward off elephants and snakes. Lachlan watched the sparks spiral into the sky and lit a cheroot to keep away the insects. He listened to the birds roosting in the trees.

The jackals came out of their daytime hiding places looking for food. Their high-pitched howls were answered by another pack on the other side of the river. The noise built to a terrible clamour, stopped suddenly, then started all over again. Then it was cicadas' turn to add to the night-time din, the clicking rising to a crescendo, falling off, then building again.

Tommy looked about nervously, but Lachlan liked the sounds of the jungle. It reminded him of Delgoa Bay. All that was missing was the beating of the drums.

'Are you alright, Tommy?'

'Been in my fair share of battles, sir, but I still can't abide lots of trees and animals.

'I find it strangely comforting. Reminds me of home. Some evenings I'd go down to the river. I'd see the animals come down to drink. Mostly gazelles, but once I saw a lion, an old battle-scarred male. He was as close to me as those trees over there.'

'If that had been me, I think I would have needed a new pair of trousers from the quartermaster.'

'At least I knew where he was and what he was. There are plenty of predators in this damned country would have you believe they are gentlemen, and you may not know what they really are until they pounce.'

'But this talk of hanging you. They can't do that.'

Lachlan didn't answer.

'Sir?'

'It depends on whether they think I'm a traitor or merely scandalous. Drake doesn't like me, and he doesn't like my reputation. If things turn bad in Bengal, he may be looking for a scapegoat.'

'But these two women you've brought with you. They said they'll vouch for you, isn't that so?'

'Or Drake may decide to send them straight back to Murshidabad to curry favour with the nawab. We'll see. Everything will be decided when we get to Calcutta.'

By noon the next day, they were close to the French fort at Chandernaggar. Although they were flying the British Company flag, Lachlan was expecting no trouble. Unless someone had declared war in the last four days, they would be free to sail past unhindered.

It was that breathless hour when even the birds appeared exhausted, sitting open-beaked on the branches of the trees. He stood on the deck, hoping for the faintest zephyr of breeze. He didn't know how the four women tolerated it downstairs in their airless cabin.

They crept along the mudflats past cormorants drying their wings on the branches of dead trees. French troops in blue uniforms stood on the banks and shouted cheerful insults when they saw the red and white striped flag.

Tommy nudged Lachlan's arm and pointed to a barge heading towards them. Lachlan recognised the colours flying at its stern. The boat belonged to Aziz Khan. As they got closer, he saw the general himself standing on the foredeck. There was someone with him. It was Kilcannon.

Lachlan waved and smiled. 'I have your sister-in-law and your daughter on board you lying, two-faced bastard,' he shouted, knowing that at that distance they could not hear him.

Aziz Khan waved back and said something to Kilcannon. They both laughed.

No doubt the joke was at my expense, Lachlan thought. Well, he would be laughing on the other side of his face when he got home and found Yasmin and Nafisa gone. He watched the barge until it was out of sight.

'I grant you,' Tommy said, from over his shoulder, 'that was a lovely moment.'

'Thank you, Tommy. I thought so too.'

Lachlan couldn't sleep. Every bone in his body ached. All he could think about was the rosewood box with his opium pipe, hidden away in his luggage. But there was nothing he could do about it. He would have to sweat it out.

He stood at the rail, staring into the dark, rehearsing in his mind what he would say to Drake, when he heard the rustle of silk and the creak of decking boards. There was a tentative footstep and the hint of fragrance.

'Yasmin.'

A breath.

He turned around. She was standing behind him in the moonlight, her arms and head covered with a pashmina shawl.

'You startled me,' he said.

'I was watching you from the shadows.'

'Nafisa would not approve of you being up here.'

'She can disapprove of me in her dreams.'

The crew were all asleep, huddled in a heap around the main masts. Someone was snoring. It sounded like a warthog in rut. He supposed that would be Tommy.

Yasmin joined him at the rail of the ship. 'What are you thinking?' she said softly.

'I was thinking about the future.'

'It is all the will of God. Not even the greatest king or the humblest beggar knows if they will see tomorrow. The future is only ever something we imagine, isn't it?'

'I suppose it is.' He thought about two sets of footprints on a lonely beach on the other side of the Persian Sea, his and Catia's. They had talked about the future then as if they were the masters of it.

It had been a warm midnight like this one, there had been the sound of drumming from a Xhosa village, and the moonlight on the waves had looked like a stairway to the dark horizon. Those footprints had long been washed away by the sea, and their future had been as real as a promise. Already, it was gone.

Yasmin covered his hand with hers. He looked down, startled by her touch. It was a stranger's hand, tattooed with complex henna patterns, with rings on every finger.

She let the veil slip away. Her face was half in shadow. The other side was lit by a silver light. He could make out the soft pulse in her throat.

Something broke the surface of the water, a fish gasping for air possibly. His heart was racing. He told himself not to be foolish. So many things could go wrong. It was madness to hope.

'You are still in great danger,' he said.

'Yet I have never felt so alive. Freedom is worth any risk, any death. Don't you think?' She leaned closer.

He felt the warmth of her and did not quite pull away. I have to keep her at arm's length, he thought.

'I did not believe it when they first told me,' she said, 'that you smoked opium. But I can see it is true. You have the look.'

He said nothing.

'My father says that those who dedicate their lives to it become like shadows.'

He turned his head to stare out at the water. 'It helps me,' he said.

'Nafisa says it is because of what happened to you. That grief has made you a little mad.'

He looked back at her. 'If she thinks I am mad, why did she put your life and hers in my hands?'

Yasmin laughed. 'It's probably why she chose you. Only a man who is a little mad would think to abscond with Aziz Khan's daughter.'

He laughed with her. 'You have a point.'

She searched his face and put a hand to his cheek. 'All I wanted to say,' she said, 'was that perhaps we could rescue each other.'

Then she slipped away.

Lachlan had heard much about Calcutta and had expected it to be at least as impressive as Murshidabad, so his first sight of it was a grave disappointment.

At a distance it was as ill-conceived a place as he could have imagined - a confusion of grand mansions, straw huts, and crumbling warehouses without order of any kind. The fortress that had been such a focus of contention between Alivardi Khan and Drake looked to be falling into the river.

The harbour was a knot of masts, and he wondered how any skipper could find passage through it. He wrinkled his nose at the smell of mud and ordure that reached them even this far upriver.

'Tell the captain we will make anchor here,' he said to Tommy. 'I shall go ashore alone.'

'I should go with you, sir.'

'You have been a great help and a formidable adjutant,' Lachlan said. 'But I fear you can lend me no assistance with a man like President Drake. Stay here and keep an eye on the women for me. And if tomorrow you see me hanging from a gibbet on the walls, there's a bottle of gin in my kit. It's yours.'

CHAPTER 35

Calcutta

President Drake of the British East India Company, Calcutta, sat behind his rosewood desk in his black coat and freshly powdered wig and regarded Lachlan with what seemed like both contempt and immense satisfaction.

Nothing like an upstart finally being brought down to size, Lachlan thought.

Outside, garrison redcoats were drilling on the parade ground. They were almost outside the window even though Drake's office was on the second floor. It was a peculiarity about Fort William - the parade ground was on the roof of the godowns. From Lachlan's military experience, it seemed to him it would leave the garrison horribly exposed in the event of a siege.

Drake's high-backed mahogany chair appeared to be the Company's more sombre version of a peacock throne. He didn't invite Lachlan to sit. He kept him standing at attention on the other side of the desk. 'You have single-handedly caused irreparable damage to both the Company's reputation and finances in India,' he said.

'I have done nothing that-'

'You will have the chance to have your say at your court martial.'

Lachlan stared into the distance.

'Alivardi Khan claims...' Drake waved a letter in his right hand as if it were a judgment from God himself. 'He claims that you dishonoured a Mughal princess, the daughter of one of his closest military advisors, and also apparently, a descendant of their Muslim prophet. In so doing, you have disgraced the Company, and you have disgraced yourself. You have also caused incalculable offence to the nawab, to his religion and to the people of Murshidabad.'

Lachlan shook his head. 'The nawab has been deceived. It was a political manoeuvre to shift the balance of power inside the *durbar.*'

'Well, it worked. You allowed yourself to be played.' Drake jumped to his feet and went to the window. 'A few days after writing this letter, the nawab went to meet his Maker. Your timing could not have been worse.

'Alivardi Khan is dead?'

'His grandson, Siraj-ud-Daulah, has taken the throne. The first thing he did was attack our factory at Cossimbazar. In reprisal for your actions, no doubt. God knows how we will repair the damage you have done.'

'He will attack here next.'

Drake looked as if such an eventuality had never occurred to him.

'You must be prepared for that.'

'He wouldn't dare.'

'I have had the opportunity to study Siraj at close quarters. I can tell you that he is ruled by his temperament, which is both fiery and foolish. He would most certainly dare.'

'On what pretext?'

'He believes, as his grandfather did, that you should have sought his approval before repairing the fortifications here at Fort William.'

'I don't need his approval!'

'Technically you do. He's spoiling for a fight, and this fort will be his excuse to start one.'

'The fortress belongs to the Company. He cannot tell us what we can and cannot do.'

'It stands on his lands. So, he believes he can.'

'The French are doing exactly the same at Chandernaggar.'

'Yes, and with respect, Alivardi Khan said the same thing to them. They did the politic thing, apologised profusely for causing him offence and promised to tear down the new fortifications. And then they went ahead with building the new earthworks anyway.'

'I'm not going to grovel to a native.'

Lachlan took a deep breath. He realised he was doing himself no favours, but something had to be said. 'What I don't understand is why you went over my head-'

'Over your head?'

'With the letter that you sent to Alivardi Khan. You deliberately antagonised him by claiming you had the right to rebuild the fort on your own terms.'

'I do have the right.'

'If you think that, then why didn't you do it? Any fool can see from even a cursory inspection, that the whole place is in utter disrepair.'

'You have no right to question me, McKenzie.'

'Fort William is falling into the river. If Siraj attacks, you are doomed.'

Drake shook his head. 'If he attacks, it is because you dishonoured a lady of the royal house.' A vein bulged in his temple. 'If it was up to me, I'd have you thrown in gaol for what you have done. I have been persuaded instead to keep you under house arrest until I can convene a court martial.'

He rang the bell on his desk. The doors were thrown open and an officer entered, his tricorn under his arm. 'My secretary, Mathieson, has agreed to vouch for you while you're here. You're damned lucky. I know no one else that would.'

Lachlan felt a wave of relief as Charlie Mathieson walked into the room. At last, a friendly face. 'Good God,' he said. 'I'm glad to see you.'

Lachlan followed Charlie out into the black and white marble tiled reception hall. The heavy rosewood doors to Drake's office slammed shut behind them.

'Well, it looks like you made a good first impression,' Charlie said.

The clerks eyed Lachlan surreptitiously from their desks.

'Why are they looking at me like that?' he said.

'You have the distinction of being both famous and notorious. They're not sure whether to applaud you as a war hero or curse you as a scoundrel who shamed a lady of a Mughal royal house.' Charlie smiled and clapped him on the shoulder. 'We'll talk about this over a cigar and a cool drink. Let's get you out of here.'

There was a *tonga* waiting in the street outside. Two sepoys with muskets at arms attempted a ragged stamp of their feet as they went down the marble steps and jumped in.

'It's good to see you, Charlie. You don't know how good.'

'Not the warmest of welcomes from our president, then?'

Lachlan laughed. 'Not exactly. He wants to throw me in gaol. But what are you doing here?'

'I'm Drake's private secretary these days. A promotion, of sorts. They sent me up here from Madras about a year ago. It's bloody murder, to be honest. The man's insufferable. But it's a step up the ladder so I try to make the best of it.' The *tonga* set off at a clip through the gates. 'Drake looked bloody furious when I walked in. What did you say to him?'

'I said that he'd allowed the fort to crumble into disrepair and that he wasn't doing his job. In the light of recent events, I can see how that might not have gone down well with him.'

'Recent events are all that Calcutta is talking about. What on earth happened?'

'Do you want the short version or the long one?'

'There's more than one version?'

'The short version, then. The Mughal princess, as Drake insists on calling her, is here in Calcutta with me.'

Charlie raised both eyebrows.

'She and her aunt are presently on the *pinnace* you see anchored there in the harbour.'

'God's sake man, he's been telling everyone that you dishonoured her by force.'

'It's unlikely that they would have come with me if I had.'

'Why are they here?'

'What?'

'Why on earth would you do that?'

'I admire the young woman. She wants to make her own way in the world, instead of having someone choose her life for her, and she has the courage to do something about it. Also, I have my own personal reasons for helping her. Aziz Khan played me for a fool, and I decided to return the favour.'

Charlie shook his head. 'Well, it's your business, I suppose, but I think you're playing with fire. I'll help you as far as I can.'

'Thanks.' Lachlan leaned back in his seat and let out a breath.

Out on the river, a frigate weighed anchor and made its way towards the Sunderbans. It fired one of its guns to signal its departure and the boom of the gun echoed around the dock.

'It's been a long time, Charlie. Haven't seen you since Madras. How have you been doing?'

'Life's been good to me. I seem to have had better luck than you.' There was a shadow behind his eyes.

No doubt he's heard the rumours about my opium smoking, Lachlan thought. Word gets around. 'I know how I look, but I haven't smoked any poppy for almost four days now. I'm trying.'

Charlie hesitated then he said, 'You know about Napoleon Gagnon's daughter?'

Lachlan nodded.

'Fitting, I'd call it.'

'Her death won't bring Catia back.' Lachlan looked up at the earth ramparts. They looked even less formidable at close hand than they did from the river. 'Can we stop here?' he said.

They walked down to the wharves. A group of sailors staggered out of an alehouse, bumping and shoving the native porters who tried to make their way past, backs already bent under bulging calico sacks. An ox cart piled with bales of silk and cotton jostled with others in the filth along the quay. The whole waterfront stank of bilge and salt.

They came upon a dozen cannons, twelve-pounders, that had been left abandoned on the dock. A seabird had built a nest in one of the barrels. It flew away, squawking in protest, as they approached.

Lachlan ran a hand across the metal. The capsquare was rusted to the trunnion, and the wooden fore and hind trucks were rotted through. 'How long have they been here?' he said.

'Since last year before the monsoon.'

'No one thought to move them into the fort?' He shaded his eyes against the sun and looked up at the bastions. He counted ten guns at each corner. 'What about the cannons up there?'

'They look imposing, but only a handful are safe to use. They can't be moved because the platforms are eaten through by termites, or else they have truck wheels missing.'

'What about powder?'

'Madras sends us regular supplies, but Minchin, who's in charge of the defences, didn't give any thought to keeping the stocks dry through the last monsoon, so much of it is useless.'

'Is there nothing you can do?'

'I've told them, but they won't listen to me. Too busy with their own business ventures on the side.'

Lachlan looked up at the north-west bastion, where the red-and-white striped Company flag whipped in the hot wind. The red was faded to a dull pink by the sun. It looked like an old rag.

'The fort is virtually falling to bits,' Charlie said. 'You can see from here, the earthworks are crumbling away. And see that wall over there? Drake had parts of it pulled down because he said it made his office too dark.' He pointed along the wharf. 'The worst of it is the godowns. You can't see them from here but there's a row of warehouses abutting the south wall. The roofs overlook the fort. Imagine what enemy snipers could do from there. The Company engineer, O'Hara, told Drake and the Councillors to pull them down, but they wouldn't have it. They said it would be too costly. It's madness.'

'Yet Drake put Alivardi Khan into a rage by insisting he had the right to do whatever he wanted.'

'He told me it was a matter of principle, so he argued about it but didn't actually do it. He made some half-hearted attempts to shore up the river wall, that's all. He didn't want to do anything that would eat too deeply into the profits.'

They went back to the *tonga,* and Charlie showed him the city as they rode south along the river - the silted banks on one side and the native bazaars and European mansions clustered together on the other. Far to the south were the mangrove swamps of the Sunderbans.

They passed what Charlie called 'the park' - a wide expanse of gardens and tanks - and then they were riding through narrow streets lined with mud huts and palm thatched roofs. Skinny men in *dhotis* snoozed on charpoys strung under the eaves of their houses while their wives, in dust-stained saris, headed back from the market with baskets perched precariously on their heads.

Hawkers sold *paan* or brass pots or bananas. A barber shaved his customer in the shade of a palm tree. Holy men smeared with ash and mud made their way through the streets ringing bells for alms. Mangy dogs barked furiously from the shadows of the houses.

Suddenly, they reached a walled mansion with uniformed guards patrolling the gates.

'Home,' Charlie said.

CHAPTER 36

Charlie's home was set in sprawling gardens overlooking the river, with stables and servant quarters clustered around it. They drove through the gates and up a long driveway to what appeared to be a Greek temple. The façade had been painted a blinding white, and there were wide, shaded verandas under the porticos.

Charlie has done alright for himself, Lachlan thought. His due reward for being a good Company man. Unlike me. I suppose I was marked down for trying to assassinate people in my own time and deflowering Moghul princesses.

They were met by liveried servants.

As they climbed down from the *tonga*, a beautiful young Indian woman came forward and held out her hand. Charlie kissed it like a gallant. 'This is Muttubby, my *bibi*,' he said. 'Don't know where I'd be without her.'

'McKenzie *sahib*,' she said with a dazzling smile. 'Charlie has told me so much about you.'

Lachlan bowed. 'He saved my life once. Your husband is a very brave man.'

'You don't need to flatter him for my benefit. He has recounted all his exploits to me, and I don't doubt they are all wildly exaggerated.' She gave Charlie a mischievous smile.

Charlie turned to Muttubby. 'Lachlan will be staying with us for a few days,' he said.

'I'll have a bedroom made up. We have plenty of room. You are most welcome.'

'He also has some ladies with him who should remain in *purdah*.'

'They can have the summer house. No one will trouble them there.'

'There's also my adjutant,' Lachlan said. 'I hate to impose on you further, but I can't leave him on the boat.'

'Of course,' Charlie said.

They went inside. The lofty ceilings and tall Venetian windows took Lachlan's breath away. There were marble tables, gilt mirrors, luxurious silk couches, and woven bamboo fans on the ceilings. It might have looked like a palace if not for all the children running everywhere.

'They're not yours, are they?' he said.

'Oh goodness no,' Charlie said. 'They belong to the servants. I just give them all a little rice and let them run around. I'll send someone down to the river to fetch your guests. Why don't you and I go up to the roof and have a cigar.'

Charlie leaned against the terrace wall.

'How did you meet Muttubby?' Lachlan said.

'A colleague. She was his *bibi*. I used to visit him at his house quite often when I first came up from Madras. I was taken with her right from the off. You can see why. When he left to go back to England, he left her behind. I invited her to come and live here and she accepted. I have grown quite fond of her. Quite fond.'

'Most of the other senior men in the Company hide their mistresses away.'

'Well, she is different in that regard. She'd never stand for that. Are you thinking of taking this Mughal woman as your *bibi*?'

'That is the plan. I can't mourn forever. There's one problem, of course. I don't think they allow *bibis* in prison.'

Charlie shook his head. 'It's damned rich of Drake to be moralising to you. He's been having an affair with his own sister. The whole of Calcutta knows about it, and no one here will give him the time of day. But the Company insists on keeping him as governor. They'll pay for it in the next weeks when we lose our place here.'

'You think that will happen?'

'Drake didn't tell you everything. It was not his intention, but he saved your life by recalling you. Your replacement in Murshidabad has not been heard of since Alivardi Khan died, and our factor at Cossimbazar barely escaped with his life.'

'Watts? What happened?'

'The first thing Siraj did when he took the throne was attack the trading post. He took the entire garrison prisoner, but Watts managed to escape. He arrived back in Calcutta only a few hours after you. He says Siraj has amassed a huge army, fifty thousand strong by his reckoning, and is marching on Calcutta. Drake has sent a ship to Madras begging Channing for reinforcements, but by the time it arrives, it will be too late.'

The roof terrace overlooked the river and afforded a panoramic view that left Lachlan feeling both astounded and dismayed. It was obvious no one had taken charge of the burgeoning city for a long time. The Europeans and the rich merchants had thrown up their mansions and palaces wherever they liked, and ramshackle clusters of tumbledown hovels had grown up around them. It was a chaos and impossible to defend.

'How many men do we have?'

'Two hundred and fifty by my count. But half of those are mercenaries - Portuguese and Armenians and the like - with questionable loyalties. We don't even have enough muskets to arm them all. We have no ready-made cartridges, limited ammunition for those cannons that are still serviceable, and large stocks of our gunpowder are too damp to use.'

'Who is in command?'

'Captain Minchin. He is a friend of Drake's. That should tell you everything you need to know.' Charlie pointed to the bazaar and the jumble of native dwellings clustered around the park and the Anglican church. 'There's two hundred thousand people live down there. If Siraj comes, where are they going to go? They'll be on their own, God help them.'

'And us?'

Charlie shook his head and frowned. 'You and I have no choice, of course, it's the women and children that are the concern. I've tried to get Muttubby out of here, send her to Madras for a few months to wait things out. But she won't go.' He stared out at the river. 'So, you tell me. You've met their new nawab. Is he bluffing or are we all dead men?'

Lachlan stubbed out his cigar on the stone. 'The latter, I'm afraid.'

CHAPTER 37

The heat was unbearable.

The local people looked to the skies, praying for the monsoon rains. The *punkha-wallahs* worked furiously, but Lachlan thought it made little difference. Sweat poured out of him and there didn't seem to be enough air to breathe. Another cramp almost doubled him over.

Opium withdrawals.

Drake was not the same man he had encountered a week ago. He paced the council chambers, his powdered wig askew, and his long face pale and drawn. Minchin was there also, staring vaguely at the charts that he had spread on the polished table.

Drake stopped pacing and looked resolutely out of the window. 'You were right, McKenzie. Siraj's army has moved into position across the river. It seems they're getting ready to attack.'

Lachlan looked at Charlie. This wasn't news to either of them.

'As you've some experience in these things from the siege at Karimkot, I'm ordering you and Mathieson to assist Captain Minchin with the defence of the settlement.'

'I thought I was under house arrest,' Lachlan said.

He heard a hissing intake of breath from Minchin. 'Don't be insubordinate. This is a chance to salvage something of your reputation.'

'It's not *my* reputation that's at stake now.'

Drake turned to him. 'What's your advice?'

'Well, first we need to tear down all the warehouses that abut the walls. It should have been done a long time ago. Should they fall into the hands of the enemy, their snipers will have a clear field of fire into the fort itself.'

'We have neither the time nor the manpower for such a thing,' Minchin said.

'We could blow them up,' Charlie said.

'Our stocks of gunpowder are low enough as it is.' Minchin looked to Drake for support.

The president took out a linen handkerchief and mopped at the perspiration on his face. 'It's an absurd suggestion,' he said. 'The Company would never countenance such unnecessary destruction of its own property.'

Lachlan wiped his eyes. They wouldn't stop watering. God, he needed that rosewood box.

'Are you alright?' Minchin said.

He realised they were all staring at him. 'Just a touch of fever.'

'If I may make a suggestion,' Charlie said.

Drake nodded.

'Siraj may not wish to attack. Perhaps he is merely looking for concession.'

Drake looked startled. 'What sort of concession?'

'Something in the way of a grovelling apology,' Lachlan said. 'Siraj is ruled by his own inflated estimation of himself. In this situation, a little self-abasement on behalf of the Company would be wise.'

'Apologise to a bunch of coolies?' Minchin said.

'Captain Minchin is right, I can't do that,' Drake said. 'Perhaps a monetary concession will do it. I'll send Watts. Tell him to offer anything Siraj demands on condition that he gives his army the order to retire.'

'Sir, I strongly advise you not to do so,' Minchin said. 'He may form a blockade around the settlement but that is all. He would not dare attack our guns.'

'Nevertheless,' Lachlan said, 'we must evacuate everyone in the European settlement outside the fort's perimeter and move them inside Fort William.'

'That will cause great dissatisfaction,' Drake said.

'Being dissatisfied is better than being dead.'

Minchin frowned. 'It won't come to that.'

'Are you sure?' Charlie said. 'Because according to my reports, Siraj's troops have been sighted near DumDum heading towards the Maratha Ditch. Once they are over it, they will be in the northern suburbs of the town and free to make any sort of mischief they want.'

'They won't get over the Ditch,' Minchin said. 'It's seven miles long and twelve feet wide. It kept out the Marathas and it will keep out Siraj.'

'With respect,' Charlie said, 'the Marathas are bandits. Siraj has an army with war elephants and cannons.'

'We should at least evacuate the women and children,' Lachlan said. 'There are enough ships out there in the river to get them all away from here.'

'It's too soon to talk about evacuating the fort,' Drake said. 'What will they say in London?'

'Do we care what they say?' Lachlan could feel his voice getting louder. 'They are not here. We are short of muskets, cannons and gunpowder, and at least half the garrison are mercenaries who cannot be relied on in a fight. Whatever you say, Captain Minchin, I would say our situation is dire!'

They all looked at him.

'We do not evacuate yet,' Drake said and dismissed them.

The riding lights of the warships and freighters standing offshore blinked in the dark, and the night buzzed with the sound of beetles and the soft whine of mosquitoes.

It was too hot inside the house and Lachlan couldn't sleep or even think. Whenever he closed his eyes, all he could see was the rosewood chest in his kit. Just one pipe, a voice in his head whispered. It's medicinal. You'll feel so much better afterwards.

He needed some fresh air.

He dressed and made his way across the lawn to the summer house. Camphor candles were burning in the windows. Two liveried servants stood guard at the doors. He waited while one of them went to fetch Nafisa.

She finally appeared, holding an oil lamp. 'What do you want, McKenzie *sahib*?' she said.

'Are you well?' Lachlan said. 'Are the accommodations satisfactory?'

'Your friend has been very generous. His *bibi* has shown us great kindness. Is that what you came here to ask at this hour?'

Lachlan shook his head. 'I have bad news.'

'Aziz?'

'He is here with Siraj's army. They are gathered just outside the city at the Maratha Ditch. I believe Siraj intends to sack Calcutta.'

'Did you ever doubt it? It's why Aziz and the other generals have supported him all these years. They have been spoiling for a fight.'

'I would have liked to have given them one.'

'Can you British not withstand an assault?'

'No,' Lachlan said. 'The defences are in bad shape and there are not enough men or guns. It looks very bad.'

Nafisa sighed and shook her head. 'If only Alivardi Khan had lived a little longer.'

'I'm sure he felt the same.'

'I have made a terrible mistake. I should not have brought Yasmin here.'

'She knew the risks. You did not hide them from her. If the old nawab had lived a month more, and Drake had been more reasonable, she might have got away.'

'What now?' Nafisa said.

'Everyone living outside the fort has been ordered to quit their houses and take up residence inside Fort William.'

'We can't do that,' she said. 'If Siraj's soldiers sack the fort and find us there, you can imagine what they will do. They will not ask who we are or how we got there. I must take her back under our own terms, secretly and by night.'

'No! That's unthinkable.'

'Yet it is what I think. If we are fortunate, Aziz will not want our family's shame to be known publicly. His punishment will be private, behind closed doors. He will blame me, not Yasmin.'

'There is another way. Drake has not yet ordered a general evacuation, but I am sure he can be persuaded to find you both berths on one of the merchantmen out there on the river. I can put you on a boat to Madras. You will be beyond Aziz Khan's reach there.'

'What about you?'

'I cannot leave. I am a Company officer. That would be desertion.'

'You would fight for the British, even though they want to hang you?'

'That is an entirely different matter. I am not a coward.'

'If we go to Madras without you, then what? We know no one, we have just the few trinkets that we have brought with us, and when they are sold and the money gone, what then? Will my Yasmin become a whore or a beggar?'

'It won't come to that.'

'I'm afraid it will. A Muslim woman has no future without a man to take care of her. If you cannot come with us, then we must go back.'

'I cannot leave here,' Lachlan repeated. He looked at the window and thought he saw Yasmin's shadow moving inside. 'May I see her?'

Nafisa shook her head. 'That is not possible, not now. You cannot protect her, and I will not have her treated like some common *nautch* girl.' She laid a hand on his arm, but briefly. 'You did what you could, but fate has decided against us. It is our karma. We are no longer your responsibility. Thank you for everything.'

She went back inside.

Lachlan returned to the main house. As he stepped onto the veranda he saw the glow of a tobacco pipe. 'Good evening, Tommy. Still awake?'

'I'll sleep when I'm dead, sir. You've been visiting the ladies?'

'I had to speak with the begum.'

'Did you tell her about Siraj?'

'I told her things don't look good.'

'What's to become of them now?'

'I don't know. Our own future looks scarcely better.'

'We had a saying in Limehouse. Life is hard, then you die. Look on the bright side. We're almost through the hard bit.'

'Thanks for that, Tommy. Somehow, you always manage to keep my spirits up.'

He went inside. He was tired. He fell into bed and did not even glance once at the rosewood chest.

CHAPTER 38

Siraj's camp filled almost the entire valley of the Bhagirathi River.

Kilcannon made his way through the chaos, deafened by the shrill ululations of the *nautch* girls, the trumpeting of elephants and the coughs and snarls of the camels. The stink was as bad as the din. The soldiers' tents at least were laid out in orderly rows, the pikes and spears stacked outside in pyramids of four.

A subadar pointed the way to Aziz Khan's impressive silk tent. Orange and white banners hung limp in the heat either side of the entrance. Two bodyguards stopped him as he approached, until a captain recognized him and let him through.

The general clearly liked to go to war in style. His campaign tent was furnished with thick carpets, silk drapes and velvet cushions. Candles in small silver cages provided a warm flickering glow. Aziz Khan was leaning on a bolster on his *divan*, a water pipe bubbling beside him. The air was thick with scented tobacco smoke.

Kilcannon salaamed from the waist and sat down on the cushions beside him. A *wallah* brought him a water pipe.

'So, here we are,' Aziz Khan said. 'I got rid of the Englishman as I promised. Siraj is our new nawab, and we are at the gates of Calcutta. I kept my half of the bargain. Now you must fulfil yours. What news of this Ashin Das?'

Kilcannon bowed his head, acknowledging the debt. 'My spies tell me he has already bought passage out of Calcutta on one of the British ships. Before he left, he hid most of his wealth in a cellar under his palace. No one will find it unless they know where to look. But my man in his household will show us where it is and how to break in.'

'What will we find in this cellar?'

'Bales of silk. Gold and silver bars the size of bricks. Everything too heavy or too bulky for Ashin Das to take with him because of the limited space on the ships. I would guess that there is more in his vault than the British have in their entire treasury.'

'How do you propose that we liberate this wealth?'

'We'll need at least half a dozen wagons.'

'That many?'

'Yes, that many.' Kilcannon lowered his voice. 'Imagine them all creaking with gold. Half for you, half for me, as agreed. We're going to be the richest men in Bengal. Almost as rich as the Jagad Seth!'

The water pipe bubbled furiously. Aziz Khan blew the smoke out through his nose. 'Good,' he said.

Lachlan, Charlie and Tommy stood behind Minchin on the parade ground as he reviewed his troops. The sight didn't fill any of them with confidence.

'What a hopeless shower,' Tommy said. 'I wouldn't have them as chuckers-out in a brothel. Half of them don't know which end of a musket to hold.'

'It may not matter,' Charlie said, 'we don't have enough ammunition to go round anyway.'

Lachlan did a quick inventory in his head. A quarter of the Company regulars were unfit for duty, either laid up in the hospital with fevers or some sort of rot. It left them with less than two hundred men in uniform and only fifty of those were British. The rest were mercenaries.

Minchin had hastily formed a militia from the Company clerks and re- cruited some sailors he had press-ganged from the waterfront. That added another three hundred men to the defences, for all the good it would do them. None of them had been in a proper fight before.

Minchin turned to Charlie. 'President Drake has ordered me to defend the fort to the last.'

'I thought he was going to negotiate,' Charlie said.

'Negotiate with natives? Where's your spirit, man?'

'Charlie was with me at Karimkot,' Lachlan said. 'He lacks nothing in spirit. But at that engagement we were in command of well-trained and well-armed men, and you couldn't poke holes in our fortress wall with your index finger.'

Minchin waved a hand dismissively. 'Don't worry about the fort,' he said. 'They won't get this far. I shall engage the enemy with my artillery at the Maratha Ditch. I fully expect that to be the end of it. As a precautionary measure, I intend to deploy the rest of the guns around the park, at the prison and either side of the main tanks this side of the Chowringhee Road.' He nodded to Lachlan. 'I have been authorised to commission you with the rank of lieutenant and put you in charge of the militia. I want you and Mathieson to take fifty men and start erecting palisades on the main thoroughfares into the city.'

'You said they won't get this far.'

'Just do it.'

'Very well,' Lachlan said.

'Get on, then.' Minchin left the parade ground and went down to the maidan to supervise the gun carriages as they were limbered to the horses.

Lachlan turned to Tommy and nodded towards the new recruits. 'So, Sergeant, this is our new unit. What do you think of our chances?'

Tommy reached for his pipe and tapped it on his boot. 'Well, sir, I'd say we're fucked and far from home. Pardon my French.'

Nafisa hugged her arms across her chest. 'I won't let you do this,' she said.

'What does it matter now?' Yasmin said.

'There's still a chance your father will take you back, but only if he thinks you are intact.'

'He's not going to take me back. We both know that.'

'He will punish me, not you. You are still useful to him.'

'I don't want to be useful to him.' She came to stand beside her aunt at the window. 'Don't take this on yourself. I don't blame you.'

'You should. Look at the trouble I have led you to. I should have been firm with you. Making this arrangement with the Englishman was a foolish thing to do.'

'I am happy to face whatever fate has in store for me. But I will have this night.'

Nafisa took her by the shoulders. She wanted to shake some sense into her. But wasn't it too late for that? 'Why throw yourself away on him now?'

'I am not throwing myself away. I liked him from the first.'

'You liked him because he was English. You saw a chance.'

'I won't be denied in this. I want to live my way or not live at all.'

'You are impossible.'

Yasmin put her arms around her aunt. 'Thank you for trying, but I am not frightened of what will happen. I want a life on my own terms. If I thought otherwise, then I would ask you to buy us passage to Madras.'

'You are so brave,' Nafisa said. 'The Englishman has no idea what he has lost. Very well. I will go and find him.'

Lachlan stared at the rosewood box lying on his bed. He closed his eyes and imagined the pungent ecstasy of the smoke, and the blissful dreams that brought the great forgetting and took away the pain in his shoulder, in his leg and in his soul.

He swayed on his feet, the heat in the room draining his strength. Turn your back, he told himself. Find Charlie and go up to the roof with a bottle of *arrack*. Do anything but give in.

A gentle tapping on the door brought him out of his reverie.

'A moment,' he said. He slipped on a shirt and opened the door.

It was one of the houseboys. 'Excuse me, *sahib*,' he said. 'But you are wanted at the summer house. The lady begum says she must talk to you.'

'I'm coming,' Lachlan said. He slid the rosewood casket back into his kit and hurried into the garden.

As he crossed the lawn, he saw Nafisa standing under one of the camphor lamps. 'Is everything all right?' he said.

'No, it is not,' she said. 'It is definitely not all right.'

'What has happened?'

Nafisa paced the lawn. 'She wants to see you.' She stopped pacing and stared at the riding lights of the British warships on the river.

He followed her gaze. 'It's not too late to get away,' he said.

'But it is. Far too late.' She turned back to him. 'We both know you will die here. Her only hope now is to return and to throw herself at the feet of her father.'

'He will have her killed. And you.'

'He is capricious. He might not. We will weigh an uncertain fate against an inevitable doom.' She pointed to the two servants standing at the door, under the lamps. 'Go in,' she said. 'She is waiting for you at the end of the corridor.'

The shutters were closed. The only light came from the dozens of candles that were scattered about the floor.

Yasmin was sitting on the edge of a charpoy. She removed her *hijab*, stood up and came towards him. Her perfume filled the room. She put her hands on his shoulders and her lips brushed his cheek. Her touch sent a shudder through him.

Another woman I am letting down, he thought. For a long time, he had felt he had no right to be happy. Now he had a chance to start again, and he couldn't take it.

'Take us to Madras with you,' Yasmin whispered.

He desperately wanted to. 'I would if I could.'

'Don't you like me?'

'Of course I do. More than you know.'

'I don't understand your loyalty to the British. They want to put you in prison.'

'It's not about the British or the Company. It would be cowardice for me to leave now. Charlie has to stay. Tommy has to stay. I can't just run away and leave them behind to die. Please Yasmin, go to Madras. When this is over, I will find you there. I promise.'

'If you stay, you will die too.'

He took her hands. 'You can't go back to your father.'

'I have no choice either.' She looked away, making up her mind. 'It's strange. I want so badly for you to take me to Madras, but there's a part of me that is proud of you for not doing it.'

He let go of her hands. 'It seems we have only this moment. Tonight, at least, you are free to choose.'

She placed the palm of her hand on his chest. 'And I choose you,' she said and led him to the bed.

CHAPTER 39

Gudachatram

Adelaïde watched the light on the thatched bamboo roof change from morning's pale yellow, to the ochre of noon, to the fathomless black of night, then back again to yellow.

Day after day after day.

She drifted in and out of roseate dreams. Shapes moved about the hut. Sometimes they made her drink something foul, forcing the liquid down her throat even when she spat it out. Anonymous hands undressed her, washed her with wet rags, and whispered to her in Tamil.

Then one day, without warning, hell began.

She moaned and cried, riding waves of pain. It was the drink, she realised. They had stopped giving it to her. She begged for more, but when she opened her eyes, there was only Aravinth sitting beside her, inscrutable.

No matter how loudly she screamed and pleaded with him to do something, he just patted her hand and smiled. When she finally passed out, exhausted, he changed the poultices on her face and body. And then she would wake, and it would start all over again.

One day, although the pain was not gone, it was somehow bearable. She lay on her charpoy listening to the noises from outside. She could hear children playing, the bleating of goats, the tinny ring of a cow bell.

It was the smells that told her where she was - smoke and dung and dust and rotting fruit, and every now and then, the waft of human excrement.

Her face felt strange. It was hard to move her jaw. Aravinth was still there, but she couldn't see him clearly because of the thick bandages over one eye. She managed to get out some words, though her voice no longer sounded like her own. 'What happened?' she said.

'A tiger has sharp claws,' he said. 'My bearers saved your life. They were very brave, braver than your *jemadar*. The tiger would have killed you if they had not chased her with their drums and trumpets.'

She reached up a hand to her face. Her head was swathed in bandages and there seemed to be a soft moist mass underneath them. There was a nauseating smell.

'It is medicine,' Aravinth said. 'Herbs.' He reached out his hand and gently moved her fingers away from her face. 'You should not touch.'

She looked down. There were flies crawling all over the dressings on her body. Aravinth was keeping them away with a fly whisk made of feathers.

'You must rest,' he said. 'You have been with us for a cycle of the moon. It will be many more before you can go home.'

'Narain?'

'He rode away.'

'Did he not come back for me?'

'Yes, the next day. He had a *sahib* with him. They brought soldiers and searched the forest all day looking for you. We didn't tell them you were here. We said the tiger took you.'

For a moment she was confused. Didn't tell them? Then she remembered Narain's face as he pointed the musket at her head. The tiger had saved her from him even as it almost took her life.

She closed her eyes, and the silence stretched. He had betrayed her.

'Have you done something in this life that you are ashamed of?' Aravinth said finally.

Adelaïde said nothing.

'You have not caused harm to another that would bring this great misfortune on you?'

A moment's hesitation. 'No.'

'All misfortune comes from something we have done in this life or a previous one. It is karma.'

Adelaïde tried to move her head. Even the smallest movement brought pain and bright lights flashing behind her eyes.

'Then perhaps it was in another life. But you must accept what has happened and know that you have now paid a debt that had to be paid.'

She motioned him towards the door. She didn't want to listen to this.

'You should have died,' Aravinth said. 'Injuries such as yours, almost always they mean death. Yet you are alive. It means your soul is not ready for its next life.'

She tried to get up, but it brought on an excruciating spasm of nausea and pain. She lay back on the charpoy, heaving and fighting for breath. She rode the blinding waves for as long as she could before finally surrendering to the void.

When she opened her eyes, Aravinth was still there. 'I am not keeping you here,' he said. 'Your body is keeping you here. Healing takes time. Much time.' He bent over her. 'I am sorry I cannot give you any more opium juice. Soon the pain will pass, but if you have too much, the need for the opium will stay. So now you must suffer a little, and you must try to sleep.'

The next time she opened her eyes, there was another man with him. Aravinth said he was the village healer and that he was the one who had stitched her wounds after they had brought her in from the forest. It was time to remove the poultices.

How long had she been here? It could have been weeks, even months. She remembered the village women coming every day to wash her and change her. Until now, she had been indifferent to her humiliation. This morning was different. She felt strong again.

The old man gently lifted the sticky messes from her body. She looked down. There were three raised cicatrices from her collarbone to her waist, where the tiger's claws had raked her. The sutures he had used to bring the lips of the wounds together looked like the rough stitching on a horse's saddlebags.

'That's good,' Aravinth said. 'There is no more infection.'

The healer reached for her face.

She knocked his hand away. 'Get out.'

'But it needs to come off.'

'I don't care. Just go!'

The two men retreated.

She pulled up the foul cotton sheet they had given her as a blanket and covered herself. She lay there for a long time staring at nothing.

In Pondicherry, she thought, they would all believe she was dead, and Gerard would have found a way to profit from it. She tried to sit up but gasped and lay back down again. It felt as if someone had taken a giant pair of scissors and torn her from her cheek to her breastbone.

Why had Narain done it? There could be only one reason, she supposed. Money. It was the only reason anyone did anything. Gerard must have got to him.

She inched her legs over the side of the charpoy and slowly sat up, clinging to the frame until the dizziness cleared. They had left her a sari to put on. It was ragged but clean. Her own clothes were still piled in the corner, torn beyond saving and covered in blood and flies.

She stood up. It was like standing on a boat in a rough sea and she struggled to find her balance. After she put on the sari, she put a tentative hand to the poultice on her face. It was kept in place by a thick bandage they had wrapped around her head. It was time to see what was under it.

She ventured a step outside the hut, squinting in the bright sunlight. There was a tank at the edge of the rice paddy, and she made her way towards it, still unsteady on her feet. Some village children were playing in the dirt, shrieking with laughter. As soon as they saw her, they fell silent and stared.

She went down the steps of the *ghat* to the water's edge. When she reached the bottom step, she dropped to her knees. She unwound the bandage and gingerly removed the poultice. It was foul and stinking. She tossed it aside and traced the outline of her cheek with the tips of her fingers. A part of her face seemed to be missing. The skin around her eye and the side of her mouth felt numb and tight. Everything else was bumps and ridges.

She leaned forward to look at her reflection in the tank.

Afterwards, she made her way back to her hut. She lay down on her charpoy and closed her eyes.

Night fell. A full moon rose over the jungle, huge and bright, framed by the doorway of her hut. It was as if someone was holding a lighted torch near her face. She got up and went back outside.

A peepal tree loomed above her. The heart-shaped leaves seemed to shiver in the silver luminescence, and the murmur of breeze through the branches sounded like falling rain. The villagers, being superstitious, worshipped the tree as holy. She had seen some of the young wives praying in front of it believing that it would help them to conceive.

Aravinth had said that ghosts hid in the high branches, but she didn't need a sacred tree to conjure ghosts. She could do it herself without any effort at all.

The moonlight cast long shadows.

'I need to go back now,' she said to the darkness.

She had arrived in the village on the back of a pure-bred white Arab. She had not imagined then, that when she left, it would be on the back of a bullock cart, sitting on a pile of watermelons, shoulder to shoulder with three village women.

They set out just before dawn and arrived at the canal on the edge of the Black Town in the heat of the day. She climbed down and walked away without looking back. Aravinth flicked the reins, and the two white bullocks shuffled in their traces, heading for the market. He called to her, but she did not turn around.

She crossed the canal and made her way along the Rue Romain Rolland with a headscarf covering her face. She had always attracted stares from the other European women in the quarter because she was half caste. Now that she looked like a native, no one spared her a glance.

She turned down the Rue Dumas to Gerard's villa. There were two *topasses* guarding the gate. She knew them well. She approached the first, her veil held across her face, and said, 'Luis, do you know who I am?'

He looked her up and down. 'Go away, woman. There's nothing for you here.'

She moved the veil so that he could see the right side of her face. She didn't want to frighten him by showing him her scars.

He started as if he had seen a ghost. He looked at his fellow sentry and then back at her. His face screwed into a frown of confusion and fear.

'It's me, *Madame* Kilcannon.'

'It could be her,' the other guard said.

'It can't be, she's dead,' Luis said. 'Show us your face properly.' He reached up a hand to snatch her veil away, but she stepped back, out of his way.

'I need to see the *m'sieur*. Tell him I am here.'

The two men hesitated.

'He's not here,' Luis said, 'and we can't let you in.'

'You know who I am. Let me pass or it will be the worse for you.'

'You're dead. Everyone says so.'

'Clearly, I'm not.'

'Get Narain,' Luis said to the other guard. The man turned and ran inside the house while Luis stood resolutely in front of the gate, his musket at slope, ready to stop her if she tried to get past. He looked terrified.

Narain, she thought. The last time she had seen him, he was holding a musket to her face. There was no point in taking this further. She had no friends or allies here.

'You and your friend are both dead men,' she said and turned away.

201

CHAPTER 40

The sun was setting over the city, leaving a dirty violet stain. Adelaïde crouched in the shadows near the fortress. There were two sepoys in blue *Compagnie* uniforms standing outside the gate. She had not troubled to approach them. If her own guards would not help her, what chance did she have with these two?

She would wait for the only man who might yet be her lifeline, even if she had to wait all day.

In fact, it was just on twilight when she saw Fontaine's palanquin approaching. It was so hot he had left the curtains open. He lay back on the cushions, in his silk stockings and brocaded jacket, furiously fanning himself with a peacock feather.

She jumped up and stood in front of the bearers. They tried to go around her, but she didn't let them.

'*M'sieur* Fontaine, it's me, Adelaïde!'

Fontaine's jaw dropped in alarm. His shock changed to confusion when he realised a ragged native woman was addressing him in perfect French. He told the bearers to stop. He got out and stared at this strange apparition.

She let the veil drop so that he could see the uninjured half of her face.

His mouth fell open. 'Adelaïde?' he said.

Adelaïde sat on a bentwood chair in front of the bureau that dominated Fontaine's private study. Oil lamps had been lit around the room. The only sound was the humming of a mosquito.

Fontaine paced the boards, gulping Madeira and rubbing his face with his hand. 'You say you have been in the village this entire time? It's been three months!'

'It was that long?'

He stopped his pacing and looked at her. 'Let me see your face.'

She drew back the veil. He didn't even attempt to hide his horror. She didn't blame him. Her upper lip was drawn up in a permanent snarl on one side, making it look as if she was baring her teeth. The flesh from her left eye to her chin was raw, knotted and twisted. She thought she looked like a half-eaten cadaver.

He turned away before she had a chance to cover herself again. His hands shook. He gulped another glass of Madeira and looked steadfastly out of the window. 'Kilcannon said you were dead. Eaten by a tiger. Your *jemadar* corroborated his story. So, you were declared dead.'

'Where is my devoted husband now?'

'He left for Bengal a few weeks ago. Soon after the British declared war on us. In Europe-'

'Then I am ruined,' she said. Kilcannon had outmanoeuvred her.

'Don't you have resources?'

'Before this, I had ample resources. But Narain was my legal guardian, and he knew where those funds were deposited. With my death, they would have passed to my husband. With Narain's help, of course.'

Fontaine drained his glass. 'What really happened that day?'

'What happened was that Narain tried to kill me. It seems obvious to me now that my husband paid him to do it. The last thing I remember was him pointing my own musket at my head.'

'You mean this.' He went to the wooden chest in the corner, opened it and took out her prized Toradar. He laid it on the desk. It still had bloodstains on the stock.

'The tiger attacked just as he was about to pull the trigger.' She ran a finger along the barrel. 'When they said I was dead, and you couldn't find my body, did no one think it suspicious?'

'Everyone thought it was suspicious. Of course they did. But there was nothing to be done.'

'Wasn't it obvious what had happened?'

'There was no actual proof of anything. But Kilcannon had every reason to...'

'Tell me.'

'It seems he had lost everything...' He took a breath. 'A shipment of guns and cannons coming from France, that he had underwritten, had sunk in a storm off the Malabar coast. The *Compagnie* had already given him a downpayment on these armaments, and de Leyrit was demanding to have his deposit returned. It was quite a considerable amount.

'Your death solved all of Kilcannon's problems. There was nothing anyone could do. The governor just wanted his money back, and once Kilcannon had paid him, he washed his hands of the whole affair. I will inform the governor of this development, of course. There will be an enquiry.'

'How long will that take?'

Fontaine shrugged. 'I must tell you that it seems unlikely that much will come of it. De Leyrit still needs your husband, and he never liked your father. He will not overly concern himself on your account.'

'Of course.'

'What will you do?'

She didn't answer.

'Let me give you some money. You can buy passage back to France.'

'What is in France? I have never been there.'

'I can give you money anyway,' he said. He unlocked a drawer in his desk and took out a handful of silver *fanams*. He put them in a leather purse and passed it to her. When she reached out, their fingers almost touched. He pulled his hand away as if she were a leper.

Peasant women in ragged saris squatted on mats on the ground hawking cold chapatis. A boy with twisted limbs squealed at passersby from a ledge on a wall, looking for all the world like a pale and malevolent spider. A cow with a garland of flowers hanging from one of its horns munched happily on some greens from a street stall while the shopkeeper raged and howled. Cows were sacred, so he was powerless to stop it.

Adelaïde had never come to the Black Town without Narain. But today she felt quite safe. Who was going to bother her now, for her money or her sex?

She followed the crooked alleyways into the heart of the bazaar, stepping over the filth, accustomed now to the overpowering melange of smells - curry and animals and rosewater and human waste.

She heard wailing from a Ganesha temple and the clash of cymbals and flutes. The temple roof was a riot of gods, the brightly coloured plaster statues jostling each other for space. Clouds of incense poured into the street. A man passed a coconut over his body three times, so that it would absorb his sins, then hurled the coconut at the wall. It smashed into pieces, releasing his sins into the firmament.

If only it were that easy.

A mile from the outskirts, she came to a huddle of decrepit shacks. She crossed an open drain. Pi-dogs were fighting over some morsel they had dragged from a stinking pile of rotting garbage.

A wraith appeared in a doorway. She looked like a turtle, with no nose and no lips. She raised a hand to warn Adelaïde off and gave a strangled cry.

'Hello grandmother,' Adelaïde said.

'Who are you?'

'It's me, Adelaïde.'

The woman shook her head. 'You're not Adelaïde.'

'No, I'm not, not anymore. But I used to be. And now I need your help.'

.

Part 4

THE DAY OF THE TIGER

CHAPTER 41

Calcutta

  Lachlan peered through the blinds. The moon had set. It was still dark, but dawn was not far off. He heard the high-pitched whistle of a kingfisher down by the river as he turned away from the window. The candles had gutted and died, and the only light came from the flickering glow of an oil lamp in a niche high in the wall.

'I should go,' he said.

'Yes,' Yasmin said.

Lachlan could only make out her silhouette. He opened the door, and hesitated. 'I know what Nafisa says. But what if she's wrong, what if there's still a way out of this? If you go back, your father will kill you.'

'It is perhaps what I deserve. I have broken every rule. I have offended him, I have offended the Prophet, and I have offended God.'

Men make laws, not gods, he thought. But he knew it was pointless to contend with her about religion. So instead, he said, 'Wait a few hours and I'll get you on a ship for Madras. You and Nafisa can wait for me there. I promise I will get through this and come and find you.'

'It would be good to think so.'

'I mean it.'

'I had this one chance and took it. I knew this could happen. My only regret is that Nafisa will suffer for my wilfulness. I will never forgive myself for that.'

'We all make mistakes. We can't carry them forever.'

'You do,' she said. She got up from the bed and crossed the room.

He hadn't realised he was that easy to read. He wanted to hold her but didn't trust himself to let her go again. 'I don't know what to say.'

She put her finger to his lips. 'Then say nothing.' She kissed his cheek. 'You will be in my heart for always.'

'Goodbye,' he said. 'I'm sorry.'

He walked slowly across the lawn, slumped under his burden of guilts. First Catia, now Yasmin. He tried briefly to persuade himself to escape with her to Madras. He reminded himself he bore no allegiance to an England he had never seen or to the Company he despised.

But he could not leave Charlie or Tommy alone at the ramparts. He could never live with himself if he did.

Perhaps it was karma.

The next afternoon, standing at the palisade, Lachlan listened to the boom of cannon fire in the distance. Minchin's artillery at the Maratha ditch had been joined by the heavy guns of the *Prince George,* which had taken up position on the river west of the emplacements. Flashes of orange flame illuminated the evening clouds, followed by a shock wave that shook the ground under them. He wouldn't want to be on the receiving end of any of that.

He and his men had used anything they could find to build a barricade big enough to block off the street, upturning native carts and wagons, collecting barrels and lumber and even bare rocks. They had left a gap in the roadblock wide enough for the artillery limbers, should they need to fall back. He hoped they wouldn't have to use it.

As dusk fell, the streets emptied. Nothing moved except stray dogs and a single lost cow. Most people had already fled towards the fort, but Drake had shut the gates on them. Some had tried to get out of the city on boats or on foot, hoping to find a way through the blockade. The rest of the population now huddled inside their shacks and shophouses, praying to their gods to be spared from the cataclysm.

Lachlan peered over the barricade. It was eerily quiet. The cow was contentedly eating a cabbage it had found in one of the garbage piles at the side of the road. Two cats were fighting over a chicken bone.

He yawned, as tired as he had ever been. His limbs felt too heavy for his body. It was always like this before a battle, before the adrenalin kicked in.

It was strange to be back in a field uniform. He had promised himself he would give up warring after Kaveripauk, but it seemed that life had other plans for him. They had given him standard kit, the same as Charlie - a white canvas haversack slung across his right shoulder, a short sword on his left hip.

There was a water bottle on a leather strap across his other shoulder. He gulped at it. His mouth was gummy and dry.

Tommy leaned against one of the timber stakes and tapped the bowl of his pipe against the heel of his boot. 'I'm sorry for your troubles, sir.'

'What's that?' Lachlan said.

'I heard she and her aunt left last night. Went back upriver.'

Lachlan nodded.

'There was nothing you could have done.'

Behind them, a Company clerk, barely out of his teens, sighted his musket along the road, repeatedly checking the frizzen pan for powder. Charlie growled at him to take a deep breath and calm down.

'What do you make of this Captain Minchin?' Tommy said.

'I think he's overconfident and foolish,' Lachlan said.

'So, you don't think he can hold them at the Ditch, like he said.'

Lachlan turned to Charlie. 'What do you think? Is the Ditch as impregnable as Minchin makes out?'

Charlie shook his head. 'There's a gap near a place called the Bread and Cheese Bungalow where the Ditch was never completed – something else Drake and Minchin overlooked. Once Siraj's men find it, they'll walk straight through.'

'So, there's nothing between Siraj's army and us.'

Tommy filled his pipe, swatting distractedly at the flies. 'I don't think I'm ready to die,' he said.

Charlie nodded. 'I don't suppose anyone is. What about you, Lachlan? Ready for heaven?'

'I don't know if I believe in such a place.'

Tommy looked around for something to light his pipe. There wasn't anything, but he put it in his mouth anyway. 'Do you think like these Hindus, sir, that we keep coming back over and over in different bodies?'

'Perhaps.'

'I hope I get a better one next time. I'd like to be taller. But I think it would get tedious, having to learn to walk and talk again every few years and in different languages and such. I think if I had a choice, I'd be a Muslim. They reckon that if they're martyred fighting for God, they'll go to Paradise and be waited on by a hundred virgins. Don't know that I've ever seen that many all in one place. Certainly not in Limehouse.'

'You should convert,' Lachlan said.

'I'd like to, but I can't. I was baptised Church of England. You can't change sides in the middle of a battle. Besides, a hundred virgins aren't going to stay virgins forever are they? There's always a catch.'

The sun had barely fallen below the horizon, when they saw riders coming fast down the road. Lachlan held up his hand and stepped out, in case one of his raw recruits was too quick to open fire. The leading rider was wearing a red Company coat.

As he came closer, he saw it was one of Minchin's artillery officers. He was wide-eyed and red in the face. He reined in his horse long enough to shout, 'The enemy cavalry has outflanked us. We must retreat in good order to the fort!'

With that, he dug his heels into his horse's flanks and galloped back towards Fort William. The rest of the artillery came thundering down the road, riding too fast for their loads, limbers bouncing over the detritus in the street.

This is nothing like good order, Lachlan thought. This is sheer panic. He took out his spyglass and brought it to his eye. There were more redcoats on the road, gunners who had been left behind in the retreat.

As the moon rose over the hills, a glow spread above the roofs of the city. Soon it lit up the whole of the northern sky. A short time later, they saw people running down the road, some carrying babies and little children.

They poured through the gap they had left in the barricade. Others vaulted over the top, running and stumbling towards the fort.

'Do you think Drake will open the gates for them?' Lachlan said.

Charlie shook his head, his face grim.

'What do we do now, sir?' one of the young clerks shouted.

'You hold firm,' Lachlan said. 'Nothing's happened yet. And stop waving that musket around, boy. You'll hurt someone.'

He watched the gate through his spyglass. It was chaos already, people clamouring to get inside. He thought about Yasmin and Nafisa and said a silent prayer for them to a god he no longer really believed in.

Siraj's encampment, outside Calcutta

Tallow candles had been placed around the tent, and the smell of burning wax was overpowering. A plaited black whip lay beside Aziz Khan on the carpet. A servant brought him coffee. It was very hot and very sweet. He breathed in the steam that rose in tendrils from the surface as he contemplated what to do with his sister-in-law and his daughter.

Death, a beheading, would be appropriate for both of them, but he had promised his brother he would take care of Nafisa. And Yasmin, well, that would be too good for her. He was determined to break her spirit first. She had humiliated him, and he could not forgive that.

Yet he did not wish to bring attention to this scandal. It was best dealt with privately. A public shaming would tarnish his own reputation. If people thought that he could not control his women, what else would they think about him?

He clapped his hands.

Guards dragged the two women into the tent and forced them onto their knees. Earlier that day, they had arrived at one of the outposts on foot like common beggars and announced themselves to one of the pickets. They were fortunate they had not been shot, although on reflection that might have been the best solution. It would have solved his problem for him.

Nafisa would not meet his eyes, but Yasmin had the effrontery to raise her head and glare at him. The guards pushed her head down.

Aziz Khan sighed and sipped his coffee while they stared at the carpets. 'What have you to say for yourselves?'

'It was not Auntie's fault,' Yasmin said.

'Don't listen to her,' Nafisa said. 'I was the one who persuaded her to do this. It was for my sake, not hers.'

Aziz Khan shook his head. 'I don't believe either of you.' He turned to Yasmin. 'Do they not say, "When God made desire, He made it in ten parts. He gave one to man and nine to woman." You are wanton and you have brought shame to yourself and to me. I could take your head now.'

'Then do it,' she said.

He would have liked to. He wanted to see how long her defiance would last when she knelt in the executioner's shadow. But if things somehow went badly with Siraj, he might need her. He could still use her as a bargaining chip with the British, but a hostage was no good to anyone dead.

'If there is disgrace,' Nafisa said, 'you invited it into your house, not her.'

A red mist descended. He jumped to his feet, lashing down with the whip once, twice. Nafisa's screams were balm to his pride.

Yasmin threw herself over her aunt and tried to protect her from the blows. But by now he was in a rage. He wielded the whip in a frenzy, not caring where the stripes landed. Their cries only enticed him more.

He only stopped when he was too exhausted to carry on. He tossed the whip aside and walked from the tent feeling better and calmer than he had in a long time.

CHAPTER 42

Calcutta

Smoke rose from the Bhag bazaar. Thick black clouds billowed into the air, turning day into night. They had filled the gaps in the barricades with whatever they could. Now all they could do was wait.

As the hours passed, the carnage crept closer, and by the time Lachlan could see the flames, there were no more people running from Siraj's army. Either they had realised the Company wasn't going to help them, or they were dead.

He sniffed the air, sensing something else over the acrid taint of smoke. Blood had a distinct coppery smell, and he knew it would not carry to him at such a distance, unless the streets of the Black Town were awash in gore.

He could see them now, the irregulars that Minchin had called 'rabble.' They came on in a din of trumpets, unfurling their banners as they ran, a mass of coloured robes and turbans. He saw the dull flash of metal from their spears.

There was a tapping behind him. He looked around. One of the Company clerks was shaking so badly, his musket was rattling against his coat buttons. Another of his boys - for that's all they were – turned aside and retched.

'Stand fast, you lads,' Tommy shouted. 'Remember the drill I taught you.'

Lachlan had split their company into three sections. The first section would fire from the top of the barricade, while the second section was reloading, and the third section was getting ready to take their place.

Thanks to Drake and Minchin, they had no ready-made cartridges. Before they could fire their Brown Bess muskets, each man would have to measure powder from a flask and ram the wad down on it. Then he must get a lead ball from the pouch at his side, wrap it in a greased patch, and rod it down the bore after the powder and wadding. Finally, after he had primed the pan and snapped the steel lid shut, the gun would be ready to fire.

Seasoned, well-trained regulars would find it hard work under fire. But these were not seasoned men. They were mostly pimple-faced clerks and a handful of sailors who had never held a musket before.

One of the lads on the barricades brought his Brown Bess to his shoulder.

'Not yet,' Lachlan said. 'Wait till they're closer.'

He watched them, loose-robed and ragged, waving spears and rusted swords. A trumpeting grey elephant lumbered behind them in silver-plated armour. There were spikes on its head plates, and its tusks were painted blood-red to make it appear more fearsome. Its *mahouts* stood on the *howdah* on its back, beating drums and goading it forwards.

He let them get close.

Closer.

'Fire!' he shouted.

There was a crash of musketry followed by a single hang fire. They were all enveloped by clouds of stinking black smoke from the gunpowder. The first section scrambled down and were replaced by the next. Charlie was screaming at them to hurry.

I'm going to choke on the powder smoke long before any of Siraj's men reach the palisade, Lachlan thought.

Now the third section.

As they clambered back down, he could see that the first section wasn't ready. Some men had spilled more powder on their breeches than in the firing pans. A young clerk dropped his musket in his panic. Finally, a dozen of them scrambled to the top and loosed off a ragged volley.

Now the second section. Better.

The third section. Worse.

'They're going to come right over the top of us,' Charlie said.

The elephant seemed to fill the sky. It was so close, Lachlan could hear the leather straps of the *howdah* creaking as it swayed precariously on the animal's back. He snatched a loaded musket from one of the clerks and aimed. He wished he still had his hunting rifle.

The *mahout* was wildly prodding the elephant's ear with some kind of spear. This is from me, Lachlan said under his breath, but also from your elephant. He fired, aiming at the *mahout's* chest.

A moment later, the man fell forward and rolled down the beast's trunk. He lay prone in the dirt.

A stray musket ball hit the animal in the shoulder, and it reared and screamed. Panicked without its *mahout,* it turned away from the volley of musket fire and retreated, trampling the mass of foot soldiers still surging towards the barricade.

Lachlan watched the carnage, both horrified and fascinated, as the massive beast charged blindly back through the ranks. Men screamed and threw themselves out of the way. The rest ran.

The rush at their palisade was halted for now, but he knew the respite would be brief. 'Head for the park,' he shouted. 'Tommy, get our boys back to Minchin's trenches!'

Tommy started to shepherd the men along the narrow street of tumbledown shacks.

Lachlan and Charlie ran into a shophouse with two of the clerks. They battered loopholes in the mud brick and *chunam* with the butts of their rifles. The shopkeeper and his family were crouched in a corner. The man had his arms around his wife and two children. The smallest of the children was crying.

'Run!' Lachlan shouted at them in Bengali. 'Run for your lives!'

But they didn't move.

Siraj's men were clambering over the barricade. They made easy targets. The first half dozen or so fell back under a withering barrage of musket fire from Tommy's men. But there were too many of them. Soon they were over the palisade and marauding towards them down the street.

'We have to pull back,' Charlie said.

As the two clerks stepped out onto the street, a Mughal soldier with an orange robe and dark blue turban leaped off a cart in the middle of the barricade and ran at them, his *talwar* raised above his head. The young lads had their bayonets fixed, as Tommy had shown them, and turned to face him.

They had been drilled to work in pairs, but they had not learned the drill well enough. The bayonet had a longer reach than any sword, and a veteran might have dealt with the threat, but the first lad missed his thrust, and the edge of the blade deflected off the soldier's tough leather *target*. It was a fatal mistake. The *spahi* buried his sword into the boy's neck up to the hilt.

As he fell, he blocked his friend from driving forwards with his own weapon. The *spahi* sliced backhanded. Blood sprayed up the *chunam* wall behind him, and the lad went down clutching at his throat and drowning in his own blood.

By the time Lachlan got there, they were both dead. He swung at the *spahi*, but his sword bent double against the other man's chest without inflicting any kind of wound. Useless. He tossed it aside.

As the *spahi* swung his *talwar*, Lachlan stepped inside the blow and grabbed his wrist. He stabbed his splayed fingers into his eyes and brought his knee up into his groin. The man screamed and momentarily lost his grip on his sword. Lachlan wrestled it free and plunged it into the other man's belly. It seemed Mughal steel was more efficient than the Birmingham tin the Company had given him.

The *spahi* slumped to his knees. He looked up at Lachlan and cursed him, spitting blood at him through his teeth. Lachlan hacked down as hard as he could. The man's head rolled into the dirt.

Damn it, Lachlan thought. Another ghost for my dreams.

He looked around. The fight was going on all about him, and it was desperate. Siraj's infantry was still pouring over the barricade. He saw Tommy hauling two of the clerks away down the alley, trying to shake sense into them as he went. They were catatonic with terror. 'Move!' Tommy was shouting. 'Move!'

Charlie was still fighting off a turbaned infantryman with his sword.

Another *spahi* leap down from the barricade and thrust at Lachlan with a spear. Lachlan hacked down at the shaft and sliced off the spearpoint before it could find its target. He sliced again backhanded and didn't wait to see what damage he had done.

By now, Charlie had disabled his own man, and Lachlan grabbed him by the arm and hauled him away, following Tommy and the others in the retreat to the park.

CHAPTER 43

There comes a point, Lachlan thought, when death appears inevitable, but you have to keep going because there is nothing else to be done. He had felt this way at other battles and survived, so perhaps if he held on long enough, another miracle might come along.

He looked at the sword he had taken from the *spahi*. It had a cross guard and a simple knuckle bow. The curved blade was rigid as iron and razor sharp. It had taken off the man's head like cutting off a tree branch. He winced at the memory of it. Yes, it was him or me, he thought, but that doesn't make it any easier.

What was left of his militia were huddled in the trench alongside him. Some of them were shaking and crying and really would be of little use now, while others were still eager, had even found a taste for it. A couple of spindly Company clerks looked as if they would like to lick up the spilled blood if they could. They'd never get them back to the ledgers and the counting house after this.

He crouched down and caught his breath. His uniform was filthy and sweat-stained, covered in blood and dust, and the heat was stupefying. He would have ripped his jacket off, but he didn't want to get shot by any of these wild-eyed clerk boys who might mistake him for Siraj's infantry.

He gulped at his water bottle and looked around. The ditch was filled with bloodied bandages, shattered ramrods, sponge pails and empty shot bags. A few yards away from their position, Minchin's gunners were sluicing down the barrel of their cannon to cool it.

He had lost count of how many charges Siraj's men had made across Chowringhee Road. For the time being it was quiet. He peered over the top of the ditch into the copper haze of the afternoon.

'What's happening?' Charlie said.

Bodies were piled in hedgerows in front of their position, and the vultures and carrion birds were circling, waiting for their opportunity. There was a fine feast to be had out there all right.

He saw movement through the drifting smoke. Dear God, would they never give up? They were waving their war flags, the green and white of Islam, the orange of Aziz Khan. They poured out of the Black Town and towards the park, a seething, yelling mass of banners and *talwars* and ferocity. Their fish-scale armour shimmered like mercury in the heat.

'Here they come again,' he said.

Tommy bird-dogged over the lip of the trench and shouted to the boys still in his command to wait for his signal to fire. Let the cannons do the work first, he told them. Their job was to pick off any stragglers who made it through the hail of metal.

The gunnery captain away to their right gave the order to load the twelve-pounders with shot. Each canvas bag contained dozens of small lead balls that spread out as they left the barrel and went through massed infantry like a scythe, shredding flesh and bone as they went. One volley could kill or maim scores of men at a time.

It was bloody, gruesome and hellishly effective.

The cannons roared, jumping on their trucks one after the other. The gunners reloaded quickly, swabbing the barrels, bringing up more bags of packed shot and tamping them down. By the time Lachlan had counted to thirty, they were ready to fire again.

He knew that Siraj's own gunners could fire just one shot every quarter of an hour. The *spahis* thought that was usual. He supposed they could not comprehend the level of training they were up against.

The guns ranged along the ditch roared and jumped, and another iron hailstorm swept the park. The smoke cleared, leaving black powder trails drifting over a litter of twitching, lacerated bodies. The last volley had even punched holes in the shacks on the other side of the road. As he watched, one of them collapsed in a cloud of *chunam*, mud and rattan.

The massed line of attackers wavered and fell back. A lone *spahi* stumbled around in circles, dazed and lost. One of the clerks aimed his musket at him. He fired and the man tottered and fell. The clerk grinned and made a fist at his companions, who gave him a wild cheer.

There was an argument going on between the captain of the gunners and his crew. One of the men was gesticulating at the limber. Lachlan sent Tommy to find out what was going on.

He came back a few minutes later and said, 'They're almost out of powder.'

'What are they going to do?'

'The gunners are all for retreating, and their officer had to draw his pistol on them. I don't think he can keep them there for much longer.'

Lachlan looked across the park. He saw shadows, indistinct, moving among the heat and dust and powder smoke. They quickly resolved into yet another infantry wave, leaping wild-eyed with opium and fervour over the mounds of bodies, waving their banners as they ran.

The gun crews resorted to using langrage - grapeshot made from nails, horseshoes and coins that they had salvaged in desperation over the last couple of days.

Lachlan covered his ears. There was a burst of flame as the cannons fired another barrage, and everything was obliterated by the smoke. He was momentarily deafened.

He looked over the lip of the trench. More piles of mutilated men. More nerve-wrenching screams. As the smoke began to clear, he thought they had finally given up. Then he saw another wave forming on the other side of Chowringhee Road.

Tommy was right about the gun battery. They were out of ammunition. The gunners threw down their ramrods and sponges and ran. They didn't even stop to spike the guns. Already some of them were halfway across the maidan, sprinting for the fort.

'Pull back!' Lachlan shouted to his own boys.

As he jumped to his feet, a musket ball zipped past his head. Siraj's officers had brought up snipers with long-barrelled matchlocks. Beside him, Charlie gave a moan and went down. Blood blossomed over the front of his tunic.

Lachlan pulled him upright and hauled him up over his shoulder. He stumbled back across the park, Tommy jogging beside him.

'Run and save yourself!' Lachlan shouted.

'Can't sir,' Tommy said. 'I'm your adjutant. Must stay close at all times.'

'That's an order!'

'Can't hear you, sir. The cannons made me deaf.'

Lachlan kept going. He didn't dare stop to see how close Siraj's men were. Any moment he expected to be felled - a musket ball in the back perhaps, or a sword slash as one of Siraj's men caught up with him.

Charlie was a dead weight. He must have passed out, Lachlan thought. He could feel hot blood leaking down his chest. He concentrated on the fort, just a hundred yards away now. He wasn't sure that he could make it.

Tommy kept his musket at the ready. 'Keep going, sir. We're nearly there.'

Lachlan could tell by his voice that he didn't really believe it. There was another concussive blast, and he staggered as the shock wave hit him. One of the cannons on the east gate had opened fire on the enemy infantry behind them. Two more cannons joined in from the south bastion. He staggered, the muscles in his legs turning to jelly.

'I've got him,' Tommy said and manhandled Charlie onto his own shoulders. They were just twenty or so paces from the gates now.

Lachlan grabbed Tommy's musket and turned around. He saw a turbaned infantryman loping towards them through the smoke. He raised the musket and fired, then ran after Tommy into the shadow of the gates.

Suddenly, they found themselves inside the fort. They both collapsed in the dirt. Lachlan eased Charlie up against the wall. His head was slumped on his chest, but at least he was still breathing. He tore open his jacket and found the bloody hole where the musket ball had entered just below his collarbone.

He reached for his canteen and handed it to Tommy, then gulped a mouthful himself. He looked up, wiping the sweat from his face with the sleeve of his jacket. A copper sun hung halfway down the sky above the western wall. He realised they had been fighting through most of the day. It seemed like just a few minutes.

He dragged himself back to his feet. 'We have to find Charlie a doctor,' he said. They grabbed him by the arms and legs and carried him past the barracks, shouting desperately for a surgeon.

CHAPTER 44

The Sunderbans, downriver from Calcutta

The body, bloated and half burned, bobbed ghastly against the riverbank. Long black hair spread out in a fan on the current, and the remains of a red sari clung to the blackened flesh. A woman, then. Vultures and crows vied with the village pi-dogs over this fulsome meal. Their growling and squabbling were wearying on the nerves.

Just a few weeks ago, Narain had been enjoying the peace and the quiet in the *sahib's* villa in Pondicherry. He wished he were back there now. The dead had been floating down the river all day, sometimes three or four at a time logjammed against a sand bank. It seemed that Siraj's infantry, like their commander, had little time for restraint. They must have massacred thousands.

He grimaced at the bitter taste of smoke in the air. It hung in a black shroud to the north, clinging to the roofs of the city. He could hear the muted roar of the battle even down here at the borderlands of the Sundarbans.

The ruined *chhatri* where he and Ashin Das's man had agreed to meet was safe from prying eyes. The only witnesses to their conversation were the bats and tigers in the mangrove swamps.

'As a precaution,' the man said, 'my master moved his treasure. He was convinced someone would know about the secret vault.'

'He was right,' Narain said.

'There is a headstone in the walled graveyard of the old church. It is for a Lieutenant Henry Smith. The treasure is buried directly beside it, between the grave and the wall.'

'How do you know this?'

'Late one night, my master had the servants load everything from the vault into four carts. He left with six men and when they came back the carts were empty. It was my job to cut the men's throats so no one would ever know where the treasure was buried.'

'How did you find out what they had done?'

'I told one of the men that if he gave up the secret, I would spare his life.'

'And once he told you?'

'Well, then I cut his throat. It was a mercy. He was too stupid to live.'

'Where is Ashin Das now?'

'He has left on one of the British ships. He took with him his women and his most precious jewels. But his gold and silver are all buried in the churchyard.'

Kilcannon *sahib* will be pleased with this news, Narain thought. And I get a one fifth share.

'And what will you do now?' he said.

'Give me what we agreed, and no one will ever see me again.'

Narain nodded and reached inside his robes. He took out a leather purse. It was suitably heavy, but nothing like the fortune that was waiting for them in the churchyard.

'You could have asked for a lot more.'

The man looked inside the purse, at the darkly nestled jewels and coin. 'It's greed that gets a man killed. There is enough to live out my life in comfort here. With luck I won't have ever to cut another man's throat again.'

'A modest ambition,' Narain said.

'The key to a long life is modest ambition.' The man put his hands together, his thumbs towards his chest, and bowed. '*Namaste.*'

Calcutta

Drake's face was a sickly grey and he couldn't sit still. He paced the council chambers drinking brandy. There was a trace of vomit on his shirt.

225

'The situation is dire,' Captain Grant, the fort commander, was saying. 'The enemy forces are at the eastern gate, camped in front of St Andrew's church.'

Lachlan looked across at Minchin, but he would not meet his eyes. He sat at the end of the mahogany council table with his arms crossed, staring at the floor.

'We did not expect our batteries to be so suddenly quitted,' Drake said.

'You were misled,' Lachlan said.

Everyone turned and stared at him except Minchin who continued to study the carpet with great determination.

'How long can we hold out?' Drake said.

Grant hesitated. He looked around the room before delivering the bad news. 'We have only two days of ammunition left.'

'Two days?'

'Perhaps three.'

There was deathly silence.

He went on, 'Some of Siraj's men have French muskets, flintlocks. They have occupied the warehouses at the southern wall. Their snipers have been firing directly onto the bastions and ramparts, making it impossible to stand at the guns in some places.'

Lachlan lost his temper. 'We told you this would happen.'

Drake chewed his lip.

'Can't we use sandbags?' someone said.

It was left to Lachlan to answer. He stood up and put his fists on the table. 'We could, but there is a shortage of men to drag them up to the ramparts. We also have no lascars to carry shot and powder, or repair the gun carriages, and there are not enough cooks to supply food to the garrison.'

'Why not?' one of the councillors, Frankland, said.

'Because they've run away.'

'I cannot abide disloyalty!'

Lachlan turned on him. 'Neither can I. But it seems the natives you employed for these tasks have suddenly quit the fort. They did so on account of seeing their relatives slaughtered by Siraj's army when President Drake ordered the gates locked on them. Why a man cannot on occasion see his wife and daughters raped and murdered by invaders without becoming difficult about it, I cannot imagine.'

Drake glared. But he needed him. He turned to Grant. 'What do you advise?'

It was clear that Grant didn't want to be the one to say it. He settled for, 'The men are exhausted. They have been fighting two nights and a day with no rest, no food and not enough water.'

Lachlan grew impatient and broke in. 'What he means is, the men who are still willing to fight are done in. The rest are mercenaries, and if you'd like to take yourself down to the cellars you may hear them singing bawdy songs. They are all dead drunk.'

'Is this true?' Drake said to Grant.

'Sir,' Lachlan said, 'the drums beat to arms three times this morning, when Siraj's men attacked the walls. Barely any men came up to the ramparts to assist those already there. It is only a matter of time before we are overwhelmed. We must quit the fort.'

'I will not be the man who loses Calcutta,' Drake said. 'What will I tell the Board in London?'

Lachlan struggled to keep his temper. 'You will tell them that you did it to save the women and children who put their lives in your care. There are enough ships to get everyone away safely, but we must stop dithering. Get the longboats onto shore and get everyone out!'

Drake turned his back on the room. His shoulders heaved. Lachlan wondered if he was having a fit.

Finally, he mumbled, 'Very well. Frankland, you and Councillor Manningham take care of it.'

'So, we are agreed?' Lachlan said.

There was a deafening concussion. A timber from the roof slammed across the long mahogany council table splitting it in half, and the room filled with powdery white *chunam* dust from the ceiling.

Lachlan recoiled, choking.

When the dust cleared, he saw that the doors had been blown out. He staggered into the reception room gasping for breath while the councillors and officers hurried away down the stairs. He looked up. There was a massive hole in the roof. A cannonball must have come right through.

Well, that was it then. He supposed Siraj's men had made his point for him.

CHAPTER 45

T he hospital had been established in a basement storage room under the armoury. There were no windows, and the only light came from a few dozen tallow candles. As Lachlan came down the stone steps, the smoke from the candles made his eyes sting, and he almost recoiled at the smell of blood and waste.

Muttubby was kneeling on the filthy stone floor next to a wooden charpoy. Charlie lay on his back, his eyes closed, his jaw slack. He had not regained consciousness since he had been shot.

Lachlan could hear him trying to breathe from the other side of the cellar. He had brought him here thinking that it was a just a shoulder wound, but the surgeon had said the ball had severed an artery below his collarbone and damaged a part of his lung. He had removed the lead slug and cleaned the wound as best he could. The rest, he had said, was up to God.

They were words Lachlan never liked to hear. In his experience, God was notoriously unreliable.

Business in the makeshift hospital was brisk. He saw two orderlies hurry to fetch pails of water to sluice down the operating table and get it ready for the next casualty. The surgeon was working alone around the clock in a bloodied apron. A saw lay in an enamel bowl next to him, and soiled bandages and a discarded pair of forceps littered the floor at his feet.

The corpses of two dozen men lay side by side in the corner, some unmarked and looking almost peaceful, others mutilated beyond recognition.

The wounded lay moaning on cots or on the floor. A soldier was begging for someone to shoot him. There was nothing the surgeon could give them to ease their distress. Drake, with typical foresight, had shipped their stocks of opium on a merchantman just the week before.

'Muttubby,' Lachlan said.

She turned and looked up at him and somehow managed a smile.

'We have to get you out of here,' he said.

'I won't leave without Charlie. The surgeon says he can't be moved. It will kill him.'

If Charlie stays, Lachlan thought, that means I must stay. He was ashamed for feeling disappointed. He had allowed himself to believe there would yet be a way out of this.

'Very well,' he said. 'But if you stay, and the fort is taken, you will have to look like a *mem'sahib* and not a *bibi*. It will go better for you. You will be treated properly.'

'I won't wear stays. I'd rather die.'

'No stays, then.'

'Where will you find Englishwoman clothes?'

'I'll find a way, but you have to promise me that you'll wear them.'

She nodded.

He looked down at Charlie. There seemed to be no improvement. He was almost the same colour as the corpses piled up in the corner, and it sounded like he was trying to breathe underwater.

'He'll be all right,' he said. 'He's tough as old boots.'

Muttubby smiled but the look in her eyes told him a different story.

On the way out, he stopped and handed the surgeon his rosewood box with the last of his opium inside. 'For the young lad in the corner who wants someone to shoot him,' he said.

The surgeon took it gratefully. 'Where did you find this?'

'The man who owned it doesn't need it anymore.'

Lachlan couldn't sleep. He patrolled the bastion, exhausted and aching.

'You should keep your head down,' a voice said.

He peered into the dark. 'Is that you, Tommy?'

Tommy sucked on his pipe. The tobacco crackled as it burned, glowing in the dark. He offered it to Lachlan. 'I always find it relaxes me. Even when people are shooting at me.'

'No thanks,' Lachlan said.

'It's a different kind of pipe you're wanting, isn't it, sir?'

'I'm alright.'

'You're worrying the men, sir. You're as twitchy as a cat in a dog parade. They think you're scared. If the Tiger of Karimkot is frightened, they think they should be too.'

'Tell them I'm fine.' He crouched down behind the sandbags.

The north-west bastion was one of the safest places to be in the fort. The cannons had been largely abandoned, as there was no more powder and no lascars to haul the sacks up there even if there was. But the bastion served as an observation post to see what Siraj's men were up to on the north side of the fort.

He peered into the dark. Siraj's army had taken over the Black Town and the glow of their campfires stretched far to the north. He could see the silhouettes of the twelve cannons just below, the ones that Drake had left to rust on the wharf. He didn't want to think about how useful they could have been right now.

There was a sudden concussion and the platform shook. Smoke rose from the eastern gatehouse, blotting out the moon. He heard panicked screams and someone somewhere yelling in agony. Another one for the surgeon's knife.

They had barely enough men left to man the walls, though it scarcely mattered now. Siraj showed little inclination to storm the ramparts. He knew he could slowly reduce the place to rubble at little cost. When the batteries in the park had been overrun, the crews had neglected to spike the guns, so Siraj had turned the captured guns on the fort.

Lachlan and his men couldn't even move unhindered inside their own walls, because Siraj's snipers and archers were using them as target practice from the roof of the godowns.

'Is there a plan?' Tommy said.

'Drake has agreed to quit the fort. He's getting the women and the children on the boats first, then we're to follow.'

'Thank the Good Lord.'

Lachlan looked at the river. There were lights everywhere along the wharf. He could make out the dark shapes of longboats heading towards the merchantmen. It looked as if the evacuation was finally underway.

Suddenly, the sky lit up as fire arrows traced an arc over the city. Several landed in the shrouds of the ships, setting them alight. One of the merchantmen drifted away from the others, heading upstream.

Tommy peered over his shoulder. 'Do you know what that is,' he said. 'That is them leaving us all behind.'

Narain led the string of camels through the shattered ruins of the churchyard. The church itself had been abandoned long before the siege. The roof had fallen in years ago and now trees sprouted from the walls.

A single wayward shell had landed in the churchyard during Siraj's assault on the city, leaving a crater of upturned earth and shattered headstones scattered among the tombs. A skeletal arm protruded from a recent grave – a corpse reaching out for the living as if hoping for a reprieve.

Kilcannon shuddered. He took out a scented handkerchief and held it to his nose. He kept looking over his shoulder. No one is watching us, he told himself. They have other things on their minds. Aziz Khan will never find out.

It had taken longer to get to the church than he had anticipated. The promenades and gardens outside the fort were pitted with shell holes and littered with bloated bodies. Even the camels had found it heavy going. The crack of musket fire sounded uncomfortably close.

Narain had hand-picked six men from a native regiment, men who were too scared or too stupid to ask questions. They stumbled along beside the camels, dumbly grateful for such an easy commission. This was better than being made to charge the cannons and get torn to bits by British iron.

The plain marble cross that marked the resting place of Lieutenant Henry Smith's mortal remains was surprisingly untouched by the battle. Kilcannon pointed to a spot between the grave and the wall. Narain put his men to work.

They were illuminated briefly by a fiery glow as a cannon shell exploded on the eastern gatehouse of the fort. It momentarily lit up the church and the hellscape of the cemetery.

Kilcannon supposed the old bones he was standing on would be justifiably outraged. They had been promised they would rest in peace, but that was unlikely here in Hindustan. There was no peace anywhere. Not when there were fortunes to be made for the living.

Narain's *sepoys* were enthusiastic at their work. He had offered them extra pay if they got the job done quickly, and the freshly turned earth came up easily.

Finally, one of them let out a shout as his spade struck something solid. Very soon they had uncovered the iron bound chests from Ashin Das's vault. It took six men to lift one out of the hole. Narain bent down next to it and wrenched open the brass lock with an iron bar.

Kilcannon held up a flaming torch and peered inside. 'Holy Christ,' he said.

All that gold and silver. There was a king's ransom just in this one chest. And there looked to be another two dozen buried down there about the same size.

How did a man like Ashin Das make so much money in his life? It was surely not possible to earn it from honest labour. He had earned a sour reputation for cheating others in his business dealings, and now he was about to be cheated himself. How poetic was life.

He thought briefly about his promise to share the treasure with Aziz Khan but dismissed the thought. Thanks to Narain's spy, and Ashin Das's excess of caution in moving his wealth, this entire fortune would be his as long as he kept his nerve. He smiled to himself. Things always had a habit of working out.

The rest of the chests were hauled to the surface. The camels grunted under the strain as the loads were lifted onto their backs. One let out a scream and jerked on its rope.

Kilcannon snapped out an oath to the leader of the string. 'Get them under control or it's your head!'

Finally, it was done.

Kilcannon took Narain aside. 'Head straight for the French fort at Chandernaggar and load these chests on the first ship to Pondicherry. Wait for me there.'

'What about guards?'

'The more guards you have, the more people will think you have something to hide. And don't be tempted to open any more of them.'

'I wouldn't.'

'You wouldn't be a man if you didn't think about it. But if you do, I'll know.'

'You can trust me.'

'I don't trust anyone. But your share of this is more money than you can spend in ten lifetimes. Let me down, and I'll hunt you down like a dog.'

CHAPTER 46

L achlan knew death when he smelled it, and Charlie had that smell about him. But Muttubby wasn't going to leave him while there was breath in him.

He put a hand on her shoulder. 'Has he said anything?'

She shook her head.

'It doesn't look good,' he said, preparing her.

'I know.' She looked up. Her eyes shone. 'He was very good to me.'

The cellar shook and mortar dust fell from the ceiling. Men started to choke. For a moment, Lachlan thought the building was about to come down, but the surgeon didn't even look up from his operating table in the corner.

'If we get out of here,' Lachlan said. 'I'll take care of you.'

'There is no way out, McKenzie *sahib*,' she said. 'We both know this.'

Trumpets sounded the alarm. Another attack. Lachlan left her and ran up the stairs to the yard.

Tommy was waiting for him. 'Siraj's men are mustering under the south wall,' he said. 'In the carpenter's yard.'

Siraj must be losing patience, Lachlan thought.

Tommy was holding an oil lamp. He held it up so that Lachlan could see the men he had brought with him - two regulars and four militia. One of them looked as if he had never shaved.

'Is this all the men we have?'

'It should be enough for what I have in mind, sir. We can take cover by the south-west bastion.'

They had to run the gauntlet along the south wall. Lachlan led them in a crouching run. He saw the flash of musket fire from the godowns, and several balls cracked into the wall either side of him. He was relieved to finally throw himself down behind the sandbags at the corner bastion.

The others all made it, except for their fresh-faced volunteer. A sniper found him out halfway along the curtain wall. They watched him stagger back, clutching at his belly, and drop into the yard.

'Poor bugger,' Tommy said.

There were two gun crews crouched in the embrasure. They pointed down to the carpenter's yard below. Lachlan dared a quick glance over the sandbags. Siraj's men had thrown scaling ladders against the walls, and now they were milling around below, ready for the assault.

He ducked down again.

Tommy reached into a bag he had brought with him. He handed each man a grenade. They lit the fuses from the gunnery captain's lamp and at Lachlan's command threw them down into the yard. They counted the explosions, one after the other. There was an eerie silence, followed by the yells of the dying.

They waited.

'How many more grenades do we have?' Lachlan said.

'Five,' Tommy said.

Lachlan chanced another glance over the wall. Dear God. Even in the moonlight, he could see what a mess they had made. 'We won't be needing them. I think that should discourage them for now. Keep an eye on things, Sergeant.'

He ran the gauntlet back to the hospital, thinking to say his final farewell to Charlie.

But he was too late. By the time he got back to the basement hospital, Charlie Mathieson was dead.

Lachlan waited on the riverbank with Muttubby. She stood ramrod straight beside him, not saying a word. She had a faraway look in her eyes. He felt he should say something to comfort her, but he couldn't find the words. No one had ever found words enough to console him after Catia died, so he suspected it was pointless to try.

Loss. It was the great trick that life played on everyone. It seemed to be Fate's great pleasure to bring someone into your life who filled you with joy, then wait for just the right moment to snatch them away again.

When he buried Catia, he had vowed that in future he would keep everyone at arm's length so he wouldn't have to suffer. Yet somehow, he had been duped into caring again.

He looked out over the river. Where were the ships to take them away from here? Half the merchantman fleet appeared to have gone.

Captain Grant was standing in full fig further up the strand, legs akimbo. A crowd had gathered around him, demanding rescue. Most were women with children, but there were also a few dozen mercenaries, still drunk on Company wine.

Lachlan went over. 'Where are the ships, Captain?' he said.

Grant looked like a man caught in a lie. 'The *Dodaly* got in trouble last night. Siraj's men set fire to her shrouds with burning arrows. She had to seek shelter further downstream. Some of the other ships followed.'

'And left the women and children behind?'

Grant did not respond.

'Where's Manningham and Frankland?' Lachlan said. 'They were supposed to be in charge of this.'

Grant nodded towards the *Dodaly,* now almost out of sight.

'They are on board?'

'They felt it too dangerous to return.'

Lachlan felt his frustration growing. 'Of course it's dangerous. That's why we're evacuating everyone.'

A dozen longboats were heading to the shore from one of the packet ships still standing off, and a crowd of women and children started to stampede towards them.

Lachlan saw Drake and Minchin skulking further down the beach. He ran after them. 'Someone needs to take charge of this,' he shouted.

Neither of them answered.

As the longboats pulled into the shallows the crowd surged forwards. Lachlan saw one of the Armenians barge into Muttubby and send her headlong into the river. He raced over, grabbed the man by his jacket and hit him, knocking him down. The man looked up at him in surprise and then scrambled straight back to his feet and waded towards the nearest boat.

Lachlan scooped Muttubby up in his arms. Everywhere people were being trampled in the panicked rush for the boats. One of the painters was already full to the waterline. As it pushed off, a factory clerk swam after it and tried to jump in. His weight made it capsize, and everyone in it went screaming into the water.

Lachlan saw a small child go under. Christ Jesus. He hesitated.

'Save him first,' Muttubby said and jumped down out of his arms.

He swam out and ducked down after the child. It was hard to see anything in the muddy water, but his outstretched hand found the boy's shirt, and he hauled him back to the surface. He dragged him into the shallows.

'Where's your mother, boy? Where's your mother?'

A woman grabbed him from his arms without a by your leave and disappeared back into the melee.

He watched the remaining boats row out to the deeper water. Some of them were only half full, but he doubted they would come back now. He looked around for Drake but couldn't see him anywhere. Muttubby grabbed his arm and pointed.

Drake was with Minchin and Grant, hunched in the stern of one of the longboats.

Muttubby stood dazed in the water, blood dripping from her chin from where the mercenary had struck her with his elbow. 'Do you think they will come back for us?' she said.

'Of course,' Lachlan said, though he knew it was a lie.

An hour later, he watched the remaining ships weigh anchor and drift slowly downstream towards the mangrove swamps of the Sunderbans, headed for the distant coast beyond.

The sun had throttled the life out of the day, and the afternoon sky was bleached white like a bone. Lachlan sat with his back against a sandbag, trying to find what little shade he could. Bodies lay decomposing on the parade ground in the heat. He watched a vulture tear a strip of flesh off a dead man's back with its beak and gulp it down.

'I once saw a snake swallow a lizard whole,' Tommy said. 'It looked a lot like that.'

One of the clerks brought his musket up to his shoulder and aimed. 'Don't,' Lachlan said. 'Number one, save your ammunition. Number two, even a marksman couldn't hit it with a smooth bore at this range.'

'But it's disgusting,' the lad said.

'It's a vulture,' Tommy said, 'doing what vultures do.'

Metal green clouds of flies hovered around the bodies, their steady hum a constant backdrop to the late afternoon. The stink got worse.

Lachlan closed his eyes. They would have to surrender soon, even if just to get away from the stench. His face was sticky with sweat and dust, his lips cracked by thirst and sun. He shrugged out of his red uniform jacket. He was too hot and tired to care if any of his own lads shot him by mistake.

He thought about Charlie and then he thought about Yasmin. They had both so nearly found the life they dreamed of, only to have it snatched away at the last. It didn't seem fair.

Well, I won't have it, he decided. Someone has to dodge the traps that life has laid, and it might as well be me. I'll not give up yet. Somehow, I'll get through this and find a way to live and be happy, just to show it can be done.

He heard singing coming from the writers' building. Some mercenaries had taken up residence there with a cask of Madeira. One of the officers had gone down to order them to the ramparts. They had threatened him with bayonets. No one had been foolhardy enough to risk it a second time.

All day long, signal flags had been raised on the north-west bastion requesting assistance from the handful of ships still moored offshore. So far there had been no response.

'I cannot believe that Drake and Minchin would behave like this,' Lachlan said, 'leaving women and children behind in order to save themselves. What sort of men are they?'

Tommy sucked noisily on his pipe. He had run out of tobacco the night before. 'You might well be surprised sir, but speaking as a common man, I must admit my astonishment is not as great.'

'How do they live with their conscience?'

'Very well, I should think. Perhaps a slight case of indigestion after their good dinner tonight, but after a cigar and a glass of porter, they'll soon recover their spirits.'

'Are we going to die here?' one of the clerks said.

'I don't know, son,' Tommy said.

'I think I'd rather die than be taken prisoner. I heard they impale their prisoners on sharp stakes and cut off their privates.'

There was a long silence. Just the murmur of meat flies.

'Give me your musket, lad,' Tommy said.

'Why, sir?'

'Because I'm going to shoot you with it.'

CHAPTER 47

After Drake had abandoned his post, command had fallen to the city magistrate, a man named Holwell.

There was little glory attached to his sudden promotion. In Lachlan's view, all that was required was someone capable of organising a surrender. But with fewer than two hundred men, Holwell had insisted that they fight on through the day.

Lachlan and his small band of clerks and sailors ran from one wall to the next, filling breaches with bales of cotton for want of anything more solid. But soon, there were few places on the ramparts where they were safe from the snipers on the roofs of the warehouses.

As the attrition mounted, Lachlan ordered his men back to the roof of the writers' building to make a last stand. One of them brought with him a flintlock he had taken from a dead *spahi*. It was a Charleville. Lachlan wondered where Siraj had got them. It could only be from Kilcannon.

He sent his wounded down to the surgeon only if they were unconscious. Otherwise, they were propped up behind sandbags and put to work reloading muskets for those men physically able to fight on. But by late afternoon, just five of the fifty recruits who had stood with him at the palisades two days before were still fit for duty. Even Tommy had a bloody bandage around his head where he had been hit by stone fragments after a shell had exploded close by.

Lachlan upended his leather water bottle. Empty. 'How much ammunition do you have left, Sergeant?' he said.

Tommy fumbled in the canvas bag at his hip. He pulled out three lead balls.

'Powder?'

Tommy shook his head.

Lachlan looked at the others - four clerks and an old seaman. They had barely five rounds between them.

'Look,' Tommy said.

Someone was hauling a white flag up the pole on the north-west bastion.

A few minutes later, a courier appeared on the roof. 'Mister Holwell sends his compliments,' he said to Lachlan, 'and requests that you cease firing.'

'Stand down,' Lachlan said to his men. 'It's all over.'

Smoke rose into the air from the North Gate. The Mughal infantry had set fire to the cloth bales they had used to plug breaches in the walls.

One of Siraj's soldiers ventured into the yard below. More followed. Soon there were hundreds of them swarming across the parade ground.

'I have to find Muttubby,' Lachlan said.

Siraj ud-Daulah sat on a white Arab stallion, surrounded by his officers and bodyguard. He was wearing a turban of pure white linen, with an aigrette feather held in place by a fat red ruby clasp. It was impossible to look at him without being momentarily blinded by the glare from his chain mail. His horse was beautifully caparisoned in gold and silver cloth.

He surveyed his prisoners with weary disinterest. He looked straight at Lachlan but did not seem to recognise him without his ceremonial uniform. He seemed in no hurry to get down to things.

Lachlan imagined he wanted to give them all sufficient time to admire him before they got down to business. He turned to Tommy. 'He's well turned out, as usual.'

'Tie a pink ribbon around elephant dung, and it's still a giant turd, begging your pardon, sir.'

Lachlan looked for Aziz Khan and was relieved not to see him among Siraj's deputation of officers.

'What do you think will happen now?' Tommy said.

'They'll keep us as hostages,' Lachlan said with a confidence he did not feel, 'then squeeze the Company purse for whatever they can before they set us free.'

Well, perhaps, he thought. That's the best case.

More usually, when a Mughal army captured a town or city, their habit was to execute some, impale others, and send the young women to the nawab's harem. Those that weren't raped on the spot.

He looked at Muttubby standing beside him. She had still been crouched over Charlie's body when he had found her in the basement hospital. At first, she had refused to leave, and Lachlan had been forced to gather her up and carry her out in his arms.

She was now almost unrecognisable as a *bibi*. The women who had managed to escape on the ships had been forced to leave most of their belongings behind, so it had been easy enough to scavenge a dress for her.

It was calico, with a high neck, and it was far too long. Its hem trailed around her ankles, but that was to advantage. Her hair was hidden under a bonnet. It would have looked ridiculous to anyone who had seen her the day before in her silk sari, but it would serve its purpose. She held a handkerchief to her face to hide her complexion.

Holwell was carried into the yard on a stretcher and set down in front of Siraj's horse.

'Name,' Siraj said.

'John Zepheniah Holwell. I am the magistrate.'

Siraj frowned. 'Where is this President Drake?'

'He has left the city. I am now the senior man here.'

Siraj stared at him. He shook his head. 'You must show me where he has hidden his gold.'

'I have to inform you that the treasury is virtually empty. President Drake had everything loaded on board the merchantmen when you arrived at the gates.'

'That is impossible.'

'I assure you, it's not.'

Siraj flicked a finger in dismissal. He turned to the officers around him and shouted at them in Parsi, telling them to search the fort for Drake's treasury.

A captain asked him what he should do with the prisoners. The guards were standing over them with their rifles and spears, scowls on their faces.

'Untie them,' Siraj said. 'If they're not British, send them home. Lock up the rest until I decide what to do with them.'

He rode off.

Even though the sun had dropped behind the fortress walls, it was still unbearably hot. The yard was filled with smoke.

We must look a sorry lot, Lachlan thought, ragged and half-starved. Most of the men around him had filthy bandages on untreated wounds. A few leaned on ramrods or timber palings as makeshift crutches. Some of them would scarcely make it through another night.

Some *spahis* appeared and ordered them to get into a line. They marched them to the veranda at the south-east bastion. One of the guards took pleasure in jabbing Lachlan in the ribs with the muzzle of his rifle. Lachlan turned on him, his fist raised. The man grinned with betel-stained teeth, delighted to get the reaction he had been looking for. He let him know in Bengali that it would be his personal pleasure to shoot him if he wanted. Tommy grabbed Lachlan by the arm and dragged him away.

There was a platoon of Armenian mercenaries already gathered under the arched veranda, the same men who had raided the Company stores for liquor. Siraj's troops had been unable to get their booze off them, and now the men were rowdy and even more belligerent. They began taunting their guards with obscene gestures.

'This is not going to end well,' Lachlan said.

The captain of the *spahis* ordered his *jemadar* to take the brandy bottle away from them. One of the Armenians jumped to his feet and pushed him. The *jemadar* reached for the pistol in his belt, but the soldier was quicker, despite the drink in him, and knocked him down. He jumped on top of him. As they struggled for possession of the pistol, it went off. The *jemadar* gave a small cry and lay still, a lead ball lodged somewhere in his brain.

The *spahi's* captain immediately drew his sword and took the top of the Armenian's head off. When he saw his *jemadar* was dead, he was incensed.

This is it, Lachlan thought. We're for the slaughter as well.

Instead, the captain shouted to his men and pointed to a dark and stinking room next to the barracks. He held his sword at Lachlan's neck. 'You. Go in there.'

'Why me?' Lachlan said.

'All of you. Get in there!'

The rest of the *spahis* raised their muskets or brought out their *talwars*. They were angry about losing their sergeant and now they meant business.

'You can't put us all in there,' Lachlan said. 'Some of these men need a doctor.' He pointed to Muttubby and another woman, the wife of one of the merchant captains who had somehow also been stranded inside the fort. 'There are women with us.'

The captain nodded to the man who had been taunting Lachlan with his musket earlier. He brought up the butt end of his rifle and slammed it into Lachlan's stomach. He crumpled to his knees, fighting for breath. Tommy lunged forward to protect him, but two of the *spahis* held him back, their spears at his chest.

Lachlan held up his hand and shook his head at Tommy. He wanted to avoid any more bloodshed. Resistance was pointless now. 'Sergeant, don't,' was all he could manage, still winded.

'God's holy blood,' Tommy said.

'What is it?'

'They mean to put us all in that guardroom. It's for other ranks when they're on a charge. It's meant for three men, four at most.'

Lachlan stared into the cell. They couldn't possibly cram everyone in there in this heat.

'For pity's sake, man,' he said.

But the captain's eyes betrayed no pity at all. In fact, the man had a certain look about him. Lachlan had seen it many times before on the faces of sergeant majors counting out the stripes at a flogging. That sort had a rapacious hunger for suffering, providing it wasn't their own.

The *spahis* charged at them, using their spears or the butt ends of their muskets, herding them towards the door. One of the Armenians was speared through the thigh with a bayonet, but he carried on kicking and fighting until Lachlan finally dragged him inside the guard room to save his life.

As more and more people were forced into the cell, Lachlan, Tommy and Muttubby were pushed against the back wall. Soon, everyone was packed in so tightly they couldn't even move their arms. They all sobbed and cried out in panic.

The *spahis* threw their shoulders to the door to wedge it shut and slammed the wooden bar in place.

The captain shouted something through the door. Lachlan couldn't make out what it was, but several of the *spahis* laughed, and one of them fired his rifle into the air to celebrate.

CHAPTER 48

A shin Das's palace looked like a Greek temple that had been painted with turmeric. The gardens must have looked beautiful once, Kilcannon thought, but the rose beds had been flattened by Siraj's cavalry, and there were bodies floating in the fishponds.

The looting was well underway. A *subadar* came down the grand marble staircase with a mirror in a gilt frame. Another soldier ran behind him with a heavy jute bag over his shoulder that jangled with every step. A five branched silver candlestick was poking out of the top of it.

Two cavalrymen were arguing over a gaudy statue of a heathen god. One of them ended the disagreement by taking out his dagger and inserting it adroitly into his rival's stomach. Another soldier - Kilcannon supposed it was the wounded man's comrade - saw what had happened and pulled his sword from his belt.

Fools, he thought, let them kill each other.

The Greek portico was streaked with ash where some soldiers had lit a campfire the night before. He went into the echoing entrance hall. Narain had already told him that the house had been thoroughly ransacked. He had also reported that the Georgian furniture, family paintings, and even a harpsichord that had once belonged to the Duke of Savoy, had been burned as firewood.

An ornate mahogany door hung loose on its hinge, and there were torn silks and velvets littered around the marble floors. He looked up. The crystal chandeliers were still in place. You'd need to climb on the back of an elephant to reach them. No doubt someone would think of that later.

A white sculpture stood in the middle of the floor next to the staircase. A Michelangelo, or so he'd been told, and it probably weighed more than a fully grown buffalo. Not an easy thing to put over your shoulder and run off with, which was why it was still there, he supposed. The vile sort who fought in Siraj's infantry would not have known what it was anyway.

He went down some steps leading to a basement. It was a long way down and the air was cool and dank. He saw torches at the end of a tunnel and headed towards them.

'Where have you been?' Aziz Khan said when he saw him.

'Trying not to get killed,' Kilcannon said. 'Your men are lawless.'

'It's their payday. What do you expect?'

'Have you found it?'

Aziz Khan pointed to the wall. 'The mortar's still fresh. I'd say these bricks have been laid in the last few days.' He turned to the two men he had brought with him. They were holding heavy sledgehammers. 'Take it down.'

The men went to work. There was only a single layer of brick and knocking it down was the work of just a few minutes.

The general didn't wait for them to finish. As soon as the hole in the wall was wide enough to step through, he snatched a torch from one of his soldiers and went in.

Kilcannon followed.

The room had been cut from the bare rock. Water dripped from the ceiling, and the walls were covered in a green lichen slime. Aziz Khan swung his torch around. It hovered over some dark shapes in the corner.

Kilcannon sniffed the air and knew what they had found. There were six bodies neatly stacked one on top of the other. They were natives, peasants by the look of them.

'What is this?' Aziz Khan said.

Kilcannon knelt down. The corpses all had dirt under their fingernails. Nothing unusual in that of course, but significant if you knew they had spent their last hours burying their master's iron-banded treasure chests in the Anglican graveyard.

Aziz Khan roared in frustration and kicked one of the corpses. 'Where is the gold?'

Kilcannon took his time standing up. He looked around the room as if in disbelief. 'I have no idea.'

'What about Ashin Das?'

'My man said he escaped on the British ships.'

'Your man? If he knew so much of Ashin Das's affairs, how is it he didn't know that the treasure was gone?'

'Ashin Das must have taken it with him after all.'

Aziz Khan grabbed his arm. 'You said the British ships would not take such a cargo. We had a deal! My help for half this treasure!'

'Ashin Das has fooled me as well,' Kilcannon said. He watched a hundred emotions play on the other man's face and for one heart-stopping moment he thought he was going to draw his sword.

Aziz Khan glared at him and Kilcannon cooly met his stare.

'I suppose he did,' the general said finally.

Kilcannon discreetly drew breath. I've done it, he thought, as he watched him stamp away. I've fooled one of the biggest crooks I've ever met and walked away with a fortune.

It was as much as he could do to stop himself smiling until he was safely away from the palace.

CHAPTER 49

The mosquitoes were swarming. The only air came from a single barred window high on the wall, and the stench was insufferable. No one had washed or changed their clothes for days in the boiling heat. The stink mingled with the bad-egg smell of the black gunpowder they had been using in their smooth-bore muskets. Their clothes, their hair, their skins were steeped in it.

Lachlan was wedged at the back of the cell. He couldn't move and he could hardly breathe. The heat was stupefying. Someone cried out for water. Then someone else. In moments those closest to the door were hammering on it with their fists, water, water, water.

'Well sir,' Tommy said. 'Been nice knowing you. I'd shake your hand if I could move it.'

Lachlan could feel him laughing. 'What on earth could you find funny?'

'I was thinking about when I was little.' Tommy could manage only short sentences between gasps for breath. 'I had eight brothers and sisters. We all had to share a room. I was always whining how it was too cramped, and my old mum said I didn't know how lucky I was. I suppose this proves her right.'

'That's funny?'

'If you think about it.'

They were pressed against the wall furthest from the window. Lachlan considered trying to elbow his way closer, but everyone was trying to do that. He decided that staying where they were and toughing it out was their best chance.

Soon, the fighting started. It was hard for men to swing a punch when they could barely raise their arms from the crush, but they managed somehow.

He watched through the haze of his own suffering. He saw men who had remained resolute at the walls during the siege, toughs from the east end of London and the slums of Birmingham and Liverpool, fighting with proper English gentlemen in wigs and frock coats.

They used their elbows and knees, some even headbutting and biting, to get to the window. Once a man was there, he clung to the bars with all his strength while his former comrades tried to tear him away, clawing at his face and eyes with their nails.

How do they have the strength, he thought.

They screamed at each other, desperate for the one stale breath of air that they imagined would save them. It was the same clamour he had heard countless times on the battlefield.

They begged the guards for water. The guards just laughed and jeered.

After a while, some slipped to their knees, exhausted. The men behind stood on them with their boots.

They surged forward and surged again.

One man close by was trapped against the walls, his eyes bulging as he fought for breath. Lachlan could only watch on as the life was squeezed out of him. He died standing up.

Holwell shouted at them from somewhere in the darkness, but he couldn't make himself heard. They would have paid no attention anyway. All order had been lost the moment the door had slammed on them. Lachlan closed his eyes and concentrated on staying calm. Panic was the enemy now.

With so many pressing towards the window, it gave him and Tommy and Muttubby a chance. Perhaps there was less air at the back of the tiny cell, but there was at least room to move a little.

'We'll stay here,' Lachlan said. 'Get your uniform jacket off if you can, Tommy, and take small calm breaths. There's nothing anyone can do for these other men. They are all going to kill each other sooner or later.' He turned to Muttubby. 'Are you alright?'

'I can't breathe,' she said and started to struggle. 'I can't breathe! I need water.' Until that moment, she had managed to stay calm, but now she began to lose control. She kicked and twisted. It was as if she was drowning right next to him.

Finally, she exhausted herself and went limp. She would have fallen but she was wedged in.

Lachlan managed to get a hand free. He took off her bonnet and undid the hooks of her dress so that she could breathe easier. This was a fight for life now. Her disguise didn't matter anymore. Neither did modesty.

He and Tommy held her up between them. She rested her weight on their shoulders.

Time meant nothing. Like a fever dream, Lachlan was no longer sure what was real and what was not. He fought the urge to shout and struggle like the others.

He passed out once. Or perhaps he passed out many times. He couldn't be sure. But sometime during the night, he was aware that the screaming had died down. It had been replaced by the low moaning of men too far gone to fight anymore.

He had enough space finally to slide down the wall. He sat with his back against it, his mouth open like a beached fish. He spared a glance to his side. Muttubby had slumped to her haunches beside him. He couldn't see her face, but she didn't seem to be moving. He turned to his left. Tommy opened his eyes and winked. It was all he could manage.

He could no longer see the window because of all those standing on the litter of bodies on the floor and blocking out the light.

Everyone who dies leaves more air for us, he thought. He was ashamed of the thought, but it was true.

Someone shouted that one of the guards was coming with water. A few men made a renewed effort to get to the window. They started fighting again, but it made no difference. The guard couldn't get the water bowl through the bars. Someone grabbed for it and spilled it. The water splashed onto the floor. One man tried to lap at it like a dog before he disappeared under the crush.

Light crept through the high window. A redcoat stood there, his hands in a death grip around one of the bars. It was impossible to tell if he was alive or dead.

It must be close to dawn, Lachlan thought. Grey shapes were entangled with each other in a gruesome pile. He wondered if the torture was over, or if they intended to leave them all in here until they were dead.

He looked down at Muttubby. Her mouth was open, but her eyes were glassy and grey like the fish at the market. He turned to Tommy. For a moment, he thought he was dead too, until he saw him raise one finger and nod.

A guard threw open the door and ordered them out.

Incredibly, there was no rush for the door. Everyone was too weak and too exhausted. Those who could, crawled or dragged themselves into the yard. Lachlan and Tommy pulled Muttubby out between them. A guard pointed to a trough of filmy warm water, and Lachlan flung himself at it and drank until he was sick.

Afterwards, he collapsed against the veranda wall and watched the soldiers carry out the dead. They laid them in rows in the middle of the courtyard.

It was not until later that Siraj made another appearance. When he saw the bodies, he flew into a rage. 'I did not order this!' he shouted at the captain in charge of the *spahis*.

'Most of them were wounded and would have died anyway,' the man said, his nose pressed into the dirt. 'And it was a very hot night.'

Siraj pointed to Holwell. 'Send him to Murshidabad. He is a prisoner of war. I want him alive.'

He walked his horse forward and saw Lachlan. Recognition came slowly. When it did, his face twisted into a cruel smile. 'Well, it is the English Resident. I did not know you without your fine red coat.' He turned back to the captain. 'This one is my prisoner, too. And his servant,' he added, pointing to Tommy.

'Adjutant,' Tommy said.

Part 5

THE KILL

CHAPTER 50

Murshidabad, a year later

'What day do you think it is?' Lachlan said.

'It feels like a Sunday.'

'Every day here feels like a Sunday.'

Tommy sat up and studied the scratchings he had made on the wall. He counted the rows and made a quick calculation. 'We've been here almost a year by my reckoning.'

Lachlan peered out of the high, barred window. The clouds were streaked with pink, but he couldn't see the sun. It was only ever visible for a few hours around midday. 'I wonder what's happening out there?'

He had supposed at first that they would be traded as hostages, but as time went on that hope had faded. Their jailers would tell them nothing. He feared now that the Company had been thrown out of Bengal, perhaps even out of all Hindustan. If that was true, then they had lost their value to everyone as hostages. They might be left here to rot.

All they had seen of the jail was the courtyard above, twelve paces by five, where they were allowed to exercise for an hour each day. It was surrounded by a ten-foot-high wall, with two armed guards in the watchtower. They had seen no one else since they had been brought here from Calcutta. He had no idea what had happened to Holwell.

'When is your baptismal day?' he said.

Tommy lay back on his charpoy, his hands behind his head. 'I've no idea. No one ever told me and I never asked. I just plopped out on the floor, I reckon, and that was it.'

'We had a tradition when I was living in Africa. My mother had kept a record of all our birthing days, and when that day came around, she made us reflect on our lives over the previous year and write down our plans for the future.'

'That must have been nice. My mother just kept a count of how many of us there were and tried not to lose any.'

'Well, let's suppose this is your birthday. What are your plans for the coming year?'

'Number one, I'd like to get out more.' Tommy closed his eyes. 'And if we get out of here – and to be honest, sir, I don't hold out much hope – then I will be due a not untidy sum of back pay. I will spend it on a juicy leg of mutton and a proper ale if I can find one. That's the only thing I still miss about home. The food and the ale.'

'Is London really as bad as you say?'

'My end of it was. The thing I remember most was the soot and grime from all the chimneys everywhere. It was so bad we had candles to light the house in the middle of the day. And at least here, the locals go down to the river to do their business. In Limehouse they just chuck it out the window. Imagine that when winter comes and the streets flood. And you've seen nothing till you see the butcher's stalls round the Tower of London. They throw the guts wherever they like. All you need then is some nob in a carriage to go splashing past with a team of horses on a wet day, and there you are, you're covered in it.'

'What about your family? Don't you miss them? You told me you had ten brothers and sisters.'

'Only half of them were still alive when I left, and there'll be less than that now.'

'You lost five brothers and sisters?'

Tommy nodded. 'Four died from the cough and such when they were mites, and my big brother went to heaven when I was twenty.'

'What happened to him?'

'He was hung for thieving. That was what made up my mind to take up with the army. I only had two choices, me. Get my neck stretched likewise or serve John Company in some place other than England. It wasn't a difficult choice.'

'Funny, Channing made England sound like paradise. He told me that after a few years I could go over there and live like a lord.'

257

'Well, living like a lord is the only way to live, that's a fact. But you need money for that, and it's the one thing poor people don't have.'

Lachlan sat down on his charpoy and stared at the window. 'If we don't get out of here soon, I'll go mad.'

'I reckon that shag bag they made nawab of the place has probably forgotten about us.'

'Once he realises we're no use to him anymore, perhaps he'll let us go.'

'You really think so?'

'You never know. My mother used to say that every man has a bit of good in him.'

'Your old mum. Get out much, did she?'

'She had a good heart.'

'A good heart is like a three-legged horse. It's a novelty to show your friends, but it's not much use in the real world. Can I ask you something of a personal nature?'

Lachlan toyed with the lace of his boot. 'You're going to ask me about Catia.'

'Well, a man hears all sorts of stories over the years.'

'I know what you're going to say, and yes, the bullet was meant for me. It was an act of revenge.'

Tommy thought this over, then said, 'You know what they say, sir. If you go out looking for revenge, first dig two graves. They'll get what's coming.'

'I wish I could believe that.'

Suddenly, they heard shouts outside and a scream cut short. Something heavy tumbled down the stairs.

Lachlan went to the door and peered out through the grill. There were three men standing outside, the tails of their turbans wrapped around their faces. He saw the steel glint of a sword.

So, this was it. Assassins. Someone had decided they were of no more use. He stood back from the door.

Tommy jumped to his feet. He shrugged and puffed out his cheeks. 'Is this it?'

'Looks like it.'

'Well, it was good serving under you, sir. If you get to heaven before me, put in a good word.'

A key rattled in the lock and the door burst open. But as the first man came in, he simply nodded and sheathed his sword. He was dressed in rich silks and expensive mail armour. Elite cavalry, through and through. No assassin this.

The man stood aside and pointed up the stairs. 'Hurry,' he said in Parsi, 'we don't have much time.'

'It seems we have been granted a reprieve,' Lachlan said. He saw the jailer sprawled on his back with his throat cut. He jumped over his body and followed the other two men up the stairs to the courtyard, Tommy behind him.

He blinked in the bright sunlight and looked around for the two guards. One lay crumpled on the ramparts. The other was sprawled like a rag doll in the dirt at the foot of the watchtower.

There were five horses waiting for them. One of the soldiers tossed him and Tommy robes and turbans like theirs. They dressed quickly, climbed on the two spare mounts and followed the three men through the gates.

Their saviours were an intimidating sight with their rich cavalry robes and liveried horses, silk scarves over their faces. People in the street outside averted their eyes and hurried to get out of the way.

Lachlan saw a sprawling wooden palace to their right and realised that for the last year they had been imprisoned within a stone's throw of old Alivardi Khan's residence. His mind raced. He still wasn't convinced this wasn't a trick.

They galloped through one of the triple gates to the river.

Ever since he had been taken prisoner in Calcutta, his world had been circumscribed by a courtyard wall. He reined in his horse and pulled back his scarf for a moment, to breathe in the tang of the river. The quicksilver of the water and the colours of the peacock boats dazzled him. He wanted to shout out with relief.

Then one of their rescuers turned around and scolded him to cover his face, and they hurried on.

They rode through a red brick gate into a large compound. Behind the high walls were gardens, tanks and pavilions. On one side, there was a white temple with a conical roof decorated with gold leaf. They dismounted in front of a pond filled with lily pads, a Greek statue at its centre.

'Well, this is more like it,' Tommy said.

Their escort ushered them up the steps of what appeared to be an Athenian palace. It had an emblem on its façade, two golden lions rampant. There was more Greek statuary on the roof. After the dank prison cell, the opulence was disorienting.

They went inside. A marble floor, polished to a mirror-like sheen, reflected the white pillars supporting the cedar roof beams. There were gilt framed mirrors around the walls and a dozen or more lacquered Oriental vases, almost as tall as a man.

They were taken to a bathing room. Servants shaved their beards and combed their hair. They were allowed to soak in two steaming marble baths and then given clean white Mohammedan robes.

'Where's my uniform?' Tommy said.

Lachlan spoke to one of the servants in Parsi, then turned back to Tommy. 'He says it was home to a family of lice. He burned it.'

'Burned it? How will I explain that to the quartermaster?'

Lachlan laughed. 'That's what I love about you, Tommy. An army man through and through.'

CHAPTER 51

Their benefactor was waiting for them in a pavilion in the court-yard. He was wearing a gold silk robe with a white turban. A string of pearls hung around his neck and rubies glittered on his fingers. A servant sat behind him with a fly whisk.

'Mir Jafar,' Lachlan murmured under his breath as they walked in.

Tommy looked puzzled. 'Who is he?'

'He's one of Siraj's generals. It was his men who were taking pot shots at us from the roof of our godowns in Calcutta.'

'So, what does he want with us?'

'We'll soon find out.' Lachlan bowed in the British manner. 'My lord.'

Mir Jafar said in Parsi, 'You know who I am?' His voice was surprisingly reedy and thin.

Lachlan nodded.

'Be at ease. No one knows you are here. This house belongs to the Jagat Seth. Not even the nawab would dare to come here uninvited.' He indicated they should sit next to him on the cushions.

'We owe you a debt of thanks for our release from prison,' Lachlan said.

Mir Jafar nodded in acknowledgment.

'May I ask why you did it?'

'Because I need your help.'

'My lord, that seems unlikely, considering my present predicament.'

'I understand your confusion. But much has happened while you have been enjoying the nawab's hospitality. For instance, your Mister Clive has come up from Madras with a fleet of ships and a small army and retaken Calcutta.'

Lachlan was shocked but tried not to let it show on his face. He had assumed that Bengal was lost. But if Clive was here, that changed everything.

'Not content with that,' Mir Jafar went on, 'he has also taken Chandernaggar from the French. It is impressive.'

'He enjoys a fight.'

'I hope so. I hope so very much.' Mir Jafar clapped his hands for refreshments. 'But I suppose you are wondering how this situation came about?'

'I suppose I am.'

'Our new nawab does not understand the finer points of business, such as the trade in saltpetre, silk, cotton, pepper and muslins. These are things that Bengal has in abundance, that the whole world is eager to buy from us. It is your British East India Company ships that makes this trade possible.'

'To our mutual profit.'

'Siraj thinks he can organise it on his own, with a little help from the French.'

'I very much doubt that. Besides, my country will not relinquish their part in the trade without a fight. Many of our lords in England own a large share of the Company. Captain Clive himself is heavily invested.'

'Alivardi Khan said you people were just merchants and not much to be feared. Everyone thought he was right when Siraj took Calcutta. But now, your Mister Clive has retaken the city, thrown the French out of Chandernaggar, and forced Siraj to the negotiating table. I warned our fledgling nawab that this would happen, but he would not listen to me.'

'So, you no longer believe that Britain is just a nation of shopkeepers?'

Mir Jafar smiled. 'I never did think that. Even before you came here, I was following your career, and that of Mister Clive, in the Coromandel. I saw how he brought the supposedly mighty French to the treaty table there as well. You yourself are lauded as the Tiger of Karimkot. Am I right?'

'A lot has been made of my part in that action. There were many brave and resolute men who fought with me.'

'I agree. You British have been much underestimated.'

A servant brought them *sharbats* on a silver tray.

'You like the cup?' Mir Jafar said.

'It's very handsome.'

'Look inside. What colour is it?'

'Silver.'

'Good. It changes to a copper colour if the contents are poisoned. You can never trust anyone these days.'

Tommy stirred his *sharbat* with a finger and took a long, second look.

'Here is some more news you will not have heard while you were shut away in Siraj's prison,' Mir Jafar said. 'A war has started in Europe between you English and the French. Of course, that means you are at war with them here in Hindustan as well.'

'We will prevail.'

'I think perhaps you will. But whatever the outcome, it would not trouble us unduly if it were not for our new nawab.'

'You are afraid Siraj is going to draw you into the war on the French side.'

'He already has. Your Mister Clive has named Siraj as his principal enemy in Bengal.'

'It's not too late. Siraj could negotiate a way out of this.'

'And a wise man would do so. But Siraj is not a wise man. Being vicious is not a virtue when you are weak. He is also ignorant, reckless, unreasonable and arrogant. Some say it is because he is young, but others think that even if he lives to be two hundred years old, he will still be as stupid as he is now.'

'And you are one of them?'

A nod.

'So how may I be of assistance,' Lachlan said, his mind moving over a thousand possibilities, trying to catch up.

Mir Jafar put up a hand. 'In a moment. First, let me ask you, how do you British reward your generals after they have won you a great victory?'

'Promotion. Financial rewards. Medals.'

'It is the least a great man should expect, yes? After I besieged and captured Calcutta, I expected the same from Siraj. Instead, he gave the governorship of the city to one of my greatest rivals. A man I personally detest.'

'Aziz Khan?'

'Yes. I see you were paying attention while you were Resident here. I am not the only one aggrieved by Siraj's conduct. I and many of my fellow generals fought the Maratha invaders for his grandfather, year upon year, keeping them from ravaging our cities and our homes. And what thanks do we get from Siraj? He screams and shouts at us in foul language and blames us for every reverse.'

'He has always been so. While I was Resident, I tried to persuade Alivardi Khan, may God bless him and grant him repose, to make a different choice for Crown prince.'

Mir Jafar nodded. 'I am not the only powerful man he has disappointed.' He looked around the marble room where they were sitting. 'The Jagat Seth believe he is going to move against them soon. He wants their money, all of it. He demanded thirty million rupees a year from them to pay for his war against you British. When they refused, he slapped Mehtab Chand, the head of the family, around the face. He did this in the *durbar* in front of everyone.'

'That was very unwise.'

'It was shocking and stupid beyond words. What Siraj has never bothered to learn, is that wars are not fought by soldiers. They are fought by bankers. And the Jagat Seth is the greatest bank in the world.'

'So, you and the Jagat Seth want to get rid of Siraj ud-Daulah.'

Mir Jafar nodded. 'Yes. And you are going to help us.'

'We have to act quickly,' Mir Jafar said. 'Your Mister Clive is getting ready to leave Calcutta and return to Madras. My spies say he is worried about a French attack in the Coromandel.'

'So, what do you want from me?' Lachlan said.

'I need you to go to Calcutta and talk to him. Persuade him to come north to Murshidabad and help us remove Siraj from the throne. We are prepared to offer twenty-eight million rupees to your Company for this service.'

'But that's the entire annual revenue of Bengal.'

'In return, once Siraj's forces have been defeated, Mister Clive will confirm my position as the new nawab. I am prepared to offer a further one hundred thousand rupees a month to pay for Company troops to ensure my protection.'

Lachlan stared at him, stunned.

'In addition, your Company will be permitted to create their own mint in Calcutta, and all trade in and out of Bengal will be duty free.'

'That is an extravagant offer.'

'I would also be prepared to offer your Company ten million rupees in compensation for the loss of Calcutta and another five million to those European inhabitants inconvenienced by our incursions.'

Lachlan took a deep breath. It was a vast sum. Clive's eyes would water at that. But even if Mir Jafar became nawab, he could not stand surety for this kind of money. He was only a puppet. The Jagat Seth must be behind it.

'Is this even possible?'

'Siraj is at his weakest right now. He cannot deploy all his army against Mister Clive, because he must guard his northern border against the Marathas. He owes them arrears on the annual tribute we pay them to keep them from invading us.'

'If you want me to ask Captain Clive to take his forces against Siraj, he will want to know what he is up against.'

'Siraj is presently at Plassey, thirty miles to the south of here. He has with him fifty thousand men, mostly irregulars. He also has fifty field guns and a battery of French artillery.'

'He has Frenchmen with him?'

Mir Jafar nodded. 'Another Frenchman called Kilcannon has supplied Siraj's army with Charleville muskets.'

Kilcannon, Lachlan thought. That bastard seems to pop up anywhere there's blood on the floor. 'We will be hopelessly outnumbered,' he said, 'even without the French cannons.'

'You must tell Mister Clive not to concern himself with these numbers. I will shortly be riding to Plassey to take command of my troops there, and so will several other generals sympathetic to our cause. At a key point in the battle, my forces will turn around and attack Siraj from the flank.

My fellow generals will do the same and turn the tide of the battle in your favour.'

'And this offer will be in writing?'

'The document is being prepared as we speak. You must be ready to leave here as soon as it is dark. You must reach Mister Clive before he sails back to Madras.'

CHAPTER 52

A fter the slop they had been served while they were in prison, the meal that Mir Jafar had prepared for them was like a king's banquet.

Servants brought in earthenware pots piled with roasted lamb, stews spiced with saffron, cardamom and cinnamon, along with pickled vegetables and thick lentil gravies.

There were baked flaky flatbreads oozing with ghee, and when they had eaten their fill and thought they could eat no more, the dishes were replaced with candied fruits, exotic sherbets, and silky sweetmeats flecked with precious silver leaf.

Afterwards, Tommy leaned back in his oversized kaftan and patted his belly. 'Well, that's done it. Something terrible's going to happen.'

'What do you mean?' Lachlan said.

'Stands to reason. Whenever something this good comes along, life has to balance it out somehow. So we're for it, mark my words.'

'That's a very grim view of life.'

'Just stating the facts, sir. So, tell me what Mir Jafar had to say. I didn't understand a word.'

'Well, to begin with, it seems this palace doesn't belong to him. It belongs to the Jagat Seth.'

'Who's he?'

'It's not a *he*, it's a *they*. They're a family of bankers. Years ago, one of the Mughal emperors made Jagat Seth their official title. It means bankers to the world. They have enormous power here. They may not be the nawabs, but they are the nawab *makers*. They have their own mint, and they control the exchange rates. It's said they could dam the entire Cossimbazar river with gold bars. With that much money, they can pretty much make or break anyone in Bengal.'

'Must be nice not to worry about money.'

Lachlan smiled. 'But they do worry, Tommy. They have so much of it, all they ever do is worry. Worry they're going to lose it.'

'So, where does this Mir Jafar come into it, then?'

'Mir Jafar is a general with no talent for politics whatsoever. He's just the front man for the Jagat Seth. They are frightened that Siraj has become so unstable, he will try to steal their bank. They're going to get rid of him before he can do any harm. But they need the Company to help them do it.'

'What do they want you to do?'

'Mir Jafar wants me to persuade Clive to invade Bengal, depose Siraj, and basically do their dirty work for them.'

'Will Captain Clive do that?'

'I think there's a very good chance he will. If it was about glory or land, he might hesitate. But this is about money. It's what everyone fights over.'

'I don't.'

'No, you don't. You're just a soldier.'

Tommy frowned, unsure if he'd been insulted. But he knew Lachlan better than that. 'And you, sir?'

'Me, I'm only the messenger boy. What the Company does, or what the Jagat Seth do, doesn't interest me. There's only one reason I'd ever want to come back here, and it has nothing to do with glory or money.'

The lamps had already been lit about the house and gardens when Mir Jafar and his son, Miran, handed Lachlan a rolled parchment, duly signed and notarised, outlining their offer to the Company. Afterwards, both men took an oath on the Koran to solemnify their treaty obligations.

Lachlan hid the scroll inside the folds of his robes.

When it was done, Mir Jafar jumped to his feet. He looked nervous. He was a military man and not made for intrigue. 'If that gets into the wrong hands,' he said, 'it is death for all of us.'

'I understand,' Lachlan said.

'I have made arrangements to get you safely out of Murshidabad. May God shine upon our purpose, but let darkness be your friend.'

'Before I go, I have one thing to ask of you.'

Mir Jafar looked irritated. 'I have already done a great deal.'

'It's about Aziz Khan's daughter.'

Mir Jafar shook his head. 'There's nothing I can do for you.'

'Can't you even tell me what has happened to her?'

'What goes on in another man's *zenana* is a matter for him and him alone. That door is closed. Matters of the heart do not concern me.'

'You have heard no word of her at all?'

Mir Jafar shook his head, his face a mask.

So that's it then, Lachlan thought. She must be dead. But he wasn't ready to let it be. Not yet.

A donkey cart, loaded with melons and pumpkins, stood under the burning torches at the gateway. Two dark-skinned men in white turbans held the reins. Lachlan and Tommy stood to one side, waiting to get into the back of the tray.

Mir Jafar looked them over. He frowned and shook his head. 'No, this will not do. You look like English *mem'sahib*s straight off the boat. Whose idea was it to give you baths?'

He said something to one of the servants and the man hurried away. He returned with two pails of freshly dug earth and was about to put some on their faces, when Tommy took a step back.

'English,' Mir Jafar said. 'This is for your own protection. Have you ever seen a peasant *ryot* with skin as white as yours? And don't strut around with your head in the air like that. Drop your eyes. Hunch your shoulders. That's better. If you don't look like a beaten dog, you'll get robbed before you even leave the gates.'

Mir Jafar's servant smeared handfuls of damp soil over their faces, necks, arms and feet – every patch of skin that was bare to the world.

'Mister Clive is camped just outside Calcutta,' Mir Jafar told Lachlan while this was being done. 'You have a long journey in front of you.'

'Is this it then?' Lachlan said. 'No escort?'

'I want you to look like simple villagers on the way to market. You must be your own bodyguards.' He pushed aside the melons and showed them a wicker basket in the back of the cart. Inside were two pistols, a musket, two swords and two canvas bags of powder and ball. 'I hope you will not need these.'

Lachlan climbed into the back of the cart. Tommy jumped up beside him.

'By morning, you will be far from Murshidabad,' Mir Jafar said. 'These men know the way.'

The driver cracked his whip, and the cart bounced away through the arch.

As they reached the city outskirts, Lachlan looked back just once at the silhouettes of the mosques and palaces, crouched in the darkness under the crescent moon.

He promised himself he would be back.

CHAPTER 53

The road tracked the grey and turbid surge of the Cossimbazar river, which they could sometimes glimpse through the banana palms and tamarind trees. The land was flat, with rice and cotton paddies on either side.

They were seldom alone. Women in dusty saris passed by, earthenware jugs or wicker baskets of fruits and vegetables balanced on their heads. Hordes of bullock carts and other hackeries trundled up and down.

The villages they saw were mostly a jumble of miserable clay cottages with thatched roofs. Old men lay under the eaves, one leg hanging over their string charpoys, while mothers and grandmothers fanned themselves with palm leaves or brushed the dirt from their doorways with bunches of twigs.

No one seemed to notice them. They wore the ends of their turbans around their faces, but two men riding in the back of a cart were unremarkable and rarely attracted a glance.

They slept that first night at the side of the road. Their two companions kept themselves apart. Occasionally, Lachlan heard them speaking in whispers. They seemed to acknowledge no difference between Lachlan and Tommy and their load of pumpkins.

The next morning, they set off on a lonely stretch of road. The cart swayed wildly as it bumped over the potholes. One of the drivers shouted an oath as a huge water buffalo rose from a mud wallow, where it had been lying half submerged, cooling itself from the deadening heat of the afternoon. It darted in front of them, braying in protest.

They passed a holy man, mostly naked except for a rag passed between his legs and held up with string. He had rubbed himself head to foot in ashes made from mud and cow dung, which gave him a strange, blueish appearance. He was so thin as to be almost skeletal, his fingernails like the talons of a long dead bird. His hair was matted, and he wore the filthy pile on top of his head, wrapped loosely in a turban. He carried a trident and a drum.

'Primitive,' Tommy said lying back in the nest he had made in the pumpkins.

'Primitives like him invented mathematics,' Lachlan said.

'Sir?'

'Two thousand years ago, one of their astronomers explained gravity and algebra. They also invented the number for nothing.'

'What good's that?'

'Without it, mathematics would be impossible. And without mathematics, you wouldn't get paid every month.'

'You're pulling my leg.'

'Compared to these people, we're barbarians. It's just that we have better cannons and better military tactics. That's what makes civilizations great in the end. It's not architecture or education or literature. It's having a bigger gun.'

'Sometimes I'm not sure which side you're on.'

Lachlan laughed. 'Neither am I, Tommy. Neither am I.'

On the third morning, Lachlan suddenly sat up, feeling the hairs prickle at the back of his neck. He looked around. A sixth sense told him that something was wrong. It was unusually quiet. He wiped the sweat from his face with a neck cloth.

'What is it, sir?' Tommy said.

'I don't know.'

Just as he said it, there was the crash of a musket shot. They stared at each other, wondering which one of them had been hit. Then their driver toppled backwards on top of them, a bloody hole in the middle of his chest.

Lachlan leaped from the cart. There was a man standing almost out of sight, in the heavy shade of a mango tree at the side of the road, trying to reload an ancient blunderbuss. The man was not skilled. He dropped half the powder onto the ground.

Lachlan ran towards him. The man looked up and froze, open-mouthed. It seemed not to have occurred to him that unarmed peasants might fight back. Lachlan had a knife inside his robe, and he hit him over the head with the blunt end of it using as much force as he could. The man dropped like a stone.

Another *dacoit* was standing no more than ten feet away, a matchlock rifle aimed at Lachlan's head. At that range, he could hardly miss. There was a crash and a cloud of white smoke, and Lachlan felt the lead ball whizz past his ear. For a moment, he was too stunned to move. He couldn't believe he was still alive.

There was another crash, and a red hole appeared in the middle of the man's forehead. A bead of blood oozed out of it and ran like a carmine tear down his face. He crumpled where he stood.

Tommy was standing on the running board holding one of the muskets Mir Jafar had given to them. Smoke drifted from the barrel. 'Behind you!' he shouted.

Lachlan span around. A third *dacoit* ran at him with a rusted sword. Lachlan picked up the rifle lying at his feet and swung it. It caught the man under the chin. There was a loud snap as his jaw broke, and he rose up in the air and landed on his back. His head cracked on a tree root. He lay still, staring at the sky.

All that was left now was a young boy, no more than nine or ten years old by Lachlan's reckoning, holding a long knife. He was skin and bone and shaking with fear.

Lachlan took the knife out of his hands and jerked his head. 'Go on, lad. Be off with you,' he said.

The boy turned on his heel and ran away through the trees.

'Bandits,' Tommy said. He jumped down off the wagon and examined the three bodies. 'This one's still alive.' He pointed to the one Lachlan had hit with the butt of his knife. 'What shall we do with him?'

'Leave him,' Lachlan said.

'Do you think Siraj sent them?'

'If he wanted to stop us, he'd have sent a regiment, not three old uncles and a boy. No, these are just *dacoits* looking for an easy mark.' He turned back to the road. 'Where's our cart?'

'Oh, the loveless bastard,' Tommy said.

The cart was gone. It was almost out of sight already, their driver's matey boy keeping the donkeys to a steady canter down the path.

'He's left us here,' Lachlan said.

'Do you think we can catch him?'

'In this heat?'

'Perhaps he just panicked. He'll wait for us in the next village.'

'Of course,' Lachlan said with a sigh. 'I'm sure he will.' He put the knife back in his robe. 'But if he doesn't, I suppose we'll have to walk.'

CHAPTER 54

Calcutta

For two days, they had been living on fruit they foraged from the trees at the side of the road and drinking water from the river. Occasionally, they rested in the shade, fighting the desperate urge to fall down and sleep. If they did, Lachlan worried they wouldn't ever get up again.

By the third day, all he could do was put one foot in front of the other, trying not to think about opium or Yasmin or Catia or eating proper food.

Finally, they saw the white haze of campfires from Clive's camp in the distance. They knew there would be pickets placed around the perimeter, but the two soldiers they came across were busy talking and smoking pipes, their muskets resting against the trunk of a peepul tree.

Tommy swore under his breath. 'What are those two clowns doing?'

They were almost past them, when one of them looked up and shouted out in alarm. He scrambled for his musket. 'Where are you going, Mohammed?'

Lachlan took off his turban to reveal his curly blonde hair. The men stared at him in shock.

Tommy marched up to the one with the musket and stood in front of him, legs akimbo. 'What do you think you are doing, son? You are a disgrace to the uniform!'

The boy's face fell, shocked at being upbraided by a Hindustani peasant with an East London accent.

Tommy turned to the other man. 'What are you looking at?'

The soldier started to raise his musket, then lowered it again.,

'I said, what are you looking at?'

'Who are you?'

'What does it look like? I am a sergeant in the First Madras Regiment, so when you speak to me, I expect you to call me Sergeant, *sir*. You got that?'

The sentry nodded.

'Again!'

'Yes, Sergeant sir! But why are you dressed like that then?'

Tommy put his face close to the young man's. 'It's none of your business how I am dressed, son! You are supposed to be on picket duty, not lazing around smoking and scratching your hairy balls! Do you hear me?'

'Yes, Sergeant, sir.'

'That's better.' Tommy said. He took off his turban and put it under his arm as if it was his dress shako. 'Now, will you please inform your commanding officer that Lieutenant Lachlan McKenzie and Sergeant Thomas Baker of the First Madras Regiment are reporting for duty. Got that? Right, off you go.'

Lachlan and Tommy were brought into Clive's tent, still wearing their Mohammedan robes. Tommy saluted smartly, even somehow managing to click together his sandalled feet. Lachlan threw off a reluctant salute.

The man likes his comforts, Lachlan thought, looking around. The floor of the tent was covered in a silk carpet of burgundy and royal blue. Clive was sprawled in a canvas chair, drinking brandy out of a silver cup. His lieutenants and secretaries hovered in his wake.

'The Tiger of Karimkot!' he shouted. 'I have not had the pleasure since Kaveripauk. You made a good account of yourself as I remember. And now, here you are, escaped from the maw of the beast. You, sir, are a remarkable young man.'

'Thank you, sir,' Lachlan said, aware that he was being charmed. It made him wary.

'How did you escape from Murshidabad?'

'We were assisted by one of the nawab's generals, Mir Jafar.' He reached inside his peasant robes and produced the scroll in its leather tube that Mir Jafar had given him. 'He asked me to give you this, Captain.'

'It's Colonel now by the way,' Clive said. He took it and read it through quickly. 'Good Lord,' he said and then read it through again. 'Good Lord.' He looked up. 'Do you trust him?'

'As well as I would trust any traitor. But he is not the guiding hand behind that document. I believe the funding for the offer comes from the Jagat Seth. Mir Jafar told me that they fear they will lose everything if Siraj has his way.'

'What to make of this, I wonder? It is a great opportunity. Unheard of. But it may also be a trap. I shall have to call a council of war to discuss this with my officers. You had better attend, McKenzie. I believe they will have questions for you.'

'It's a trap,' one of the younger officers said as soon as Clive had finished reading out the document.

'And yet they are the ones who have it all to lose,' Lachlan said. 'I know from my time at Murshidabad that Siraj despises the Jagat Seth. He is jealous of their power and their money.'

'The sums they are offering are fantastical.'

Lachlan shook his head. 'To you, perhaps. To them it is nothing if it secures their future.'

'Yet these bankers won't be on the battlefield at the critical moment.'

'Bankers are never on the battlefield, gentlemen,' Lachlan said, 'but you fight to the death for them every day.'

There was a chill in the room when he said that. Even Clive looked discomfited. A captain from the Green Linnets shook his head and frowned.

'Captain Bennett,' Clive said. 'You have something to say?'

Bennett turned to Lachlan. 'Lieutenant, to be clear, you didn't speak to these mysterious bankers though, did you? You spoke to Mir Jafar.'

'That's right, sir.'

'And didn't Mir Jafar command the Mughal forces that invested and looted Calcutta?' Bennett knew the answer and didn't wait for a reply. 'Isn't he our bitter enemy?'

'If you count things as black and white,' Lachlan said, 'then you do not understand the first thing about politics in Bengal.'

Bennett looked angry at being rebuked by a mere lieutenant.

As Lachlan listened to himself, he wondered why he had chosen to argue so vehemently on Mir Jafar's behalf. He didn't give a damn about the Company. This was about his own unfinished business.

Bennett persisted. 'The Company's instructions to us were to defend our interests from the French. We do not have the remit to start a possibly disastrous war with the Nawab of Bengal.'

Clive could not keep the expression of distaste from his face. Lachlan knew what he was thinking. Since when had blowsy men in powdered wigs sitting in an office in Leadenhall Street told him what to do?

'Besides, it is fifteen miles to Siraj's capital, and it will soon be the monsoon season,' Bennett went on. 'How will we bring up our supplies?'

'We have the barges that brought us across the river,' Clive said reasonably.

'You intend to tow our cannons and ammunition upstream?'

'Why not?' Clive said and smiled. 'The fact is, this is no longer just Company business.' He turned to a man dressed in full fig who had been keeping his own counsel in the shadows at the rear of the tent. 'Is it, Admiral Watson?'

Watson stepped forward and his commanding presence intimidated the younger men in the room. 'What Colonel Clive says is true. We are now at war with France, and it is our bounded duty to distress them at every opportunity. As it now appears that Siraj is their client prince, he can be also counted as French for our purposes.'

Clive turned to face the rest of his staff, stabbing his forefinger on the table to emphasise his words. 'Our intelligence says that Siraj has met with the French commander in Bengal, Jean Law, and asked him to persuade the Marquis de Busy to bring his army north from his base in the Deccan to join him in attacking us.'

'How do we know this?' Bennett said.

'We captured a French courier. He had letters on him from Law.'

Bennett turned to the admiral. 'Will you be coming with us, sir?'

'I wish I could,' Watson said, 'but the river is too shallow for my warships.'

Bennett looked at Clive. 'Not having Admiral Watson's guns puts us at a considerable disadvantage.'

The major standing at Clive's side had been growing increasingly red in the face but had so far said nothing. Lachlan knew him by reputation. Eyre Coote was young for such a senior commission, not much past thirty, but he had a fearsome reputation.

'What do you say, Major?' Clive said.

Coote had been eager to voice his opinion and his voice was unwavering. 'Ever since we landed at Calcutta, we have taken the fight to Siraj ud-Daulah, and we have prevailed despite his superior numbers. Aggression and daring always win the day. I am with you, Colonel Clive. Should we turn back now, we shall give heart to the enemy, and I believe such timidity will lead inevitably to the Company's destruction in Bengal.'

A gunnery captain from the Bengal Artillery nodded. 'My men are itching for a fight. They were the lucky ones that escaped when Calcutta fell. Many lost their comrades in the Black Hole.'

'Is that what they're calling it?' Lachlan said.

'You were there,' Clive said. 'Do you have a better name?' He turned to the rest of the men in the room. 'This is no longer just about protecting the Company's interests, nor is it about our country's war against the French, though I know that every true patriot among you must be eager to answer the bugle call.

'No gentlemen, we are taking up arms in the name of justice and freedom. We have the opportunity to exact retribution for all those poor souls who lost their lives in the Black Hole at Calcutta. The enemy ranged against us are nothing better than savages. We have God on our side, I have no doubt of it.'

Lachlan stared at him, astounded.

Clive's eyes shone with a fervour that was both daunting and disturbing. 'We must bring this villain to account for his foul deeds in Calcutta,' he went on. He turned to Lachlan. 'Do you not agree, sir?'

Lachlan thought about Muttubby and nodded.

'You are a hero, sir, and a fortunate one.' Clive looked at the others. 'Councillor Holwell tells us that one hundred and forty-six souls were imprisoned on Siraj ud-Daulah's orders in a cell barely large enough for half a dozen. Only twenty-three walked out alive the next morning.'

Lachlan could not believe his ears. By his count, the number was less than half that, and Siraj, for all that he was no friend to the British, had had nothing to do with it.

'It is decided, then,' Clive said, with a hard stare at everyone in the tent. 'We go to Murshidabad!'

Lachlan realised that this council of war had been merely an imprimatur. Clive had made up his mind what he was going to do the moment Lachlan gave him the letter from Mir Jafar.

As everyone filed out of the tent, Clive called Lachlan back. 'So, what now for you, Lieutenant. You have served the Company well. Back to Madras for a well-earned rest? I'm sure the Board in London will be very generous in their reward for your efforts.'

'If it's all the same to you, sir, I should like to accompany you on the rest of the campaign. I want to see this through to the end.'

Clive seemed gratified with the reply. 'That's the spirit, McKenzie. A man after my own heart. Men like us don't know the meaning of fatigue, eh? I shall be glad to have you along.' He pursed his lips in thought. 'I'm giving you command of one of the sepoy regiments. They're a rough lot, untouchables from Bihar, but they know their business. Think you can manage?'

Lachlan smiled and nodded. 'I'll manage,' he said.

Murshidabad, he thought. At last I'll find out what happened to her.

CHAPTER 55

R edcoats squatted next to their cookfires, cleaning their muskets and sharpening their hangers with stones. In a few yards, Lachlan heard a dozen languages and dialects - Urdu, Hindustani, Irish, Brummies, Scots. These men had come from everywhere to fight in Clive's army, and he would wager it wasn't justice or freedom that had brought them here.

'What did you think of all that?' he said.

Tommy tilted his head. 'Colonel Clive's little speech, you mean? Well sir, to be honest, when I hear men with wigs and braided coats talk about law and civility, my fundament starts to squeak.'

Lachlan laughed. 'I know just what you mean. Let's get a drink.'

Clive had organised a tent for Lachlan not far from his own. It had a portable camp table, a chair, a rattan cot and a washstand. More importantly, there was a cowrie basket full of basic supplies. Underneath the packets of tea and sugar and wax candles, Lachlan found a bottle of brandy. He opened it and splashed some into two enamel mugs.

He handed one to Tommy. 'You don't have to stand to attention in here. Now drink this. You've more than earned it.'

'Thank you, sir. Nice drop.'

'Black Hole of Calcutta. I wonder who thought of that. Siraj has played right into their hands.'

Tommy frowned. 'It was bad enough as it was without doubling up the numbers.'

They finished their cups of brandy and Lachlan poured two more.

'Don't mind me asking, sir, what's your plan?'

'The plan is to serve the Company and its interests the best way I can.'

'No, really.'

Lachlan smiled. 'My plan is to get to Murshidabad, go to Aziz Khan's palace and discover what has become of Yasmin and Nafisa.'

'And then what?'

'It's my guess that they have both been murdered by that brute.'

'But if not?'

'I haven't thought that far.'

'You're a terrible liar, sir. I have been your adjutant for four years now, and I would say you have planned your next move to the finest detail.'

'Perhaps you're right.'

As he swallowed his brandy, Lachlan felt the tension draining out of him. What he needed now was a good dinner and a long sleep. Knowing Clive, he doubted that he would get either. 'Have you ever thought about going home, Tommy?'

'This is my home, sir. The regiment is my family, so to speak. It's not much but I don't know what I'd do without it.'

'You've never thought to live to an old age surrounded by your adoring grandchildren?'

'I shall more likely expire in middle age with my boots muddied in the middle of god-awful nowhere. If it's quick and painless I shan't mind.' He finished his brandy. 'I should best be getting to bed, sir. You know what Colonel Clive is like. He'll get us up in the middle of the night and march us to Persia and back. Best sleep while we can.'

After he'd gone, Lachlan lay down on his cot. Exhaustion over-took him. In moments, he was asleep and dreaming about Africa. He thought about a white beach, and a woman's footprints following the wave line beside a frothy lace of surf. He ached to go back.

A second chance to get it right. That was all he wanted.

Everyone had been praying for the monsoon. There had been months of unremitting heat, with towering banks of cloud surging up the sky higher every day. At night, sheet lightning flickered over the plain as the monsoon clouds taunted them with the promise of cooling rains that never came.

But finally, that night, the first storms arrived. Lachlan woke to a rush of wind slamming against the canvas of his tent a few inches from his head. He heard horses neigh in panic, and a moment later, the rain slammed down.

He got out of his cot and looked outside. A flash of forked lightning lit the valley as if it was day. A tent that had not been properly secured was picked up and dragged through the camp by the wind. It was followed by a crash of thunder so loud he thought for a moment he was back at Calcutta standing next to the guns.

'One more battle,' he said to the darkness. 'One more battle and let fate decide.'

A bugle sounded the *reveille* well before dawn. The storm had cleared as quickly as it had come. They woke to a full moon, crisp and clear.

Overnight the land had changed from a dusty plain to a glutinous swamp of red mud. It was too wet to light fires for *chai* or to heat last night's curry for breakfast, so the men made do with cold chapattis and water from their canteens.

It was still dark when the European regiments in their red coats trudged wet and dispirited up the gangplanks onto the small boats that were waiting to ferry them upriver.

The plan was to be break camp early and avoid the heat of the day. But wrangling the field guns and the rest of the ammunition and supplies onboard took much longer than planned, and it was midmorning by the time they were under way.

There wasn't room on board for the native regiments, so Lachlan and his sepoys followed the flotilla on foot as it wound upstream, along embankments and through muddy villages with more goats and ducks than people.

The previous night's rains had woken the crickets and frogs, and the din seemed to drown out every other sound. New seedlings sprouted above the shimmering squares of water in the rice paddies. It was a steaming, green world that even left some of his sepoys gasping and bathed in sweat.

It was slow going. The Cossimbazar had almost flooded its banks, and the men at the tow ropes slid and skidded in the mud, cursing as the barges skewed from side to side in the current. Some of the men jumped into the river up to their waists and tried their luck in the water instead.

Clive was sitting under an awning at the prow of one of the lead boats, his staff with him, still wearing their wigs and red frock coats.

'You could be there, smoking a cheroot with his nibs,' Tommy said.

Lachlan shook his head and pointed at the ragged line of sepoys marching behind them along the muddy bank. 'Tomorrow or the next day, I will have to ask these men to risk their lives in battle. I believe they may be more welcoming to the idea if they know I am prepared to share their discomforts along the way.'

'Don't mind me saying, sir, but you're not like any other officer I ever met.'

'I find you remarkable also, Tommy. I don't know how you do it.'

'Do what, sir?'

'How you keep so bloody cheerful all the time. You have the same disposition if you are dying of thirst in a Calcutta dungeon or half drowned in a swamp.'

'Well, I've nothing to be glum about. I'm a lucky man.'

'How's that?'

'Because whenever I feel a little gloomy, I remind myself that I'm not living in Limehouse or hanging from a gibbet. It's all how you look at things, isn't it.'

Later that day, word came down the line. Clive had called a halt to the march at Paltee.

A town called Katwa lay between them and Plassey. It was held by a small garrison of Siraj's troops. Clive sent Coote ahead with a regiment of sepoys to take possession of it.

As they were making camp, there was another cloudburst. Lachlan was still trying to dry off inside his tent, when one of Clive's staff officers appeared out of the dark. Coote had met little opposition and Katwa was theirs.

And Colonel Clive wanted to see him.

CHAPTER 56

Paltee, south of Murshidabad

Lachlan trudged through the mud, his serge coat soaked through. He had his tricorn pulled down around his ears, and the rain dripped off the peak. He shivered, the rain and wind stinging his sunburned face. A union jack hung limp in the rain outside Clive's tent. A sentry guard lifted the flap for him. He ducked inside.

The tent was crowded and stank of wet wool and unwashed bodies. The entire officer staff were huddled inside, along with Clive's adjutant and his quartermaster. Rainwater trickled steadily through the canvas onto the fine carpets and the map table. Even Clive's wig was sodden. This miserable country.

The mood was tense.

'Ah, Lieutenant McKenzie,' Clive said. 'I'm glad you could join us. I am debating with my officers on whether we should proceed to Murshidabad or wait here for further developments.'

'I thought we were decided,' Lachlan said.

'Some of my officers still have misgivings,' Clive said. 'They are against crossing the Cossimbazar when we are at such a disadvantage. They advocate fortifying ourselves at Katwa and waiting out the monsoon.'

Bennett seemed to have been made spokesperson for the malcontents. 'We do not need to venture as far as Plassey,' he said. 'We can comfortably hold our position here until after the monsoon and then make contact with the Marathas in the north. They would be more than amenable to an alliance. If they attack Siraj from the north as we come from the south, we will crush him easily.'

'And then what will happen in Murshidabad,' Lachlan said, 'after the Marathas have raped and slaughtered and pillaged all the treasure?' He saw the look on Clive's face and knew that his point had been well made. There was only one thing their colonel was interested in, and it wasn't avenging the men and women who had died in Calcutta. He might turn a blind eye to rape and slaughter, but he wasn't having the Marathas beating him to Siraj's treasury.

'I agree with Lieutenant McKenzie,' Clive said. 'An alliance with the Marathas may not be to our ultimate advantage.'

'Besides,' Lachlan went on, 'the city should be our goal, not simply defeating Siraj. May I remind you, Captain Bennett, that the Company has been offered a handsome reward for its time and trouble from Mir Jafar and his allies. I very much doubt that they will pay us twenty-eight million rupees to see their capital sacked by bandits.'

'But what if we are defeated?' Bennett said.

'Rather, what if we are victorious,' Clive said. 'Defeat Siraj, and we can instal a new nawab in Bengal who is sensitive to the Company's needs. *And* we will have the richest men in Asia in our debt. Risk little, gain little.'

Now it was Coote's turn. He was fresh from his victory at Katwa and looked none the worse for his exertions. In fact, it seemed to have cheered him no end. 'Colonel Clive is absolutely right,' he said. 'Our latest intelligence says that Marquis de Busy has moved his troops out of the Deccan to Cuttack on the coast. I have no doubt he is preparing to attack us with Siraj's help. We have not a moment to lose.'

Bennett was intractable. 'But we have just three thousand men,' he said, looking around the tent for support. 'Two thousand of them are natives. We have just eight guns. We are outnumbered by twenty to one.'

'You forget,' Clive said, 'that Mir Jafar has committed to our side. He held up the document that Lachlan had brought with him from Murshidabad. 'He also says that other generals may well follow his lead, such is the enmity that Siraj arouses among his own people. When the battle gets under way, the odds may instead be in our favour.'

'Also, Siraj's men are ill-trained and underpaid,' Coote said. 'Their heart is not in it. At Katwa they ran from us without a shot fired.'

'I still say it's a trap,' Bennett said. 'We cannot trust this Mir Jafar.'

'This is madness,' Coote said, showing his frustration. 'We cannot hold off now.'

Bennett turned to Clive. 'Sir, if this Mir Jafar proves faithless, what happens to Calcutta, what happens to Madras? It will leave those cities undefended. Lose here and we could lose all of India.'

Suddenly everyone was shouting at once.

Finally, Clive held up a hand for silence. 'Leave me all of you. I need to think. Go!'

Chastened, everyone began to file out of the tent. Lachlan turned to leave as well, but Clive called him back. 'A moment of your time please, Lieutenant McKenzie.'

After the others had gone, Clive's customary expression of unbridled optimism slipped off him like a wet cloak. He looked suddenly bereft. He turned to Lachlan with the air of a condemned man. 'I fear Captain Bennett is right,' he said. 'We may be betrayed. I have received this from your friend, Mir Jafar.'

My friend, Lachlan thought. He's no friend of mine.

Clive reached into the pocket of his frock coat and handed Lachlan a letter. The ink had smudged in the damp heat, but he could still read most of it.

He read:

On the news of your coming, the nawab was much intimidated and requested at such a juncture that I would stand his friend. On my part, agreeable to the circumstances of the times, I thought it advisable to acquiesce with his request, but what we have agreed on must be done. I have fixed the first day of the moon for my march. God willing, I shall arrive.

Mir Syed Jafar Ali Khan Bahadur.

'What is his meaning?' Clive said. 'Could he be more ambiguous?'

'Perhaps he is being closely watched. It is more to our advantage that he does not show his hand too early.'

'What if he does not show his hand at all? Siraj will have us at his mercy. The only way we might be victorious is if Mir Jafar keeps his promise. How certain are you that he will be faithful to us?'

Lachlan turned his mind to the conversation that day in the Jagat Seth's palace. The man had been convincing enough then.

'We are just a day's march from Plassey,' Clive said. 'My scouts say there are fifty thousand natives waiting for us there as well as a battery of French artillery. Without Mir Jafar's assistance, we are doomed.'

Lachlan shook his head. 'I believe he is waiting to see what we will do. It may be that if the battle goes against us, he will not come to our aid. But if he sees an opportunity, he will seize the moment. That is the nature of the man.'

'I shall not sleep easy tonight,' Clive said.

This wasn't what Lachlan wanted to hear. He knew Clive to be bluff, reckless and venal, but until now, he knew where he stood with him. No one wanted a commander who wavered in his decisions, whether they were right or wrong.

Clive had thrown his weapons onto the table in front of him when the meeting had started. Now he dragged his flintlock pistol towards him and ran a finger along the barrel. 'Did I ever tell you that I once held a pistol to my own head? I had just come to Madras and the prospect of spending my days in the counting house so depressed my spirits that I sought to end it all.'

Lachlan didn't know what to say. Clive was the last man that he thought would be subject to such melancholy. 'But you changed your mind at the last.'

'No.' Clive shook his head. 'No, I didn't. I pulled the trigger, but the pistol misfired. I remembered my father had once told me that persistence should be rewarded, so I reloaded and fired again. Another misfire.' He stared at his hand as if he could still imagine holding the errant pistol in it. 'I have never decided whether I am alive today because God wished me for greater things, or if I had merely drunk too much *arrack* and was in no fit state to load a weapon. Have you ever been so low that you considered oblivion in a favourable light?'

'No,' Lachlan lied. He listened to the rain patter on the canvas over his head.

Clive looked suddenly disconcerted at having revealed so much of himself. 'Then you are a fortunate man.' He straightened his jacket. 'I have befuddled you with this. You may leave me now.'

'Have you come to a decision about Plassey?'

'Yes. I think Bennett is right. I do not trust your friend, Mir Jafar, and there is too much risk in going further. We shall wait here for further instruction from Calcutta. Leave me now.'

Early the next morning, Lachlan woke to the sound of bugle and drum. Clive had changed his mind.

They marched into a watery world of shimmering fields and lily ponds, the heat making the land appear to float above the flooded rice paddies. The mud stuck to their boots and made every yard an effort. Water buffalo watched warily from their mud wallows.

Towards evening, they saw the thatched roofs of a native village nestled among the bamboo groves and giant banyan trees. Clouds of parakeets screeched into the air in protest as they approached.

Close by, in the crooked elbow of the river, was a small brick hunting lodge shaded by an orange splash of flowering palash trees. The local villagers said it belonged to the nawab. It had started to rain, so Clive set up his headquarters inside.

Lachlan and his sepoys took shelter in their hastily erected tents in the mango orchards behind the lodge. He and Tommy shared a cup of brandy before turning in.

'I still don't understand why nought is a number,' Tommy said.

'What was that?'

'When we were in the back of the cart, coming from Murshidabad, you said the Hindustanis invented a number for nothing. But it can't be a number. Because it's nothing.'

'And that is why the Hindustanis are cleverer than us.'

'Well, let's hope they're not cleverer than us tomorrow.' Tommy drained his cup. 'We're in enough trouble as it is.'

CHAPTER 57

P lassey

  Kilcannon listened to the rain beat down. Aziz Khan seemed un-perturbed by it. Two servants sat either side of him, holding *chatras* above his head to keep off any rain that found its way through the many layers of silk that encompassed the roof of his tent. His banyan appeared dry and snug, and he had his water pipe and a pot of hot, spiced coffee on a brass tray in front of him.

Kilcannon sat beside him on the carpets. He tried to keep his voice reasonable. 'I have supplied the modern guns you asked for. I need payment.'

'You will get your money.'

'Ah, but when. I have overheads. Bribes to pay. Porters to be reimbursed.'

Aziz Khan leaned in. 'We have them.'

'What?'

'The British. They are camped in the Laksha Bagh mango tope. Your French compatriots will start the battle with a bombardment, and then our cavalry will drive them back to the river. We will fall on them as they attempt to board their barges and retreat. They cannot win. They are outmanned and outgunned.'

'Are you listening to me?' Kilcannon raised his voice. 'I have no interest in the outcome of this battle. That is your concern. What I want is my money.'

Aziz Khan waved a hand dismissively. 'And you will have it.'

'When?'

'When this is over.'

'That was not the arrangement.'

'Now is not the time to bother me with this.'

Kilcannon heard trumpets outside. A cavalry troop rode past on black Arabs. The *mahouts* brought up the general's elephant with an escort of barefoot infantry. Some had ancient matchlocks and swords, others had spears. Most had just bows and arrows.

What happened to the thousands of muskets I sold him, Kilcannon thought. Probably onsold to the Marathas for profit.

You couldn't trust anyone these days.

It was dark, and the trees were still dripping from the previous night's downpour, when Lachlan arrived for the war council. Clive's staff officers were gathered around the map table. Clive entered, still struggling into his red frock coat. Just as he was about to start speaking, they heard trumpets and drums close by.

Clive cocked his ear. 'It seems we have found our quarry,' he said.

They went up to the roof terrace. As the sun rose over the plain, they saw Siraj's army almost encircling them to the north and east.

Lachlan held his breath. No one spoke.

'Good God,' someone said, finally.

Lachlan realised that they had almost stumbled straight into Siraj's camp the night before. His army was only about a mile away, drawn up along the length of some hastily prepared earthworks. They ran inland at right angles to the riverbank for about two hundred paces before sweeping around to the north and disappearing into the heat haze.

Between Siraj's army and their position were two tanks, one larger than the other, surrounded by mounds of earth. Lachlan could make out the blue uniforms of a French artillery unit at the larger tank. He counted six guns.

The rest of Siraj's army ringed the redoubt behind them, ragged, colourful and terrifying in their flowing robes, waving their green and white battle flags. Armour flashed up and down the line. It hurt the eyes when it caught the sun.

He heard the screech of war elephants. He took out his spyglass. Siraj's men were bringing up their massive cannons on wooden platforms drawn by teams of forty or fifty oxen. An elephant stood behind each gun, nudging it into position with its forehead. Ingenious but slow.

He swung his spyglass to the east. He smiled grimly when he made out another mass of troops carrying Mir Jafar's banners. 'Can we trust you?' he said under his breath.

'What was that, Lieutenant?' Clive said.

'I said it's a beautiful morning. I love how clean everything looks after the rain.'

There was a stunned silence, then Clive roared with laughter. Only Coote joined in.

'I see no reason for merriment,' Bennett said. 'They have us almost surrounded. I count fifty cannons. We are no match. And if we move forward, we leave our rear totally exposed to Mir Jafar's cavalry.'

'Mir Jafar is committed to us,' Lachlan said.

'You'd trust the word of a native?' Bennett said. 'Dear God. This could turn into a massacre.'

'I think the question of whether or not we can trust Mir Jafar is now moot,' Lachlan said. 'It's too late to retreat. We're committed.'

Clive leaned on the parapet and watched the enemy troops form up. 'Move the troops forward,' he said to Coote. 'Company troops in the centre, three six-pounders on each side. Keep the sepoys in two divisions on the flanks. Place our two other guns with our howitzers there and there to oppose the French guns.' He pointed out two emplacements where the artillery would be partially protected by some brick kilns.

'I'd better get back to my men,' Lachlan said and turned to go.

Clive called him back. 'You're right, a fine day,' he said, 'but it looks like rain later.' He pointed to the clouds lurking on the horizon to the north.

He seemed positively cheerful. Of the man who had spoken about doing away with himself the night before, there was no sign.

Perhaps I imagined it, Lachlan thought.

CHAPTER 58

The sepoys were drawn up in their battle lines in front of the mango tope. Tommy stood ahead of them, his musket at slope. Lachlan made his way towards him through the mud. 'How are the men, Sergeant?'

'They're terrified. There's only one thing keeping them here, sir. That's our Colonel Clive's reputation. They think he knows what he's doing.'

'Well, they're wrong. Today's outcome indeed rests entirely on one man, but it's not our trusty colonel.'

'You mean that cove Jafar? Me, myself, personally, I wouldn't trust him an inch.'

'Now you say.'

'I'm other ranks. Who cares what I think?'

Lachlan told the men to rest and wait. Some of them slumped to their haunches and peeled fruit or took out their clay pipes. There was even some nervous laughter.

He went up to one of the *jemadars* and offered him a cheroot. The man took it as if it were a gold coin, holding it reverently in the palm of his hand until Tommy came up and lit it for him with his pipe.

'What's your name, *Jemadar*?' Lachlan said in Hindustani.

'Hatem Ali, *sahib*.'

'Where are you from?'

'Calcutta, *sahib*.'

'Do you know what nought is?'

'It is an Indian number,' Ali said. 'The most important number there is.'

'And why is that?'

'If you have ten enemies shooting at you and you shoot nine, then you have one enemy left, and he can shoot you back. But if you shoot ten, then there are no enemies left, and that is the perfect number because no enemies can hurt you. So, nought is the most important number there is.'

Lachlan smiled and turned to Tommy. 'There, Sergeant. Nothing is a number. Do you see?'

Lachlan took out his spyglass and watched the relay of smoke along the enemy redoubt, followed by the boom of the cannons as they fired their first salvo.

'Are you sure you'd rather not cosy up to the colonel in the hunting box, sir?' Tommy said. 'It would be safer.'

Lachlan laughed. 'I thought you'd need someone to hold your hand, Tommy. This could get dangerous.'

Their own field guns answered the salvo. As Bennett had been at pains to point out, they were completely outgunned. There could only be one outcome to this. Fortunately, Siraj's Indian gunners lacked training. They were slow and most of their cannonballs exploded harmlessly in the mango grove behind them.

'They can't shoot for shit,' Tommy said. 'Pardon my French.'

Lachlan saw another puff of smoke from the French guns away to his left. Unfortunately for them, the French knew what they were about. The salvo exploded near the centre of Bennett's Green Linnets. A dozen men fell, but they kept their formation. 'We need to get back behind the embankment,' he said.

The French had just four field guns at the tanks, but with each barrage their fire became more accurate and more devastating. Shot after shot fell into the ranks of the infantry facing them.

Lachlan winced and tried to shut his mind to the screams. He turned and looked at the hunting lodge. He saw Clive silhouetted against the sky. 'Come on,' he said, under his breath. 'This is hopeless.'

At last, the order came through. Retreat.

Lachlan followed his men back to the mango grove. It was enclosed by a mud wall which provided natural shelter. He jumped down behind it and caught his breath. He could hear raucous cheers from the enemy lines. They thought they'd won.

Siraj's artillery fired another salvo. Their shot ranged too high, and Lachlan and his men were showered with branches from the tops of the trees.

Their own artillery finally had some success. As Lachlan peered over the wall, he saw one of Siraj's massive field guns blown to pieces by a direct hit. Another shell hit an ammunition wagon. A fireball mushroomed into the sky with a series of loud cracks. Now it was the redcoats' turn to cheer.

But the cheering didn't last long. Within minutes, the French cannonade began again, and Siraj's *spahis* came bellowing down the slope. Lachlan could almost feel the men around him sweat. He waited.

'Sir?' Tommy said.

'Not yet,' Lachlan said. He watched them come. They were mostly ragged peasants. He couldn't see a single one of them with a musket or a decent sword. He tasted bile in the back of his throat. This will be carnage, he thought, but it's them or us.

Closer.

'Sir?' Tommy repeated. There was real urgency in his voice.

'Now!' Lachlan shouted. He aimed at one of the orange-robed men running towards them and fired. Hundreds of muskets barked up and down the line, enveloping them in smoke.

At least this isn't like Calcutta, he thought. This time, every man in his command had a full canvas bag of cartridges. Bite the end, tip some powder into the pan and lock, then ram the rest of the cartridge down the muzzle along with the ball. Lock, aim and fire. And again. A series of quick, mechanical movements.

A cannon ball exploded not twenty paces away, showering him with dirt. A man slumped down, blood spouting from his neck where his head should have been. He prayed it wasn't Tommy. He rammed another ball down his musket, jumped up, aimed and fired.

There was a roar from the gun battery to their left and a salvo of case shot swept through the ranks of Siraj's infantry. When the smoke cleared, the slope was covered with broken and bleeding bodies. A few survivors scattered back towards the native lines.

'Thought we were done for that time,' Tommy said.

Lachlan sagged against the wall and stared at his sergeant, who didn't have a mark on him. 'You're alive.'

'For now, sir. But our *jemadar* copped it.' Tommy pointed to the decapitated corpse between them.

One of Clive's runners came towards them in a crouching run and tapped Lachlan on the shoulder. 'Colonel Clive wants to see you.'

Tommy raised his eyebrows. 'Time for morning tea, sir.'

'Stay here,' Lachlan said, 'I'll bring you back a tiffin cake.'

There was a war council in progress on the roof. Lachlan heard Clive say to one of his runners, 'Tell the gunnery officers to get their powder and fuses under tarpaulins if you please.'

He looked up and saw black thunderheads billowing up the sky. Lightning flashes shimmered among the dark cumulus. Clive was right, there was another downpour coming. He went inside and was hurried up the steps by one of Clive's junior officers.

'We should try to seize their cannon,' Bennett was saying

'That's impossible!' Coote shouted. 'The embrasures are too far apart. We'll run out of men long before they run out of guns.'

'I agree,' Clive said. 'Any frontal attack on their emplacements is doomed to fail.'

'Then what are we going to do?'

Clive tapped his spyglass against his thigh. He looked as if he were trying to solve a difficult chess problem. 'Without knowing Mir Jafar's true purpose, there is nothing we can do. If he does not make his move, we must hold our position here until nightfall. As soon as it is dark, we shall put our muskets over our shoulders and force march back to Calcutta.'

Bennett looked at Lachlan. 'You said we could rely on this Mir Jafar. He's betrayed us. I said he would.' He didn't say, *I told you so,* but it was written all over his face.

Clive held up his hand. 'We don't know that yet,' he said, but the look he gave Lachlan said it all.

Lachlan looked around at the others. They thought they were doomed too.

It was growing darker by the minute. Clouds mushroomed over the plain, and thunder cracked around the sky. It was becoming difficult to distinguish the sounds of the weather from the blast of the guns.

A grey curtain of rain rushed towards them across the paddy. Lachlan could hear it hissing as it approached. Suddenly it swept over them. In moments, they were all drenched and standing ankle deep in rainwater.

Huge drops dripped off Clive's nose. 'Get back to your men, gentlemen,' he said. 'That will be all for now. I need to change. I cannot run a battle in wet clothes.'

CHAPTER 59

Kilcannon sat on a black Arab, unsmiling and unmoved. He had around him two dozen sepoys of his own personal bodyguard. They wore blue uniform jackets and white turbans, their brass buttons and horses' trappings polished to a shine.

The rain had finally eased, leaving the world steaming hot, drenched, misty. He fingered the scar above his eye, following the ridge along to the hairline at his temple. Life and death, he thought, it was all about fine margins.

Aziz Khan formed up his cavalry, ready for the final assault. The horses skittered with excitement, while the men laughed and shouted encouragement to each other, convinced that this was their moment of glory. A forest of spears and swords shimmered in the storm light.

The general raised his sword. The point of his blade was directed at the thin red line at the edge of the tope below.

Allahu Akbar.

They charged. The thunder of a thousand hooves shook the earth. They closed on the British line. Any moment, they would be through the infantry.

Kilcannon watched on, his face impassive.

Suddenly, there was a blossoming of flame as the British guns roared to life. The cannons were immediately enveloped in a drift of white smoke.

Well, that was unexpected. Aziz Khan had told him the British guns would be useless, their powder ruined by the monsoon storm, just as theirs had been.

As the smoke cleared, he saw a litter of men and horses in front of the guns. The second wave thundered over the top of them. He wondered if the British gunners were as good as he had been told. Could they reload that quickly, with horses and steel thundering down on their position?

He heard the booming of another salvo, one gun after the other, and saw more of Aziz Khan's horses fall, before his cavalry was again enveloped by the smoke. So, he supposed his question had just been answered in the affirmative. Moments later, the third wave turned their horses and galloped back to their lines.

He looked for Aziz Khan but did not see him among the survivors. The fool had insisted on leading the charge, thinking it would be glorious. It was incautious of him, to say the least. He took out his spyglass. He focused on the British batteries, saw the redcoats working with clockwork precision as they raised their elevations.

Another salvo raked the embrasures. One of the wooden platforms that Siraj's artillerymen had used to transport their cannons exploded into firewood. A massive barrel catapulted through the air. Men scattered, screaming.

Well, he thought, Aziz Khan has only himself to blame. He had not foreseen the possibility of rain, even though it was the beginning of the monsoon season, and their enemy had. Perhaps it was because they were British, and they never discounted the weather, no matter where they were.

One of the war elephants, panicked by the cannonade, turned and charged back towards the rear. The *howdah* on its back lurched sideways, throwing the *mahout* and several archers into the mud. Kilcannon froze, thinking the beast was heading straight for him, but at the last moment it veered away, trumpeting in alarm, leaving a wreckage of bullock carts and trampled tents in its wake. He saw a body stir in the mud then lie still.

A team of oxen was struggling to pull a massive cannon free of the quagmire, bellowing under the whips of their overseers.

One of the gunners saw something heading towards their redoubt. He shouted a warning to his comrades and started to run. The rest of the gunners leaped from the platform and followed him.

A British infantry regiment was headed up the slope.

The trickle of deserters became a flood. Barefoot soldiers threw down their spears and fled. An officer on a white horse slashed at one man with his sword, trying to make him go back. He swung again and again, but the man ducked and swerved and kept running.

Kilcannon looked away to the left. Mir Jafar's cavalry should have been closing in on the British flank. Instead, they were still at station. What was he up to?

He trained his glass on the other flank, closest to the river. Several more cavalry regiments were riding away in perfect order, their muskets strapped across their backs.

No panic there. The men were clearly obeying their officers' orders and returning to the city.

He turned to his *jemadar*. 'I believe it is time for us to return to Murshidabad.'

If Aziz Khan was dead, well that was unfortunate, but he had a plan for such an eventuality. One way or another, he intended to get the money that was owed to him, and perhaps even a little bonus on top.

The afternoon was dull and hot, the low grey clouds pressing upon the earth itself. The red coated gunners were keeping up a steady fire. Lachlan watched them working and took a moment to admire their skill and discipline. At every count of thirty, the nine-pounders coughed orange flame and jumped back on their limbers.

Still there was no answer from Siraj's guns.

He raised his head over the wall and brought up his spyglass. The ground between their position and the enemy line was littered with the bodies of men and horses. Some of them were still alive, but God alone knew how. It was another butcher's yard like Calcutta. How did men make a profession of this sort of thing?

A messenger, a young ensign, made his way through the tope, his boots sticking in the cloying mud. He shook the water from his oilcloth cape and saluted. 'Colonel Clive's compliments,' he said. He reached inside his jacket, took out a leather pouch and handed it to Lachlan.

Lachlan opened it and examined the scribbled orders from Clive. He turned to Tommy. 'We are to hold our ground.'

He trained his spyglass on the redoubt once more. The native batteries in front of their position seemed to have been abandoned.

'Are you thinking what I'm thinking?' Tommy said.

'Indeed I am. Tell the men we are about to advance.'

'But, Lieutenant,' the runner said. 'Colonel Clive told me to impress you on that his orders must be followed to the letter.'

'Look son,' Lachlan said, though the runner was not much younger than him, 'here's what you do. You run back to the lodge and advise Colonel Clive that you delivered his orders into my hand, and I screwed them up and used them as wadding for my flintlock. By the time you get there, I'll either be in possession of that redoubt or I'll be dead. Either way, it won't matter to me anymore what Colonel Clive has to say about the matter.' He turned to Tommy. 'Get the men ready.'

Tommy shouted an order.

The sepoys rose from behind the wall as one and began to march through the drifting smoke. Their drummer beat out the steps. A *jemadar* raised the Company colours as they advanced up the hill.

Lachlan led them, making the count in his head. He reached thirty and waited for the cannonade that would signal their doom. Nothing.

Another thirty count. He had hoped they would already be at the redoubt by now.

'Fix bayonets!' he shouted.

This was too often what it all came down to - close quarter butchery. But only if he and his men could survive the next few minutes.

If he was wrong, and the native gunners were still up there, they would be loading their cannons with canister shot. One blast at this range could cut a swathe thirty yards wide through the ranks behind him, turning uniformed men into dog meat in an instant.

'At the double!'

They started to run.

There were some who said a commander should force his men to proceed at a steady walk right up to the mouths of the guns. Otherwise, the men would be too exhausted to fight hand to hand when they got there. But Lachlan had always believed there would not be a man standing if he ever tried that. The quicker they could cover the distance to the guns, the less men he would lose.

Right to the last, he waited for the hail of chain and nail that would rip him and his men apart. It never came.

He scrambled over the earthworks and looked around, his lungs bursting. The guns had been abandoned. Cannonballs and case shot were neatly stacked. Ramrods, sponges and pails had been left trampled in the mud. The charges were a sopping mess, soaked by the rain, black powder leeching through the canvas.

He looked over to his left and saw the French cannons limbered up and churning away towards the rear, their horses staggering for purchase in the mud.

'They know they're outflanked,' Tommy said, gasping for breath.

Lachlan sank to his haunches, wondering that he was still alive. The noise of the battle around him seemed to be coming from very far away. Meanwhile, his men jumped onto the gun platforms, cheering. One balanced on a massive cannon barrel, his arms in the air.

Lachlan looked back at the battlefield. He saw the first and second battalions charge forward with their field guns and take possession of one of the tanks the French had just surrendered. 'Sergeant,' he said, 'tell the men now is not the time to rest. Get ready to defend our position.'

'Yes, sir.'

A runner toiled up the slope below. 'Where is Lieutenant McKenzie?' the boy said.

Lachlan called him over. 'What is it, lad?'

'You are to report to Colonel Clive immediately,' he said, panting from his exertions.

'About to get knighted in the field,' Tommy said. 'We should get an extra ration of gin for this.'

'Or I'm about to be court martialled and shot. Depends on the mood our Colonel Clive is in.'

Lachlan followed the man back down the slope and through the mango grove. Clive was on the roof of the lodge with his staff officers. As soon as Lachlan got there, he rounded on him, red in the face. 'What in God's name were you doing?'

'I was overrunning the enemy position, sir.'

'They were not your orders!'

'Well, they should have been!'

There was a stunned silence. The two men glared at each other. Then Clive put his hands on his hips and laughed. 'That's the spirit!'

'Look, sir.' His adjutant handed him a spyglass.

A battalion of grenadiers had dragged four field pieces up to the tanks and taken possession of the embrasures either side of the battery that Lachlan's men had taken. Clive had wasted no time in pressing his advantage.

Clive swung the glass to the right, then handed it to Lachlan. 'What do you make of that, Lieutenant?' he said.

Mir Jafar's divisions were circling around behind the mango tope.

'I think he means to attack our supply wagons at the rear,' someone said. It was Coote, his jacket spattered with blood, his wig askew. 'It seems all the assurances he gave you amount to nothing.'

'I cannot believe he would do that,' Lachlan said. 'Not now the tide has turned in our favour.'

'Well, seeing is believing.' Clive said. He called one of his couriers and told him to order one of the field guns to redeploy to check Mir Jafar's advance.

'I should get back to my men,' Lachlan said.

'I will come with you,' Clive said. 'Captain Coote, get the rest of the field guns up to the redoubt. It is time to take the battle to the enemy.'

'So, I'm not on a charge, then?' Lachlan said.

'Good lord, no,' Clive said. 'You're insubordinate and reckless. I like that in a man.'

'Wait,' Coote said. He pointed.

Mir Jafar had not advanced on their flank. Instead, he had detached his divisions from the main body of Siraj's army, and they were riding off.

'So, you were right,' Clive said. 'He means not to betray us after all.'

'No,' Lachlan said. 'Not anymore, at least.'

'Then our flank is safe,' Clive said. 'Let us have at them.'

He drew his sword and turned to Coote. 'Bring up the men from the rear. We are going to advance. I believe we will carry this day.'

CHAPTER 60

L achlan stood on the battlefield feeling the heady bloodlust drain out of him. The clouds to the west were streaked with mauve and pink as the sun dipped below the rice paddies. The day had passed so slowly and yet so quickly. There had been minutes that had felt like days, and hours that had gone by without his notice. And now it was done.

His knees felt suddenly weak, and he sat down hard on an ammunition box. He thought about what he had said to Tommy about growing old surrounded by his grandchildren. He realised that was his dream, not his sergeant's. He was sick of blood, and he was sick of fighting. He prayed this battle was his last.

Some of his sepoys stood along the redoubt, arms in the air, cheering Clive as he strode among them accepting their acclaim. Others were more intent on picking their way over the battlefield, finishing off the wounded with their swords and helping themselves to whatever they could. The usual business of war.

He looked up when he heard roaring behind him and saw a bullock up to its haunches in mud, trapped by the traces that tied it to one of Siraj's cannons. He drew his hanger and cut it free, hacking through the ropes.

And then he saw him.

He lay on his back next to his horse, a ragged flag of flesh where his leg should have been. He was barely breathing.

At first, Lachlan thought he was dead. His face was already sickly grey, the colour of a corpse. Then he saw his eyelids flicker. His fingers tightened on his sword. This was his chance to finish him. But there was something he had to know. He knelt in the mud beside him. 'What did you do with Yasmin?'

Aziz Khan drew back his lips in a grimace. There was blood on his teeth. 'If I do not return...' He started to choke.

Lachlan held his head and fumbled for the leather water canteen on his belt. He poured a little of the water down his throat.

Aziz Khan coughed a fine pink spray from his lungs and took a long, rasping breath. 'If I do not...' He trailed off.

'What? What if you don't return to Murshidabad?'

'My men. Kill her.' Another grimace. He was laughing at him.

Lachlan raised his sword. One thrust would shut him up. It would be easy enough. How many men had he killed hand to hand in his short life? But that was the problem. Without the terror of battle, he had no taste for it. Besides, it would change nothing, not now.

He stood up and turned away.

He had gone no more than a few paces when he heard the crack of a musket. He wheeled around. Tommy stood over the general, smoke rising from the barrel of his Brown Bess. The back of Aziz Khan's head was gone.

Now he saw what Tommy had seen. The general had a pistol in his hand. Where had that come from?

'You should never turn your back on them, sir,' Tommy said. 'Not until they're deader than dead.'

Lachlan stared at the pistol, then at his sergeant. 'I couldn't finish him. Not in cold blood.'

Tommy shook his head. 'You're a strange one, sir. I don't think you're cut out for this game.'

That night in the lodge, Clive was in an expansive mood. Bennett did not look quite as cheerful. No man likes to be proven wrong.

Clive had Mir Jafar's letter open on top of his charts, a compass and a brass tobacco box as paperweights. A large tallow candle spluttered and smoked in the middle of the table.

'You are to be commended, Lieutenant McKenzie,' Clive said. 'You showed initiative and sound tactical sense. You remind me of me in my younger days. Yes, you do, by God. Where are you from, sir?'

'My father was from Berwick in the borderlands,' Lachlan said. 'I grew up in Africa.'

'Africa? My God, man. That accounts for the savage in you. I can use a man like you. What do you say?'

'What is it you want me to do?'

'I want you to take some men and ride ahead to Murshidabad. Go directly to Siraj's palace. I want to make sure the treasury is intact when I get there. We were offered a great deal to secure Mir Jafar the throne. I intend to be paid in full.'

Lachlan nodded. He didn't give a damn about Siraj or the treasury, but this was his chance to get to Murshidabad before anyone else. 'I'll do my best, Colonel.'

'Good.' Clive clapped him on the shoulder. 'You have the makings of a good Company man, McKenzie.'

CHAPTER 61

Murshidabad

When Aziz Khan had left for Plassey, he had ordered the guards on the south gate of his palace to lock the gates and open them to no one. So, when the guards saw a dozen riders approaching on horseback. They got ready for trouble.

'Open up, quickly,' one of the riders shouted up at the gatehouse. 'It is the general. He has been wounded.'

The two guards looked at the men's uniforms and at their orange and white banner. One man was hunched over the saddle of a beautifully caparisoned Arab. There was blood streaked down the animal's flanks.

'It's Aziz Khan,' the older guard said. 'Let them in.'

The gates creaked open and the riders galloped through.

As soon as they were inside, four of them swung down from their saddles and hacked the two guards into bloody pieces.

Kilcannon straightened in the saddle and threw back his hood. Four donkey carts trundled into the tiled court. He hoped they would be sufficient. His spies had told him that Aziz Khan had a fortune in gold hidden underneath the palace, enough to pay ten times what he owed him. The treasure was not as great as the one Ashin Das had hidden in the churchyard at Calcutta, but he expected it would be enough to turn a tidy profit.

He waited for the rest of his detachment to appear from their hiding places in the surrounding streets. 'Find the rest of Aziz Khan's men,' he said. 'Kill them.'

The room where Aziz Khan had kept Yasmin and Nafisa locked away was never intended for use as a prison, yet neither was it fit accommodation for even the poorest *zenana*. The carpets were threadbare, and the only furniture consisted of two charpoys strung with rattan for sleeping.

The walls were made of delicate marble lattice, inlaid with polished and precious stones. The two women could gaze out over Aziz Khan's harem yet remain unseen. Yasmin wondered if this was meant as a comfort or a torment.

Now they ran to the lattice and peered out in horror. They heard screams coming from the courtyard and the clash of steel.

Nafisa looked at Yasmin and took her hand. 'Do you remember the secret hiding place?'

Yasmin nodded. When her great, great grandfather had built the palace, he had told the architects to build a room that he and his family could use in times of war. They had put a stone in a blank marble wall which looked identical to those around it but was much lighter and much thinner.

She had learned about it when she was still a child. She knew how to lever the trick stone aside and wriggle through the gap into the dark crawl space on the other side. Once the stone was pulled back into place, it became invisible to anyone who didn't know about it.

'As soon as this door is opened,' Nafisa said, 'you must run as fast and as hard as you can. Find the hiding place and stay there.'

'What about you

'I will find you.'

The sound of fighting got closer. They heard men outside, hammering at the door, attacking it with staves and hammers. It trembled and bent on its hinges. Nafisa grabbed Yasmin by the arm and dragged her to the side.

Finally, the lock snapped and the door swung open. Nafisa darted out between the soldiers, pulling Yasmin with her.

There were three of them, turbaned sepoys in blue and white jackets. Only one of them was alert to what was happening. He caught Nafisa by the arm as she dashed past. Yasmin was quicker, but when she realised that Nafisa had been caught, she stopped halfway along the cloister and turned back.

'No!' Nafisa shouted at her. 'Run!'

The other two sepoys were about to go after her. Nafisa raked her fingernails down one of the soldier's eyes and cheek. He yelled and put his hands to his face to protect himself. She pulled a curved dagger from his sash and slashed at the man holding onto her. He screamed as blood spurted from his arm.

The man's companions stepped back to avoid the blade as she slashed again and again. Then one of them drew his sword, and with a single practised stroke, left her lying on the marble in a spreading pool of blood.

When they looked around, Yasmin was gone.

Kilcannon stared at the *zenana* gardens one last time. He heard a scream as one of the women ran across the grass trying to get away from two of his men. They caught her within a few yards, and one of them bent her over the silver swing while the other held her wrists.

He had never understood why the rougher sort took such pleasure in rape, but it was what they wanted and expected after a battle, and he had to give it to them. Loot and lust. That was their wages.

He left them to their torture and butchery and made his way back to the courtyard. His servants had finished loading the carts with the contents of Aziz Khan's treasury. It was time to leave.

He wanted to be well away from the city by sunset. Mir Jafar was hunting down Siraj's supporters. He couldn't afford to get caught up in any of that. Clive wouldn't be far away, and once order was restored, all opportunities for businessmen like himself would be gone.

He had heard Siraj had escaped the city, but that didn't matter now. The tide had turned, and sooner or later, the British would find him and put his head on a sharpened stick. That was the way in Hindustan. You either had a crown on your head or a crow pecking out your eyes. No middle ground.

He calculated that Narain should be in Pondicherry with Ashin Das's riches by now. Thanks to Aziz Khan's thoughtfulness in dying prematurely on the battlefield, he had another king's ransom on the back of the carts.

He told his *subadar* to tell the men the fun was over and to cut the throats of any women still alive. There were to be no witnesses. Time to get to the coast and get out of Bengal. The French were finished in Hindustan.

CHAPTER 62

The road to Murshidabad was littered with the seemingly endless baggage of a fleeing army - broken cannon limbers, upended hackeries, and the bloated and stinking corpses of men and horses. Mir Jafar's men may have seen little action at Plassey, but they had been more than enthusiastic in slaughtering the remainder of Siraj's army as they fled back to Murshidabad.

The killing had clearly continued unabated inside the city as well. By the time Lachlan and Tommy reached the outskirts, a pall of smoke hovered over the rooftops, and the stench of death hung in the air. Every man had his sword drawn and pistols cocked. The streets were lawless. There were pools of blood everywhere and bodies lay in the dirt like piles of rags. It was so dangerous that Mir Jafar sent an escort out to meet them.

As they got closer to the medina, they heard cheering and shouting. Crowds of people lined the streets. The captain in charge of their escort pointed ahead at a procession slowly making its way towards them along the main thoroughfare. It was led by a gaudily painted elephant and guarded by a squadron of smartly turned-out cavalry in Mir Jafar's colours.

Lachlan tried to make out who was riding in the elephant's *howdah*. For a moment, he thought it might be Mir Jafar himself. But as it came closer, he realised it wasn't him.

It was Siraj.

He had been tied upright on a painted throne and fixed in place by the simple artifice of tying his long black hair to the chair. His head lolled like a puppet's with every jarring step the great beast took.

He was naked and flies buzzed around his empty eye sockets. His carcass was badly mutilated. Someone had clearly taken to him with a sword for longer than was necessary. There seemed to be several parts of him missing.

Tommy frowned and shook his head. 'Oh well,' he said. 'He was never an oil painting to start with.'

When the procession had passed, their escort continued towards Siraj's palace at Mansurganj, where Mir Jafar was waiting for them. But Lachlan told the captain he had more important business to attend to first. He sent them on ahead.

'Where are we going, sir?' Tommy said. 'Aren't we supposed to go with Mir Jafar's lads?'

'It can wait,' Lachlan said. 'This way, Tommy. Bring the men.'

The gates to Aziz Khan's palace were wide open, and the bodies of his men lay scattered about the courtyard. As Lachlan and Tommy rode in, a crow that had been perched on one of the corpses lazily spread its wings and flapped away.

They climbed down from their horses.

Dust devils twisted across the flags as they entered the *zenana*. A silver swing creaked. A body lay half in and half out of one of the fountains, turning the water pink. It had been so badly mutilated that it was impossible to tell if it was a man or a woman.

A girl lay on her back, eyes staring, her guts spilled green and grey on the marble, a feast for the flies. Two more lay in an arbour, where they had died huddled together trying to protect a child. The stink in the furnace heat was overwhelming.

'Dear God,' Lachlan said.

'The Devil has been here in person,' Tommy said.

The men gathered behind them. No one spoke.

The first time I saw this place I thought it was a paradise on earth, Lachlan thought. Now it's a horror. He saw a bloody handprint smeared across the glazed tilework.

As he wandered among the ruin of bodies, it was clear to him that there had been little restraint. Harem girls and servants had been treated with the same disregard. Most were naked.

'Sir?'

He turned around. It was Tommy. He had an old woman with him.

'Who is this?' Lachlan said.

'She's a servant,' Tommy said. 'One of the lads found her hiding in the kitchens. She says that she was by the river getting water when the soldiers came. Because of the rioting in the city, everyone thought it was too dangerous to leave the palace. They drew straws and she got the short one. It was bad luck turned to good for her.'

'You saw what happened?' Lachlan said to her in Bengali. The old woman was still shaking. He told Tommy to give her some water.

'I hid under the bridge when I saw the soldiers ride up to the gate,' she said, when she had calmed down enough to speak. 'I heard much screaming from the other side of the walls. It seemed to go on for hours. I was frightened. I stayed by the river until they were gone.'

'Why did they come here?' Lachlan said.

'For the general's treasure,' the woman said, as if this must be obvious to anyone. 'When they left, they needed four bullock carts to carry it all away.'

'Do you know who they were, mother?'

'They were sepoys, but there was a white man, a *sahib*, leading them.'

'Can you describe him?'

She shrugged as if this was a strange question to ask. All *sahibs* had white skins and hats. Finally, she found inspiration. 'He had a scar,' she said and pointed to her right eye. 'Here.'

'Thank you, mother,' Lachlan said. 'You may go now. Don't be afraid. My men will make sure you come to no harm.'

He had underestimated Kilcannon. He had met countless men of easy charm in his life before and been fooled along with everyone else by their wit and devil may care airs. But looking at the mutilated bodies of these helpless women, he knew that the good looks and flashing smile were just a cheap disguise. He was a devil through and through.

'If they had four hackeries with them,' Tommy said, 'they can't have gone very far.'

'Where do we think they were headed?'

Tommy pointed to the bridge. 'Not east, because he's crossed the river. Marathas are to the north, so he must be headed south-west towards Orissa. My guess he's hoping to meet up with the French army. Do we chase after him or let him go?'

Lachlan shook his head. 'We're now at war with France, Tommy. Our orders are to engage the enemy when opportunity presents. Leave four of your men here to give these women proper burial according to their religion. Tell them to find some linen for shrouds. Then take the rest of the men and go after Kilcannon.'

'What about you, sir?'

'My orders from Clive are to keep an eye on the Company's investment at Mansurganj. But first I'm going to find Yasmin.'

'Look at the state of these bodies. How will you even recognize her? Bloody animals.'

'I will recognise her, Tommy, no matter what they've done.'

He found Nafisa in a gloomy corner of the harem. She looked as if she had been torn apart by a frenzied animal. Only her face was untouched. He crouched down and covered her with a corner of her bloodied veil. He felt the bile rise in his throat.

For a moment, he remembered himself crouched in a native canoe, staring at his family's burning wooden stockade, vowing to take vengeance on the man responsible.

What now, he thought. Will I start another murderous quest?

He heard someone call his name. He turned around.

A figure approached from along the cloister. She appeared to shimmer in the heat rising from the marble stones, like a spirit, a *djinn*.

She stopped in front of him and drew back her veil.

'I thought I'd never see you again,' she said.

CHAPTER 63

Mansurganj

It was late afternoon and the cumulus clouds were stained with mauve and molten gold. Lachlan walked his grey along a shaded path, the lake on one side, a lush jungle of palms and mangoes on the other. People lined the way, silently raising their hands and their babies towards him, hoping for a few silver coins.

As he entered the estate with his escort, he was surprised at how peaceful it looked. It was eerily quiet after the chaos of the city. There had been no wholesale destruction here. The pleasure gardens and the sprawling pile of marble that Siraj had built for himself seemed merely empty and a little sad. The complex of domes and lakes had only recently been completed, but Siraj had had little time to enjoy his new palace.

He was struck by the smell of elephant. There seemed to be hundreds of them lining the approach, and despite their silks and panoplies, the stink of them was overpowering.

Mir Jafar waited in the shade of a pillared arcade at the top of the palace steps, one hand resting on the jewelled *talwar* at his side. His turban had two large aigrette feathers and a diamond clasp, and his moustache, freshly waxed and curled, had never looked as magnificent.

It was only a pity about the body floating in the tank. Someone must have forgotten to remove it.

As he walked up the steps, Lachlan tried to fathom Mir Jafar's mood. The man was probably wondering if he had made the right choice. Not that he ever really had a choice.

They greeted each other formally.

Lachlan felt like someone whose presence reminded Mir Jafar of a sordid episode from his past. 'I saw Siraj on my way here,' he said. 'He has looked better.'

'They stood in line to do the deed. He had few friends at the end.' Mir Jafar lowered his voice. 'Can I trust him? Your Mister Clive, I mean.'

'Yes, you can trust him. If he's standing right in front of you, and you have a gun to his head.'

'What I did was very necessary. Siraj would have led us all to disaster.'

'The treasury is intact?'

There was a moment. Mir Jafar had the look of a man who had just bought a purebred Arabian stallion, and now he was mounted, was thinking of galloping away rather than pay the trader his hideously expensive price.

'Colonel Clive will be here in the next few days with his army,' Lachlan reminded him. 'It would be unwise to disappoint him.'

'It was never my thought,' Mir Jafar said with practised ease. He led the way through the empty and echoing halls of the palace to one of the inner sanctums. A long corridor led off it, with a large iron gate at the end. A guard opened it with a key from a ring on his belt.

Beyond this was another door. Mir Jafar unlocked it with a key he had secreted inside his tunic. He told the guard to turn his back.

'Are you ready?' he said.

Lachlan nodded and followed him inside.

He had never seen anything like it. As some men stored chattels in a basement, Siraj had what seemed like the wealth of the world stacked side by side inside a cavernous cellar the length of a parade ground.

There was a four-poster bed made entirely of gold next to a solid silver dressing table. There were innumerable caskets, brimming with pearls. On the shelves that lined the walls, he saw a coronet of diamonds, a tiara of rubies, parures of emeralds and sapphires, priceless necklaces, and so many jewel-encrusted bracelets and rings that looking at it all became monotonous.

When Mir Jafar spoke again, there was both bitterness and apprehension in his voice. 'I hope I have not promised too much for my throne. Do you think Mister Clive will be satisfied now?'

Lachlan did not know how to answer. If I know Clive, he thought, he hasn't even started his looting yet.

The trees and grasses bent to the wind, and the clouds rushed across the sky in the face of it. Tommy and his men were blasted by leaves and palm fronds. But there was not a drop of rain, the first afternoon since Plassey that there had been no cloudburst in the afternoon.

Tommy held up a hand and peered ahead into the teeth of the monsoon. He thought he saw something and took out his spy glass.

Up ahead was a slow-moving river with a long wooden bridge. At its approaches, one of Kilcannon's wagons was blocking the crossing, bogged in a mire up to its axle. Sepoys were hauling on ropes, while others pushed from the back, trying to get the spoked wheels free of the mud.

'Got you,' Tommy said. He urged his horse into a gallop and signalled for his men to follow. But as they got closer, he started to feel a sense of unease. Something was not quite right.

Then he saw what it was. The two men at the back of the wagon were wearing blue uniform jackets to make them look like sepoys, but they were also wearing *dhotis* like village peasants. He hadn't noticed it until now because they were half-covered in mud from the splashback of the spinning wheels.

He shouted a warning and reined in his horse. Too late.

Suddenly, the oilcloth over the back of the cart was thrown back, and half a dozen blue-coated sepoys jumped to their feet and brought up their muskets. A volley of shots rang out. Two of the men riding beside him slipped from their horses.

Tommy swore under his breath. It was a trap, and they'd galloped straight into it.

He saw another flash of musketry from the tamarind tope away to their left. More of his men fell from their saddles. He had only a heartbeat to think his way through their predicament. They couldn't go back. They would have to rush the wagon and get under cover. He drew his sword.

'Charge!'

He galloped forward, mud spraying from his horse's hooves, and hacked at the sepoys in the wagon's tray before they could reload.

But the blue jackets were ready. They had fixed their bayonets and lunged at them from the backboard. One of them had saved his round and now aimed his musket at Tommy as he turned his mount and charged back at the cart.

Tommy ducked at the last moment and heard the ball zip through the air near his head. He slashed again with his hanger and the edge of the blade hit the man full in the face. He lurched off the back of the cart into the mud.

There was another crash of musketry from the trees.

For one mad moment, he thought about Lachlan and his daft idea that he would die of old age in a feather bed surrounded by his adoring grandchildren. No, this was more like it, slaughtered in the middle of some foreign nowhere, left face down in the mud with no one to bury him. He'd never expected anything else.

He saw more of his men topple from their saddles. His *jemadar* lay in the mud with a dead horse on top of him. All order was gone. There were no more than half a dozen of his lads still fighting. They were looking to him, but he couldn't see a way out of this.

His horse screamed and staggered sideways. The poor old girl was hit, and he let go of the reins and leaped clear as she went down. He felt a jarring pain through his knee and wrist and blacked out.

He couldn't have lost consciousness for long, because when he opened his eyes the fight was still going on. He rolled to his left and was about to put his weight on his arm to haul himself up again. God's holy blood, his hand and wrist were bent outwards.

There were fierce stabbing pains in his left knee, and he knew he'd crippled himself in the fall. He crawled, desperate now, into the tall stands of *kans* grass next to the river.

When he was out of sight, he looked back once over his shoulder. There was nothing to be done. The firing had stopped, and he realised all his lads must be dead or wounded.

Time to save yourself, Tommy boy.

But he hesitated, something making him linger. He supposed it was the voice in his head shouting, *you fool, what have you done?*

He hadn't given Kilcannon credit. Just because he was pursuing him, didn't mean the bastard couldn't pursue him back. He should have known that. When the lieutenant found out how he'd fallen for one of the oldest tricks in the book, he would be bloody dark about it.

The mud before the bridge was littered with dead and wounded horses and men. His men.

Kilcannon's blue jackets were busy with the looting now, going through the pockets of his sepoys. Any still breathing, they finished off with their knives.

He saw Kilcannon, remembered him from the day outside Aziz Khan's palace. He had the sort of cold smile you'd expect to see from the executioner when you mounted the gallows. He watched him ease himself out of his saddle and draw the pistol at his belt.

He could see what he was about. His *jemadar* lay on his back next to his horse pleading with him for mercy, telling him he had a wife and family at home. Kilcannon cocked his pistol and shot him through the head before moving on to the next man, who was so badly wounded he could barely raise a hand in supplication.

Kilcannon put away his pistol and drew his sword. He hit the poor fellow hard on the side of the head with the flat of the blade, then plunged the tip between jaw and breastbone, leaning on the pommel to ensure it went all the way in.

You won't get away with this, Tommy thought. We'll settle with you, me and the lieutenant, pay you in kind for my men here today and for what you did to those women in the palace. We'll hunt you down like the dog you are.

He crawled to the river, favouring his left arm and leg. He unbuckled his sword belt, struggled out of his uniform jacket and eased himself in. The water was tepid and brown. He let the current take him downstream.

CHAPTER 64

T he coronation procession for Mir Jafar followed the same route that Lachlan had taken a few days before. It was led by two bearers on horseback. One wore green robes and carried the nawab's standard. The other was a Company ensign in shako and red coat, holding the red and white striped Company flag.

Behind them came Clive and Mir Jafar, riding side by side in the howdah of one of the royal elephants, which had been painted and caparisoned in silks for the occasion.

Mir Jafar wore a turban with a fat ruby and a tall yellow aigrette. Clive had on a cocked hat with a freshly powdered wig. He wore a ceremonial red frock coat, with a waistcoat and white silk stockings. The heat was insufferable as always, and his face was bright pink and shone from the sweat rolling down his cheeks.

Lachlan followed behind. He rode to the beat of the mounted kettledrums, along with another dozen hand-picked Company officers. A detachment of the nawab's cavalry rode beside them in shining mail.

Siraj's palace loomed ahead.

Lachlan had expected the elephant to kneel at the foot of the palace steps to allow its celebrated passengers to dismount, but that was not the Moghul way.

Instead, the beast climbed the last few steps to the entrance and stopped under the white marble colonnades. There it discharged a thick, yellow stream of urine that splashed over the robes of the two dozen courtiers who had gathered for the ceremony. Clearly, no one had informed the elephant of the proper etiquette.

Clive's escort, drawn up in ranks with muskets at arms, did not flinch. It was an impressive display, but then these men had endured far worse at Plassey.

They had been told to load their muskets with live rounds. No one on the general staff was convinced that Mir Jafar would not even now change his mind and renege on his deal.

Lachlan followed Clive and Mir Jafar into Siraj's palace. The golden throne that Mir Jafar had coveted for so long was directly ahead of them on a raised *masnad*.

They paused. Clive shot out a hand to help Mir Jafar ascend to be formally crowned.

By this one simple act, Clive demonstrated to everyone looking on, who the real kingmaker was. He turned away, caught Lachlan's eyes, and gave him a wry smile.

Clive stood with his hands on his hips and surveyed the contents of Siraj's vault. He looked like a landlord with troublesome tenants. No, his face said, this just isn't good enough.

'You realise,' he said, 'that there is probably not enough here to pay the Company's commission.'

Lachlan stared at him. 'What?'

'Not even two crores, I'd say. It will leave a massive shortfall. I have had a meeting with the Jagat Seth. They have promised to organise loans so that Mir Jafar can meet his obligations.'

'But this is a king's ransom.'

Clive smiled. 'Lieutenant, have you so little imagination?' He picked up a shoulder sash made up of thirty strings of pearls. 'I quite like the look of this.'

'Are we taking it all?'

'An agreement is an agreement. We have played our part.' He turned his attention to one of the coronets. He picked it up and examined it more closely. The centrepiece, a cabochon cut ruby, caught the light from an oil lamp. Its bloody heart dazzled. 'I am about to become one of the wealthiest men in all of Europe. Imagine that.'

'I'm not sure that I can.'

'And this is just the start. Of course, in the future I shall need someone with me I can trust.'

'Sir?'

'Do I have to spell it out to you, man? I am offering you a golden opportunity here. Look on it as your just reward for all you have done to further the Company interests in Bengal. Join with me and I will make you rich beyond your wildest dreams. What do you say?'

Lachlan thought about a wood panelled office in Madras and another man promising to make him absurdly rich.

Clive was staring at him, waiting for an answer.

'Thank you for the offer, sir, but I shall have to say no.'

'What?'

'I'm resigning my commission, effective immediately.'

'Are you mad?'

'Quite possibly,' Lachlan said and turned away.

Pondicherry

The sky was black and the palms along the promenade were bent over by the gale. A two masted sloop rocked wildly at its moorings at the end of the jetty. It had just arrived from Orissa and was lucky to have made port before the full force of the storm bore down.

So, it's true, Fontaine thought as he watched Kilcannon make his way unsteadily down the gangway. The bastard is back.

Kilcannon did not possess his usual sartorial splendour, he was pleased to note. He was unshaven and there were salt stains on his jacket and breeches. And something else. Vomit possibly, hopefully.

'*M'sieur* Kilcannon. I had heard you were on board. I hope you had a good journey.'

'Ah, Fontaine,' Kilcannon said, as if addressing a tally clerk. 'How pleasant to see you again. *Au contraire,* the journey was exceedingly unpleasant. But I suppose you already guessed that.'

'We had not expected to see you back in Pondicherry. Will you be gracing us with your presence for very long?'

'Who knows what I will do.' Kilcannon lowered his voice. 'And what fucking business is it of yours anyway?' He turned his back and made his way down the jetty where Narain was waiting for him.

Fontaine stared thoughtfully at the sloop. He had been told that when Kilcannon boarded her at Orissa, he had four wagons laden with cargo brought into the hold. It seemed his adventures in Bengal had been profitable.

Of course, he could have the hold searched and the inventory seized by the *douane* on some pretext, should he so choose.

But not yet.

The tricolour whipped in the monsoon gale and the halyard vibrated against the flagstaff. He turned and walked back to the *Gouvernement*.

Later that morning, Fontaine stood at the window of his office, watching a company of sepoys drilling on the maidan. There was a knock at the door. One of his secretaries ushered in a small, bony native.

Dukki had the look of a beaten dog. He would do almost anything for a few *fanams*, which was what made him valuable. Fontaine went to a wooden chest in the corner and took out a large musket. Dukki gaped at it. It had a painted stock and a squared, gold damascened barrel.

'It's called a Toradar,' Fontaine said. 'It belonged to a friend of mine.' He wrapped it in oil cloth and handed it to Dukki with an envelope. It had a name hand-written on it in his elegant script.

Dukki shook his head. 'Please, *sahib*, no. I don't want to go there.'

'I can get someone else. Men like you are easy to replace. What is it to be?'

Dukki stared at the package as if it were a live snake. He hesitated then turned for the door.

'Make sure both items are safely delivered,' Fontaine said. 'Otherwise, it will be the worse for you. Understand?'

CHAPTER 65

C alcutta

Calcutta was still largely in ruins and the military hospital had been relocated to one of the merchant palaces near the river. The palace had been thoroughly looted. All that was left of any value were the crystal chandeliers on the high wooden ceilings.

The grand *durbar* hall was crammed with charpoys, mostly filled with Europeans who had come down with the latest bout of fever, as well as a handful of wounded from the battle at Plassey.

The place had a unique smell to it, the scent of flowers mingling with the sour odours of death and stale sweat. Lachlan wondered what Ashin Das would say if he could see his chequered tiled floors covered in filthy enamel bowls and stained bandages.

He followed a long corridor to the courtyard garden. It must have been grand once, he thought, looking around at the ornate galleries and intricate Corinthian columns. But many of the flower beds had been trampled by Siraj's soldiers, and the trees had been stripped bare of branches for firewood.

Tommy was sitting on a bench in one of the arcades, his arm and knee encased in thick bandages. A crutch was balanced against the wall behind him.

'Tommy.'

He looked up. 'Sir,' he said and made an effort to rise.

Lachlan knew things must be bad with him when he didn't jerk to attention and salute. He put a hand on his shoulder and eased him back down onto the bench. 'What have you done to yourself?'

'I'm alright. Broke my wrist a little bit and twisted my knee. Rest up for a few weeks and I'll be good as new.'

'Do I need to carry you out?'

Tommy smiled.

Lachlan sat down and they stared at the ruined garden in companionable silence. 'So, what will you do now?'

'Back to the regiment on light duties, they reckon, until I'm alright to march again.' He held up his left hand. 'This might take a little bit longer. Lucky I salute with my other hand.'

'It's not your only choice, you know.'

'Well, it is. I only have two hands.'

'I mean, it's not your only choice about what to do.'

'I don't think I quite understand your meaning, sir.'

'I mean why don't you come with me, Tommy?'

'To Africa?'

'With me and Yasmin.'

'She's alive?'

Lachlan nodded. 'Nafisa wasn't so fortunate.'

'Those bastards.'

'You're lucky we're not burying you as well. Time to think of your own future.' When Tommy didn't answer, he went on, 'I'll need a new overseer. I imagine the place has run down after all this time, so there'll be a lot to do. You'll have your work cut out. But we're leaving on this afternoon's tide, so I'll need an answer now.'

'What about Kilcannon?'

'What about him?'

'He killed my lads in cold blood. And what about all those women, what he let his men do to them.'

'Tommy, there has to be an end to it. I can't kill every evil bastard in the world.'

'But what he did. We can't let him get away with it.'

'Gagnon is dead,' Lachlan said. 'So is his daughter. I've had enough Tommy. I'm not a soldier. I just want to go home. Come with me. What do you say?'

Tommy shook his head. 'It's good of you to come back for me, sir. But this is my family. The Company. Only family I've ever known.'

'The Company treats you like dirt. They take advantage of you, and you get no reward for anything you do.

Tommy nodded. 'Like I said, they're family.'

'I can show you a better life.'

'Thank you, sir, but I like this one well enough.'

Lachlan stood up. 'I wish I could change your mind.'

'Good luck, sir. It was a pleasure serving with you.'

Lachlan hadn't expected this. He had supposed Tommy would jump at the chance. But then Channing and Clive had seemed just as mystified when he turned down their offers of riches.

'Take care of yourself, Tommy,' he said.

As he was walking away, he heard Tommy call after him, 'You'll be back one day.'

'Perhaps,' he said, but in his heart he knew that would never happen.

He had his second chance. And he was going to take it.

Pondicherry

The night steamed. The monsoon downpour had lasted most of the afternoon. At least it had made the ground soft and easy to turn. Narain held up the *flambeau*. The coolie was digging furiously but not fast enough.

'Tell him to hurry,' Kilcannon said. 'The *Modeste* is sailing with the tide first thing in the morning. We have to be aboard tonight.'

He heard the man's spade hit metal. There, that would be the last of it. In that chest were his gold reserves from his dealings in the Coromandel. It wasn't a fortune, but he wasn't about to leave it any of it behind.

The real fortune was already on the *Modeste* or loaded on the four hackeries waiting outside the villa gates. Once he had the combined wealth of Ashin Das and Aziz Khan safely stored in a vault somewhere in France, he could live the rest of his life like a king.

No, he could do better than that. He could buy himself lands and a title and become a king *maker*.

It was what he had always dreamed of. No longer a penniless count, but a duke with real power and wealth behind him. It would be the culmination of everything he had worked for.

There was just one more ocean to cross.

'Hurry,' he said again to Narain and went back inside the villa.

He stood at one of the louvred windows, staring at the darkened gardens. A part of him would miss this life, miss the anarchy of it all, the challenge of pitting himself against men like Aziz Khan and Siraj ud-Daulah. He had outlasted and outwitted them all.

He heard a noise behind him.

A woman stood in the doorway, a long elaborately painted musket cradled under one arm. She was dressed in a dirty white sari and her feet were bare, cracked and filthy like a beggar's. She had a white scarf wrapped around her head so that only her eyes were visible.

'Hello Gerard,' she said. 'Have you missed me?'

A breeze rustled the leaves of the banana palms.

Kilcannon froze. There was something about her voice that was familiar to him. It couldn't be. 'Adelaïde?'

'Are you leaving without me?'

She brought the Toradar to her hip and pointed it at his chest. She had a piece of cord in her left hand. It was glowing at the tip. She blew on it and placed it in the gun's serpentine. There was a loud click as she cocked the trigger.

He couldn't see her face, but he recognised that look in her eyes. He only had seconds to think of something. He panicked. What was her weakness, what could he say?

'I know where McKenzie's gone,' he said. 'He's got a new wife. Did you know? I can help you find him. You're not going to let him get away, are you?'

She blinked slowly. 'It's good to hear you whine,' she said, 'but I'm afraid I'll have to stop you there.'

The Toradar was loaded with tiger shot, and the blast at such close range sent him hurtling backwards into the drawing room wall.

The room was full of smoke. She waited a moment for it to clear then walked over to make sure he was dead.

A voice called from outside.

Narain. Good. This was working out well.

She reloaded the musket - fourteen seconds by the count of the longcase clock in the hall. Satisfactory.

Suddenly he stood in the doorway, his face blackened with smoke from the *flambeau*. He stared at Adelaïde in astonishment.

'You have made a big mistake,' she said.

He dropped to his knees. 'I'm sorry, *mem'sahib.*'

'That is what you said last time.'

She brought up the musket and fired.

She winced at the recoil. Her hip would be sore in the morning. She would have her grandmother rub in some ointment.

She sighed. There were pieces of her husband everywhere, even on her clothes. Kilcannon stared at her with sightless eyes.

'It's called karma,' she said.

She licked her finger and thumb and extinguished the burning cord in the serpentine. Then she put the Torador under her arm and stepped carefully over the bodies, closing the door quietly behind her.

Author's Notes

When I was a boy growing up in England, there was a map of the world on the wall of our classroom, and large parts of it were coloured in with red – denoting those countries that still basked in the glow of being part of the British Commonwealth. India was dead centre.

And when my parents took me on a day trip to London, I remember seeing the statue of a man called Robert Clive. He looked brave, wise and forbearing. A true hero of Great Britain.

It was only when I was older that I learned that Clive of India was not quite the hero I imagined. The historian William Dalrymple called him 'a vicious asset-stripper.'

When he died in 1774, apparently from suicide, his contemporary Samuel Johnson wrote that he 'had acquired his fortune by such crimes that his consciousness of them impelled him to cut his own throat'.

Clive was a servant of the British East India Company, the world's first multinational corporation. As a private company, it built an army twice the size of that of Britain, and following the Battle of Plassey, it ruled large parts of India for a hundred years, answerable only to its shareholders. The results were catastrophic for millions of human beings. It should have been a lesson to future generations about the consequences of greed.

But we tend not to learn much from history. It's a pity because often it's a vision of the future.

Here are some notes about the historical events described in the book.

The Black Hole of Calcutta remains a controversial topic among modern historians. One of the survivors, John Zephaniah Holwell, afterwards testified to the House of Commons that there were one hundred and forty-six people crammed into the cell that fateful night, and twenty-three survived. These numbers now seem to have been inflated for propaganda purposes and are hotly disputed. The most painstaking recent survey of the evidence concludes that sixty-four people entered the so-called Black Hole and that twenty-one survived.

The president of the British East Company at Madras between 1750 and 1755 was Thomas Saunders.

The British called the Bhagirathi River the Cossimbazar after their eponymous fort near Murshidabad, so I have used this term when talking about the river from their perspective.

The Battle of Karimkot is my invention, based on loosely on the Battle of Arcot.

The intrigues leading up to the Battle of Plassey have been simplified here. The intermediary between Mir Jafar and Robert Clive was in fact the Chief of the British Factory at Cossimbazar, a Mr. William Watts.

The engagement at Plassey was not considered a major action at the time. British losses were just twenty-three killed and fifty wounded.

The spontaneous attack on Siraj's cannons was instigated by Clive's deputy, one Major Kilpatrick. At the time, Clive threatened to arrest Kilpatrick for insubordination. Kilpatrick's initiative turned the tide in the Company's favour.

Though the battle itself does not compare to Agincourt or Waterloo, the result changed the course of Indian history. Had Clive been defeated at Plassey, it is likely the British East India Company would have been thrown out of Bengal and ultimately out of India. Instead, Mir Jafar and his backers became the Company's puppets, and the Company's pre-eminence was assured.

The Battle of Plassey took place on 23rd June 1757. Siraj ud-Daulah escaped with his gold, his women and his elephants. He was caught soon afterwards while trying to flee upriver to Patna, betrayed by a man whose ears he had ordered cut off a few months previously. He was not killed until 2nd July. These two events have been condensed in this novel so that Lachlan could witness Siraj's body being paraded through the streets of Murshidabad and describe the scene for the reader.

Things did not end well for Mir Jafar. The five crore of rupees that he promised Clive in compensation for his services eventually bankrupted Bengal. In an effort to repay the debt, he imposed onerous taxes on the Bengali population, which made him a deeply unpopular figure. He was deposed two years later by Clive.

His successor, Mir Kasim, incensed at the treacherous role the Jagat Seth had played in the Plassey debacle, murdered two members of the family by throwing them off the ramparts of the Monghyr Fort.

By then, Clive had already returned to England to much fanfare. He was awarded an Irish peerage and bought a seat in the House of Commons.

In 1912, they erected a bronze statue of him in Whitehall for later generations of schoolboys like me to gaze up at in awe.

About the Author

I have been a writer all my life. It's all I ever wanted to do, except for a brief dream of being a pro footballer. I started out in advertising as a copywriter, then worked as a journalist, a magazine columnist and a script writer for radio and television before becoming a full-time novelist.

I love adventure and travel and that has shaped the kind of books I write. Early in my career I developed a passion for Wilbur Smith novels. I also love Cornwell and Follett.

When I publish a book, I'm hoping to share it with other readers like me, who crave adventure, and stories with action and twists, but who also love something else – exotic locations, long ago times and unforgettable characters. The kind of stories that stay with you well after you finish the last page. It's what I read and it's what inspires me to write.

I try to travel to all the places I write about to experience the smells and sounds that you just can't get from Google, and I have written many chapters in airports, on planes and in cafes in cities around the world. I am completely in my head when I'm writing and it doesn't matter where I'm sitting. Stories play like movies in my mind. I press play and pause as I write.

I was born and raised in London, but these days I live in Fremantle, Australia, with my wife and spaniels. I post regularly on my Facebook page if you'd like to see behind the scenes or ask a question.

Thank you for reading my books and sharing my adventures.

Colin Falconer

ABOUT THIS SERIES
Part thriller. Part history. All adventure.

Special offers
Colin Falconer books are often selected by Amazon to be in Kindle deals. To stay in the loop on deals and new releases, follow Colin on Amazon or sign up for his mailing list at colinfalconerbooks.com

Enjoy this book?
You can make a big difference by adding a rating or writing a short book or series review on Amazon. Thank you!

The Epic Adventure Series
Multi-bestselling historical adventure thrillers
Stand-alone stories that can be read in any order
35,000+ five-star Amazon reviews
Exclusive to Amazon
Kindle, Kindle Unlimited and paperback

SELECTED BIBLIOGRAPHY

- *A History of Murshidabad District* – JHT Walsh, 1902

- *A history of the military transactions of the British nation in Indostan* – Robert Orme, 1763

- *Begums, Thugs & White Mughals* – Fanny Parkes (republished 2002)

- *British government in India* – Marquess George Nathaniel Curzon of Kedleston, 1925

- *Clive* – C. Brad Faught, 2013

- *Early records of British India* – James Talboys Wheeler, 1879

- *Murshidabad Kahani* – Nikhil Nath Roy, 1897

- *Murshidabader Iitihas* – Nikhil Nath Roy, 1902

- *Original letters from India* – Eliza Fay, 1780-82

- *The Anarchy* – William Dalrymple, 2019

- *The Diary of Ananda Ranga Pillai* – Anantarankam Pillai, 1900

- *The Early annals of the English in Bengal* – C. R. Wilson 1963

- *The Good Old Days of Honorable John Company* – W. H. Carey 1906

- *The History of the Bengal European regiment* – Percival Robert Innes, 1885

- *The Masnad of Murshidabad* – P. C. Majumdar, 1905

- *The Rise and Fall of the Jagat Sheths* – Joseph Rozario, 2015

- *The Road to Plassey, A Reappraisal of the British Conquest of Bengal, 1757* – the Proceedings of the Indian History Congress, 1998

- *Three Frenchmen in Bengal* – Samuel Charlies Hill, 1903

- *White Mughals* – William Dalrymple, 2002

GLOSSARY

- *angvastra* – shoulder cloth worn by Hindu men

- *arrack* – alcohol made from sugarcane

- *anna* – copper coin equal to one sixteenth of a rupee

- *baksheesh* – tip or bribe

- *begum* – honorific title for woman in South and Central Asia

- *bibi* – Hindu word for a high-class woman. In colonial India, became a synonym for 'mistress'

- *brinjal* – aubergine

- *budgerow* – slow moving barge

- *chador* – garment worn over the head and body leaving only the face exposed

- *chai* – tea made with spices and milk

- *chaise* – horse-drawn carriage for one or two people

- *charpoy* – traditional woven bed

- *chatra* – ceremonial umbrella

- *chhatri* – elevated dome-shaped pavilion

- *chitty* – pass or voucher slip

- *choga* – long-sleeved cloak worn by men

- *chunam* – type of plaster made from shell lime and sand

- *Compagnie des Indes* – French equivalent of the British East India Company

- *dacoits* – in India and Burma, member of a band of armed robbers

- *dhoti* – loose piece of clothing wrapped around lower body on men

- *divan* – long, upholstered seat

- *djinn* – spirit with magical powers from Islamic theology

- *durbar* – ceremonial court or audience chamber

- *dubash* – 'middleman' between European and native merchants.

- *fanam* – small gold or silver coin

- *feringhee* – derogatory Asian word for a foreigner

- *fonctionnaire* – French term for a civil servant

- *foule* – French word for a large crowd

- *frizzen* - L shaped piece of steel positioned over the flash pan on a flintlock weapon

- *howdah* – seat or covered pavilion for riding on the back of an elephant

- *huqqa* – water pipe used for smoking tobacco

- *jama* - a long coat worn by Mughal nobles

- *jemadar* – Indian army officer rank corresponding to a lieutenant in the British army

- *kans grass* – wild sugarcane that grows up to three metres

- *kohl* – black powder used for eye make-up

- *kurta* – loose, collarless shirt popular in South Asia

- *livre* – currency of France until 1794

- *masala boat* – flat bottomed, high sided boat used off the coast of Madras

- *maghrib* – Muslim sunset prayer

- *mishti* – term of endearment in Hindi and Bengali

- *Moghul* – Muslim dynasty that ruled India from 16th to 19th centuries

- *naan* – round flat leavened bread

- *nautch* girl – professional dancing girl

- *nullah* - watercourse

- *paan* – mixture of areca nut, betel leaves and slaked lime chewed as a stimulant

- *pajama* – loose fitting trousers

- *pilau* – spiced rice dish similar to pilaf

- *pinnace* – small boat that often served as tender to a much larger warship

- *porte-cochere* – covered entrance to a building

- *purdah* – curtain used to screen Muslim or Hindu women from strangers

- *prazo* – large estate leased to colonists in Portuguese Africa

- *punkha* – large swinging fan, suspended from the ceiling and operated by a servant using a cord

- *sati* – act of a Hindu woman being burned to death on her husband's funeral pyre

- *sepoy* – Indian native employed in a European army

- *sharbat* – Persian word for drink made from sugar and water

- *shikar* – wild game hunt in India

- *spahi* – infantryman in the army of the Mughal empire

- *subadar* – senior rank in Indian army, above *jemadar*

- *talwar* – from Persian, type of sabre

- *tank* – from the Hindi *taanka*, a reservoir

- *target* – round shield, often made of extremely tough leather

- *tonga* – two wheeled horse-drawn carriage

- *topass* – soldier of Indo-Portuguese descent serving in British army

- *tope* – grove of trees

- *veshti* – everyday garment, similar to a *dhoti*

- *zenana* – women's quarters in South Asian household

Printed in Dunstable, United Kingdom